Black Hamptons

Black Hamptons

Carl Weber

with

La Jill Hunt

www.urbanbooks.net

Urban Books, LLC
300 Farmingdale Road, NY-Route 109
Farmingdale, NY 11735

Black Hamptons
Copyright © 2022 Carl Weber with La Jill Hunt

ISBN 13: 978-1-64556-470-6
ISBN 10: 1-64556-470-3

First Hardcover Printing September 2022
Printed in the United States of America

10 9 8 7 6 5 4 3 2 1

Distributed by Kensington Publishing Corp.
Submit orders to:
Customer Service
400 Hahn Road
Westminster, MD 21157-4627
Phone: 1-800-733-3000
Fax: 1-800-659-2436

Carolyn Britton

1

I stepped off the elevator on the 36th floor in a black Armani silk blazer and pencil skirt, Manolo Blahnik heels, and the red Hermes scarf that made me feel powerful whenever I wore it. Behind me were my pride and joy, my two handsome sons. Malcolm, the oldest, was tall, lean, and quite brilliant when it came to business. His younger brother, Martin, was muscular, athletic, and especially easy on the eyes. Unlike his brother, who was more of an introvert, Martin was a true people person. He could charm the panties off a nun if he had to, which could be useful when it came to closing deals.

"Mother." Malcolm gestured toward a row of benches, where Jeffrey Bowen was seated. He was married to my niece, Leslie, and he was also our family attorney. He jumped up from his seat the moment he saw us, closing the gap between the bench and the elevator in five long strides.

"Aunt Carolyn." He kissed my cheek, then nodded at the boys. "You're right on time. Follow me."

Jeffrey led the way through double doors and into a small courtroom, where a middle-aged African American judge sat on the bench. I had to stifle the urge to call out, "Hello, Robert," reminding myself that we were in his courtroom, not at one of the numerous dinner parties in the Hamptons we'd both attended over the thirty years that I'd known him. Judge Terry, however, didn't seem to have any trouble separating business and pleasure. He kept his head down and didn't acknowledge me in any way as we took our seats at a table facing the judge's bench.

"Mr. Bowen, as the attorney of record for Amistad Bank, I see that you have made a motion. Would you like to elaborate?" Judge Terry spoke formally into a microphone, still not even glancing in my direction.

Jeffrey rose to reply. Like his father and grandfather before him, Jeffrey was a highly respected attorney. His practice was mainly in New York, but he had also spent time working in the office of the White House legal counsel during President Obama's second term. "Your Honor, we move that the conservatorship of Amistad Bank be removed and that the Moses Britton Trust be turned over to Carolyn Britton and the Britton family, so that Mrs. Britton's status as acting chairwoman and CEO of Amistad can be made permanent. Thank you, Your Honor."

Judge Terry placed his glasses on his head and began thumbing through the paperwork on his desk. After a minute, I started to feel restless. He was taking way too long for my taste, especially considering the fact that the outcome of this little horse and pony show had been determined weeks ago over drinks at my summer home in Sag Harbor. Judge Terry, along with a few key Democratic figures, had agreed to release the conservatorship in a wink-wink, nod-nod agreement. In exchange, Robert's son would receive a one-percent interest rate on a mortgage for a summer residence next door to the judge, and some up-and-coming Democratic candidates would receive generous campaign support from the bank.

"Any objection from the government, Mr. Lee?" Judge Terry glanced over to our right at Matt Lee, a small, well-dressed Asian man. He was a pain-in-the-ass federal banking regulator, and he sat next to Sara Wilson, an assistant deputy U.S. attorney.

"No, Your Honor," Mr. Lee replied. "The Brittons have met all the terms of our agreement."

Judge Terry removed his glasses and closed the folder. "Then I see no reason not to grant your motion, Mr. Bowen. The conservatorship over Amistad Bank is hereby relinquished and returned to the Britton family, along with all assets belonging to the Moses Britton Trust. Good luck and godspeed. Case dismissed." Judge Terry slammed down his gavel.

"Thank you, Your Honor." Jeffrey turned to me, offering his hand. "Congratulations, Aunt Carolyn."

"So, that's it? The bank is mine?" Although I knew this proceeding had merely been a formality, it felt good to finally be over the finish line. After four years of Donald Trump's government trying to take what was ours, I had struggled to believe we'd ever get full control of the bank again.

"Well, technically it belongs to the family trust, but you run the trust, so yes, the bank belongs to you. That's what your husband wanted, for you and your boys to have the bank and continue his legacy."

"Well then, Jeffrey, you don't deserve a handshake. You deserve a hug for a job well done." I wrapped my arms around him and squeezed him tightly. This had been a long time coming.

Jeffrey turned and shook the boys' hands, then we exited the courtroom and got back on the elevator. Down in the lobby, we were greeted by Kimberly Simmons, our family's chief of staff. I admired Kimberly, whose rare combination of stunning beauty and whip-smart intellect was sure to take her far in life. She was just starting to come into her own as a businesswoman, and my plans were to one day have her marry my son Martin whenever he finally grew up and stopped hoeing around.

"Well, I assume from all the smiling faces that things went well?" Kimberly had a naturally happy energy about her, although when she had to, that girl could be a shark—which was why I liked her.

"Phenomenal," Malcolm replied. "Jeffrey got the regulators off our asses, and now we can get back to making real deals instead of all this small business loans shit."

"SBLs and minority loans have been the backbone of Amistad since its inception, Malcolm. Never forget where you came from, son, because when you do, it will bite you in the ass every time. I promise you that," I replied.

"You're right, of course, Mother. I'm just looking forward to doing some big money deals like Daddy used to," Malcolm said.

Malcolm had always been a daddy's boy, and his dream was to one day run Amistad like his father and grandfather had. He had the brains for it, that I could never deny, but he hadn't proven he had the balls for the job yet. I guess now that we had full, unregulated control over the bank again, time would tell.

"Malcolm!" A familiar voice interrupted us.

We turned our attention to David Michaels, a wiry, brown-skinned man who made his way excitedly across the lobby. He gave Jeffrey, Malcolm, and Martin brotherly handshakes then turned to me and gave me a quick hug.

"How are you doin', Mrs. Britton?"

David came from an old money family that had made their fortune in construction and real estate during the seventies. He'd attended Hampton University and graduated at the top of his class in accounting, passing the CPA exam on his first try. The man was a whiz with numbers. My husband, Moses, had tried to recruit him to work at the bank when he graduated, but surprisingly, David had declined. He accepted a job offer from a big white accounting firm instead. I swear, sometime these young people think the white man's ice is colder.

"I'm doing fine, David. What brings you to the federal courthouse?"

"I'm with my boss, filing patents." He turned around and spoke to a man seated on a nearby bench. "Hey, Anthony. Look who's here!"

I watched as the man rose from the bench. If this was his boss, then it appeared David had left his job at the white accounting firm. This man was tall and handsome, with a smooth milk chocolate complexion. There was a woman with him. She was good looking also, although her too-tight outfit detracted from her overall look. If he was the boss, he should consider asking his secretary to dress a little more professionally.

They approached us, and David made the introductions.

"Mrs. Britton, have you met Anthony and Sydney Johnson? They live a few doors down from you in Sag Harbor."

So she was his wife, not his secretary. I couldn't help but let out an accidental chuckle when the girl reached back and pulled an obvious wedgie from her skirt. The men didn't hear it, but she sure did, and she shot me the most evil look in response.

Oh, well. Too bad, honey. Next time wear something a little more appropriate.

Anthony offered his hand. "We've met briefly at one of the homeowners association meetings, Mrs. Britton. Nice to see you again."

"Ah, yes. The new owners who bought the Petersons' house. You're the tech guy, aren't you?" I said. I must have met him soon after he bought the house, but he couldn't have made much of an impression on me, because the memory was quite vague.

As he shook my hand, I looked over at his wife again and got a good look at her dress, which, in addition to riding up her backside, revealed too much cleavage to be considered tasteful. From the cut and quality, I guessed it was an off-the-rack find from some mid-range mall store. I was not impressed. From what I understood, her husband's tech company was extremely successful, yet she dressed as if she were married to a manager at Best Buy. Poor thing probably didn't know any better, though. I wouldn't be surprised if he'd met her on Instagram or maybe even at a strip club.

She narrowed her eyes at me slightly, as if she could feel me judging her, so I slowly let my eyes return to Anthony Johnson's face. He was smiling at me.

"The tech guy. Yes, some people do call me that," he said.

After Jeffrey introduced Anthony and his wife to my sons, he announced, "Well, ladies and gentlemen, my job is done, and I'm going to take my leave." He gave me a quick hug. "Hopefully I'll see you folks out east this weekend?"

Since it was Memorial Day weekend, the official start to the summer season in our beloved beach community, I would normally have already been out there preparing the house for weekend guests, but I had one more task to complete before I could go. I'd had Malcolm call a special meeting of the board of directors in anticipation of the judge's ruling. I couldn't wait to see the surprise on their faces when half of them found out I was replacing their disloyal asses. Only after that was complete would I be able to relax and enjoy the opening of summer in the Black Hamptons.

"We'll be out tomorrow," I replied. "Your wife has me helping out with refreshments for the HOA meeting. I'm making crab cakes."

"Well, I was supposed to go sailing," Jeffrey said with a grin. "However, if you're making crab cakes, perhaps I should reschedule."

"Perhaps you should."

"We're going to take off, too, and see if we can get ahead of some of the traffic," Anthony said as he took his wife's hand. A look of relief passed over her face, as if she was pleased to be getting away from us. "See you in the Black Hamptons."

Anthony Johnson

2

"What's the matter? You still upset about Carolyn Britton?" I glanced over at my wife, who had just let out a long sigh.

"You didn't see the way that woman was looking at me, Anthony." Her voice was starting to take on that Brooklyn edge that always crept in when she was annoyed. "She was looking down her nose at me."

"Syd, what does she have to look down her nose at you about?"

Despite her annoyance, she gave me the cutest smile. "You know, for a man so smart, you can be so naive sometimes. Women like Carolyn Britton don't need a reason to be petty. It comes naturally," she replied just as I slammed on the brakes to avoid a car swerving into our lane. "Watch out, babe!"

"Look at this jerk!" I yelled, tightening my grip on the wheel. "Dude! You're not gonna get there any faster."

"God! I can't believe this traffic," Sydney groaned, fidgeting in her seat. "How long until we get there?"

Sydney hated riding in a car. Anything over forty minutes and she would be shifting in her seat like a little kid. My Sydney was a city girl through and through, born and raised in Brooklyn and proud of it. She preferred the bus or the subway, although she tolerated the drive from the city to Sag Harbor because she loved our home on the water so much. Normally we could make the trip in two hours, but it was the Friday before Memorial Day weekend, and traffic was backed up like a son of a bitch. We'd been on the road almost four hours, and Sydney was about to lose her mind.

"It'll clear up once we get past the Southampton split," I replied.

"And how long is that going to take?"

"Maybe twenty or thirty minutes." I glanced over to see her arms folded and bottom lip poked out. It was pretty obvious she was about to have a tantrum.

"What's wrong now?"

"I'm bored. I'm tired of being in this car, and I'm horny as hell. You didn't finish what you started this morning."

A smile crept up on my face. This morning was pretty special, or at least it had been until a call from an important client interrupted us. When you own your own business, sometimes you have to make sacrifices to keep things running smoothly, and that includes answering phone calls even when you're busy trying to get it in.

"I know, and I'm sorry about that, but what was I supposed to do, Syd, miss Victor Singh's call? But we can take care of that as soon as we get to the house."

"I'm horny now, Anthony," she snapped.

"Syd, there's nothing I can do right now for you. We'll be home in a bit, and I will service all your needs. I promise."

"Hmph. Maybe there's nothing you can do now, but I'm a take charge kinda girl." She turned to me with a devilish smile, then unhooked her seat belt. Sydney had hiked up her dress and slid off her panties, spinning them on her fingers sexily. I swear my wife knew how to fuck with me.

"Are you trying to make me run off the road?" I asked.

"Keep driving. You ain't seen nothing yet."

I glanced over to see what she was doing and had to do a double take.

"Are you . . . are you masturbating?"

"Yup."

"You can't wait until we get home? Traffic's starting to move."

"Nope. I've been in this car almost four hours, Anthony, and I'm bored as shit, so keep one eye on the road, and the other on me so you can watch the show." She just kept doing her thing like I wasn't even there.

"How many times do you think I can make myself come before we reach the house?" She let out a loud moan, and I exhaled, shifting my eyes every few seconds from the road to my sexy-as-hell wife. Her performance had woken the other Johnson in the car, the one between my legs.

Twenty minutes later, I was still fully erect, and Sydney had taken the liberty of releasing me from my boxers and giving me a massage. By the time we pulled into our neighborhood, I was the one squirming in my seat, about to lose my mind.

"What the fuck?" I snapped as we turned down our block, which was more crowded than I'd ever seen it.

"What?" Sydney lifted her head from my lap, peeking over the dashboard. "Where'd all these cars come from?"

"Looks like someone's having a party," I replied as I stared at the rows of cars parked on both sides of the street.

"Who?"

"I don't know, but it better not be our kids."

Syd and I had two college-aged kids, a son, Tyler, and daughter, Gabrielle. They'd come home from Virginia State University a couple weeks ago and headed straight for the beach house. Now I wondered if it had been a mistake to let them stay out there by themselves until Memorial Day weekend. They were good kids, but they were still kids.

Sydney and I adjusted our clothes. As we got closer to the house, I could hear the music booming so loud through my closed windows that it sounded like it was inside the car with us.

She looked as nervous as I felt. "Anthony, I hate to say this, but it might just be our kids," she said. There were young people who looked to be in their late teens and early twenties headed down the block in the direction of our house.

"It better not be," I growled.

As we pulled up in front of our driveway, I realized with relief that the teens were walking past my property.

"Well, that's a relief. It looks—"

"Son of a bitch!" Sydney yelled, interrupting me. "Do you see that? Those little shits ran over my geraniums!"

"Well, the good thing is the party is not at our house. Looks like it's over at the Brittons," I said, trying to remain positive as I pulled into our driveway.

Just as I'd feared, though, Sydney was not going to be placated. "I don't give a shit. I just planted those geraniums. It took me two days to put those things in," Sidney said, stepping out of the car to inspect her flowers.

By the time I got out of my seat, she had already pulled her phone out of her purse and was dialing.

"What are you doing?" I asked as I approached her.

"I'm calling the cops."

"For what?"

"For my geraniums. Those things cost like eight hundred dollars," she said angrily.

"Put the phone away, Syd. I'll buy you some more geraniums."

"I don't want you to buy me more flowers. That's not the point," she said. "I spent two days of my life putting those flowers in, and you can't give me back that time. Some little bougie-ass kid just trampled all over my flowers, and I want someone to pay for that disrespect."

"Babe, I know you're upset, but stop and think for a minute. I don't want the police in front of my house with flashing lights over some flowers."

Sidney lowered her phone, giving me a look of recognition and understanding.

"Maybe we could just go over there and talk to the Brittons," I suggested.

She paused, and for a minute, I thought I'd won, but then she smiled devilishly. She lifted her phone again and pressed the button to make the call.

"What are you doing?"

"Calling the police." She chuckled.

"Why?"

"I don't want the police in front of our house either," she said. "But I do want them in front of the house where all the noise is coming from. The house with rude guests who ruin my flowers."

"Syd, that's a bad idea . . ."

She was already talking on the phone before I could finish my sentence.

"Yes, I'd like to make a noise complaint."

It was too late to stop her, but I knew without a doubt that my wife had just opened up a big-ass can of worms.

Jesse Britton

3

"What's up, Black Hamptons!"

I stood on the master bedroom balcony at my beachfront home and raised a bottle of champagne high in the air. The loud cheering from the crowd of onlookers was all I needed to know that I'd done the right thing in throwing the season-opening party. Yeah, there was always the risk that some fool would end up tearing my family's place apart, but the pluses of rising to the top of the popularity charts far outweighed the minuses of a few broken vases or a scratched-up coffee table. Besides, I'd hedged my bets by hiring my cousin Kenny and his Q-dog fraternity brothers as security.

"Now, we got good music, plenty of drinks, and my man Beast Boy over there has all the weed you can smoke!" There was another round of cheering. "So, what I'm tryna figure out is why I see people without cups in their hands. And you ladies over there wearing pink and green ain't dancing. This ain't no sorority meeting, ladies. This is a damn party, so let's party!" I lifted the champagne bottle again, and the crowd roared. "DJ Riot, hit the damn music!"

Right on cue, the music began blasting again, and I watched with a satisfied smile as the young ladies I'd pointed out grabbed red cups from a nearby server and began dancing.

"Nice party."

I turned to stare at the dark chocolate face of Tania Maxwell, whose tiny white bikini barely covered her Kardashian-like curves. I had to force myself to stop imagining what was underneath and make eye contact with her.

"I had to think of some kind of way to get your attention," I said. I was trying to keep it cool, but I'd been infatuated with her since the ninth grade. Tania lived in New Rochelle and came out on the weekends and summer, until four years ago, when her parents got divorced. That's when she moved into her summer house with her mom and lived here year-round. "So, I figured throwing the season-opening party might do it."

She smiled at me. Her smile always made me weak. "I guess you were right," she said. "But now that you have my attention, what are you going to do with it?"

Before I could even formulate a response, her mouth covered mine. She wrapped her arms around my neck. I slipped my tongue into her mouth and immediately recognized the taste of Hennessy. The kiss was everything I wanted it to be and more, and the moan from Tania indicated that she was enjoying it just as much as I was.

"Damn, if I would've known I was gonna get all that, I definitely would've tried to get your attention earlier," I said when we stepped back from the kiss.

"Well, like I said, you've got it now. So, you gonna stay up here all night? Because I'm trying to get my dance and drink on, and then maybe a little more."

"Shit, you ain't gotta tell me twice. Let's roll." I grabbed her hand and led her back down to the yard.

The party was in full effect. Drinks were flowing, the music was popping, asses were twerking, and I was enjoying every minute of it. Based on the way she was dancing on me, Tania was too.

"I see ya, cuz!" Kenny yelled from across the pool. "But I got something for you."

Kenny gestured to the DJ, and then the beat dropped, and "Atomic Dog" started playing. It was the unofficial theme song of Kenny's fraternity, Omega Psi Phi. Girls squealed as Kenny and the members of his fraternity got into formation and began stepping. The crowd went wild, and I knew it was time to make my move.

"Let's go back inside," I said, whispering to Tania as I hugged her from behind.

"Now?" She turned and gave me a weird look.

"Yeah, we can see better from up top. We'll be back in a little while." The seductive look I gave her was enough motivation for her to take my hand and follow me. I grabbed a bottle of champagne and led her back through the house, up to the balcony.

Unfortunately, our escape to somewhere more private was short-lived. We'd just gotten back to the balcony, and I went in for a kiss. It didn't last for more than a minute, though, before we heard a commotion down below with lots of angry shouting.

I released Tania's hand and leaned over the balcony to see what was going on down there. The music scratched to a halt, so I could clearly hear a verbal altercation.

"I'm saying, man, you need to leave. This is a private party!" Kenny shouted.

I saw him standing in front of four guys. It was a pool party, so all of my guests were wearing bathing suits or cover-ups, but these guys were all fully clothed, making it obvious that they didn't belong there. All of them were white, except one tall dude, who looked like he spent most of his waking hours lifting weights. This muscle-bound brother seemed to be the ringleader.

"Don't nobody give a shit about this whack-ass party. I'm looking for my girl. Her car's parked out front," he said.

Kenny, now backed by five of his frat brothers I'd hired for security, took a step closer. My cousin is short, but he's stocky as hell, and he is far from a punk, so I expected they would take these guys out quickly and we could get back to partying. But I underestimated the strength of our party-crashers. The white guys hung back a little, but I don't think it was because they were scared. It was probably because they knew their ringleader could handle it without their help. He picked up Kenny's ass and effortlessly tossed him in the pool like he was a child.

"Damn!" I said to myself. "Fucking townies. I shoulda known they'd crash my shit." Little did I know they were about to fuck up more than just the party. They were going to fuck up my chance to finally get with the girl I'd been lusting after for years.

"I'm a townie," Tania said.

"No, you're not. You're one of us. You live in the Black Hamptons."

"Tania!" the big brother shouted, catching me by surprise.

I turned and looked at Tania. She just stared at me with a look somewhere between annoyance and embarrassment.

"Tania! Where the fuck are you? I know you're here!" The guy continued yelling as he walked through the crowd. After seeing how easily he handled Kenny, everyone stepped back to give him a wide berth as he passed by. "I saw your car."

My head swiveled from her to the guy then back to her. "You know this clown?"

"Yeah," she said, exhaling loudly. "His name is Peter. He's kinda my boyfriend."

My eyes widened and my lower lip dropped. Now that was a fucking surprise.

"You got a boyfriend?" I asked, feeling deflated.

She nodded sheepishly, and I stared at her as I tried to make sense of what was happening. Tania had come on to me, not the other way around, so why the hell was I finding out now that she already had a boyfriend? It was kind of disappointing. I had always wanted her, but I'd never imagined she was that kind of chick.

I was in my feelings for a minute, tuning out the background noise of Peter's yelling as I tried to process, but I snapped back to the present when I heard water splashing again. I looked over the railing and saw two of Kenny's frat brothers bobbing in the pool. Peter was standing at the edge in a defensive posture, like he was waiting for someone else to step to him so he could throw them in too.

"Shit, I'll be right back," I said. I'd have to deal with Tania later.

I turned to leave, but she grabbed my arm. "Jesse, I wouldn't start a fight. He's a Golden Gloves champion."

I didn't try to hide my annoyance. "I don't give a shit about that. Dude crashed my fucking party, and he's gonna get the hell off my property."

"Jesse—" Tania tried stopping me again, but I pulled away and rushed back in the house and down the stairs.

By the time I made it to the pool, Tania's man had tossed another guy into the pool and was grabbing the collar of a fifth. I maneuvered my way through the crowd gathered around, witnessing the mayhem that was unfolding.

"Hey, my man, time to leave or I'm calling the cops." Now that we were face to face, I realized I'd underestimated exactly how big dude was. He was about five inches taller than me, and his frame was forty percent bigger and made of solid muscle.

Peter looked me up and down, probably sizing me up before he would toss me into the pool too. "Call the cops? Do I look like I'm afraid of the police?"

The guys behind him laughed as if they knew something I didn't.

"I ain't going nowhere without my girl."

I glanced around the crowd and saw from their expressions that if they had been placing bets, their money would be on the other guy to beat my ass. I couldn't lose their respect, especially right at the beginning of the season. I'd spend the rest of my summer getting roasted as a punk. I took a step closer to him and puffed out my chest, even if it was still nowhere near as swole as his.

"Well, I'm sorry to tell you this," I said, "but she ain't coming. Now, I'll make sure she gives you a call tomor—"

"Tania! I ain't playin wit' yo' ass!" Peter shoved me in my face and walked around me. Tania was now standing in the doorway to the patio, and he took a step in her direction.

If you're gonna stop him, you'd better do something quick. This is your house. You're the king of this castle.

My arm was up in the air before I even realized it, and the champagne bottle in my hand came crashing down on Peter's head. He stumbled, and for half a second, I believed I'd handled him and saved my reputation. But as I waited for him to fall, he regained his footing and turned around to face me. The average person would have been flat out on the ground after being hit with a bottle, but I swear this dude was superhuman.

"Oh, shit." I mumbled. I can't lie; I thought about running. Unfortunately, before my feet got the message from my brain, Peter struck me in the stomach with such force that my body folded like a tent. I hit the ground, gasping for air.

Sergeant Tom Lane

4

Ten minutes. That's how long I had left on my shift as one of two sergeants of the Sag Harbor police department. Not that the night had been very eventful. Even though it was the start of the Memorial Day weekend, the official start of the busy tourist season in the Hamptons, it wasn't like the town was a hotbed of criminal activity that required active policing. The most exciting thing I'd done for the past nine hours was hand out a few speeding tickets on Route 114.

I wasn't complaining, though. I'd only been working in Sag Harbor for two months, and I much preferred the quality of life here to the wild-ass blocks I'd patrolled as a member of the NYPD for the past twenty-two years. For the first time since my son had been born, I had no real fear that I might not make it home one night.

The dispatcher's voice crackled through the radio. "Sergeant Lane, we have a complaint for a noise disturbance at 234 Bayside Drive."

Damn. A party. Aside from traffic violations and the occasional DUI, this was the other thing I'd been warned was pretty common out here during the summer months. In the Hamptons, there was always a party somewhere. In the winter, when the tourists were gone and there wasn't shit else to do, bored local teens partied. I had already broken up a few of those events in the short time I'd been working. In the summer, I was told, it would be all the rich folks who had second homes out here. The location at Bayside Drive told me this party was one of theirs.

I tried to keep the irritation out of my voice as I responded. "I've got ten minutes left on my shift. I'm not looking for any overtime, Jenny."

"Chief says anything east of Bay Street off of 114 is yours and that you'd know why," she responded.

"Yeah, because it's in the Black Hamptons," I mumbled to myself. I was the lone Black officer on the force, so the chief had let me know when he hired me that I'd be the one answering calls in the Black neighborhood. Since most of the houses there were summer homes, they'd been empty until this weekend, so this would be my first official call to the neighborhood.

I pushed the button and replied, "Ten-four. En route."

"Copy that. Officer Nugent will meet you there."

Six minutes later, I arrived at the east entrance to Bayside Drive and realized this wasn't just some little beach party. Both sides of the street were lined with illegally parked cars, and even with my windows rolled up, I could hear the music from three blocks away. It was a miracle that we hadn't received multiple complaints.

I pulled up to one of the most impressive houses I'd ever seen and stepped out of the car just as another cruiser came charging down the west end of the street with its lights flashing and sirens blaring. Officer PJ Nugent, a young, thick-necked guy who'd lived his whole life in Sag Harbor, hopped out of his cruiser and came rushing toward me.

"Really, Nugent? Really?" I pointed to the flashing lights.

Before he could respond, a group of Black kids came running from the side of the house. Some of them jumped into cars, and some ran down the block. It was pretty obvious none of them wanted anything to do with the police, which probably wasn't a bad thing.

"Was all that necessary?" I asked Nugent.

"It worked, didn't it? See, no music, and the party is dispersing." He pointed at the kids running down the block. "Might as well get out of here and call it a night. I have a fishing trip to Block Island early tomorrow morning," he said.

"We're not going anywhere until I speak to someone and make sure they keep down the noise." I started walking toward the house. My suspicion was that this party was being held by a bunch of young people whose parents weren't home. If this was going to be my beat, I wanted folks to see that I was hands on and things like this would be taken care of.

"You sure about this, Sarge? I mean, it looks like they got the message. And more importantly, our shift is over. It doesn't have to be our problem."

I'd been a policeman for more than twenty years, and I'd do anything for one of my fellow officers, but it never ceased to amaze me how much these white boys just didn't get it. "These are Black kids, Nugent. As a Black man, they are my problem." I was sure there would be talk behind my back at the station about my comment, but I didn't give a shit. I was taught as a youngster that it takes a village to raise a Black child, as a single father raising a Black son, I was a willing participant in that village. Hell, if it hadn't been for a Black cop steering me down the right path when I was a teenager, who knows where I'd be?

"You afraid of a couple of Black kids, Nugent?"

"I wouldn't say that, but they have us outnumbered probably fifty to one, and we both know how young Black kids feel about white cops. I'd rather avoid an incident than create one." He patted his holster. "But if you want us to go in, then I'm ready for anything."

"This is not the OK Corral, and we're not here for a gunfight, Nugent. Keep that gun holstered, and make sure your body-cam is on," I replied. I wanted to tell him to just go home, but that was against department regulations. "Now, come on."

I opened the back gate and entered the most spectacular backyard I'd ever seen. It looked more like a resort than the back of someone's home. The pool was huge with a waterfall at one end, a slide in the middle, and two Jacuzzis. There was a gazebo with a six-person bar, plus an outdoor kitchen with two jumbo gas grills, an outdoor TV twice the size of the one I had at home, and a pizza oven. All of this was overlooking a spectacular view of the beach. The moon reflecting off the water just completed the picture of wealth and luxury. I'd driven by some of the homes in the Black Hamptons during my patrol, but this was even more impressive than I could have imagined. I had to admit I felt proud to know that it was Black people who owned it.

"More cops! Let's get the hell outta here!" someone yelled, and the stragglers who hadn't scattered before took off now— except for a small group near the pool. They were looking down at the ground, where we saw a young man trying to get up. He looked like he might be hurt.

Nugent and I made our way over and pulled him to his feet.

"You all right, son?" I asked.

"Get off me!" he said with an attitude that took me by surprise.

"Okay, settle down. You have too much to drink?" I asked, letting go of his arm.

"No. Just got the wind knocked out of me."

"And how exactly did that happen?"

He hesitated, still holding his stomach. "I fell down."

"Okay, I'll accept that for now," I replied, although I knew it was bullshit. I looked around at the young people still there. "Whose house is this? Who's in charge here?"

"It's my house. And why are you here?" The answer came from the one who'd been on the ground.

"We're here because we've gotten some complaints about the noise." I usually tried not to judge young people, especially young Black boys, since I had a son of my own, but there was an arrogance about this kid that tweaked my nerves. "I'm not sure if you're aware, but Sag Harbor has a ten o'clock noise ordinance."

The young man, who appeared to be feeling better, gave a sarcastic apology. "Ooops, sorry, *officer*. Just having a little fun." He gave my arm a patronizing pat, and I had an urge to swing on him and put him right back on the ground. Then, he turned and took a red plastic cup from a young lady standing nearby and smiled at me as he sipped from it. To make matters worse, I could almost feel Nugent off to my right, judging me. I was trying to give these kids a break, but this one wasn't making it easy.

"For the record, these stripes mean I'm a sergeant." I took a cup from another girl and sniffed the contents. "This smells like alcohol. How old are you, young lady?" I asked.

"Twenty-one." Her voice was barely above a whisper and her eyes wide with fear. It was evident she was lying.

"Let me see some ID."

"Uh, it's at home," she replied weakly.

"Well then, why don't we take a trip to your house and get it?" She kept staring at the boy with the cup, and he kept looking away. I unhooked my cuffs. It was a bluff, but it usually worked. "It'll be fun. I might even get to meet your parents," I taunted her.

The suggestion of her parents brought tears to her eyes. "Officer, I'm seventeen. This is the first time I ever drank, and the only reason I'm here is because Jesse invited me." She glanced at the smart-ass kid again. "Please don't tell my parents."

Satisfied that she would think twice about going to another party soon, I turned back to the guy. "You did say that you were in charge, right?"

"Yeah," he said confidently. "And just so you know, I am twenty-one, and I do have ID. Now, the music is turned down, so you guys can go. I know my rights."

"You know your rights, huh?" I'm not gonna lie, I wanted to smack his arrogant ass for that.

"Yeah, I do," he said, then sipped from his cup like he didn't have a care in the world. "So I'd appreciate it if you'd leave."

"Sure thing. Why don't you take that ride with me?"

I grabbed his arm, and in one swift motion, twisted it behind his back and locked the cuffs on his wrists. I'd had enough of being nice.

"What are you doing?" he demanded.

"I'm placing you under arrest for contributing to the delinquency of a minor, giving alcohol to a minor, and I'm sure I'll think of about five other charges by the time I reach the car."

He no longer had a superior smirk on his face, but he still didn't look humbled. In fact, he looked downright pissed off.

"You have the right to remain silent. Anything you say can and—"

"Yo, yo, Deputy Dog, back up off me!" he yelled. "Do you know who I am? My family probably owns your mortgage. You might wanna rethink this shit."

"Nope. I don't know who you are, and I don't care. Oh, and for the record, I don't have a mortgage. I rent," I informed him. "But one day, I'd like to have a place like this," I said sarcastically. "Let's go!"

"You can't arrest him! He's twenty-one!" someone shouted.

"Yeah, he ain't do nothing! Leave him alone!" another person yelled.

"Yo, Sarge." Nugent leaned toward me and whispered, "You sure about this? We might wanna let him off with a warning."

"*Warning* my ass. I tried to be nice and cut him a break, but this big-head bastard needs to be taught a lesson. Now, do your job. Check the IDs for these kids and call the parents of the underage ones and have them picked up. I have a feeling this will be the last party around here for a while." This had not been my intention, but this kid had pushed things too far. Not only was he trying to embarrass me in front of his peers, but also my fellow officer.

Fear and shock appeared on the faces in the crowd as I began walking the cuffed party host out the back gate. By the time we made it to my cruiser, several neighbors had gathered in their yards. I was placing him in the back of the car when the headlights of an approaching car hit my eyes.

"What are you doing with my grandson?" a woman asked after she stepped out of the Rolls Royce and approached me.

"If you're referring to this hooligan, he's being arrested," I answered.

"Arrested for what?"

The young man spoke. "Grandma, I—"

She held up her hand and gave him a threatening look that shut him up. Okay, this was promising. At least he had someone of authority in his life, which meant maybe there was hope for him after all. Perhaps the two of us could scare this kid straight and make sure he stayed on the right path.

I was wrong about that. Grandma let me know in a hurry that she wasn't thinking the same way, which was disappointing.

"Officer, let me make something clear. You are going to remove those handcuffs from my grandson right now or you'll be looking for employment in the morning. Have I made myself clear?"

I did a double take. Did this woman think she was Michelle Obama or Vice President Harris? From the commanding look she gave me, it was obvious that she fully expected me to heed her warning, which pissed me off. Did anyone around here have respect for the uniform?

"Ma'am, these cuffs are staying right where they are, and if you don't get out of the way, you'll be wearing a matching pair. Now, have I made *myself* clear?"

"Crystal clear." She took a deep breath and stepped forward. Her voice was calm, but there was fire in her eyes. "However, I almost feel sorry for you, because you have no idea of the consequences of your actions."

"I'm doing my job, and I'm not going to warn you again. Interfering with a police officer is a serious charge," I grumbled.

Her eyes remained on me, but she called another name. "Martin!"

A younger man in a suit stepped past her and held his hand out, offering me his cell phone. I stared at it, my hands still at my sides.

"You might want to take this," he said.

Was he serious? "What, you work for Verizon? You giving out free phones?"

He gave me a very insincere smile. "No, but this might be the most important call of your life." He gestured again for me to take it.

"Why would I take that from you?" I asked.

"Because it's your boss on the line," the woman said. "Chief Harrington."

No way in the world that could be my boss. I wasn't taking the phone. They weren't gonna punk me.

"If I were you, I'd take it, Sarge," I heard Nugent say from behind me.

Something about the tone of Nugent's voice told me he believed it really was the chief on the line. I took the phone and brought it to my ear.

"Hello."

"Lane, what the fuck are you doing?" Chief Harrington's voice boomed through the phone. "How the fuck did a simple noise complaint end up with Carolyn Britton's grandson in cuffs? Have you lost your mind?"

"Chief, it wasn't a simple noise complaint," I tried to explain, still shocked that he was actually on the phone. "There were underage teens here drinking."

"Drinking on private property, Lane. Did you have permission to enter the backyard?" he asked.

"Well, no, but I had reason to believe—"

"This is not New York City, Lane! Your job is to keep the peace, not start a damn war."

He wasn't wrong about one thing: this was definitely not New York City. My old bosses never would have told me to just look the other way if I came across a party full of underage kids drinking. I guess they did things differently out in the Hamptons.

"Chief, I just thought—"

"I don't give a shit about what you thought! You're not paid to think. Release him now and apologize for the misunderstanding, then leave," Chief Harington instructed. "Am I understood?"

The chief's voice was so loud in my ear that the woman who I now knew was Carolyn Britton probably heard every word. She had a satisfied smirk on her face.

"Yes, sir, I understand," I told him.

"Good. Now, put Carolyn on the phone."

"Yes, sir." I extended the phone to her. "Chief Harrington would like to speak to you."

She gave me a condescending smile and then said in a friendly voice, "Hello, Chief Harrington. No, no need to apologize. I can see he's new. Let's just make sure it doesn't happen again. Oh, and tell the mayor I'm looking forward to golf with the two of you on Thursday. I've been working on my swing. See you then."

I listened to the conversation as I took her grandson from the back of the cruiser and removed the cuffs. Who the fuck was this woman, and how did she have so much damn power?

"You're free to go," I told the kid.

"Thanks, *officer.*"

I closed the door and looked at the small crowd of onlookers, who seemed to be amused by the situation.

"All right, Nugent," I said. "Let's get out of here."

Nugent gave me a sympathetic nod. He walked over to my patrol car with me and said quietly, "Rule number one of policing the Black Hamptons. Stay clear of the Brittons."

I glanced back at the house, which looked bigger than my whole precinct building back in Brooklyn, then back to the Brittons, who were standing in front of their mansion, staring at me. I didn't know who these people were, but something told me that if the chief expected me to patrol this area, it would be in my best interests to find out who they were in a hurry.

Martin Britton

5

By the time the fiasco with my nephew Jesse was over, it was after eleven o'clock, and I was extremely late for an event I'd been planning to attend all week. Marjorie Kincaid was a fine arts dealer who had been pursuing my business for quite a while. She was twenty years my senior, refined, and had quite the body for a woman her age. However, it was her reputation in the art community and her knack for finding unique artistic talent that drew me to her and her gallery. We'd done business in the past, but both of us were looking to expand upon that and more. So, when I received her handwritten invitation to an exclusive showing, I didn't hesitate to accept.

Once my mother had calmed down, I showered, changed into a pair of black slacks and a crisp black shirt, then made my way to East Hampton to the address on the invitation. I arrived to find that there were still quite a few people at the beachside home, indulging in the beautiful view of the water, open bar, jazz quartet, and exclusive art. The artwork on display was quite impressive, and several pieces caught my attention.

Art had been my passion ever since I was a child. My grandfather used to take me to art galleries, and he had taught me an appreciation for art with the same enthusiasm many fathers have for teaching their sons about baseball and basketball. To me, at times, a good piece of art could be more seductive than a beautiful woman—and a hell of a lot more expensive.

I'd wanted to major in art when I was in college, but my old man wasn't having it. He'd made it clear that I was to major in business and get an MBA in economics so I could work at the bank, which I ultimately did. However, an art minor had served me and our family well over the past five years as I'd acquired a valuable collection of art by African American artists.

"Eclectic, isn it? I see it caught your eye," a soft voice said.

I'd paused to admire a stunning oil painting of a couple dancing in a subway station. I turned, and my eyes fell upon a stunningly gorgeous dark-skinned woman standing beside me. Her makeup was flawless, and her dimpled smile was as captivating as the picture in front of us.

"Yes, it's breathtaking. I have to have it," I replied, referring to the painting but also meaning her. "I love the curves. They make me feel as if I can just reach out and touch them."

"They really do, don't they?" She took a step closer.

I wasn't quite sure who she was, but I liked her. She had an energy about her that was sexy.

"Who knows? For twenty thousand you just might be able to take it home," she said.

"I guess I'll have to check and see if I have an extra twenty K lying around," I responded flirtatiously.

"Well, if you do, see if there's another twenty lying around for me," she flirted back.

"Do you really think you're worth twenty thousand?" I said boldly.

"I most certainly—"

"Martin, you're here!" Marjorie shouted from across the room.

I turned to her, and her silicone-injected, Jessica-Rabbit figure sashayed across the room. Don't get me wrong. She didn't look bad, but there was no way that figure was anywhere close to being real.

Marjorie made her way over and gave me a hug. "I didn't think you were coming."

"My apologies for being late. The traffic from the city was hell," I said, giving her a kiss on each cheek.

"I can imagine. I absolutely hate traffic," she said. She motioned toward the young lady I'd been speaking to. "I see you've met our featured artist, Jade Sinclair. Jade, this is Martin Britton. Martin is the vice president of the largest African American–owned bank in the country."

"We haven't officially met," I replied, offering my hand. "However, we have discussed the price of this magnificent piece. Sorry for being late."

Jade smiled as she took my hand. "With an introduction like that, you can be late any time you like, Mr. Britton."

"Please, call me Martin," I replied, kissing her hand. "I think your painting would look magnificent featured in our Harlem headquarters."

I could see the excitement in Jade's eyes, but Marjorie didn't look pleased at all.

"Well then, let's talk about it over drinks," Marjorie said. "Jade may be the artist, but my gallery handles all her work exclusively." Marjorie jealously placed her arm in mine and began to tug me away. It was obvious she did not want me around Jade.

"Nice meeting you," Jade said with a look that made me want to stay and continue our conversation.

"Same here, Jade." I smiled, making sure we made eye contact. "I'll catch up to you later."

"Looking forward to it."

Marjorie's grip on my arm was tight as she forcefully guided me toward the bar. "So, Martin, if I can get you a twenty percent discount on her little painting, will you allow me to bring the Franklin piece I sold you last year to market? I have three motivated buyers."

"I'm not sure if it's for sale," I lied. I'd been planning to sell the painting for almost six months because my mother couldn't stand it and actually had it taken down from our Queens branch lobby.

Marjorie gave me a disappointed look. "I see. Well, you paid twenty-five thousand for it only last year. I can get you fifty thousand by the end of the weekend, along with a bonus."

"Seventy-five would be better. Three buyers sounds like a bidding war to me."

"I like the way you think."

"I thought you might. Now, what kind of bonus were you talking about?"

"You're not an unattractive man, Martin, and I've seen the way you look at me. Perhaps I could sweeten the deal by letting you spend the night."

I couldn't help but chuckle. Marjorie had been trying to get in my pants for the past five or six months. I hadn't bitten because older women like her had a tendency to become a bit possessive, and the last thing I wanted was a stalker. But now that she'd offered a twenty percent discount on Jade's painting and possibly triple the price of a painting my mother couldn't stand . . . Well, I had never been against taking one for the team.

There was only one problem. Jade. Despite my being whisked away, we'd continued to make eye contact, and our eyes were talking in ways my lower half could understand. I wanted her, I wanted her bad, and I was sure she wanted me. I stood there contemplating my decision for a moment, until I remembered the number one rule my father had drilled into me and my brother practically since birth. Business always comes first. I needed both the painting and the sale, which meant Marjorie was going to have company that night.

Marjorie stuck to me like glue for the rest of the event. She finally excused herself to talk to a client who was leaving, and I took that time to scan the room, hoping to get a glimpse of Jade. Unfortunately, she was nowhere to be found, and I felt a twinge of regret.

"If you're looking for Marjorie, she's over there."

I turned to the voice and was surprised to see Kimberly, our family's chief of staff, holding a glass of wine and staring at me. "Not like you to be played so close, Martin."

"What are you doing here anyway?" I asked, a bit annoyed. I liked Kimberly, and she had proven her loyalty over the years, but she always seemed to pop up at the most inopportune times. "Did my mother send you to spy on me, or have you suddenly developed an interest in art?"

"My interests are your interests, Martin. I serve at the pleasure of not only your mother, but the entire Britton family. I came here to support you," she replied.

"This is an art show, not a board meeting. Why would I need support?"

"Marjorie Kincaid has had you on her radar for quite a while. I'm here to make sure whatever happens between you two ends up in the family's best interest."

"I'm not a child."

"Neither is Marjorie Kincaid." She placed a hand on my shoulder. "I'm not here to stop you from having fun, but a woman like her with a body like that is right up your alley."

"What is that supposed to mean?" I was borderline offended.

"It means you like women, Martin. Young women, old women, dark women, white women. Hell, you'd probably like alien women if you could find one. You like women. They're your weakness, and unfortunately, they seem to like you as well," she stated matter-of-factly.

I nodded in agreement. "Touché. It's a blessing and a curse sometimes."

"Yes, but let's not let your blessing become a curse." Her words were so on point they gave me a chill.

"Don't get it twisted, miss know-it-all. There may be an exchange of bodily fluids, but this is also business. Marjorie's offering a twenty percent discount on the painting I want, and she has three clients lined up to buy the Franklin painting, which means a bidding war may ensue, and we may end up with five times what we paid."

"All money isn't good money, Martin." Kim looked directly at me and asked, "Now, let's be honest, shall we?"

"Aren't we always?" I replied.

"It's Ms. Sinclair's artwork you're really interested in, along with the woman herself."

I couldn't help but laugh because she was always one step ahead of me. "You don't miss a trick, do you?"

"No, I can't afford to. It's my job. Now, just so you know, unfortunately Ms. Sinclair's car is in the parking lot with a flat tire. She's going to need a ride. I suggest it be you." She said that shit so confidently that I knew she was behind the convenient scenario.

"Kim, did you flatten that girl's tires?" I asked, shaking my head.

The devious grin she gave me was priceless. "I only did what needed to be done."

"What about Marjorie?"

"I think she is best left alone. From what I hear from her maid, Marjorie Kincaid is leaving her male friends with a parting gift they can't get rid of. Herpes isn't sexy, Martin, and we need you to be sexy." Kimberly finished her wine and placed the empty glass on the bar.

"Herpes?" I damn near choked on the word.

"It is the gift that keeps on giving. Now, go find Jade and offer your assistance."

"Good looking out," I replied. "But what about the paintings?"

"I'll deal with Marjorie."

I chuckled. "I'm sure you will."

"May I suggest you entertain her on the yacht? Your brother's entertaining a guest, but I'm sure he won't mind. It is a rather large ship. I think you two should be able to stay out of each other's way. After what happened with Jesse and the police, I'm sure your mother isn't in the mood for house guests."

"To say the least," I replied. Mother had always said how special Kimberly was, and every day, she seemed to give me another reason to believe it.

Jeffrey Bowen

6

Golden fingers of sunlight reflected on the water as it lapped against the hull of my pride and joy, The Lady Leslie. She was a 38-foot Catalina sailboat named after my wife. The boat was docked but still rocked gently. I was waiting impatiently for my guest to arrive.

"Glorious morning." Everett Simpson strolled down the dock.

"You're late."

Everett shrugged. "You said sunrise."

"I said I was trying to catch the sunrise. The sun rose thirty minutes ago." I usually didn't take people out on my boat for this very reason. After a long winter, I couldn't wait to get out on the water, and now Everett's inconsiderate ass was holding me up. The only reason I'd invited him was because I was the attorney of record on his father's estate, and we had unfinished business to take care of that he insisted on doing this weekend.

"Jeez, Jeffrey, you sound like a whiny-ass woman. It's not like you have a hundred-fifty-foot yacht and we're going out to have eggs Benedict and mimosas. It's a forty-foot sailboat. As far as I'm concerned, it might as well be a dingy. We can conduct our business right here."

I pushed aside the urge to curse out his pretentious ass for wasting my morning as he climbed aboard. The sailboat he was putting down had cost me 250 grand, so he could kiss my ass.

I'd known Everett since my family first started summering in the Black Hamptons back when I was in grade school. His father, my father, and my wife's uncle Moses Britton were good friends and did a lot of business together, but Everett certainly wasn't what I'd consider a friend, mainly because he was an asshole. His grandfather was one of the founding fathers of the beloved community where we'd grown up every summer, and in Everett's mind, that made him superior.

"Well then, how can I help you, Everett?" I asked. I'd already missed sunrise, so maybe I could conduct business quickly and get rid of him to sail in peace.

He handed me a manila envelope. I opened it and scanned the contents.

Looking up at him, I asked, "Are you sure you want to do this? This is part of your family's legacy."

"I wouldn't have called you if I wasn't. My family's legacy will never die in this neighborhood. We built the Black Hamptons," he boasted. "There's no need for me to hold onto a senseless piece of property when it can fund my future. I'm not selling the house. Besides, you know I've always preferred living in The Bluffs where things are a little more . . . settled."

"Settled? What does that even mean? We both know you're selling the land because you need the money, Everett." I could see that he felt insulted by my words, but before he attempted to deny it, I said, "You know what? It doesn't matter. How would you like this to proceed? I can broker a private deal with a buyer, and you'd still get asking price. You also wouldn't have to pay a real estate commission. Just my fee."

"I don't want a private buyer, Jeffrey. Let's give all the folks in the community and their friends the opportunity to make the purchase. I'm sure someone will have interest. It's not often prime beachfront comes available. Perhaps we can get a bidding war started." Everett folded his arms and leaned against the railing. "Even though I'm selling, I want the Black Hamptons to remain Black. That's important to me, and that's the real legacy you were talking about, the legacy my family is so proud of: A whole fucking oasis of Black excellence."

"I'm proud to hear that."

There was constant pressure from outside the community, trying to tempt owners with significant cash offers for their properties. It was always a relief when a seller was interested in "keeping it within the family," so to speak.

"No one is gonna say that Everett Simpson fucked that up. I will not be known as one of the culprits who sold their property and it resulted in the gentrification of our community," he said.

Hearing him refer to the same neighborhood that he felt wasn't classy enough for him to live in as "our community" was hypocritical, but I didn't point that out.

"I respect that, Everett, and as a longtime resident, I appreciate it too. I'll have my wife put out feelers and a sign later this week."

"I'd like it announced at the HOA meeting later today."

"You sure about that?" I asked. "Leslie can put together a marketing plan."

"No need for all that. I can't think of a better way to let it be known." Everett's usual smug attitude returned. "Consider it my gift to the community. I want *everyone* to learn at the same time that it's for sale and have a fair chance to bid. Now, you're the estate lawyer and executor of the estate. I'm going to allow you to hire your wife to take care of this, Jeffrey, because I trust that you're the best people for the job."

"I promise we will both be on it. I'll let you know what happens," I told him. Even though I wouldn't have enough time before the meeting to give Leslie all the details, I was sure that once I told her how high her commission would be, she'd be on board.

Everett extended his hand to me. "Good. I'm going to head to the Vineyard for a week or two, but I'll be accessible by phone. I can't wait to hear the response."

"So, you won't be at the meeting?"

"No, but I'm sure you'll handle it. Just remember that you and your wife work for me." He gave me that smirk again, and my gut told me he was up to something.

Malcolm Britton

7

Despite a slight hangover, my body was still buzzing with energy after a very special night of sexual bliss with Morgan. Thanks to Kimberly, I'd "accidentally on purpose" run into Morgan at a bar in the city last night. We had a couple of drinks, talked about old times, and like I'd planned, we ended up on my family's yacht headed out to the Hamptons. The rest of the night, as they say, was history, one for the record books. Now that the night was over and the yacht was moored in the Hamptons, I had to leave my true-life fantasy behind and drag my ass out of the bed and back to reality.

I'd hoped a hot shower would bring me down from my sexual high so I could concentrate on business, but Morgan foiled that plan by entering the shower and kissing along my back and rubbing my lower back and ass cheeks.

"Good morning." I turned around and smiled. Seconds later, our mouths and tongues were exploring, and my penis sprang back to life.

"Well, good morning to both of you," Morgan said, glancing down at my semi-hard manhood with a seductive grin. "In fact, let's make it a great morning. Let's make it memorable."

Morgan needed no instruction whatsoever to make my body respond to every intuitive touch. The temperature of the water was nothing compared to the heat that was created between us. The foreplay session was brief, interrupted when I positioned myself so that I could enter from behind: our favorite position. I grabbed Morgan's waist with one hand, and with the other, took my swollen penis and rubbed it back and forth against the spot that I knew was most sensitive.

I was invigorated when I heard Morgan's eager moans. Entering, slowly at first, I was welcomed by a gasp and another moan that turned me on even more.

The spontaneous shower fuck seemed to be over as quickly as it began, leaving both of us short of breath, smiling, and very satisfied. I was grateful for the early morning quickie, but I had things to do ashore. Round four would have to wait, despite Morgan's pouting face.

"Are you sure there's nothing I can do to get you to stay?" Morgan, now back in bed, asked as I got dressed.

"Yeah. There's a lot of things you can do, but they'll have to wait. Business before pleasure. I'll be back," I promised. "If you're hungry, the fridge is full. You can enjoy the yacht as if it's your own."

"Be careful what you say. I may hold you to it."

I had enough sense not to react. After a quick forehead kiss, I closed the stateroom door behind me and hopped the steps, reaching the deck just in time to catch the last few moments of the sun rising against the shore. It was a beautiful, peaceful sight, the perfect view to start my day and celebrate the recent court victory of my family and our company.

"Beautiful, isn't it?" I heard a voice and turned to see Martin, my brother and best friend, coming down the stairs from an upper deck. He must have slipped on board sometime late last night after we docked. "I think I finally see why Granddaddy and them settled on Sag Harbor. Right now, it might be the most beautiful place in the world."

He handed me cup of coffee, and I took a long sip.

"Thanks."

"You look refreshed." He gave me a knowing smile. "Who is she? Anybody I know?"

I hesitated briefly before I told him. "Morgan."

My reply was met with my brother's stone face.

"Morgan?" He tried not to sound annoyed, but his rolling eyes told a different story. It wasn't hard to see that my brother did not like Morgan. In fact, sometimes I think he hated Morgan. "I thought you put Morgan out to pasture. What happened to moving on to bigger and better things?"

"Your words, not mine. You know how I feel about Morgan." I sipped my coffee with no regrets.

"And clearly, I think you should rethink your feelings," he said.

I gave him the side eye, and he understood it as the warning it was.

"Look, Malcolm, I just don't wanna see you to get hurt like you did the last time. Morgan doesn't care about you." He was referring to my breakup with Morgan last year. It wasn't pretty at all, and Morgan actually slapped me in front of him. But what Martin didn't understand was that I was the one who fucked up. All Morgan wanted was a commitment, and I wouldn't give it.

"Let's agree to disagree," I said, tiring of this back-and-forth. "What are you doing here, anyway?"

I got my answer when a beautiful, dark-chocolate woman strolled down the top deck stairs, wearing his shirt as a dress and carrying heels. She kissed him like he had changed her life. It wasn't the first time I'd seen a woman look at my brother like that.

"Jade, this is my brother, Malcolm. Malcolm, this is Jade, a very talented artist and a friend of mine."

I offered my hand. "Nice to meet you, Jade."

"Nice to meet you," she replied, gently shaking my hand. Then she turned back to Martin. "Call me?"

"Sure." Martin kissed her gently, then pointed toward the dock. "I had my guys fix your tire and bring it over here to the marina. You should be good."

"Thanks." She looked like she wanted to kiss him again but didn't. Martin watched her walk down the gangplank and kept his eyes on her until she made it to the parking lot.

"So, are you really going to call her?" I asked.

"Maybe not tonight, but I'll give her a call. We had fun." His expression was serious. "But, bro, we've got more important things to talk about after last night."

"What happened last night?"

Martin furrowed his brow. "I thought you knew. There was an incident last night."

"What kind of incident?" My heart rate doubled. "This doesn't have anything to do with the bank, does it?"

"No, the bank's fine, but it could prove embarrassing at the homeowners association meeting today." Martin gave me an intense look. "You have your phone. You may want to give Mother a call."

This made me even more nervous. It was never a good look when something upset or embarrassed my mother. There were very few women, especially Black women, who were more astute and calculating in business than she was. She reveled in her position of power and influence, and the reputation of the family was an integral part of the equation. She expected us to maintain an appearance of damn near perfection at all times.

It had been hard growing up with that kind of pressure, but at times my mother could also display genuine love and compassion for us. That was a side of her she never revealed to anyone outside of the family, and for that, she had gained a reputation for being cold and uncaring. The stress of the court proceedings over the past year had enhanced some of her worst qualities, causing her to become even more rigid and short-tempered to the point that sometimes she was downright intolerable. I had hoped that with the court returning control of the bank to us, things would go back to normal, or at least our family's version of normal. Martin's serious expression made me worry that whatever had happened last night would delay that relief.

I took out my phone and dialed her number, placing the phone to my ear.

"Yes, Malcolm," Mother answered.

"Good morning, Mother." I tried to sound cheerful.

"What's so good about it? Obviously you haven't spoken to your son, or you wouldn't be calling. You'd be home dealing with his shit!"

Jesse. I should've known. That boy hadn't even been home from school a week and he was already causing trouble. Sometimes that boy's actions made me wonder if he was even mine. He got into shit I never would have dreamed of doing at his age.

Sydney Johnson

8

I looked over at my husband Anthony, sleeping soundly next to me. The early morning sun's rays came through the blinds and landed on his handsome, chiseled face, and I couldn't help but smile. After twenty-six years of marriage, he still did it for me. If some of my sorority sisters had known he would turn out to be such a catch, they might have tried to steal him from me when we met in college.

Back then, people looked at me like I'd lost my mind when I started dating Anthony. I was a dance team captain, and with my Brooklyn swag and tight body, I could have had my pick of the most popular brothers on campus, yet I chose Anthony Johnson, the tall, awkward, overweight nerd from my chemistry class who made me laugh. He was the smartest person I'd ever met, and unlike most of the men I knew who were just trying to get in my pants, he could hold intense, deep conversations for hours. Maybe it sounds corny, but I knew he was interested in more than just my body, and that really turned me on.

My sorority sisters gave me hell for dating him, saying he was way beneath me, and after a while, I did give in to their peer pressure. I broke up with Anthony and tried dating a few athletes and frat boys. After the third time a guy tried to pressure me into sex on our first date, I began to think I'd made a huge mistake. The one guy I did end up sleeping with couldn't measure up in any way to the attentive lovemaking Anthony had given me. I'll never forget the look of confusion on Anthony's face when I begged him to take me back.

"You're the hottest woman on campus," he said. "Aren't I supposed to be the one begging you?"

More than two decades and two kids later, I had absolutely no regrets. Anthony had outgrown his nerdiness, lost eighty-five pounds, and now not only was he gorgeous, but he was a super successful tech business owner. Above all else, he was my best friend. I had truly married my soul mate.

As he woke up, I decided to show my husband just how much I appreciated him.

"Somebody's up early this morning," I said, reaching down to caress his morning erection.

"Yeah. Let me get in my cardio before breakfast," he said, instantly energetic. Anthony had always loved morning sex. He opened my legs wide, kissing my neck as he shifted his body on top of mine.

I was grateful for moments like this. Unlike many friends our age, our sex life was just as satisfying and exciting as when we first started dating.

"How about a little warmup first?" I said, maneuvering out from underneath him and straddling his middle. My kisses started at his neck and continued to his chest. I paused, biting his nipple, which had always driven him wild. He let out a low moan.

I continued my trail of kisses down his torso, teasing him with the tip of my tongue along his inner thigh. Anthony tangled his hands in my hair as he groaned in anticipation.

"Oh, Syd," he whispered.

I glanced up to make sure he was watching as I took him into my mouth. The way Anthony responded as I slowly slid him to the back of my throat was such a turn-on. I could feel myself getting wetter as he became even harder. I worked my tongue and my hands on his manhood, loving that feeling of power I had when I could pleasure him like this.

When he was just about to reach his peak, I quickly straddled him and slipped him into my wet, welcoming center. It felt like Heaven.

"Oh, shit, Syd," Anthony moaned as I began riding him. His fingers tightly gripped my ass, and he took control, slowing my pace. Our eyes met in an exchange that was both lustful and loving.

"Anthonyyyy, that's my spot," I purred. "That's it, right there. Don't stop."

Bzzzzzzzzzzz.

Anthony's phone began vibrating on the nightstand with some Bollywood-sounding ringtone. He removed his hand from my ass, and I looked down to see his attention was on the phone.

"What the—"

"I gotta get that." He reached out for it.

"Don't you dare," I warned.

He gave me an apologetic look as he moved me off of him and grabbed the phone. "Seriously, Sydney, I have to."

"And I'm serious. You'd better not," I snapped, but it was too late.

"Anthony Johnson," he answered, sounding like he was in a boardroom instead of in bed with his wife.

I pulled the comforter over my body and leaned against the headboard, pouting. "I know your ass didn't just stop fucking me so you could answer your damn cell phone. Are you—"

Anthony pressed his finger over my lips and gave me a warning look. Suddenly, he was all business. As annoyed as I was that he had picked up the phone, I had to admit that I usually found him sexy when he was in work mode. When it came to business, he delivered like a boss and commanded attention. When he spoke, people listened. For me, it was the ultimate turn-on because not only did it show power, but it resulted in money. Lots of it.

"No, no, you didn't wake me. I'm glad to hear from you. Yes, of course, sir."

I had no idea who he was talking to, but there was excitement in his eyes.

"Yes, I can have those drawn up immediately. I'm glad that you see the value of Sydney Technologies and all that we have to offer. I'm sure you will. I look forward to a long and rewarding relationship as well. Speak soon." Anthony was beaming by the time the call ended.

He turned, reaching for me. "You're not gonna believe who that was."

"I don't care," I lied and pulled away. "Nothing should be more important than what we were in the middle of doing."

"Not even twenty-five million dollars?" he asked.

"What?" I gasped. "Stop lying. You got it?"

Anthony broke into a huge grin. "I got it. I got the Singh contract."

"Oh my God, baby. That's incredible!"

"No, you're incredible."

As he reached for me again, I didn't resist. He positioned me so that I was flat on my back. The joy on his face was priceless as he kissed me first on the mouth, then moved down to my sweet spot, devouring me with his talented tongue. He always knew just how to work it to bring me multiple waves of pleasure.

"Anthony, please," I begged, grabbing at the top of his head. His tongue worked its magic and a deep wave rose from within. I tried to hold back in an effort to enjoy just a little while longer.

Bzzzzzzzzz

This time, it was the sound of my phone disrupting us. Unlike him, I ignored it. Nothing was more important than the climax I was on the verge of reaching.

Anthony paused and raised his head.

"Don't. Stop."

He followed my command, and seconds later, I erupted, whimpering and shaking as I saturated Anthony's face.

"Damn," he said proudly as he moved up to lay beside me.

"My thoughts exactly." I snuggled next to my husband, thinking again how lucky I was, lying beside my man in my dream home after he'd just landed the biggest deal of our career.

Bzzzzzzzzzz. My phone vibrated again.

"You want me to get your phone?" he asked.

"No." I sighed, knowing exactly who the caller was without even looking at the screen. It wasn't a business call for a $25-million deal like Anthony's, but it was probably about money. It would have to wait. I curled against his chest with a satisfied smile. Life was great. We were happy, and there was no need to bring up my gold-digging sister, Karrin. So, I closed my eyes and drifted to sleep.

Karrin Wilks

9

"Hello."

"What the fuck, Syd?" I hissed dramatically into the phone when my sister answered. "I've been calling you all morning. I could be dead somewhere."

"But you're not." Sydney sighed. "Now, what do you want? I'm busy."

I knew my sister well enough to know that "busy" was a code word for getting it in with that fine-ass husband of hers. The two of them had been married over twenty years and still screwed like rabbits. Sydney, like me, had a high sex drive, and had she not gotten her tubes tied, she and Anthony would have had like a dozen kids by now instead of just two. Right now, though, I didn't have time to ponder their sexual activity or even why my numerous calls had gone unanswered. The only thing that really mattered was that Sydney was on the phone now, and I needed a favor.

"This'll only take a minute. I need your help."

"If by *help* you mean that you need to borrow some money, the answer is no."

Damn! She didn't even let me get it out my mouth.

"Please, Syd. I'm in a bind, and I need thirty-five hundred dollars."

"Thirty-five hundred?" Sydney repeated. "Have you lost your mind? I just gave you three thousand dollars last week to catch up on your rent."

"Damn, was that last week?" I asked coyly. I had actually used that money to cover the cost of the spa day I treated myself and my girls to, along with lunch and a couple of YSL bags.

***

"Yes, and the week before that, it was for your car note."

It looked like my standard excuses—rent, car note, overdue light bill—were already used up, so I had to think of something fast. In order to get what I needed out of my sister, I was going to have to pull on her heart strings.

I let out a long, exaggerated sigh. "Sydney, this is life or death."

This one got her attention. "What's wrong?" Sydney sounded alarmed.

"I've got people around me, so I'm going to have to explain later, but this is some serious shit. Please. I don't have time to be explaining myself right now. I just need my big sister's help." I choked out the last few words so she'd think I was on the verge of tears. My goal was to sound panicked enough for her to worry, but not enough to jump in the car and ride to Brooklyn. I ain't need all of that. I just needed some damn cash.

"Karrin, are you okay?" Sydney asked. "Did somebody put their hands on you? Do I need to drive to the city?"

"No, no, Syd! I'm okay for now, but I won't be if I don't get this money."

"Sis, I can't keep giving you money without explanation. You're going to have to tell me something."

Shit. I'd overplayed my hand, and she was taking it there. Next thing she was going to say was that I needed to get a job. But not to worry. I still had one bullet in my gun: the guilt card.

"You know what? Forget it," I snapped. "Thanks for nothing. If it was me that had money, you wouldn't have to worry about shit. What was I thinking about asking tight-ass Sydney for help? I told Momma before she died that you only act like a sister when it suits you."

The line went silent for a moment, and then I could hear my sister mumbling to herself. I knew I'd hit the right nerve. She hated for people to think she was cheap.

"Fine, I'll send it," Sydney finally said. "But this is a loan, Karrin, and don't say nothing to Anthony about it."

"I won't," I quickly responded, giving her the lie she wanted to hear. "I know it's a loan, and I promise I'll pay you back. With interest. Thank you. Love you!"

"Love you too."

I ended the call and put my phone down.

"You good?" my friend Bri asked, standing beside me in the checkout line at the Louis Vuitton store on Fifth Avenue. Bri had a cute bag she was buying, and our friend Rita had a pair of last year's shoes from the clearance rack. Not to be outdone, I had a bad-ass Louis Vuitton leather jacket and a pair of shoes to match.

The chime of my CashApp seconds later was like music to my ears, and I looked at my phone to see the deposit sitting in my account. I happily placed my stuff on the counter.

"I'm better than good. I'm great," I answered Bri.

"You damn sure are," Rita agreed.

"Shit, I wish I had a rich-ass sister to spoil me," Bri said.

I gave them both a big, cheesy grin. "I guess I'm the lucky one."

Having Sydney as my big sister may have been my stroke of luck, but marrying Anthony was hers. When she brought him home to meet our family, I thought it was a joke. Sure, he kissed her and my momma's ass, but I just didn't see it. My sister was cute, and there was only one way to describe this guy. He was dorky. In my eyes, they just didn't go together. But Sydney swore he had potential, and he promised my momma he was going to make Syd the happiest woman in the world. I didn't believe any of that shit. Never in a million years would I have thought that he would become the owner of a multimillion-dollar company. Even more surprising was that over the years, he had actually started to grow into himself, and now he had the sex appeal to match the fat bank account.

By the time I left the Louis Vuitton store, my CashApp account was deflated again, but my arms were full of shopping bags. After the mini shopping spree, we enjoyed a mimosa-filled late lunch, then spa pedicures, all my treat. It had definitely been a good day, thanks to Sydney and the loan that I had no intention of paying back.

Unfortunately, my good mood was ruined when I spotted the black Ford Explorer parked in front of my building.

"Fuck." I did not feel like dealing with the bullshit I knew was waiting inside.

My initial thought was to turn and head in the opposite direction, but it only took a second for me to realize that running would only delay the inevitable. I'd ducked him for the past three months, but I couldn't run forever. I also couldn't call Sydney and ask for more money. Instead, I reached into my purse to make sure my emergency condoms were still in there. Being three months late on my rent and not having the money to pay it would qualify as an emergency to me. The only option I had was to fuck my landlord.

Sergeant Tom Lane

10

I was awakened by the smell of freshly brewed coffee and bacon drifting through the house, and it brought a smile to my face. I slipped on my robe and slippers and headed for the kitchen, where breakfast was being prepared by my son's girlfriend, Tania. I liked Tania. She was smart and pretty, and more importantly, she was good for my son, who admittedly could be a handful.

"I swear, Tania. You're spoiling me. If Peter doesn't marry you, I will," I announced as I entered the kitchen. "You got it smelling like Sunday morning at Grandma's house."

Tania was laughing as she turned from the stove. "Good morning. And thanks."

"Oh, my bad. Good morning to you, too." I reached onto the plate in the middle of the table and snatched a piece of bacon when she wasn't looking. "Nice and crispy. Just the way I like it," I said as I settled into my seat.

"I'm glad. I would have made some pancakes, but with the trials coming up, Peter's not eating carbs. I hope you like cheese eggs."

"I like whatever you cook," I replied.

She brought over a plate of perfectly scrambled cheese eggs and put it on the center of the table beside the bacon. I didn't hesitate to make my plate.

"Been a long time since there was a woman around here. Feels pretty good."

"You want some coffee, Sergeant Lane?" She held up the pot.

"You know I do. And what have I told you about that Sergeant Lane crap? You're engaged to my son. Call me Dad."

Tania looked a little embarrassed by my suggestion. "Thanks for the sentiment, but I don't feel like that would be proper. Not yet at least."

"Well, then how about you just call me Tom?" I said, picking up another piece of bacon.

"I can do that." She poured coffee into a cup then handed it to me.

"Good." I checked my watch. "Where's Peter? He still out on his morning run?"

A look crossed over Tania's face that I couldn't really interpret. "No, he didn't go this morning. He's still in the room."

"In the room?" I sat up in my chair. "Is he sick?"

"No, he's not sick," she replied. "He just has an attitude this morning and said he wanted to be left alone." Tania poured herself a cup of coffee and sat down.

Peter and Tania had started dating almost immediately after we moved to Sag Harbor, so they'd been together for a few months now. At first I was concerned, because I felt like the only thing Peter needed to focus on was preparing for the upcoming Olympic trials. A pretty girl hanging around all the time would only distract him. But Tania had proven to be supportive of Peter—not just his workouts, but simple things like making his breakfast without any carbs. She was good for him, especially when I wasn't around. Then, when she started coming around the house more, I actually began to enjoy the feminine energy she brought to the place, not to mention the great food she cooked for us. I hoped whatever they had going on would be resolved, because dealing with Peter having a girlfriend was one thing, but my son dealing with a heartbreak would be another. Peter and I both loved hard.

"Uh oh. Trouble in Paradise?" I asked.

"Not really. Peter's just Peter sometimes. It doesn't matter. We'll be fine."

"What's going on?" I probed. My inner cop was never far away.

Tania paused for a moment, then began to explain. "You know Peter and I spend a lot of time together, but it's the beginning of summer, and now my friends and sorority sisters are back for the next few months, and I wanna hang out with them. Let's just say Peter isn't fond of that."

"I'm sure he isn't. Not that you wanting to hang out is a problem. You should be able to spend time with your friends. But Peter is kinda new to the area, and he doesn't have too many friends other than the guys at work," I said in defense of my son.

"I get that, and I've tried to include him, but he'd rather sit around here watching TV then go out."

"Peter's just not a very social guy, which is why he's a boxer and not a football player," I tried to explain. "I'll talk to him. I know he cares about you."

"I care about him too, but I'm twenty-two years old, not fifty-two." She looked sad. "Like I said, we'll figure it out and be fine."

I wasn't sure if I believed that. Peter was going to have to step up his game. For now, it was time to change the subject.

"Lemme ask you a question, Tania. You're from around here, right?"

"Yeah, spent all my summers growing up here until my parents split. My mom and I moved out here full time after the divorce."

"So, you know Jesse Britton?" I asked.

Her facial expression told me she did. "We've known each other for a while. Why?"

"I had a little run-in with him last night. He's a real prick," I said. "And he has no respect for authority."

Tania laughed. "That sounds like Jesse. The only person he's afraid of is his grandmother, but Jesse really is a nice guy once you get to know him."

"I'll pass. So, what do you know about his grandmother? Why is she the queen of the ball?"

Tania sat up in her chair. "Carolyn Britton?"

"Yeah, what's her deal?"

"There's only one thing anyone needs to know about Carolyn Britton. So, excuse my French, but she's not to be fucked with." The way Tania looked at me let me know that the statement wasn't an exaggeration, but a fact. One thing was very obvious: she was afraid of the woman.

One thing every good cop knows is that in order to be effective, you have to know your beat. I was beginning to understand that I had a lot more to learn about the Black Hamptons I'd been assigned to than what I'd been told.

Vanessa Britton

11

"She has arrived! All hail Queen Vanessa!" Tami Newton shouted to an outburst of cackling from the so-called beach circle.

I smirked as I strolled toward the ten women and four men sitting under umbrellas on the beach, drinking everything from wine and champagne to vodka and gin. Their enthusiastic—although maybe a little sarcastic—greeting was a delightful welcome to a new summer, and I basked in the attention.

"Yes, ladies, I have arrived. Freshly divorced and looking for the man of my dreams." I pretended to bow before laying out my blanket and unfolding my beach chair. I chose a sunny spot still in the circle but away from the umbrellas. I was not there to hide from the sun. I was there to tan my high yellow skin to a golden brown.

"Did you bring it?" Melissa, a cute, curvy, brown-skinned woman asked eagerly, staring at the woven beach bag I'd just put down. Melissa was a teacher, and at thirty-five, the youngest of our crew, she was also our biggest lush.

"What would Memorial Day weekend be without"—I reached into my bag and removed two large bottles—"Vanessa Britton's famous rum punch?"

You should have seen the grins on their faces as the women scrambled through their own bags to pull out their beach cups, a summertime necessity. I'd learned to make rum punch from my second husband, Bernard Hastings. He was from St. Thomas, and his family had been bootleggers back in the day. The only good thing that had come out of that relationship was the recipe for rum punch and my Black Hamptons home.

"I've been waiting on this all winter," Nadia said, holding up a cup.

I laughed. "Well then, drink up. I made two bottles, and I expect them to be empty by sunset."

The beach circle was made up mostly of women who had grown up summering in the community. Of course, as we got older, spouses and friends were welcomed to join us to sip wine, snack on charcuterie, and spill tea, but it was most definitely an invitation-only event. If you wanted to know what was really happening in the Black Hamptons, all you had to do was sit in proximity of the circle, and you'd soon find out.

"Hey, isn't that your wanna-be baby daddy, Nadia?" Tami gestured to a tall, handsome brother flanked by two college-aged kids, a boy and girl, walking down the beach.

"Mmm-hmmm, that's him," Nadia confirmed. "Fine and rich and married to a bitch. Why can't he get a divorce?"

"Girl, please. You think that wife of his is gonna let him go? Not likely. That man's a winning lottery ticket."

I lifted my sunglasses to get a better look. He did have a sexiness about him. "Who is he anyway?" I asked.

"That's Anthony Johnson. He and his wife Sydney bought the Peterson house last summer. They call him the tech guy. He owns some type of technology company," Tami shared. We could always count on her for detailed information. "Google him. You'll see."

"That's your boy David Michaels's friend. They work together," Melissa's husband Steve chimed in.

"Why's he gotta be my boy, Steve?"

"Because everyone knows David has had a thing for you since we were riding bikes out here on dirt roads," Steve replied, igniting the circle into laughter, me included. "Now, can I get some of that rum punch? I gotta get ready for the homeowners association meeting." He held up his cup.

The bottle of rum punch, which was now being passed around, made its way to Steve, and my eyes roamed back to Anthony Johnson as he made his way down the beach. Nadia might have to step to the left if that one ever became single.

"Oh, I forgot about that damn meeting," Nadia said.

"Well, I'm definitely not going. I already paid my dues, I don't have a dog, and I know not to litter on the damn beach. I'm good." I poured myself a glass of wine and sat back in my chair. I wasn't about to touch that rum punch because I knew how much 151 rum I'd put in it and what it could do to someone sitting out in the hot sun all day.

"I know that's right," Melissa agreed. "I'll leave that up to those who need to feel important. I will admit, though, your girl Leslie's doing a good job as president, Vanessa."

"I told you she would rise to the challenge," I replied. The truth was that I had wanted the presidency for myself, but I was blocked by my ex-mother-in-law, Carolyn.

"I wasn't expecting you to go anyway, Vanessa. Not after last night." Nadia looked at me with this weird, sympathetic expression.

"What happened last night?" I asked nonchalantly.

"Oh, sorry," she leaned in and said under her breath. "I get it if you don't wanna talk about it in front of everybody. My Tiffany said they were actually going to arrest Jesse until Carolyn showed up."

I sat up in my chair at the mention of my son's name. "Excuse me? What the fuck are y'all talking about?" Nadia had lowered her voice, but I knew that all of the nosy asses in the circle were still listening anyway. Half of them were wearing blank expressions, and the other half were looking into space. None of them would look me in the eyes. I removed my Gucci sunglasses. "Tell me, damn it!"

"I . . . uh, we thought you knew," Nadia said.

"Knew what?" I demanded.

"Jesse threw a party last night, and the police showed up. He was put in handcuffs and briefly taken into custody." Her words came tumbling out so fast that it sounded like one long word.

I was stunned, not only by the fact that my son had been arrested, but because no one had called to tell me about it, not even his father.

"Well, hold on." Melissa placed a gentle hand on my arm and spoke in a soothing tone. "He wasn't arrested."

That brought my fury down just a notch. "He wasn't?"

"No, he was cuffed and put in the back of the police car," she explained. "But Carolyn showed up and stopped that shit with a quickness, so they let him go."

I let out a thankful exhale. "That's what Superwoman does. She saves the fucking day," I admitted begrudgingly. Carolyn might have made my life a living hell many times over, but I had no doubt that she loved my son, and for that I was grateful.

"I'm sorry, Vanessa. If I'd known you didn't know, I would have called you last night," Melissa apologized.

"I know you would have," I lied. I knew she wasn't sorry about shit. Probably none of them were. The thing about the circle was that even if you were a member, you weren't immune from being talked about if the gossip was juicy enough.

As relieved as I was that Jesse hadn't technically been arrested, I was still pissed at the fact that no one felt it necessary to tell me anything about it, and I wasn't talking about the beach circle. I was owed an explanation from my ex-husband and his family, and I was going to get it.

Carolyn Britton

12

Easthaven Church had been a staple of the community as far back as the 1930s. Far from a grand, stately building, the small wooden structure still held charm and lots of historical significance for the Black people in the area whose families had not been welcomed to worship in any of the larger, less melanated congregations nearby. Now, the tiny church not only served as a place of worship, but also the primary location for civic meetings, such as the one we were attending today. The Black Hamptons Homeowners Association meeting was a quarterly event, and although attendance wasn't mandatory, it was highly suggested for those who understood the significance of being included when matters of importance were discussed. I had never missed a meeting.

I was greeted by Reverend Chauncey, the long-standing pastor of the church, as I entered the large, open room with my sons.

"Carolyn, how are you?" he said. "I hope those are what I think they are."

I looked over at the covered trays that Martin and Malcolm were carrying. "Yes, Reverend. Per your request, those are my crab cakes."

"Well, praise the Lord. That's what I was hoping you'd say." Reverend Chauncey eyed the food greedily as he reached for the trays. "Let me go ahead and take those off your hands, young men."

"Now, Chauncey, those are for the refreshment table, not for your personal enjoyment," I chided. Cooking wasn't my forte— that's what personal chefs were for—however, my homemade crab cakes were a hot commodity. Everyone loved them. Since I refused to share the recipe, someone always requested that I bring them to the meeting.

"Of course. I'm about to take them right over there to the table." He motioned toward the long tables where the food was being set up. "You all can go ahead and sit. Good to see you all."

"Good to see you too, Reverend." Malcolm nodded as he led his brother and I to our seats on the front row.

I politely acknowledged those already in attendance as I sat between my sons. It didn't take long for the room to become filled with residents of the Black Hamptons. I checked my watch, and right on time, Leslie Bowen, the president of the HOA walked to the podium at the front of the room.

"Ahem." She cleared her throat and looked directly at me. "Welcome, everyone. I motion that the Memorial Day weekend meeting of the Black Hamptons Homeowners Association be called to order."

"I second that motion." I gave her a nod of approval.

For years, the coveted position of association president had belonged to me, but that was before I assumed the role of CEO five years ago. Running the bank left little time for me to continue, so I announced that it was time for the position to be handed over to another community member. I found it fitting that it was another family member who took charge. My niece, Leslie, was a Britton before she married Jeffrey Bowen.

"Thank you, Carolyn." Leslie smiled. "Now, to start today's meeting, I'm happy to announce that after lobbying the village board and the mayor's office for someone more sympathetic to our special concerns to patrol our community, they have finally listened. Ladies and gentlemen of the Black Hamptons HOA, I'd like to introduce Sergeant Thomas Lane."

There was light applause, and I turned to see the same officer who had attempted to arrest Jesse the night before heading to the podium. I stared at him, still irritated by the incident. As he stood beside Leslie and waited for the room to quiet down, his eyes scanned the crowd. They settled on me, but only for half a second before he looked away uncomfortably. I was glad to see that my power move from the night before was still on his mind.

"Sergeant Lane is our new community liaison to the Sag Harbor Police Department. In most cases, he'll be the first responder to any incidents or complaints in our neighborhood," Leslie explained.

"When he isn't inciting trouble and unlawfully detaining citizens," I whispered to Martin.

"Mother, don't," he mumbled.

Leslie motioned for Sergeant Lane to step in front of the microphone. As if he could sense the disdain that I wasn't trying to hide, his eyes shifted in my direction again, and he paused for a beat before pulling himself together and addressing the crowd.

"Uh, thanks, Mrs. Bowen. I'm glad to be here and glad to be a member of the Sag Harbor Police Department. I'm not quite sure exactly what you mean by sympathetic to your special concerns, but I'm definitely qualified for the position based on my previous years in law enforcement with the NYPD," he said.

I stood to speak. "What she meant was that we requested a person of color, specifically a Black person, to patrol our community. We all felt that it would be safer for not only our sons, but our husbands. All of our Black men. They deserve to be protected, not targeted. That should not only be obvious but understood by the person who filled the position."

The applause from the crowd indicated their agreement with my statement.

Sergeant Lane, however, narrowed his eyes at me ever so slightly, as if to say, "Lady, I know you're fucking with me, but I'm still the one wearing the badge."

"Ah, I see," he said. "Well, let me go ahead and let the *community* know that I'll be treating any non-law-abiding citizen the same no matter what color they are. I don't plan on showing any bias. I'm not just a Black police officer. I'm a sworn public servant, first and foremost, hired to protect and serve." His tone was more assertive now.

"As long as you keep that gun holstered and remember that your salary is provided by this community and that you've been hired to protect and serve, we won't have a problem," I fired back at him, supported by a chorus of "Amen!"

Sergeant Lane exhaled. "Ma'am, my salary is paid by the town of Sag Harbor, not you directly."

It was obvious that he hadn't really learned the lesson he was handed last night. Well, I would just have to remind him of exactly who he was dealing with.

"I'm sure you think that," I said, "but you might want to talk to your boss, Chief Harrington, and also Mayor Steadman about that before you make such foolish statements moving forward. I'm sure they can provide the clarification you seem to need."

The room fell silent. Sergeant Lane had nothing else to say as I took my seat. Instead, he simply retreated from the podium and headed down the aisle toward the back of the church. As Leslie watched him leave, her expression told me that she was replaying the whole thing in her mind, trying to understand how that interaction had gone sideways so quickly.

"Madam President, may we continue?" I said.

She shook her head slightly like she was trying to clear her thoughts. "Oh, uh, yes. Of course.

Thank you for that clarity, Carolyn, and thank you for stopping by, Sergeant Lane. We look forward to working with you," she said to his back as he stepped out the door.

"Well, that was a bit tense," Malcolm commented.

"I think I handled it quite well," I told him.

"I agree." Martin gave a nod of approval.

"Moving on, then. We have a special agenda announcement by Jeffrey Bowen," Leslie said.

"Thank you, honey." Jeffrey stepped up to the microphone. "Good afternoon. I'd like to announce a parcel of land in the community that is recently available for purchase. My wife's real estate office will be handling the sale, and as you know, we like to keep properties among the Black Hamptons family, so if you know of someone interested, please let me know. We can only keep it exclusive and off the multiple listing service for so long."

"Where is this property located?"

I didn't recognize the voice at first, so I turned around. It was Sydney Johnson, the woman with the too-tight dress who was too good to speak at the courthouse. She was standing beside her husband, who remained in his seat. Once again, she was wearing an inappropriate outfit consisting of a tight blouse that revealed too much cleavage, leggings that didn't leave anything to the imagination, and 6-inch heels.

Jeffrey looked at the folder in his hand then answered, "Twenty-two Beach Lane."

I flinched, taken aback by the address he'd given. I leaned over to Malcolm and whispered, "That's the Simpson family's property."

"Are you sure?"

"I've never been more certain of anything," I said.

Having overheard our conversation, Martin asked, "You didn't know anything about this at all, Mother?"

"Hell no, but what I do know is that I want that property. Do you understand?" I hissed.

They both nodded. "Yes, Mother."

I did my best to remain calm and maintain my demeanor, but inside, I was seething. I hated to be caught off guard, especially when it came to business. The fact that Leslie hadn't mentioned anything to me about the sale of the property infuriated me.

"I'd like information on the property," Sydney Johnson blurted as if she were in the middle of a used car auction rather than a formal meeting. "My husband and I are *extremely* interested."

Jeffrey started to speak but closed his mouth quickly when I rose from my seat and turned around to address her.

"The property actually belongs to the Simpson family. The Brittons and Simpsons had a longstanding agreement that the property would be sold to us at fair market value should the Simpsons decide to sell," I explained.

She had the nerve to roll her eyes at me. "Then why are we having this discussion? Surely, if that were the case, the Simpsons wouldn't have hired an agent to handle the sale, nor would they have brought the opportunity to this group," she snapped, then turned her attention toward the podium. "Isn't that right, Jeffrey?"

Tension filled the room, and all eyes were now on Jeffrey. Except for mine. My focus was on the disrespectful hood rat displaying her lack of class. Who the hell did she think she was? I was going have to put this little twit in her place quickly.

"Young lady, I don't give a damn about any opportunity you may or may not think you have. That property is adjacent to my home." I made sure my tone was devoid of emotion, though I was burning with anger.

"Excuse me? I'm not your young lady. I'm a grown-ass woman, just like you. That property is adjacent to our home too, and we want to put in a pool." She looked me up and down dismissively.

Two could play that game, so I checked her out the same way, then gave her my assessment. "I was being generous because I thought 'little girl' would've been insulting." I shrugged. "However, for the record, grown-ass women don't attend civic meetings dressed like they're going to a two-for-one happy hour at the Corner Bar."

"Oh, no you didn't. Heffa—" Her eyes bulged, and she stepped toward me, about to let everyone in attendance see just how ghetto she really was.

Her husband jumped up and grabbed her. "Syd!" He guided her back to her seat.

Within seconds, my sons were by my side, ready to protect me from any kind of danger. A ripple of reactions came from the audience, a myriad of gasps and gulps. People were clearly taken aback by what was happening at our usually uneventful quarterly meeting.

Leslie tapped the microphone, attempting to corral everyone's attention. "Um, hello, everyone..." she began meekly.

I turned around and settled in my seat, holding my head high. "How much do they want for the property?"

"The estate wants five million," Jeffrey stated once it was quiet.

"We'll give them five point five." It was Anthony Johnson this time.

"We'll match that," Martin yelled.

"Six million," Anthony countered.

Again, the room reacted, buzzing with conversations. Leslie glanced over at me, and I gave her the eye. That's when she took charge. "This isn't an auction," she announced. "All bids can be submitted to my office, and the sale will proceed fairly. Now, if there is no other new business to discuss, I move that this meeting be adjourned," she said, attempting to end the shortest meeting in the history of our community.

"I second," I volunteered, wanting to get the hell out of there. Normally, I enjoyed the spotlight, but that ghetto chick had brought far too much negative attention to me that morning, and I needed to get home and strategize with my sons. There was no doubt that the Simpson property would eventually be mine.

"Meeting adjourned," Leslie said, skipping right over the part where she was supposed to get a second and call a vote on the adjournment.

My sons and I began walking toward the exit. As we passed Sydney and her husband, she gave me an ugly scowl and muttered, "This ain't over. That property is ours. Believe that."

I stopped and stared at my unworthy opponent. "Honey, you may live here in the Black Hamptons, but you're way out of your league."

With my head held high, a smile on my face, and my sons by my side, I strolled out of the same door that Sergeant Lane had passed through after his defeat. I was the queen of the Black Hamptons, and by the end of the summer, I would make sure that even newcomers like the Johnsons and Sergeant Lane understood that.

Jeffrey Bowen

13

Folks didn't waste time leaving once the drama-filled HOA meeting ended. Some left solemnly, while others left chatting excitedly, as if they'd just witnessed a great reality show, but no one hung around to socialize like they normally would. A typical meeting would have turned into a social gathering where neighbors chatted and enjoyed the crab cakes and other refreshments. Not today. The room emptied, and I was sure it was because many of them couldn't wait to have their own personal conversations on the beach about the blowup between Carolyn Britton and Sydney Johnson. I knew the announcement about the land sale was going to cause a reaction because it would be a litmus test for what property values really were in the neighborhood, but I definitely wasn't expecting the chaos that had occurred.

"Well, looks like we got plenty of crab cakes to take home." I strolled over to the refreshment table, where Leslie was packing up the food. "You said you didn't want to cook tonight."

My wife did not laugh at my lame attempt to lighten the mood. She turned and growled at me, "What in the entire fuck, Jeffrey?"

"What?"

"Don't stand there and act like you don't know what I'm talking about. You drop something this big and don't say shit to me beforehand?" She shook her head. "Do you know how stupid you made me look?"

"I just found out this morning myself when Everett brought it to me," I explained. "And stupid how? You're literally agenting a deal that's gonna bring you a six-figure commission.

You should be thanking me. Now you can get that electric Benz you've had your eye on for the past two months."

"Thanking you? You blindsided me, Jeffrey." She looked me up and down, then turned back and started carelessly tossing crab cakes into a plastic container. "I don't give a damn about a commission, and if I want the Benz, I'll buy it. With *our* money."

"You're tripping, Leslie."

"Oh, I most certainly am, and with good reason. Aunt Carolyn is livid."

"Carolyn? I should've known that's what this little tantrum is about. It has nothing to do with me not telling you before announcing it. This is about Carolyn being upset, and for what?"

My wife's aunt was feared by most residents in the Black Hamptons, including Leslie and Carolyn's own sons. Yes, she carried herself in superior way, which was enough to intimidate some people, but more importantly, when your bank owns the majority of the mortgages of the residents in the community and also controls most of the business loans of its occupants, then plenty more people had reason to be scared. Personally, I had a level of respect for Carolyn Britton, but she didn't scare me in the least. My father and I had been her husband's lawyers for many years, so I knew her Kryptonite.

"Aunt Carolyn's wanted that land for decades. She's not going to forgive me if it's sold to someone else. How could you be so stupid?"

"Stupid?" I raised my voice a little.

"Damn it, Jeffrey. You know what I mean!"

"I know what the fuck you said!" I yelled back.

"Ahem, everything okay in here?"

Leslie and I both turned to look at Reverend Chauncey. We'd been so caught up in our argument that we hadn't noticed him enter the room.

"Oh, yes, Reverend." I gave him an embarrassed smile.

"We're just packing things up." Leslie pointed to the table. "As HOA president, I wanna make sure everything's cleaned up."

"I appreciate that, but I can do it. You two seem like you need some fresh air." Reverend Chauncey's suggestion sounded more like instructions.

"Yes, Reverend. I think some air will do us some good," I told him. "Sweetie, let's head out." I reached for Leslie's hand, but she pulled back.

"No, I'm fine," she said. "You go. I'm sure Reverend Chauncey will bring me home once we've finished up."

"I will," Reverend Chauncey said.

My nostrils flared, a result of the frustration brimming inside of me. I took a deep breath to steady myself and said, "Okay, I'll see you at home."

"I'll have her home soon, Jeffrey." Reverend Chauncey shook my hand and gave me a sympathetic look.

Everett had said this sale was a golden opportunity that he'd given me, and I'd jumped on it. Now I wondered if I even wanted it.

Martin Britton

14

During the brief drive from the church to home, the tension in the car was almost unbearable. Mother, who would usually leave a meeting with plenty to say about the votes that had been taken or the neighbors who had caught her attention for whatever reason, was silent for the entire ride. Malcolm and I knew to keep our mouths shut. Experience had taught us that her silence meant she was too angry to speak. I closed my eyes, mentally preparing myself for the storm that lay ahead. Sure enough, we'd barely made it through the front door when hurricane Carolyn was unleashed.

"Why the hell didn't either of you know about that damn property going up for sale?" Her voice was so loud that it echoed through the living room and caused Kimberly to appear in the doorway with a concerned look. "What fucking good are you?"

I remained silent, knowing any answer I had wouldn't be good enough for her to accept. Unfortunately, my brother Malcolm didn't feel the same way, and threw me right under the bus.

"I've been busting my ass day and night to get the regulators satisfied and still handle the ins and outs of the bank," Malcolm replied, turning to me. "Martin is the one who handles real estate, Mother."

"Really, Malcolm? Really!" I shouted.

"I don't do real estate, Martin, and you know that. It's your job to keep the wolves off our backs. If you'd do your job instead of trying to screw everything that moves, we'd have known."

This motherfucker right here. "What the hell is that supposed to mean?"

"It means that you're the one who's supposed to have your ear to the ground." He folded his arms, looking toward our mother to get a read on her reaction. Problem is, he wasn't wrong. I should have known—not that I would ever admit it to him or my mother.

"How is this on me?" I shot back defensively. "How was I supposed to know about any of this? I found out the exact same moment that you did."

"Considering you played golf with Everett Simpson three days ago, I can't see why not, mister in-the-know. Isn't that where you said the real deals are made while I'm in the damn office?"

I paused. Everett and I, along with a few other men from the Black Hamptons community, had played a round of golf a few days earlier, but he didn't mention anything about the property or his intention to sell it. I glanced at my mother, who was simmering. Malcolm's reminder made me look even worse.

"Maybe instead of throwing me under the bus, you should focus on the damn shareholders and finding board members we can trust," I said.

"Enough! Both of you!" Mother shouted. "None of this back-and-forth bullshit is helping this situation."

"You're right, Mother, and I apologize," I offered. "Now that we do know about the property sale, we can just bid and buy it."

"We shouldn't have to bid," she replied. "Now we have to deal with outsiders who have no vested interest. They want it to put in a fucking swimming pool? You've got to be kidding."

"Aunt Carolyn?"

We all turned to see my cousin Leslie, looking as nervous as Malcolm and I had been in the car, and for good reason. This was all her fault and could have been avoided. I shook my head.

"Well, the real scapegoat has arrived," I said.

Leslie's eyes were daggers as she looked at me, then turned her attention to Mother. "I'm sorry to interrupt. I just want to tell you that—"

"Now you wanna tell me something? Seems like the time for you to tell me something was before the damn HOA meeting. You of all people know how important the Simpson property is to me, Leslie," Mother snapped.

"Yes, I know, but I had no idea. Jeffrey—"

"You're full of shit, Leslie! Your office is handling the damn listing, isn't it?" Mother got up in Leslie's face.

"Yes," she replied coyly.

"Then how the fuck didn't you know?" Mother snapped.

"She knew, she just didn't care because of that fat-ass commission she's going to get," Malcolm said.

"That's not fair, Malcolm. You know I would never put profit before family," Leslie fired back at him.

I believed Leslie and knew she wouldn't betray her family for a check, especially knowing how much that decision would piss off Mother and jeopardize future opportunities. Not to mention Leslie was loyal.

"Listen, I don't give a damn what you have to do to make sure we get that property. It's rightfully ours. No one, and I mean *no one*, can own it. As a former Britton, I shouldn't have to explain anything more to you," Mother told her.

"I understand," Leslie said with her head hanging low.

"And for God's sake, get that husband of yours in line, or I will," Mother added as Leslie scurried away.

When she was gone, Mother turned back to Malcolm and me. "I expect the two of you to do whatever is necessary. Think. If ever there was a time to use those Ivy League educations I paid for, it's now."

"Yes, Mother," Malcolm said before I could. "We'll make it top priority."

"You'd better, or I can promise nobody will have peace around here."

Vanessa Britton

15

Although it had been some time since I'd been in the Britton mansion, I strutted into the front door and through the house as if I still lived there. Oddly enough, I felt the exact same way that I had a decade ago, when I did live there: like I was home. Despite Carolyn and her disdainful attitude, there was something about the house itself that made me feel as if I was supposed to be there.

"Ms. Britton." Madeline, the housekeeper, looked up from the shelves she was dusting and nodded politely. She knew that I was no ordinary visitor and was not to be treated as such.

"Madeline. Is she on the balcony or in her office?" I asked.

"Sunroom."

The heels of my Jimmy Choo sandals echoed on the marble floors as I continued through the house. Arriving at the sunroom, I paused and took a breath before I opened the sliding door to enter.

Remain calm. Don't let her piss you off. Stay in control, I reminded myself in preparation for the conversation ahead.

"What's this I hear about Jesse being arrested? And why wasn't I informed? Don't you think one of you should've called me?" I asked as I strode into the room. For a moment I was reminded of how much I'd loved this room, with its neutral colors bathed in the natural sunlight that entered from all corners. Then I saw the woman who could make even the most serene room feel like a prison cell for me.

Carolyn was seated on the padded wicker sofa, looking stylish in a business pants suit that was more appropriate for a boardroom meeting than lounging at home. On the wicker table in front of her was a Lenox tea set on a tray complete with lemon, honey, and sugar. It was the perfect setup for an early morning gathering of friends, had she had any. As far as I knew, Carolyn did not.

She barely looked up at me as she casually replied, "Is that the proper way to enter someone's home? Then again, proper manners were never your strong suit. There was nothing to inform you about. You really need to be mindful of who you're getting your intel from, Vanessa, because Jesse wasn't arrested. He did throw a party that got out of hand, for which I took his—"

"That's still something I should've been made aware of," I said.

"No need for the dramatics this morning, Vanessa. It's not necessary, especially since you've already received your alimony check this month." Carolyn went to her first line of attack, money, the one thing she loved as much as, or maybe even more than, her sons and grandson.

"You're right. I did. However, being concerned about the welfare of my son isn't dramatics, Carolyn. That's called parenting," I pointed out.

"Come now. The fact is the only thing you're *concerned* about is how Jesse's actions will have a negative effect on you, not his welfare. Let's be honest. You covet the Britton name more than I do." Carolyn laid the book she was reading on the table in front of her.

I balked. "That's not true."

"Are you really going to stand there and act like being a Britton doesn't mean anything to you? You've been married three times and still carry our last name," Carolyn pointed out.

"I'm not saying it doesn't mean anything. It's the same last name as my son. And the point I'm trying to make is that you act like I can't show concern for my son just because you stole him away from me."

It was an argument that we'd had time and time again. It was pointless considering the fact that Jesse was an adult now, and I was sick of it. Still, I was not going to allow her to act like I was some unfit parent who had abandoned her child just to get a check. That was not the case, and no matter how many times she tried to portray me as such, I was going to stand up for myself.

"I didn't steal anything. The court ruled that Malcolm was better fit to be a parent than you were. A great decision, considering your *reputation*." Carolyn finally looked directly at me as if she wanted to enjoy the sting of her words.

My jaw clenched, but I quickly recovered, determined not to show any signs of weakness. "We both know you manipulated the judge into thinking and doing whatever you wanted him to, the Carolyn Britton way. Here's what everyone knows is true, including you. The *only* man I've ever truly loved is your son, and you can't stand the fact that after all these years and the stunts you tried to pull, including forcing him to divorce me, we are still *friends*."

The statement was factual, and the slight rise of Carolyn's eyebrows let me know that I'd hit a nerve. The reaction was hardly noticeable, but still satisfying because it meant that not only was I was right, but my words were just as stinging as hers.

She was quiet for a moment, then gave a dismissive toss of her hand. "You can lead a horse to water, but you can't make him drink. If Malcolm wants to continue being a fool, that's on him. He's a grown-ass man. I can only protect him so much. You were his choice, not mine."

"You're right. Malcolm is very much a grown man, and so is Jesse. This is a conversation I should have with each of them, not you. You really have nothing to do with this situation at all, Carolyn. Despite your attempts all these years to manipulate them into doing otherwise, both your son and your grandson love me. You've won all the battles all this time, but it looks like I won the war." I gave her a fake smile, and then I politely said, "Goodbye, Carolyn."

"Vanessa, wait," she called after me.

I ignored the inner voice in my head telling me not to stop walking. I turned back around. "What?"

"You're a little presumptuous in thinking you've won some sort of victory. I wouldn't celebrate just yet," Carolyn sneered at me with an icy stare. "You're an over-the-hill three-time divorcee with no real prosects. Where's the victory in that?"

The confidence I'd had moments earlier dissolved. The fight wasn't over. It had just begun.

Karrin Wilks

16

I arrived at my apartment just as Fred, my landlord for the last two years, was taping a piece of paper on my front door. He was only in his early fifties but looked much older. Tall, bald, and slim with a salt-and-pepper beard, he seemed like he might've been a catch back in the day, but now his face was worn, and his shoulders slumped, which made him seem shorter than his actual six-foot height. Fred always wore the same thing—jeans, an oversized T-shirt, buckwheat Timberland boots, and a Yankees cap. It was the typical NYC outfit reminiscent of a nineties rapper. He also could eat the hell out some pussy, which was one of the few reasons I didn't mind fucking him when I had to.

"Hey, sexy. You leaving me a note?" I smiled, making my way toward him.

He turned and looked at me. "Something like that. But you're not going to like it." I pressed against him as I reached for the paper in his hand. "I know this ain't what I think it is, Fred."

"It is. You gotta get out." He shook his head. "I tried working with you, Karrin, but you're four months behind now."

"You can still work with me, Fred." I crumpled up the paper. "You know I'm not working right now, but I always give you something to cover at least part of my debt, don't I?" I lowered my hand and brushed my fingers against his groin.

"Yeah." Fred's eyes went from watching me lick my lips to my exposed cleavage that I had made sure was on full display before entering the building. "I mean, I know you been trying and all, but—"

"Fred, don't be like this. Come on inside. I'll pour you a shot, and we can discuss some new payment arrangements. You can set them up exactly how you want them. Once a week, maybe even twice a week," I suggested, suddenly feeling desperate when I realized he didn't even look tempted by this offer.

"I'm sorry, Karrin, but—"

"But what, Fred?" I pressed against him again. "Look at me. Don't we always work things out?"

I should have known when he looked past me and a look of fear came over his face that something was wrong.

"Well, you ain't working out nothing this time, bitch!"

I spun around to see Fred's wife stalking toward us from the stairwell with a scowl on her face and three uniformed men behind her. I'd only met her once on the day I signed my lease, and I had immediately pegged her as one of those stuck-up, over-forty bitches who had no friends. She was the total opposite of her husband: short, dumpy, and loud.

"I knew you was a ho the first time I met you. You been fucking my husband for free rent, haven't you?" she spat.

"First of all, ain't nobody fucking, and obviously my rent ain't free because this bullshit says otherwise." I held up the crumpled paper. This bitch looked like she was ready to fight over Fred's ass.

"Yo' ho ass shoulda been put out a long time ago," she snapped, glaring at her husband.

"You can't kick me out. I know my rights."

"Do you?" She laughed, holding up another piece of paper. "Well, this says differently."

"What the fuck is that?"

"It's an official fucking eviction notice from the courts, and these three men are city marshals." She pointed at the men in beige uniforms standing behind her. I didn't realize it before, but they were all wearing guns. "We sent you a notice thirty-two days ago to appear in court, and you didn't show up. Judge said kick your ass out, and I am."

Damn it! I remembered the paperwork she was talking about, but I thought that giving Fred some bomb-ass head would have squashed that.

"Your ass ain't got no job, but you got money. I hope you got receipts because you might need to return that shit. You're screwed, and not by my sorry-ass husband."

We were now standing so close that either one of us had the option to swing first and land a punch. The commotion attracted several of my nosy-ass neighbors, who came out to see what the hell was going on. Fred tried his best to separate us a few feet, but I wasn't backing down, and neither was his bulldog of a wife.

"You have an hour to get out anything you want. Then we're going to padlock the door, ma'am," one of the marshals said.

"You really fucked up this time, Karrin," she said gleefully.

I looked down at the shopping bags I was still holding. She was right. I was fucked.

"Move." Fred's wife pushed him aside and began fumbling with the padlock.

"Wait!" I called out.

They both looked at me, but she was the one who spoke. "What?"

"Please move aside so I can go in and get my things." My calm and pleasant voice was noticeably different than the one I'd used before. I hated having to give in to the mean-ass bitch, but I couldn't take a chance of leaving my belongings and having them become her possessions. Like it or not, I had to pack up and get out.

Fred and his wife stood outside my door with the marshals as I gathered my things.

"This place ain't even worth what they're charging in rent," I announced to nobody as I stuffed what I felt was valuable enough into garbage bags and the few suitcases I owned.

It was the start of summer, my car wasn't working, I didn't have a job or a man, and now I was being evicted. This was not how my life was supposed to be. I needed a break, a change of scenery, and a fresh start. Then a thought occurred to me. Maybe the eviction was the sign I'd been waiting for. I wasn't supposed to be spend my summer in the city stuck in misery. It was time to leave and have fun, and I knew exactly where I was going.

Sydney

17

I stood frozen, staring at Leslie Bowen and Carolyn Britton standing in my doorway. I'm sure it came across as rude, but I couldn't help it. Not only was I surprised to see them, but I was annoyed by their unannounced visit. We certainly weren't friends like that where they could just stop by whenever they felt like it.

"Good morning, Sydney." Leslie gave me this phony real-estate agent smile.

"Leslie?" I said, still standing in the doorway. My eyes traveled to Carolyn Britton beside her.

"I'm sure this is a bit unnerving, but we come in peace." Carolyn's voice was pleasant, much different from the way she had spoken to me at the meeting. The stuck-up heifer even had the nerve to smile, or at least that's what I thought her pressed lips were doing.

I hesitated for a moment, wondering if I should allow them inside. Then, I decided it would make me look small if I turned them away. "Well, that's good to hear. Please come in."

"Thank you." Carolyn stepped inside. She was dressed in her typical business suit and heels. Every time I'd seen her, she looked like she was headed to work, even on the weekends.

I ushered them into the living room and motioned for them to take a seat. I noticed them both looking around, and I figured they were admiring the chic, elegant decor. Carolyn Britton probably expected to see some cheap-ass faux leather furniture. Suddenly, I was glad that I'd allowed them in to see that my home was just as tasteful as theirs, maybe even more so.

"Can I get you two anything to drink?" I offered, deciding to be a decent hostess.

Leslie looked at Carolyn before answering for both of them. "No, thank you."

"Well, I'm sure there is a reason for this visit." I folded my legs and sat in the chair adjacent to the sofa where Carolyn and Leslie were sitting.

"There is, actually." Leslie reached into the briefcase she'd brought with her and took out a folder. She passed it to me.

"What's this?"

"That is what I believe is a suitable alternative to the property that you two are both bidding on," Leslie explained. "There is actually another lot that sits adjacent to your property. It's perfect for a pool. I've already spoken with the owners, and they're interested in selling as a personal favor to me."

I opened the map and stared at the aerial photo of our home and the surrounding properties. "Interesting."

"This is actually a win-win solution for everyone," Leslie commented. "You get your pool, and Carolyn will get the Simpson property."

"Well, I was going to get that land anyway," Carolyn stated. "This just speeds up the process, that's all. This other property is much more affordable for you and your husband."

Her smug demeanor ignited the heated anger that I had felt at the HOA meeting. It was as if she thought I was too stupid to realize her condescension. The woman really believed she was better than me. To have her disrespect me in my own home was too much.

"Says who?" I asked.

Carolyn shrugged. "It doesn't really need to be said. It's factual."

"Nah, I'll pass." I handed the folder back to Leslie.

Carolyn frowned slightly and pursed her lips. My response was not the one she had expected, but she was going to learn that I was not one of these neighbors who did whatever she told them to do. I was my own woman, and I did what I pleased.

"Sydney, we just thought maybe if you all had another option, it would benefit everyone, that's all." Leslie tried to reason with me. "You and your husband seemed so anxious about wanting to get a pool, and being that the Simpson property is part of an estate, it could take months to finalize."

"Bullshit!" I jumped out of my seat.

"Pardon?" Leslie asked as if she couldn't believe what she'd just heard.

"I said this is some straight bullshit. My husband and I don't need any other options, and we certainly don't need any personal favors from you. Maybe Carolyn should buy this lot instead, especially since she won't be getting the one she's currently bidding on." I flexed my fingers, itching to punch something. "This isn't some kind of compromise. You came here to put me in my place."

"That is not true," Leslie replied.

"You think you're better than me."

"Than *I*." Carolyn had the nerve to correct me. "And I don't think. I know."

"Aunt Carolyn, please." Leslie put her hand on Carolyn's arm.

I glared at her. "I know you aren't used to being challenged by anyone, but my husband and I never back down from a good fight. We're not like these scared, bougie-ass people you're used to around here. The moment you threatened us, you made it very clear where we stood. So, keep your bullshit options and alternatives because we aren't interested."

Leslie tried to intervene once again. "Sydney, I know the two of you may have gotten off to a rocky start, but Mrs. Britton was being—"

"No!" Carolyn stood up from the couch. "I don't need anyone else speaking for me. She's said her peace, and there's nothing more to be discussed. I came here attempting to be solution oriented, but I should've expected this."

"What you should expect is to get the *fuck out of my house!*" I shouted at the top of my lungs.

"Syd, what's going on?" Anthony came rushing into the living room. He looked at Carolyn and me facing one another and quickly stepped beside me.

"Leslie and this bitch popped up unannounced and tried to disrespect me," I told him.

Leslie shook her head and looked at Anthony. "Mr. Johnson, we meant no harm. We came to discuss the matter of the property."

"I think you two should leave," he said.

"We are." Leslie quickly gathered the folder and tucked it into her briefcase. "We'll see ourselves out."

"You do that." I cut my eyes at Carolyn as she walked past.

Once she and Leslie were out the door, Anthony exhaled loudly. "My God, Syd, what the hell was that about?"

"That was about that god damn property that we are about to buy," I shouted at him, still raging. "Those fucking Brittons think they rule everyone in this damn town, but they're about to learn."

"They are kinda different." Anthony sighed.

"I want that property, Anthony. I want my swimming pool. I don't give a shit how much it costs!" I was so angry that tears began to form. "We've worked too hard, and I refuse to be treated like some second-class citizen."

"I'm on it, baby. We're gonna get it." He hugged me as he took out his phone and dialed a number. "Hey, Jeffrey, it's Anthony Johnson. We want to up the bid on that Simpson property."

I wiped my tears as I listened to my husband handle his business. I couldn't wait to see Carolyn Britton standing on her balcony and watching me enjoy my backyard oasis. Anthony always made sure I got what I wanted.

Malcolm Britton

18

After several late-night meetings in the city, I decided to stop at our Great Neck estate and pick up the Lamborghini for the weekend. I loved that car, and thanks to the state-of-the-art radar detector I had installed, I was able to make the two-hour trip to the Hamptons in ninety minutes. I'd just pulled into the driveway of our Sag Harbor estate when an alarm on my phone sounded, reminding me that my alimony was due.

"Damn. Is it really the first of the month already?" I asked myself, pulling out of my driveway and down the block to my ex-wife's house.

There had been an instant attraction between me and Vanesa the moment we met on the beach that Fourth of July twenty-three years ago, and the sexual chemistry between us was still undeniable. But that didn't mean things were easy. Our entire relationship had been placed on public display in the Black Hamptons community: a hundred-thousand-dollar engagement party, an even more lavish wedding, the scandalous divorce, the power struggle for custody of our son, and then her sudden second marriage right after our divorce. That kind of attention put stress on us that ultimately helped to erode our marriage.

Oddly enough, the divorce made us closer than the marriage, once the dust from the ugly and messy custody battle settled. The bond between us didn't just survive; it thrived, no thanks to my mother. So, our relationship was somewhat complicated because although we were divorced, we still shared a healthy amount of love, lust, and a true friendship.

When I pulled into the driveway, I didn't see Vanessa's car there. Assuming she'd be home soon, I used the code to let myself in, then deactivated the security system. I was used to making myself at home in her residence.

I went into the living room, made myself a drink, then pulled out my checkbook and wrote my alimony check. I could have gone to court to stop paying alimony when Vanessa first remarried, but the amount I was paying was so insignificant, and who the hell needed that kind of drama anyway?

I was on my second drink when the front door opened. "I see someone finally made it home," I said sarcastically when Vanessa stepped through the door.

She jumped and grabbed her chest. "Malcolm! You scared the shit out of me."

"Why? Were you expecting someone else to be here?" We'd been divorced for years, and she'd been married twice since, but I still felt a twinge of jealousy when I thought about her being with someone else. "Kinda late to be coming home from a date, isn't it? You could have just stayed the night."

"Ask me no questions and I'll tell you no lies. Isn't that our agreement?" Vanessa asked, conveniently avoiding my question as she walked past me to the bar. She took out a bottle of wine from the fridge. "Wine?"

"I already have something stronger." I held up the glass of bourbon I'd poured.

"I see. You must've had a long day for you to be drinking the hard stuff. Does this have anything to do with Jesse's recent antics?" Vanessa poured herself a glass of Chardonnay.

"Our son is just being a typical twenty-something, but his current punishment will get him in check, I believe. We took away his Porsche for the summer."

"Well, he is his father's son." Vanessa took a sip of her wine.

"And his mother's." I put my drink down and walked over, positioning myself behind her. I placed my hands on her hips. "I'm sorry I didn't call and let you know what happened. That was my fault."

"I appreciate the apology, Malcolm. You could've told me that over the phone, though." Vanessa turned to face me. "Why are you really here?"

"To make my alimony payment."

I knew she was playing with me. We'd had a standing date on the first of the month for years.

"Oh, is it the first already?" Vanessa continued her act. "I didn't even realize."

"We both know that's a lie. You expect payment in full every month, and you never forget."

Vanessa gave me a lustful smile as she put her arms around my neck. "Touché."

"The check has been written. It's on the coffee table. Are you ready for your other monthly deposit?" I felt my manhood growing hard as her body pressed against mine.

"Yes, Mr. Britton, I'm ready for you to pay your debt," she murmured against my neck.

She pulled my shirt from my pants and fumbled with the belt buckle. Within minutes, we were both naked and headed upstairs to the master bedroom.

I'd been having sex with Vanessa on or about the first of the month ever since our divorce was finalized. It didn't matter whether we were dating someone or, in her case, married to someone else. This was our special time, and we never missed a month.

"I have to admit, of all the things you asked for in the divorce, this made the most sense. We are good in the bedroom," I told her as we snuggled against one another, both on the verge of drifting off to sleep. Our monthly session had been, as usual, totally gratifying and left us both exhausted.

"Good? Oh, we're better than good. And there were just some parts of you that I didn't want to let go of." Vanessa placed her hand between my legs, emphasizing exactly what she was referring to, as if I didn't already know. "No man has ever done things that made me feel like you do. I can't help but to admit that, despite your overbearing mother."

"It almost makes you think . . . what if my mother wasn't around?"

My ringing cell phone interrupted our laughter over that hypothetical question. Vanessa reached on the nightstand and grabbed it, casually looking at the screen as she passed it to me.

"Are you fucking kidding me? You're still screwing Morgan?" She looked like even saying the name left a bad taste in her mouth. The jealousy between Morgan and Vanessa was intense.

"Ask me no questions and I'll tell you no lies," I reminded her.

"What the fuck does Morgan have that I don't have?" She pouted childishly.

I turned my head and stared at her silently because she already knew the answer. "We are not going to do this."

"Damn you," Vanessa scoffed.

"Hey." I ignored her and answered the call. "I'm in the middle of something, but give me twenty minutes and I'll call you right back."

"No worries. I'll be up," Morgan said, then hung up before I could reply.

I stood and looked over at Vanessa. Her arms were folded over her chest and her face reflected the bad mood she was suddenly in. Vanessa hated Morgan almost as much as my brother did.

"I gotta—"

"Bye, Malcolm. You made your deposit. You can leave," she said without even looking in my direction.

"Don't be like that." I leaned across the bed and tried to touch her, but she pulled away.

"Like I said, it's cool. Just go home to your momma. I'm sure she's waiting up for you." Vanessa turned over so that her back was to me. "See you next month."

I decided not to waste any more time trying to smooth things over. I felt bad about the timing of Morgan's call, but there was nothing I could do about it now. We'd both said our peace, and I'd done what I came to do. Neither Vanessa nor I had any illusions about what our relationship was. No matter how jealous she was about Morgan, she understood that we were not exclusive.

I returned downstairs, got dressed, and set the alarm on my way out. When I slid into the driver's seat of my car and looked back at the house, I saw Vanessa standing at her bedroom window, waving affectionately. Everything was cool. I waved back and smiled, already looking forward to next month.

Anthony Johnson

19

It had been a long day at the end of a long, stressful week, so I was glad when six o'clock rolled around and I could close my computer and come out of my home office. I planned to pour us a few cocktails, hoping that it would help Sydney relax a little. Despite my reassurances that I would do everything within my power to buy the property so we could put in a swimming pool, Sydney had remained in an angry funk all week. I didn't know all of what was said the other day between her, Carolyn Britton, and Leslie Bowen, but it had struck a nerve. She was now obsessed with buying the property and beating Carolyn Britton. I knew the $7-million bid was excessive, but making my wife happy was priceless. I just felt a little bad for Jeffrey Bowen because I was sure my wife had been bombarding him with calls and messages, trying to find out if we had placed the winning bid.

When the doorbell rang, I assumed it was Door Dash delivering the sushi I'd ordered for us. Instead, when I opened it, I came face to face with the last person in the world I wanted to see.

"What the hell are you doing here?" I had so much disdain for the woman in front of me that my stomach started twisting into knots.

"Damn. Well, hello to you too, Anthony," Karrin sneered at me.

It had been a while since I'd seen my wife's sister, but she hadn't changed a bit from what I could tell. Her long, glittery silver nails were sharpened into points that reminded me of talons, her weave was three different shades of blonde that hung down to her backside, and her dress was so tight it looked like it had been painted on her exaggerated curves. The six-inch stiletto heels looked like they belonged on a stage with a pole, not in an upscale beach resort town. Knowing that my money had probably paid for most of Karrin's ghetto fabulous outfit just burned me up.

Looking past her, I noticed a guy taking several suitcases out of a large SUV. *I know damn well she ain't show up here unannounced and brought some random-ass dude with her.*

"Who the hell is that?" I demanded. "Yo, my man, you can put that stuff right back in the car."

"Relax. It's my Uber driver," Karrin answered, waving the man down. "Are you gonna let me inside, or should I start unpacking on the stoop?"

"Why are you here?" I asked again, remaining in the door-way.

"Oh my God, Aunt Karrin!" my daughter Gabbie squealed over my shoulder before pushing past me. She grabbed Karrin, and they hugged as if they'd been separated for decades instead of a few weeks.

I felt a hand on my back and looked over to see my wife, who could already tell I was pissed.

"What are you doing here, Karrin?" Sydney sounded slightly annoyed, but that was probably for my benefit. As different as they were, she stayed in close contact with her sister, mostly because Karrin was the only family she had left. Sydney knew that I had no patience for her sister, and truth be told, she knew I had a good reason. So, we had reached an understanding that she could maintain a relationship with her sister however she wanted, as long as her plans didn't include me. Having her show up at our door like this was not part of our deal, and Sydney knew it, which was why she was scolding Karrin now.

"You can't just show up without calling," Sydney told her.

Karrin rolled her eyes. "My bad. I didn't know I had to call to visit my sister. Is that, like, a rule out here in the bougie-ass Hamptons?"

"Visit?" I asked, looking at the suitcases piled in front of my home. The nerve of her showing up on our doorstep with enough luggage for five people was a testament to what she'd always been: selfish, self-centered, and disrespectful. "That's a lot of bags for a visit."

"Let's call it an extended visit," Karrin said.

"The hell we will." The tone of my voice was as icy as the look on my face. "You can take your ass to a hotel."

"Anthony, stop playing. My sister is not staying at a hotel." She shooed me out of the doorway. "Now move so she can come inside. Gabbie, help your aunt with her bags."

I stepped aside begrudgingly while Karrin sashayed into my home, unbothered by my cold demeanor.

"Make yourself at home. The bar is in the den, straight through the foyer, on the right. Help yourself," Sydney told her. "And make me one too."

"Yes, because a bitch needs a drink." Karrin tapped Sydney on the shoulder. "I hope y'all have top shelf. Anthony, even with all your money, you have been known to be cheap."

I was fuming. The woman hadn't been here five minutes, and already I wanted to cuss her all the way out and send her on her way. I closed my eyes and took a deep breath.

"Why the hell did you just invite her in?" I asked Sydney. "Did you know about this? Was this planned?"

"Baby, before you start, no, this is not a plan. If I'd known she was coming, I would have told you," Sydney said as soon as the door closed. "She probably needs a break. She's been dealing with a lot."

"A break from what? You been paying her rent for almost a year now behind my back," I said, and she froze. Sometimes you just have to get things off your chest. "That's enough of a break."

"Not every month, but every now and then, yes," Sydney said as if I hadn't seen the Zelle payments come out of our bank account every month. I had figured it was a small price to pay to keep Karrin away from us—yet here she was now.

"She's here, and I'm just as surprised as you," Syd said. "What do you want me to say?"

"I don't know, but don't invite her to stay." I tossed my hands in the air as I gave her the obvious answer. "I don't want that woman in my house."

Sydney raised an eyebrow. "Your house? This is *our* house."

"You know what I meant. Don't take it there. She can stay in a hotel or an Airbnb, but not here," I continued. "Her and all eleven of her suitcases need to find somewhere else to go."

"Anthony, what do you want me to do?"

"Give her money and send her on her way, please," I pleaded. "Don't let her stay here. You know what happened last time."

Sydney blinked a few times. "That was a long time ago, and we've all matured since then. Besides, you know what I promised my mama before she died."

"I loved your mother, but that was your promise, not mine. And I damn sure didn't sign up for this shit," I said.

Suddenly, I was surprised to see my wife's eyes filling with tears. Neither one of us really liked to fight, and after the stressful week we'd had, I realized it was not the time for me to push her. In the end, it wasn't her fault that she had a difficult sister. In order to pull my wife back from the edge, I would have to give in.

"You know what, babe?" I said, removing all the fight from my tone. "You're right. She's your sister, and I shouldn't expect you not to spend time with her."

Sydney looked relieved. "Thank you, babe."

I stared for a moment, hoping I wouldn't come to regret this decision. "No problem. Let me know when she's gone. I'm going back to the city," I told her in a very defeated voice as I walked away, stepping over the pile of suitcases.

"Anthony," Sydney called after me, but I kept going. As I closed the front door behind me, I heard her yell, "Shit!"

I gave the house one final look as I pulled out of the driveway. When it came to Sydney and the kids, I'd always given in, but this was the point where I had to draw the line. As long as Karrin was in that house, I wasn't going to be there. I just couldn't.

Jesse Britton

20

The waves were always best later in the evening just before the sun went down, so my cousin Kenny and I grabbed our Jet Skis and headed out after dinner. With my grandma still on the warpath about the pool party, I'd been trying to keep a low profile, but Kenny had convinced me that it was time to venture out and enjoy the summer.

Uncle Martin and his buddies were starting to prep for the Fourth of July water show and fireworks, which was always fun to watch. Kenny was hoping that they might let us be a part of it, so were out on the water for almost an hour, showing out, trying to get the attention of Uncle Martin and his friends.

"Yo, that shit was amazing!" Kenny dapped me up when I pulled alongside him. "Where'd you learn that from?"

"Uncle Martin," I told him. "Me and him went down to Aruba for spring break with a couple of his lady friends. Bruh, that shit was amazing. I ain't never been one to accept somebody else's leftovers, but I have never had so much fun in my life."

"I can imagine," he replied. "So, what's up with the Porsche? They give it back to you yet?"

"Nah. I think they might be serious about this summer punishment shit. I don't know what I'm gonna do. You know I can't live without my car. Walking is for townies." In reality, everywhere I wanted or needed to go was in walking distance. We spent most of our time on the beach anyway. It was just that having everyone see me walking was embarrassing.

"Jesse, if I was you, I'd keep my head down and my mouth shut," Kenny said. "From what I overheard my parents say, Aunt Carolyn is beyond pissed."

"No, you're right, and my dad's pissed too. But what the fuck am I supposed to do? It was a pool party, not a damn felony."

We started to head to shore as we talked.

Kenny shook his head. "Dude, the cops were at your house and they had you in handcuffs for the whole community to see. From where I'm sitting, you might have been better off doing a murder."

"True, but listen, don't tell nobody about the car. I'm just gonna tell people it's in the shop." It was only a little white lie. Besides, it was no one's business anyway.

"I got you," Kenny told me. He pointed to the cluster of bikini-wearing sunbathers stretched out on the beach a few feet away from shore. "The hotties are out, as you can see."

"Oh, I definitely see."

We'd barely secured the Jet Skis when this girl Cherie approached Kenny. He'd been trying to get with her since the party, and I guess she was trying to get with him now. A few minutes later, she jumped on the back of his Jet Ski, and they took off. While they were riding, my attention remained on the water, watching Uncle Martin, killing it on his hoverboard.

"That looked like fun. When are you gonna take me for a ride?" Tania's voice caught me off guard.

I looked over her shoulder, then moved her to the side and checked behind her. "What are you doing out here all alone? Where's your man?" I teased.

Tania rolled her eyes. "You're not funny."

"I wasn't try'na be. There ain't nothing funny about dude rolling up to my crib and assaulting me the other night because of you. A boyfriend I ain't know shit about," I reminded her.

"I mean, you did hit him in the head with a champagne bottle," she replied. "I wouldn't exactly call that unprovoked."

I chuckled, remembering the semi-heroic moment. "I did, didn't I? Shit, I shoulda hit him in the head with a baseball bat. That big-ass motherfucker turned around and came at me like the Incredible Hulk."

"I tried to warn you to stay away from him. I told you he's a Golden Gloves champion, Jesse. Respect that."

"What? You damn sure wasn't worried about respecting that dude when you were tonguing me down." I stepped closer, giving her a seductive stare. "What was up with that?"

"Let's call it a moment of weakness." Tania gasped as my finger ran along her bare shoulder and fingered the string of her bikini top that barely covered her full breasts. "I can't help it if you make me weak. I like you, Jesse. I always have."

I lowered my voice. "I know you do, with your sexy ass. I'm glad you like me. I like you too. So, what we gonna do about dude?"

"Nothing." Tania lifted her hand to push me away. "I like you, but it's just not our time."

"Looks like the perfect time to me." I held her palm against my chest. "I'm feeling you. You're feeling me. Get rid of the Mike Tyson wannabe and let's make this happen, T."

Tania snatched her hand back and shook her head vigorously. "Now, you know it's not that simple. I'm not breaking up with my boyfriend for a summer fling with a guy who'll be gone the day after Labor Day."

"Is that what you think this is?"

"Do you really want me to answer that?"

"Come on, Tania. My family comes out all year round. It doesn't have to end just because the summer's over. We can make it work. This can be long term," I said with a straight face. A committed relationship was a no-no, especially during the summer, but I was willing to say whatever it took to have my way with her sexy ass.

I was trying my best to be serious, but Tania was amused. She laughed so hard that tears came to her eyes. "Boy, I'm not stupid. You'll be back at school screwing sorority sisters up at Brown, while I'm still here, commuting to Stony Brook all alone. Thanks, but no thanks. I'll stick with the wannabe."

"Wow. We haven't had our first date and I'm already accused of being a cheater. I'm offended right now," I told her.

"Don't be. You're still cute and sexy." Tania winked as she touched my face.

"Yeah, well, obviously cute and sexy ain't good enough." I turned to walk away.

"I mean, not as a boyfriend, but it's definitely good enough for a sneaky link."

I stopped in my tracks and took a moment to compose myself so she wouldn't see my smirk. Here I was, running game to convince Tania that she'd be more than a hook-up, but it turned out that's all she wanted anyway. And if that was the case, I had no problem giving her exactly what she desired.

"What are you trying to say?" I didn't want to sound too eager, but the thought of having the opportunity to smash Tania all summer with no strings attached was almost too good to be true, even for me.

"I'm not *trying* to say anything." Tania gave an innocent shrug. "I said it."

"Oh, really? When you try'na link up?" I called her bluff, in case she was just running her mouth to get a reaction.

"Peter has training super early every morning with his dad, so he goes to bed early. That means I'm free," Tania replied.

"All right then, how about you meet me tonight, let's say, eleven?" I put my hands on her hips. This time, instead of pushing me away, she actually pushed up on me. Her face was so close that I could smell the floral scent of her perfume.

She leaned close to my ear and whispered, "See you tonight."

My eyes were still glued to her round ass walking away when Kenny came up beside me.

"A'ight, we good for the night," he said. "Cherie's gonna hook you up with her girl Kristin tonight." He nudged me with his elbow.

"Sorry, man, but that's not happening tonight," I told him.

Kenny followed my gaze to Tania's backside, and his eyes widened. "Jesse, you're kidding, right?"

"About what?" I asked.

"That chick is trouble. I would think one ass whipping was enough. Why are you even bothering with her? Do you see how fine Kristin is?"

"Yeah, she is fine, but she ain't Tania," I told him, excited about the new friends-with-benefits situation I'd just agreed to. It was definitely the start of a great summer after all.

Malcolm Britton

21

When I saw the location tagged on Morgan's Instagram, I didn't waste any time getting over to Zen Lounge, a local hotspot. Morgan was supposed to be in the city, which made me especially curious.

The crowd at Zen was thick. When I entered, I was greeted by a few familiar faces, who all seemed surprised to see me out and about. Bars were really not my thing, especially on a weekend when the crowds were quadrupled, and it was even more packed than usual.

It took a minute, but I finally found an empty high boy that gave me a good view of the dance floor and the exit. I settled in and ordered a gin and tonic, then started scanning the room to look for Morgan. A group of women at the bar caught my attention. They were laughing so loud that I could hear them even over the thumping music. It didn't come as a surprise when I looked over and saw my brother in the center of their group.

"I'm serious. It really happened!" Martin yelled.

Women loved Martin, and he loved them. His good looks and charm worked in his favor, and he had no qualms about using them to his benefit. I might have been the older brother, but in a way, I envied him because I could never walk into a bar and do what he was doing. I was more of a relationship man, as dysfunctional as mine were. Hell, I'd only had two lovers in the past fifteen years, and I was still sleeping with both of them.

I turned back to the dance floor, and there was Morgan, right in the center. I watched for a moment, enjoying the graceful moves, until I recognized Morgan's dance partner. Everett Simpson was on the floor, his body pressed a little too close to Morgan's as far as I was concerned.

The longer I watched them, the more irritated I became, because I'd met Morgan through Everett, and he knew better. Three songs later, they finally exited the dance floor, and I was there waiting with all my pent-up anger.

"Malcolm, what are you doing here?" Morgan was obviously caught off guard by my presence.

"Just enjoying the vibe. We may invest in this place," I lied, motioning toward Everett. "What's up with this? You two a couple now?"

Morgan took a breath and turned away.

Everett gave me an arrogant smirk. "I don't think that's any of your business, Britton. You still want that drink, Morgan?"

Morgan's eyes went from Everett's extended elbow, then to me. I didn't say anything, but the look on my face was telling. Luckily, Morgan was good at reading my mind.

"Uh, you go ahead. I'll join you in a few."

"Suit yourself." Everett shrugged. "Hopefully Mr. Britton's disruption of our fun won't take too long. Some of us are here to actually have a good time. Nice seeing you again, Malcolm."

I sneered at Everett as he strolled away, then I turned back to Morgan. "I can't stand that pompous, corny motherfucker. You do know he talks shit about everybody he comes into contact with, right?"

"So does everyone else around here, including you."

I frowned. "It's not funny. What are you doing with him?"

"Dancing. What does it look like we're doing? And I'm about to get my drink on."

"You don't need to do that." I grabbed Morgan's arm. "Come on. Let's go back to the yacht."

"No thanks. I'm here to dance, not sit on a yacht waiting for you all day and night." Morgan looked me up and down. "Are you gonna dance with me, Malcolm?"

I narrowed my eyes. "You know I don't dance."

"Well, Everett does, and very well, I might add. He also has no problem buying me drinks at the bar or taking me to dinner. Oh, and he offered to cook breakfast in bed for me in the morning. Can you do any of that?"

I remained silent, refusing to answer the question. I was certain this "tell all" was simply an attempt to get a reaction from me—and it worked. Just the mere thought of them together was enough to raise my blood pressure.

"That's what I thought." Morgan pulled away.

"Don't do this!" I reached out, but another hand grabbed my arm. I quickly turned, prepared to go off, until I saw who it was.

"Relax," Kimberly said softly.

Our eyes met, and I calmed down slightly. I'd rarely seen her in anything other than business attire or a gown at the occasional formal events hosted by the family. Tonight, she was dressed in a simple black jumpsuit and heels, looking chic but classy.

"I'm not just gonna stand here and let that bastard Everett do this bullshit." I shook my head. "Morgan has no idea—"

"Calm down, Malcolm," Kim said a little more forcefully. "Everett won't be here for long."

"Why do you say that?"

"Just watch." She directed my attention to the bar.

Everett was leaning against it, trying to look sexy for Morgan. Suddenly, he pulled out his phone and answered a call. Within seconds, I could see his expression change. He was obviously getting bad news. He hung up the phone, said something to Morgan, who gave him a quick hug, and then Everett was heading to the exit.

"Looks like it's time to make your move," Kimberly said.

"Yeah, it does. What the hell did you do?" I asked.

"My job. Making sure the Brittons are taken care of and always leave on top is what I'm paid to do."

"Well, you are worth every penny, my dear."

She smiled confidently. "Now, go buy Morgan a drink. The yacht's all fueled up, and the sunrise by Montauk point is out of this world."

"Thanks, Kim."

"Don't thank me. Just have a good time. I'll see you at breakfast in the morning."

I watched her walk away, thinking to myself how lucky we were to have Kimberly on our side. She always went above and beyond for us. She was more than just an employee; she was like family.

Sergeant Tom Lane

22

"Come on, come on! Let's go! Pick those knees up!" I yelled at Peter as he ran toward me on the beach.

It was a beautiful morning. The sun was just beginning to peek over the horizon, and the cool temperature was perfect for my son's early morning workout. I stood beside one of the police department's four wheelers, encouraging him as he ran at full speed in a weighted vest.

I checked my watch as he came to a stop beside me. "You gotta move faster. You got the same time as last week," I said to him as he stood with his hands on his knees, huffing and puffing to catch his breath.

I grabbed a bottle of cold water from the saddlebags of the four-wheeler, shoving it into his hand. Peter gladly accepted it, finishing the whole bottle in one long swig.

"I . . . wasn't . . . wearing this vest last week," he said, finally able to talk.

"Excuses are monuments of nothing that build bridges to nowhere. Should I go on?" I asked, knowing there was no need. Peter was well aware of the remainder of the quote.

"No." Peter emphatically shook his head.

"Good. Now, break time is over. I'ma give you twenty minutes to get to the house. You don't make it, another hour will be added to the—" Before I could finish my sentence, Peter was already running down the beach. I smiled with satisfaction. My son was a beast. He was destined to become a boxing champion. Even without a private trainer or a fancy gym, he had beaten the odds and literally fought his way to the top, and he had a 68–1 record to prove it. I couldn't wait to see where his athletic prowess and hard work took him.

Instead of going straight home to beat Peter, I stopped and grabbed coffee for me and a protein smoothie for his breakfast. When I arrived at the house, I almost drove the four-wheeler right into a Bugatti Chiron that was parked in my space in the driveway. I had no idea why the hell a car worth three million dollars was in front of my home because I damn sure didn't know anyone who could afford it. I hopped off the four-wheeler and rushed inside the house.

A man's voice came from the living room. "We've been watching your amateur career for quite a while, and we're impressed, Peter."

I hung back out of sight in the hallway to listen. I wanted to know who he was talking to and where they were going with this because I could already see it was some bullshit. Whoever was in that room wasn't the first person to try to recruit Peter into letting them train or manage his career. We'd been bombarded with so-called offers after he'd won the light heavyweight National Golden Gloves Championship last year.

"We thought you'd disappeared until we found out last week that you'd accepted the invitation to the Olympic trials."

"Yeah, my dad thinks being an Olympian will help my career," Peter explained.

I had to smile proudly at Peter's answer because he was sticking to the company line: Olympics, Olympics, Olympics! My plan for my son's boxing career was well thought out and proven. We'd bring him along slowly, the way the great Angelo Dundee, trainer of world champions Sugar Ray Leonard and Muhammed Ali, had developed their careers. The idea was to build a brand through the Olympics and not to rush straight to the pro boxing ranks until he was absolutely ready both mentally and physically and, of course, when the money was right.

"Maybe, but not if you don't win. You know how many young cats either screwed up their careers or set it back five years because they didn't win the Olympics?" the guy replied.

"Damn, I didn't know that," Peter said innocently.

Yes, you did, I thought, but the plan was not to lose. Peter was the national champion. He'd beaten everyone in the country and could easily beat them again. Our only real concern was this southpaw Russian cat and a guy from Cuba.

"Of course you didn't. That's why we're here."

Who the fuck was this dude? I was starting to get annoyed.

"A guy like you doesn't need the Olympics, Peter. A guy like you needs to turn pro and take care of his family. I can get you a title shot within two years and a whole bunch of up-front money."

We didn't want a title shot in two years. The plan was to build a brand and be a world champion, but it seemed like this guy's smooth-talking was winning over my son.

"Really?" Peter sounded way too eager.

I couldn't take it anymore. "What's going on here?" I stepped inside the living room.

The guy looked like he was about to shit himself. I'd like to say it was my overbearing presence, but more than likely, it was my gun and my uniform.

"Dad, this is—"

"Cornelius Prince, the promoter. I know who he is."

"That's what I like to hear," Cornelius said with a smile as he extended his hand to me.

I have to admit, he was not the person I had expected to see when I walked in the room. I had assumed it was one of those flunky-ass boxing mangers looking to come up on my son's hard work. Cornelius Prince was one of the premiere boxing promoters in the country, and there he was in my living room, along with his partner, Bobby "the Beast" Boyd, the highest paid professional boxer in the game. Their presence gave validation to all the hard work Peter had been putting in for the last three years.

"Your son is quite a gifted athlete," Cornelius complimented. "He's got hands, stamina, quick feet, everything to be a champ."

Now I was intimated, but I tried to keep it together with short answers. "Facts." I nodded. "He's going to be champ one day."

"We'd love to have him as part of the Boyd Beast Team." Cornelius confirmed what I already knew.

"Dad, can you believe this? It's what we've been working for." Peter sounded hyped. "We thought it was gonna take a couple of years at least."

"Nah, you're ready right now, Peter, and we're ready for you," Cornelius reiterated, clamping his hand on Peter's shoulder.

"I appreciate the interest and you coming out here," I said, throwing cold water on their celebratory mood. "But Peter's got the Olympics on his radar right now."

"That's what your son was telling us, Mr. Lane." Cornelius sat back down and leaned forward. The diamond-crusted BBT chain around his neck was damn near blinding. "And I told him that's a great goal to have, and no doubt he'd make the team, but there's also the chance that he'll get there and lose or get injured."

I opened my mouth to object, but Cornelius continued.

"Not saying that would happen, but there is a possibility that it could. And should that happen, as an unsigned amateur, that would damage not only his stellar record, but also his reputation. Losing in an arena fight when money is on the line is one thing, but losing in front of the world to a Chinese guy is another."

"Peter is young, ambitious, and has potential. We're willing to give him an opportunity to embark on his career now, with me as his mentor," Bobby the Beast said.

I couldn't believe what I was hearing. The middleweight champion of the world was offering to mentor my son.

"And of course it would come with a hefty signing bonus to prove how much we believe in him," Cornelius announced.

"Whoa," Peter said. "Are you serious?"

"We are." Cornelius nodded. "We'll fly you out to our facility in Vegas. You'll be trained by the best, so you'll be in tip-top performance shape. Start you off with a couple of tune-up fights, then get you in the ring with some ranked fighters."

"That's what's up. What do I need to do?" Peter's excitement was building.

Cornelius opened the briefcase that was on the floor beside him and took out a manilla envelope. "We have a contract right here. You just sign and then pass a full physical, and it'll be a done deal."

Peter laughed. "You got a pen?"

"I got one right here."

I stepped closer to my son. "We're not gonna sign anything right now," I told them. "We've got to discuss this amongst ourselves and with our lawyers."

"Dad! Yo, what are you doing?" Peter's tone was full of frustration. Their offer was definitely enticing, so I understood why he was eager, but it was my job as his father to look out for his best interests. He had too much potential for me to sign anything without doing my due diligence.

"I totally understand, Mr. Lane. Take your time and talk this through, and have your attorney look over the contract so you'll see it's all legit." Bobby gave me a supportive nod, then he turned to Peter. "Peter, your dad's right. This is a big decision. I wish I had someone like that when I was coming up."

"But it's *my* decision," Peter snapped.

"Thank you guys for coming." I exhaled, irritated by my son's disrespectful, albeit understandable, behavior. "We'll be in touch."

Cornelius and Bobby shook our hands, then left. Peter stood at the window, watching as they got into the luxury vehicle and backed out. I hated to see the disappointment in his face, but I knew that I'd done the right thing.

"I can't believe you're tripping like this, Dad," he finally said. "That's Bobby 'the Beast' Taylor you just let walk out of here."

"I know who he is, and I'm not tripping, Peter. You're acting like I said no when I didn't. I said we had to discuss it before making a decision. You never take the first offer, son," I explained.

Peter shook his head. "Do you see how bad they wanted me? They wanna help me be a champion."

I put my hand on his shoulder. "Son, you're already a champion. That's exactly why they want you. But if you take this deal, you won't be able to compete in the Olympic trials, at least not this year. They'll want you even more once you've won your medal."

"Were you even listening? What if I don't win a medal? What if I get injured? Then where does that leave me?"

"None of that will happen," I assured him.

"I know what this is about, Dad. You want me to be stuck out here with you."

"No, that's not true. I would never hold you back." I tried to remain calm, not wanting to upset him any more than he already was. "Son, I don't want you under Bobby. I want him looking up at you. But you have to trust me. I know what I'm doing here."

My phone chirped a text.

"Shit. I got a call. Someone's broken into a boat. We'll talk about this tonight."

"No need. Like I said, this is my decision, Dad, not yours. I'm twenty-two, and I don't need your permission or approval."

Peter rushed out the front door.

"Peter! Peter!" I called behind him, but just as fast as he'd been running on the beach earlier, he ran down the block. There was no stopping him. What a time to have a police emergency.

Karrin Wilks

23

"Sydney, you in there?" I knocked on my sister's bedroom door.

"Come on in."

I entered the master suite and saw that it was bigger than my entire apartment and the one next door. I knew my sister's shit was nice because I'd seen pictures on social media, but the pics didn't come close to the real thing. If this was her summer home, I could only imagine how nice their primary residence was.

"That's a cute sundress," I said.

"Thanks." Sydney plopped onto the sofa near the fireplace. Yep, her bedroom was so big it had its own living room.

"You look cute too," she said. "Are those Gucci?"

I sat in the matching chair and looked down at my sandals. "Girl, no, these are Tory Burch. Unlike you, I ball on a budget."

She laughed, and I was happy to hear the sound. I missed my big sister. Too bad it took being evicted for me to remember that.

"So, how long did you take off work?" she asked.

I shrugged but said nothing. I didn't want to admit that I hadn't worked in six months. Sydney caught on right away.

"You do still have a job, right?"

Again, I didn't answer.

She groaned. "What the fuck, Karrin?"

"Syd, I tried. Really, I did. The last place just didn't work out. I hated that fucking call center," I whined. "The pay was horrible, and the hours sucked. You should get me a job with Sydney Tech."

She sat back in her chair, shaking her head. "That's not gonna happen. I can guarantee you that."

"Why not?" I didn't really want to work for Sydney Tech, but my ego damn sure didn't like the idea that she was telling me I couldn't. "Sydney Tech too good for me?"

"I'm not saying that. But I'm also not trying to get divorced fucking around with you. Anthony already left the house because you're here. I'll be looking for a divorce attorney if I try to bring you into the company."

"He's still on that bullshit? Anthony needs to get over it."

She quickly corrected me. "Uh-uh. Don't do that. Don't act all innocent. You know exactly why he's acting this way, and he's gotten over a lot of it. Hence the Cash App and Zelle you be getting. But don't get it twisted. If I have to choose you over him, baby, you'll lose every time." The tone of her voice left no doubt that she meant what she said. It kinda hurt, too.

"I don't want to work for Sydney Tech anyway!" I jumped up. "How many times do I have to tell you that? I want to paint."

"Well, good luck paying your bills. That painting and drawing shit you do is fine, but is it enough to get you rent? Because I'm not giving you any more rent money if that's why you're here."

"I don't need no rent money." I folded my arms tightly. "Fuck that raggedy-ass place anyway."

She stared at me for a second, processing my words, then her eyes went wide, and she started shaking her head. "No. No! Fuck no, Karrin. You didn't lose your place too, did you?"

Once again, I kept my mouth shut. Why talk when she already knew the answer?

"Shit, that's the real reason you're here, isn't it?" I could see her processing everything.

"I'm here because I need to be around someone who supports my dreams. I need my sister." My bottom lip began to tremble. "I know Anthony doesn't want me here, but I had nowhere else to go. My life is falling apart, and I came to the only person I have left. I only have you."

Sydney stared at me a little longer, and I watched her expression soften. Finally, she put her arm around me, and I let loose the waterworks. She rubbed my back as I sobbed on her shoulder.

"Karrin, it's okay. I got you. We're gonna figure it out."

"I'm sorry, Syd. I tried. I really did." I sniffled and wiped the tears from my eyes.

She put her hands on my shoulders and looked me square in the eyes. "Listen, you know I'm here for you, but you've gotta get it together. I'm not gonna lose my marriage over you, Karrin."

"And I don't want you to." In my mind, I added, *That wouldn't be good for either of us. I need y'all to keep supporting my lifestyle.*

"What about Anthony?" I asked. "When's he coming back?"

"I don't know, but he's been gone for two days, so I'm going to have to convince him to get back here soon. I'm gonna need you to make yourself scarce when he's home. You understand?" Her eyes pleaded with me to accept the rules. I was a little bit hurt, but I could play along if it meant a few more weeks rent-free in this playground of the rich and famous.

"Yeah, I get it. I'll stay out of his way. He won't know I'm here," I promised. "As a matter of fact, I'm leaving right now."

"Where are you going?"

"To enjoy the sun and sand." I smiled. "Who knows? I might meet the man of my dreams and be out your way for good."

"Yeah, good luck with that," Sydney said.

I left the bedroom, satisfied that my emotional breakdown had done the trick. My sister knew everything about my financial and housing situation, and now instead of being angry, she felt bad and wanted to help. A twinge of guilt came over me for manipulating my sister, but the thought about the millions of dollars my sister and her husband were sitting on made it quickly disappear. I was going to take full advantage of her hospitality for as long as she let me.

I spent the rest of the day laid out on a blanket in the sand, my skin glistening with coconut oil and sunscreen. As I sipped on expensive champagne that I'd found in Syd's bar, I watched the families on the beach. There were little kids splashing in the water and building sandcastles. Their moms were nearby, watching the kids from their circle of beach chairs. It was hard to tell which kid belonged to which mom because they all seemed to be watching over the whole crew, warning them when they started to go into water that was too deep, or scolding them when they ran by and kicked sand onto a couple laying on towels nearby. The whole scene was pretty nice. This seemed like a tight-knit community, something I didn't even know existed anymore. Where I lived, neighbors barely spoke to each other. No wonder my sister liked it here.

I decided I wouldn't mind living in a place like this. Maybe one day I could have kids of my own and be among a circle of moms like them. Of course, I would have to find a man first, one who was successful enough to buy a house for our family in this community. I only hoped that Syd would let me stay around long enough to scout out some potential men.

I took my sketchpad and pencils out of my beach bag to capture the scenery and the mood of this special place. I had loved drawing ever since I was a kid. It started with coloring books and doodling on my homework pages, which calmed me down when the noises outside our apartment in the projects were too scary for my young mind. An art teacher in high school noticed my talent and helped me refine my skills in drawing and painting. I hadn't figured out yet how to make a living doing it, but art was all I wanted to do. No matter how much chaos was happening in my life, art always brought peace to my soul.

As I looked out into the water, I spotted a gorgeous, muscular body emerging from the surf. "Well, hello there," I murmured to myself. I was thankful for the sunglasses I wore because they allowed me to stare without him noticing.

I grabbed the charcoal pencil and started making light strokes on the paper, keeping my eyes on this man's perfect physique as he stood on the sand, drying off with a towel. He sat down, and I went to work, refining the sketch, shading the curves of his muscles, and trying to capture the light the way it reflected off his wet skin. Ten minutes later, I held up the picture I'd created. I had turned the guy from the water into a sexy black Aquaman, holding a spear and wearing next to nothing.

"I might just have to frame this one," I said out loud. Just then, a gust of wind snatched the paper from my hands.

I jumped up to grab it, but I was too late. The page had flown across the sand, and I cringed as I watched it head right for the guy who'd been my unwitting model. He was watching it too, and when the paper landed, he picked up the paper and looked at my drawing.

I sat back down on my blanket and pulled down the brim of my floppy hat, wishing I could just disappear. I was so embarrassed I couldn't even look in his direction. A moment later, I felt the shadow of someone standing over me, and I looked up to see Aquaman before me, looking even better up close. Everything about him was sexy: his smooth caramel skin, athletic build, and tatted arms and chest. This man was beyond fine.

"I think this belongs to you." He held out the paper to me.

"What makes you think it's mine?"

He grinned. "Because I've been sitting over there watching you draw it."

Now I was even more embarrassed. "Oh, well, in that case, thanks." I reached out to take the drawing from him. I wanted to put it in my bag and get the hell off that beach before I died of humiliation, but he held onto it.

"How much?" he asked.

"How much what?"

"How much for the drawing? I'd like to buy it." He looked at the sketch, then back at me.

I lowered my sunglasses and looked into his eyes. "What if it's not for sale?" I was curious as to his motive and intrigued at the same time. It was the first time anyone had taken an interest in my art since high school. He actually seemed sincere about it.

"You were inspired enough to draw a brilliant sketch, but you don't want to sell it to your muse?" His eyes were as mesmerizing as his voice.

"My muse?" I giggled. "I think that would be Jason Momoa."

"Nah. Dude has long hair, but the man in the drawing doesn't." He held the drawing up beside his face as if to prove his point. "Come on. This is me. Isn't it?"

I felt myself starting to relax. This guy was flirting, and I liked it.

"Well, maybe . . ." I said.

"How about this? You let me take you to dinner and we discuss a fair price. The way I see it, it's the least you can do, especially since you used my image without permission," he suggested. "We can settle out of court."

I laughed. "Is that a threat?"

"No, it's an invitation, Miss . . . ?" He looked at the bottom of the paper. "There's no signature here."

"Karrin. My name's Karrin."

"Karrin. Nice. You can't be from around here. I definitely would've noticed you."

"Actually, I'm not. I'm here visiting family for a couple of weeks."

"So, Miss Karrin. It is Miss, I hope." He raised an eyebrow.

"Oh, it definitely is."

"Good. I'll take you out for dinner and drinks tonight at Baldwin's Seaside?"

I wanted to shout, "Hell, yeah," but I decided to keep it classy.

"If I'm going to dinner with you, I think I should at least know your name," I said.

"Oh, I'm Martin Britton." He extended his hand, and I shook it. "I'm sorry. I assume everyone around here knows me. Most of us in the neighborhood have been coming out here since we were kids and our grandparents owned the homes."

"Nice to meet you, Martin."

"So, should I pick you up at seven?" he asked, his eyes scanning every inch of my freshly tanned body.

"How about I meet you there at seven-thirty?" I strategically extended my legs to give him a full view.

Finally, his eyes met mine. "I look forward to it."

"Wait. What about my drawing?" I asked when he began walking away.

"Like I said, we'll negotiate over dinner. See you tonight."

I waited until he was out of view before I took out my phone and googled him. My mouth fell open when I found out exactly who he was and what he did. Not only was I going to dinner with one of the finest men on earth, but he was also the richest man I'd ever met. Sydney may have had Anthony, but I was going to have Martin.

Sergeant Tom Lane

24

As I pulled the police cruiser into a spot at the marina, the doors of a white Mercedes Benz opened, and my eyes were treated to a sight so magnificent that I almost crashed into another car. Stepping out of the luxury car was a woman who had to be one of the prettiest redbones I'd ever seen. She was tall, slender, and graceful, and she could've easily been a supermodel with her high cheekbones. Her age was a mystery to me, because she looked both youthful and mature in a sophisticated, grown-ass woman way. The only thing that ruined the perfect image was the scowl on her face.

I got out of the cruiser and made my way toward her.

"Jesus Christ, what took you so long? I thought you'd never get here," she huffed.

I was so busy staring at how pretty she was that it took a moment for me to realize she was the one who'd called the station.

"I came as soon as the call came in, ma'am. Tell me what's going on," I said, trying to remain professional. Unable to resist, my eyes fell to her left hand. Her ring finger was empty. Well, she wasn't married. That was a good thing, but that still didn't mean she was single.

She stared at the name tag on my uniform. "Well, Officer Lane, I—"

"It's Sergeant." I wanted to let her know that I wasn't some regular beat cop. I did have some seniority.

"What?" she asked with a scowl on her face.

"It's Sergeant Lane, not officer."

I was slightly disappointed as she dismissed my explanation with a wave of her hand. "Anyway, vandals have broken into my boat. They did it all last summer, and now they're back at it. I'm not putting up with it anymore."

"I see. Well, that's why I'm here. I'll go check your boat for you."

"Yacht," she corrected me. "It's not a boat, *Sergeant*. It's a sixty-five-foot motor *yacht*. My ex-husband made that very clear in our divorce last month."

"Oh, *yacht*," I corrected myself, though I couldn't really care less what kind of vessel she had. I was more interested in the confirmation that she was divorced.

She led the way toward a sleek white yacht with the words *Miss Necessary* displayed on the rear. Speaking of rears, she had one hell of an ass.

Damn, I wonder if she'd date a cop. After all, it is a noble profession. I might not be able to buy her a yacht, but I sure as hell would take care of her in the bedroom and wear that ass out!

"See." She pointed at the yacht's sliding door. "The door's cracked open. I never leave it open."

"Has anything been taken? Is anything missing?"

She turned and gave me a look that managed to make me feel stupid, even though the questions I asked were standard procedure.

"I don't know," she said. "I didn't think it was safe to go inside, which is why I called the police."

Suddenly, we heard voices coming from inside the yacht.

"Did you hear that? I told you. They're still in there." She grabbed my arm, seeming a whole lot more appreciative of my presence now.

I shifted into super cop mode. I grabbed the walkie talkie on my shoulder and spoke into it. "This is Sergeant Lane. I'm 10-66, with a possible robbery in progress. Requesting back up."

Her grip on my arm tightened a little. Damn, she smelled good as hell.

"You stay here and stay quiet. I'll go in and check it out," I said, gently removing her hand from my arm.

With my hand on the weapon holstered around my waist, I stepped onto the yacht, pushed the door open slowly and silently, and entered the cabin. As I looked around at the warm, rich mahogany interior, I couldn't help but have a flash image of me chilling inside here, with her mixing drinks at the bar in a string bikini.

I was snapped out of my daydream when I heard voices again, coming from behind a closed door. I cautiously approached the door, where I was momentarily confused by the sound of giggling from a distinctly feminine voice. Was this some kind of girl gang burglarizing yachts? Feeling a burst of adrenaline, I raised my gun and yanked open the door.

"Police! Freeze!"

"Don't shoot!" It was a male voice this time—one that, it turned out, belonged to a male who was already familiar to me. He was bare chested, sitting propped against the headboard with a heavy white comforter covering his lower half, which was most likely also naked. There was a form beside him, no doubt the person I'd heard giggling, but she had the covers pulled up over her head.

This motherfucker here!

"Put your damn hands up where I can see them. Now!" I shouted at Jesse Britton.

He raised them slightly, but then abruptly pulled his hands back down to his sides. "For what? I'm not doing shit wrong!"

This defiant little bastard was really plucking my fucking nerves.

"This is harassment," he said.

"No, this is trespassing. Now, I'm not gonna say it again. Put your damn hands up!" I shouted. This time, the little prick wouldn't get away. "Let's see your grandma talk you out of this with the chief."

"Man, you crazy as hell. This is my boat. And my grandma's gonna have your job!"

"You own this boat, huh?" I chuckled. "Well, tell it to the lady outside. Now, get your hands up and get your ass outta that bed before I put a bullet in you."

I might have been talking shit—I wouldn't really shoot someone for a minor trespassing situation—but my threat was enough to make him raise his hands for real this time.

Suddenly, the fine redbone appeared in the doorway behind me. "Jesse!"

"Mom, tell this clown who I am," Jesse said.

"Mom?" I glanced over at her with my gun still raised toward the bed. "You know him?"

"Yes, I know him. He's my son." She pushed past me and stepped between me and him. "And I'd appreciate it if you'd lower your weapon. This has been a big misunderstanding."

I glanced at her in disbelief. My daydream fantasy about spending time with this fine woman had just become a real-life nightmare. Fuck! What was the chief going to say about this?

I lowered my gun and secured it in the holster. "What about this one?" I asked, stepping toward the other side of the bed. "Do you know this one too?"

"Don't!" Jesse yelled, but I didn't care what he had to say.

I ripped the comforter off the bed, revealing the woman who'd been hiding underneath it. My intention was to humiliate Jesse, but I was the one who ended up feeling shame and embarrassment when I saw Tania under the sheets. I wasn't sure whether I wanted to pull out my eyes or hers.

"Oh God. No, Sargent Lane," Tania whined in embarrassment, clutching the thin sheet up around her neck to hide her nakedness.

"Tania?"

Throughout my decades as a police officer, I'd seen plenty of things that upset me, but nothing prepared me for seeing my son's girlfriend in bed with another man, especially one as arrogant and entitled as this Britton kid. I was so disappointed in her. Tania was supposed to be one of the good ones. For a moment, I wished this was just some kind of cruel joke being pulled on me, but I knew it wasn't a prank. This was real life, and somehow, I was going to have to figure out a way to explain it to my son.

"Sergeant Lane!" Nugent entered the cabin with his weapon unholstered.

Still in a state of disbelief and no longer wanting to be anywhere near this shit show, I turned away from the bed and headed for the exit.

"Sarge, where are you going?" he asked as I brushed past him.

"I'm leaving. Take a fucking report."

Karrin Wilks

25

Baldwin's Seaside restaurant was filled with the sounds of soft music and intimate conversations. Candle flames flickered from a breeze that came in through the open windows, carrying with it the scent of the ocean. This place had the perfect ambiance for a romantic evening. It was a far cry from Red Lobster, where most of my dates would take me when they thought they were being extra fancy. I knew Martin's finances were on another level, but if this place was any indication of what my time with him would be like, then I was looking at one hell of a summer. I might have to start working on ways to make this last into the fall, winter, and beyond.

I had arrived a half hour late because of my sister's interrogation on my way out the door. She started out whining about how Anthony was still not back home, and once she got that off her chest, she acted like she thought she was my momma, asking me a whole bunch of damn questions.

"Where are you going? Who are you going with? What time do you think you'll be home?"

I ignored every question because I didn't need her all up in my business, especially since this was only a first date. If something developed between me and Martin, then maybe I'd consider talking to her about it, but for now, I needed to stay focused on making a good first impression. That's why I was so annoyed that she had made me late. If Martin had gotten tired of waiting and left the restaurant, Syd would never hear the end of it from me.

Fortunately for Syd and for me, the maitre'd said, "Right this way, miss. Mr. Britton has been eagerly awaiting your arrival." He led me over to a table in the corner.

When Martin saw us approaching, he stood up with a big smile on his face. He looked gorgeous in a slim-fitting blue linen suit and a simple silk T-shirt. The outfit looked like it was custom made to showcase his muscular physique. He greeted me with a brief hug, pressing his cheek against mine, then stepped back to check me out in my form-fitting silk dress. The way his eyes lit up made me feel like a work of art.

"I didn't think that it was possible, but you're even more beautiful than I remember," he said.

"That was only a few hours ago," I replied flirtatiously as I sat down. "But I'm a sucker for a compliment, so thank you."

"You're welcome," he said as he pulled out my chair for me. I couldn't remember the last time I went out with a guy who was such a gentleman. It was refreshing.

Without being asked, the waiter brought over a bottle of wine. "Opus One, 2017 cabernet sauvignon."

I glanced at Martin, who looked slightly confused.

"I hope you don't mind," I said. "I took the liberty of ordering a bottle of wine. Do you like red? It's my favorite."

My move was bold, but purposeful. A guy like Martin Britton was refined, so I had to be prepared. I'd googled the restaurant's wine cellar and requested the bottle before I was escorted to the table. This would give Martin the impression that I was accustomed to the finer things, and also serve as a test to set the standard and see if he was willing to accept it. Even dudes with money had the tendency to switch it up and go cheap. I'd experienced it plenty of times before, although most of those men were hustlers.

"I do. I usually prefer Silver Oak over Opus, though. It's a little more pricey but worth it." Martin grinned, then motioned toward the empty wine glasses in front of us. "But, since you were kind enough to order, it's fine."

The waiter poured wine into Martin's glass first. His eyes remained on me as he swirled the deep red liquid before inhaling, then sipping. Finally, he gave a nod of approval for my glass to be poured.

Martin held up his glass. "To new beginnings."

I picked up mine and tapped it to his. "Indeed."

He stared into my eyes for a moment before putting the glass to his lips. The heat between us was undeniable.

I still couldn't believe I was sitting across from him in this five-star restaurant, enjoying the view of his perfect smile and chiseled chest that I had been obsessing over ever since we met on the beach. It had taken me three hours to decide on what to wear because it wasn't every day that I got asked out by a gorgeous, successful businessman.

In spite of our different backgrounds, I managed to hold my own during our dinner conversation. He tried once or twice to ask about my childhood, but I managed to steer him away from anything that would force me to reveal the truth about my upbringing. How could this man, who had clearly grown up among the privileged elite, relate to my stories of growing up in the hood? I didn't want to find out. So, after some casual small talk, I brought the conversation around to the one thing that I already knew we had in common—art.

"So, about that drawing on the beach," I started, feeling my cheeks get warm. "I hope you don't think I—"

He put his hand on mine. "No need to apologize. It was a great drawing, and I was flattered."

"Oh, well, in that case, you still wanna buy it?" I joked.

He chuckled. "How did you learn to draw like that?"

"I just always loved to draw. I had an art teacher in high school who encouraged me, but I've never had any formal training. I mostly just do it because it relaxes me."

"That's amazing. Your work is every bit as good as some of the artists who are selling their works in the galleries out here."

I was intrigued. "Do you visit a lot of galleries?"

"Sure do. There are so many out here in the Hamptons. At one point in my life, I thought I would go to art school, but my family squashed that because, as my father said, 'You're a Britton, and Brittons are bankers, not artists.' So, now instead of making art, I buy it. I like to visit the galleries to see what's new and current."

I stopped myself from asking how much these artists were selling their works for, but I made a mental note to find out. There was plenty of money out here in the Hamptons, so maybe selling my art could be a way for me to get my hands on some of it.

"You'll have to tell me which galleries are your favorite so I can check them out," I said.

"Or I could take you there myself."

"I like the sound of that." And just like that, we had plans for a second date.

Now that the first-date awkwardness was gone, our conversation continued to flow effortlessly. Two hours later, Martin put down his fork in front of his half-finished dessert. He sat back in his chair.

"So, I have thoroughly enjoyed your company, Karrin. What are your thoughts on how the night should end?" he asked with a hint of suggestiveness in his tone. "I'd love for you to join me for a nightcap on my yacht. It's not far from here."

A yacht. Clearly, I'd died and gone to Heaven, but I knew enough to act like I was used to this type of luxury. The last thing I wanted was for him to think I was a thirsty bitch, even though I was ready, willing, and able. It was times like this that a bitch needed some advice from an expert, and I knew just who to call.

"Um, can you excuse me for a moment? I need to visit the ladies room."

"Sure." Martin stood, helping me out of my chair as his eyes lingered on my curves.

I didn't have to turn around to know that he was staring at my perfectly shaped ass as I walked away from the table. Hell, the eyes of damn every man that I passed on my way to the bathroom was on me. Had I not been with Martin, I certainly would've had several other options to choose from. I wasn't interested in anyone else, though. My sights were set on Martin.

I entered the bathroom stall, and as soon as I closed the door, I dialed Rita, my bestie.

"Bitch, where the hell are you? I came by your crib, and your neighbor said you got kicked out," Rita said when she answered.

"Girl, niggas stay lying on me," I told her. "I ain't get kicked out of shit. Sydney invited me to stay with her in the Hamptons for the summer. I'm out here chilling."

"Oh, shit. That's what's up," she said. "I thought you said her husband stay tripping, though."

"He does, but Sydney checked his ass. But forget that. Guess where I am?"

"Uh, I hope at the club getting ballers."

"Nah, better. I'm on a date at a five-star restaurant." I took a dramatic pause, then whispered, "With Martin Britton."

"Who the fuck is that?" Rita asked the question I knew was coming.

"Google him," I replied, then waited 3.5 seconds for her reaction.

"Bitch, this nigga is fine as shit! And he's the vice president of a bank!" Rita shrieked. "How the hell did you meet him? And does he have a brother?"

"Yes, and a cute-ass nephew. They own a bank. Look it up."

There was a long pause as she scrolled through a few more links. Finally, she warned me, "Bitch, don't you dare fuck this up."

"I won't."

"Then why are you on the phone with me? You are on a date with one of the Hamptons' most eligible bachelors, according to this article I'm looking at," Rita said.

"I'm in the bathroom trying to get my shit together. He invited me onto his yacht for a nightcap."

"I hope you told his ass yes. A nightcap, breakfast, lunch, and two snacks in between, too, heffa!"

"I'm trying to be coy and cute," I said. "I don't wanna come off too thirsty."

"Keep thinking like that and it'll be some other chick taking shots with his fine ass the moment you leave. Look, Karrin, I get what you're saying, but this is a dude of a different caliber, so you gotta move different. And it sounds like you like him, so go to the yacht, enjoy that shit, and when he makes his move, act like it's some shit you don't normally do, then blow his fucking mind," Rita advised. "Don't suck his dick. Suck his *whole* dick, balls and all. You only have one chance to make a first impression, so make it memorable! You want that nigga to get a dream about you thirty years from now."

Out of all my friends, Rita was the one who always managed to score the biggest ballers and keep them around longer than any other chick I knew, so I trusted her advice.

"Real talk, girl. That's exactly what I'm gonna do."

"Okay, call me tomorrow with an update, Mrs. Britton," she said. "And don't forget me with the brother and nephew."

I hung up feeling confident. Martin Britton was in for the best night of his life.

Martin Britton

26

I had been with my share of women over the years, but none of them, and I mean none of them, had ever made love to me like Karrin. We had undeniable sexual chemistry. It was like our bodies were completely in tune with each other. She was a perfect fit, and it was scary as hell. Just lying there thinking about it brought my manhood to life, and we'd already spent half the night making love.

I opened my eyes and extended my arm across the bed, expecting to feel her warmth. Instead, I felt the coolness of the Egyptian cotton sheets. I lifted my head from the pillow and looked around the room.

"What are you doing?" I groaned at Karrin, who was sitting on the window seat with a sketch pad in her hands. "Not that I'm complaining. I wouldn't mind waking up to this view every morning."

"The way you sling that thang, I wouldn't mind it either." She grinned naughtily.

God, even the way she spoke turned me on. When she smiled, her entire face lit up, and her cheeks displayed the deepest dimples I'd ever seen. Looking at her was like staring at a Nubian goddess with the power to cause wars between men.

She stood up, and I stared at her magnificent, naked body. She had an hourglass figure with an ass so perfect that it would make a plastic surgeon jealous. I stiffened more as I had a flashback of the way her natural DDD-cups felt in my hands when she rode me. She was a masterpiece created by God, not surgery, and I wanted to experience more of her.

***

"You can get some more if you like." I sat up all the way. "I had a really good time last night."

"So did I," she said, but instead of getting back in the bed, she reached down to the floor then slid into the black lace thong that I'd removed with my teeth the night before. "Maybe next time."

"Where you going?" I asked.

"I'm about to leave." She reached for her bra.

"Leaving? Why?" I swear I'd never done this before, but I jumped out of bed. No way did I want her to leave.

"Because it's morning." She laughed as she bent down to pick up her dress. "There's a lot of activity going on out there. Best I get out of here before people start asking questions."

"You don't need to leave, though. Not yet." I touched her face softly and looked into her bright, inquisitive eyes.

"I don't know if that's a good idea." She sighed.

"Why? You have somewhere to be? Or is there someone expecting you?" I hated to even think there could be another man. After only one night together, I wanted her all to myself.

"No, neither of those." Karrin shook her head. "It's just, I mean . . ."

My hands shifted to rest on her hips as I sat on the foot of the bed. "Look, I'm sorry about us not being able to enjoy the yacht last night, but I promise we'll have plenty of other times to enjoy it."

I had been surprised and slightly embarrassed when we made it from the restaurant to the mooring spot to find that the yacht was gone. It was obvious that once again, despite saying that he had no plans, Malcolm had taken it. There was no way I wanted to end the night Karrin and I were having, so I had escorted her back to the house. We shared a few nightcaps in my master suite, and then Karrin produced a blunt from her small purse. The drinking and smoking led to kissing and touching, and then Karrin had basically turned me out.

She smiled and placed her hands on my shoulders. "The yacht has nothing to do with it. Shit, this big-ass master suite made me forget all about that. I had a perfect night in here with you."

"Good, because I don't want you to go. I want you to lay here with me. Stay, please?"

"Martin, I gotta go."

"But why?"

"Because it's almost nine o'clock."

"So what?" I asked, although I was a little surprised that it was that late. Normally, I was up by seven, but Karrin's morning surprise had taken me out for a little while.

"You said your family lives here too. I'm sure they're up by now." Karrin removed my hands from her hips and put on her dress.

I understood exactly what she was saying, but that didn't change the fact that I didn't want her to leave. There was something magical about her. Before I could stop them, the words came tumbling out of my mouth. "I'm sure they are. I can't wait to introduce you."

Karrin looked surprised. "You're inviting me to have brunch with you and your family?"

"Yes, that's exactly what I'm doing. There's plenty of food. Trust me." I rubbed her soft inner thigh.

Karrin looked doubtful. "I can't meet your family wearing this."

"Why not? I love the dress, and you already know how I feel about those sexy-ass heels." I winked. "We can take a shower, get dressed, then we'll go downstairs and I'll introduce you to them."

"You really wanna introduce me to your family, Martin? We literally just met yesterday," she reminded me.

"Yes, and I want you to meet them today," I said as I stood up. "Now, come on. Mother hates tardiness."

"Mother? You call your mom Mother?" She looked amused.

"It's a long story I'm sure you'll hear over brunch." I tugged at her hand.

Karrin followed me into the bathroom. "This is crazy. You know that, right?"

I turned around and kissed her deeply. "Yeah, but so is what we had last night. You only live once, Karrin." I hate to sound corny, but now I understood what Tom Cruise meant when he said, "You complete me," because that's how I felt about this woman.

Carolyn Britton

27

"Aunt Carolyn, I swear these have got to be the best crab eggs Benedict I've ever eaten," Jeffrey said as he devoured his food.

"That's because you've always loved her crab cakes, honey." Leslie pointed out the obvious.

I wanted to tell the two of them to give it up with the over-the-top compliments they'd been throwing around ever since they sat down at the table with me, Malcolm, Jesse, and Kimberly. First Leslie wanted to talk about how beautiful the table setting was, then how the champagne in the mimosas was divine, the shrimp and grits were to die for, and now Jeffrey had a longtime obsession with my crab cakes. They were so full of BS it was practically coming out of their ears. And it was all clearly done to avoid talking about the one thing that I would insist we all discussed before they left.

"Yeah, this is good, Grandma." Jesse reached for another biscuit.

"I'm glad you all are enjoying." I turned to my niece and her husband to address the real reason I had invited them to my home. "So, what's the status of the Simpson property?"

Leslie glanced up at me, almost choking. "Ah, well, the Johnsons did make a counteroffer."

"And why are you just now mentioning this? Why didn't you call as soon as they countered?" Malcolm asked before I could.

"I mean, I told Leslie to let you know as soon as I updated Everett, but I couldn't get in touch with him last night," Jeffrey said and then quickly looked back down at his plate. The way he was avoiding eye contact told me he was lying about something.

"Whether you could reach him or not, you should've called us," I snapped in irritation. I turned my attention to my niece. "And you know better, Leslie."

"Aunt Carolyn, Jeffrey has an obligation to let Everett know first because Everett—"

"I don't give a shit about his obligation to Everett." I focused my anger on Jeffrey. "You are not only a part of this family, but you're my attorney. That should stand for something. Or are you so far up Everett's ass that you don't understand that?"

The dining room got quiet, and all eyes were on me.

"Aunt Carolyn—" Leslie started.

Jeffrey put his fork down and placed his hand on her arm. "It's fine, honey. I'm a big boy. Technically, I'm the attorney for Amistad Bank and your husband's trust, not you, Carolyn. And I'm not up anyone's ass. Not yours, not his. I'm my own man, just like my father."

So, that was the game that little twit wanted to play? I never really did like him or his father. The day would come when I let him know how I really felt, but not before I got the Simpson land deal closed.

"Okay, that's good to know, Jeffrey," I said, turning my attention to my niece, who looked like she was about to be sick at my brunch table. "With that being said, how much is the Johnsons' counter?"

"Seven million," Leslie answered.

"That's fucking ridiculous." Malcolm spoke the exact words that I was thinking.

"Anthony Johnson has made it very obvious that he'll pay whatever he has to. He wants the property," Jeffrey stated.

Malcolm shook his head. "This makes no sense. Anthony Johnson is a smart guy. He has to know that paying that much for the property makes no sense."

"This isn't about business or him. This is all his ghetto wife's doing. It's quite personal," I explained before turning back to Jeffrey. "We'll bid seven point two five, cash."

"Mother!" Malcolm's eyes widened.

"And you'd better make it work, or those will be the last crab cakes you'll ever eat at my table."

Jeffrey looked down at his third helping sadly. "I'll let Everett know." He pushed away his plate. "Now, speaking as the attorney for Amistad, there is another pressing matter we need to discuss."

"And what's that?" I raised an eyebrow.

"The situation in Venezuela." His expression had changed. He no longer looked like a puppy being punished. Instead, he looked like he got enjoyment out of turning the table to put a little pressure on me now.

"What about it?" I sat up straighter.

"Now that control of the bank is back completely in Britton hands, it's going to take about seven million dollars to rectify that situation."

"Well, I don't have that kind of capital right now. We're just now getting the government off our backs. The Venezuela situation will have to wait another year or two," I said, ignoring the inquisitive look on Malcolm's face.

"But you just agreed to pay over seven million for the Simpson property. It's important that you set things straight with this Venezuela thing." Jeffrey was obviously under a lot of pressure to get this done, but I didn't care. I was far from ready to deal with Venezuela and the headaches it would encompass.

"Venezuela is not my priority. The Simpson property is a priority," I insisted. "That will not bring the scrutiny of the U.S. government."

"Carolyn, I don't think they're going to be happy about this." Jeffrey sighed.

"I don't give a damn how anybody feels. It's not happening, and it's not up for discussion, end of story. We can't handle that kind of heat."

"What's going on in Venezuela?" Malcolm asked.

God dammit, I was afraid this was going to happen. I could smack the shit out of Jeffery for his lack of discretion.

"Ah, nothing of concern to you," Jeffrey assured my son. He knew better than to go into detail about it, but he shouldn't have brought it up in the first place.

I was beyond frustrated, and the conversation was beginning to take its toll on me. Just as I was about to excuse myself, the appearance of a strange woman walking into the dining room stopped me.

"Good morning," she said.

"Can I help you?" I asked, confused. My eyes went from the wavy-haired wig on her head and continued along to the skin-tight, wrinkled dress that barely contained her curves, then down to the matching stiletto heels. I was trying to think of a reason why a stripper would be at my house, and then Martin appeared by her side.

"Mother, this is Karrin." Martin took the hand of the woman we were all staring at.

"Is she lost?" I looked at Martin as if he'd lost his damn mind. "What is she doing here?"

Karrin

28

"Is she lost? What is she doing here?"

For a second, I thought the old bitch sitting at the head of the table was joking, so I smiled. When I got a second look at the frown on her face and the unfriendly stares from everyone else sitting at the table, I knew that the joke was on me. Clearly none of them wanted me there. Martin, however, grabbed my hand and pulled me farther into the room.

"No, she's not lost, Mother," he said as if she was just confused instead of downright rude. "She's my friend, and I invited her to join us for brunch."

"Why?" his mother asked him.

"What do you mean, why? We're hungry."

I wasn't sure whether Martin was ignoring the tension purposely or he was oblivious to it, but this whole scene made me uncomfortable as hell. My mother always said to go with your first thought, and I should have listened to it. I knew I should have left when I said I was going to.

"We came down just in time," Martin said, still keeping a cheerful tone in his voice. "Looks like the eggs Benedict is almost gone. I'm sure you had something to do with that, Jeffrey."

"Uh, they were delicious." The guy sitting at the end of the table near Martin's mother answered.

She ignored Martin's attempt to keep things light. "Young lady, you're not from around here, are you?" she asked me.

"No, I'm visiting from Brooklyn. Bed Stuy born and raised," I answered proudly.

She wrinkled her nose like something smelled bad. "Bed Stuy. I should have known." She looked at Martin. "Martin Britton, have you lost your damn mind bringing some hood rat from Brooklyn to my breakfast table?"

There was so much venom in her voice that I took a step back, and the looks on the others' faces didn't help one bit.

Martin's smile faded slightly. "Not at all. This is my home too, and I've had overnight guests before."

"This is true. However, most of those guests are respectful enough to leave through the side door. That's where the trash goes. Not at the dining room table."

"Excuse me?" The restraint I'd forced myself to use was now gone, replaced by indignation. I didn't give a damn whose mother she was at this point. There was no way I was going to allow her to talk to me like that. "First of all, I'm not trash, and I'll leave through the same fucking door I entered. The front one. Second, from the looks of that bougie crap you're eating, I'm afraid it might make me sick anyway, so no thanks."

"Good, then we understand each other." That old bitch waved her hand at me as if she were dismissing the help. Before I could even take a first step, she asked, "What are you waiting for? I'm sure Martin has paid whatever fee you required for your services, and he's always been a generous tipper."

"Mother! That's uncalled for, unnecessary, and disrespectful." Martin stepped in front of me.

"This entire conversation is unnecessary," she told him. "And the disrespect is you bringing some random THOT to our table. You've put this entire family at risk."

"Risk for what?" Martin asked.

"Have you ever thought she could be casing it and planning to come back to rob us? She's from Brooklyn, for Christ's sake!" she said as if I wasn't standing right there.

"Bitch, you've really got me fucked up!" I yelled.

Martin tried to stop me, but at that point, I didn't give a fuck.

"I don't need none of this shit in your house, and that includes your son!"

I felt Martin tense up beside me, but that was his damn problem. His stupid-ass mother deserved every insult I was preparing to throw at her.

"Bitch!" She chuckled. "Honey, you might want to look up the definition of the word, and then look in the mirror. It might remind you of someone. You!"

The two men at the table and the young dude I recognized from the beach stifled their laughter. Instinctively, I took a step toward the old bitch. The skinny, light-skinned chick stood up and glared at me like she wanted to do something, but before I could put her in her place, Martin grabbed me. He must have known I was about to turn that place out.

"Karrin, don't," he said.

I pulled myself free and stepped toward the younger chick. "What are you supposed to be, security?"

"Sit down, Kimberly. No need to break a nail on someone so trivial," his mother said. "Martin, get rid of her before I call the police."

That threat stopped me in my tracks. No matter how much I wanted to slap the shit out of both women at that table, I knew my sister wouldn't hesitate to throw me out of her house if she heard I had the cops called on me at her neighbor's house.

"Mother, don't do this. You're embarrassing me," Martin said, but it didn't matter. Even if his mother miraculously discovered some manners and apologized, I had already decided to get the fuck out of there.

"You should be embarrassed," his mother said, and I almost felt sorry for Martin.

I turned to him with my eyes full of hurt. "It's okay. I know when I'm not wanted."

"Karrin, wait. Don't go!" Martin called after me as I walked toward the front door.

Part of me was hoping that Martin would come after me like in the movies, but he didn't, and I stepped outside into the morning sunlight alone.

Anthony Johnson

29

After three days back home in the city, I decided it was time to return to the Black Hamptons. I still hadn't talked to Sydney, who'd been calling and texting like a stalker. I did miss her, but I was not ready to deal with another conversation about her sister. So, instead of going straight to the house, I made plans with David to go out on his boat then play some tennis. I would call Sydney and ask her to meet me for dinner at Baldwin's Seaside so we could talk things out away from her sister.

After being out on the boat all morning, David and I stopped at Beach Brew to grab some lunch before heading out to the park for some tennis.

"So, what's the deal? You going back to the city tonight, or you going home?" David asked as he picked up his sandwich.

"Nah, Sydney's gonna lose her shit if I don't come home tonight. I wouldn't doubt if someone has already called and told her that I'm out here. Besides, I miss the hell outta her," I said, wishing I'd gotten what he had instead of the grilled chicken salad in front of me. Food choices had been a struggle for me my entire life. I'd been an overeater throughout high school and college, until I met Sydney and she not only taught me how to eat better, but she helped me drop eighty-five pounds. Nevertheless, David's Philly cheesesteak, homemade kettle chips, and one of Beach Brew's famous milkshakes looked like a feast for a king compared to what I had ordered.

"I can't lie. I definitely didn't expect you to stay gone this long, that's for sure." David took a huge bite of his sandwich. "She must have really pissed you off," he said with his mouth full of steak.

"Not her, her sister." Every time I thought about returning home, I remembered that Karrin was there, and I got angry all over again. I opted not to head back until I knew I was in a more tolerable mood.

He nodded. "Oh, I understand. That's how I feel about my mother-in-law."

David was a good friend, but I didn't really want to burden him with my marital issues, so I changed the subject.

"Anyway, man, on a happier note, I was able to get with legal and go through that Singh contract. With this deal, we're about to take things to a whole 'nother level. We're gonna be bringing in so much money that I might need to hire another accountant to assist you," I joked.

"That's what I'm talking about." David grinned. "I'm glad your eyes remain on the prize. I was afraid this thing at home was going to become a distraction."

"I wasn't about to do that. I've got two goals right now—securing this deal with Singh Transportation and purchasing that land for Sydney's pool."

"Speaking of the land, here comes your boy." David motioned toward Jeffrey, who'd just purchased a milkshake and was sauntering over to our table.

"What's going on, Jeffrey?" David greeted him.

"I was just driving by and couldn't resist stopping to get one of these terrific shakes. Mind if I join you?"

"Go right ahead," I told him, staring at his shake enviously.

He took a seat across from me.

"Any word on the property?" I asked.

His expression told me he was about to fuck up my mood. "Yes, well, Carolyn Britton made a $7.25-million offer this morning, and she doesn't appear to be backing down."

"Well, we're not backing down either," I stated for clarity.

"Shiiiiitttt," David groaned. He sat back and looked at us both as if we were crazy. "What the fuck is buried under that land, gold?"

"Pride," Jeffrey responded. "I understand why the Brittons want the land. It has something to do with family legacy. But you, Anthony, I just don't get. I thought you were a true businessman, a visionary. I didn't think you did things out of pure emotion. Quite frankly, I'm disappointed in you."

Disappointed in me? Who the hell did this guy think he was, my daddy?

"The land is just a means to an end. My wife wants a pool, and I'm gonna get her one. There's nothing emotional about it other than pleasing my wife," I retorted.

He set his coffee cup on the table. "I don't understand. If it's all about a pool, then why did you reject the property on Waterside that my wife suggested? It was a no brainer."

"What property on Waterside? What are you talking about, Jeffrey?" I glanced over at Dave, who shrugged.

"My wife and her aunt Carolyn approached your wife with a possible solution last week. There's actually another parcel adjacent to your land that's available," Jeffrey said. "I'm surprised your wife didn't tell you about it."

"She never mentioned it." I hated being blindsided like this. Now I understood a little more why Jeffrey thought I was being irrational.

I glanced at David, who obviously wanted no part of this conversation. He stood up and said, "Looks like you two have a lot to talk about. Anthony, I'll meet you at the park?"

"Yeah, I'll be there."

As David walked away, Jeffrey gave me some more detail. "I thought it was a great solution for everyone and ideal for you, especially since it would only cost you a million dollars instead of seven."

That number hit me like a punch in the gut. My wife was usually pretty careful with our money. I couldn't wrap my head around why she was pushing to buy a piece of land that would cost us millions more than it should.

"You said it's adjacent to our property?" I questioned, now eager to hear more details about the land. Maybe it was too small or sloped or something. I was hoping he could give me a valid reason why my wife would turn it down as an option for us to build a pool. I wanted to believe her motives made some sort of sense.

"Yes, it is. Slightly smaller, but you'd have more than enough space for a large pool, and your backyard would be significantly larger, which is what you guys wanted. It just doesn't have an ocean view, hence the cheaper price."

"I don't care about an ocean view. I already have an ocean view."

"Exactly."

The additional information didn't help any. In truth, it just made things worse, because now I feared that Sydney's reason for declining it was much pettier.

"Look, Jeffrey, thanks for letting me know all of this. It definitely sounds like a more sensible option than the Simpson property, for sure. Why don't you email me the details so I can look them over? I'll have an answer for you tomorrow morning."

"Certainly. I'll get them over to you later this afternoon." He smiled like a man who had accomplished something.

We shook hands, and I got up, threw my salad in the trash, and headed to my car. As soon as I got in, I received another text from Sydney: Where are you and why are you not answering my texts? Baby, we need to talk.

I sat behind the wheel, deciding whether I was ready to respond. I still hadn't gotten over our uninvited house guest, and now I knew about the property that she hadn't bothered to tell me about. It was a lot, and although I knew I couldn't avoid speaking to my wife forever, the only thing I desired at the moment was an extra-large milkshake.

Sydney Johnson

30

I'd been sitting on my bed for more than an hour, staring into space and feeling sorry for myself because Anthony hadn't been responding to my texts or calls. Ever since he went back to the city, the only communication I'd had with him was a brief text saying, I'm fine. When is Karrin leaving?

I knew he was upset when he left, but I'd assumed he just needed a day to cool down. I thought he'd be back the next day, but now it was going on four days with almost no contact. This was the longest we'd gone without talking since we'd been married. My emotions were a mixture of anger, concern, and loneliness. I missed my husband, and now I was second-guessing my decision to let my sister stay, especially since I was sure she wouldn't have done the same for me.

I thought about calling Anthony again, but I didn't think I could handle one more unanswered call, so I decided to do something else that was sure to get his attention. It was the one thing that he'd never been able to ignore, no matter how annoyed he was with me.

I went over to the dresser and pulled out the perfect accessory for the surefire tactic I was about to employ. I slipped my sundress off and stepped into a lacy pink thong bodysuit, then I stood in front of the full-length mirror with my phone in hand, snapping photos that would've made me plenty of money on an OnlyFans page. I left nothing to the imagination.

Let's see you not come home after I send these, I thought, clicking away. I was so caught up in the moment that I almost didn't hear my phone ringing.

"Hello?" I tried not to sound desperate when I saw Anthony's name on the caller ID and answered, but that's how I felt—desperate to end this fight between us, and relieved that he'd finally called.

"You called?" His voice was cold and unemotional. Maybe I would still have to send those photos after all.

"Yes. I've been worried about you," I told him. "I just want you to come home, baby. I'm sorry. And I miss you."

"I miss you too, Syd, but we have some serious things to discuss."

"I know, and I already decided I would tell Karr—"

"It's not just about your sister," he replied, and my stomach fluttered with nerves. "I just ran into Jeffrey Bowen while David and I were having lunch at Beach Brew, and—"

"Beach Brew? You're here?" My attitude changed instantly. "Dammit, Anthony, I can't believe you've been gone for three days and haven't come straight home to your family. Not to mention the fact that you've been ignoring me."

"I haven't been ignoring you. David and I have been working on the Singh deal."

I knew he was telling the truth. I had been watching the security cameras at our city house and at the office, and I'd seen him and David together several times. I'd also seen him check his caller ID and ignore me a few times, but I'd talk to him about that later. Right now, I wanted to hear about his conversation with Jeffrey.

"So, what did Jeffrey say about the property?" I asked, hoping for good news. I really wanted a swimming pool, and I also wanted to knock that bitch Carolyn Britton down a few pegs. She thought she was so superior, but she had fucked with the wrong one.

"Is it ours?" I asked.

"No. The Brittons made a higher bid."

I felt deflated. "Dammit. We have to put in another bid. You know how important this is to me, Anthony."

"The property or a pool?" he asked in an accusatory tone that made me hesitate.

"The pool. Why else would we want the land?"

"I don't know. But maybe it has something to do with why you didn't tell me about the property on Waterside that's adjacent to us. You know the one that's millions of dollars cheaper? I mean, what the fuck, Sydney?"

Shit! Fucking Jeffrey and his big mouth.

"I don't want that raggedy lot, Anthony. I want the Simpson property."

"Syd, this is getting way out of hand. Seven million dollars was already a ridiculous amount to bid, and who knows where this bidding war will end? I'm not spending eight million dollars on a lot for a pool when we could spend a million."

I will not let Carolyn Britton win, I thought, irritated by his sudden lack of motivation.

I tried to encourage him with sweetness that usually helped me get my way. "Baby, please. Just bid one more time. Please."

"No. It's fiscally irresponsible. We are not buying that land just because you don't like Carolyn Britton. We're putting in a pool for our family's enjoyment, and we can do that on the Waterside property. What you want us to do is just plain spiteful, and I will not be a part of it." He was using that voice I hated, the one that said I wouldn't be able to budge him.

There was only one way to fight that, and I hated to do it. It was one thing to use my womanly wiles to make up after a fight, but it was entirely another to manipulate him into spending unnecessary money to inflate my ego. However, his stubbornness left me no choice. I opened the messages on my phone, attached a couple of the booty shots I'd just taken, and hit send.

"Anthony, please don't do this to me. I know it's petty, but she thinks she's better than me. If she gets that land, I'll always have her looking down her nose at me," I whined, looking for some sympathy.

"I'm sorry, Syd, but we're better than that. You're better than that."

He was right. Normally I was confident enough not to let some bitch's disrespect bother me, but there was something about this woman that just got under my skin. I was proud of Anthony and me and all we had accomplished, and that included our house in the Hamptons. I feared that Carolyn

Britton had so much animosity toward me that she wouldn't stop at acquiring the property. She would do everything she could to run us out of the neighborhood. I didn't want to admit to Anthony how insecure she made me feel, but I did want him to keep fighting for me.

"Anthony, look at your text messages." I lowered my voice and spoke seductively. "Look at them right now."

He got quiet for a second, then he whispered, "Damn."

"Exactly. Now do you see why we need that land?"

"Not exactly, but I appreciate the visual. God knows you're sexy as fuck. But we gotta be smart about our finances, Sydney."

"Okay, okay, we can talk about it when you get home. Are you on your way now?" At that point, I knew this was not something I could convince him of over the phone. "I'll see you when you get here."

"I have a meeting to go to first, but I'll be home a little later. Promise," he said. "Hey, we're making the right decision."

"Okay. I love you."

"Love you too. Oh, and Syd," Anthony said just as I was about to end the call.

"Yeah?"

"I want you in that same outfit you have on in those pics."

"Oh, trust me. I wasn't planning on wearing anything else. See you when you get home."

Anthony hung up, and I lay back on the bed, relieved that he was coming home. I was going to have to put in overtime in the bedroom to show my appreciation and keep him distracted, not just with regard to my sister, but also to make sure he would change his mind about winning that damn property.

David Michaels

31

The weather was perfect for playing tennis, and the courts at Mashashimuet Park were full of folks who'd decided to take advantage of the gorgeous, clear sky and moderate temperatures. I'd arrived early for the scheduled match, but when I got to the court, Malcolm and Martin Britton were already there, stretching and hitting balls.

"What's up, fellas?" I called out as I entered the gate.

The three of us had spent countless hours during our formative years right here every summer, learning to play tennis. Now that we were grown men, we made an effort to play at least three or four times every summer. Individually, they weren't much better than me at tennis, but at doubles, they royally kicked my ass every chance they got. It didn't seem to matter who I got to partner with me. I just couldn't beat them. However, I did enjoy the camaraderie and friendly competition, despite my mounting defeats.

"Oh, so you actually decided to show up?" Martin said. "When we got here and didn't see you, I thought you'd come to your senses and bailed."

"Keep talkin' shit, Martin. I invited you, remember. Not the other way around." I placed my duffle bag and racket case on the bench. "Why the hell would I not show up?"

"To avoid the ass kicking we're about to give you," he suggested.

"I got a secret weapon for your ass this time," I replied.

"Oh, you're desperate for a win, so you've brought in another ringer from the city?" Malcolm teased.

"Damn, you too, Malcolm? You Brittons have some big-ass mouths," I said.

Usually it was Martin who talked the most shit. Malcolm was the more serious one. He'd always been studious and hard-working, and he stuck to the rules. He was also one hell of a tennis player, so he let his game do the talking for him.

Malcolm and I were the same age, but I had spent more time hanging out with Martin, mostly for the social opportunities. He was cool with everyone, and when he wasn't the one throwing the party, he always got us into the best clubs. With Malcolm, you knew you could make money; with Martin, you were guaranteed to have a good time. Truthfully, though, whether it was in business or on the tennis court, the brothers were a very formidable two-headed dragon.

"No ringer," I said. "He lives in the Black Hamptons, just like us."

Martin and Malcolm gave each other the eye, looking doubtful. They'd beaten just about everyone under sixty in our community.

"Who?"

I could see the curiosity was killing Martin, who never had any patience.

I laughed. "You'll see," I said, bending down to tighten my laces. "So, I hear things got a little heated at the last HOA meeting. Sorry I missed it."

"You talkin' about that shit with Anthony Johnson and his wife?" Martin asked.

"Yeah, I heard you folks were going head-to-head over the Simpson property."

Malcolm frowned. "That fuckin' guy. Forced us into a damn bidding war in the middle of the meeting. It was embarrassing."

"Don't sleep on my boy Anthony. He's a hell of a businessman," I told them.

"Yeah, well, your boy and his wife need to learn their damn place," Martin replied.

"Their place? Tell me you didn't just say that." I glared at him like he had taken a dump on the court. Martin was usually a little more politically correct than that. "What the hell is that supposed to mean? You sound like Everett Simpson. This ain't 1965, Martin. We don't use a paper bag test to vet our neighbors, and nobody gives a shit how much your grandfather or mine made back in the day. The only thing they care about is how many Twitter and Instagram followers you have and how much money you have in the bank. And for the record, Anthony Johnson has plenty of both."

The Brittons, like my family, the Simpsons, and a few other families, had been founding members of the community. I hated to admit it, but back in the day, they held themselves to be a little higher than the average black person because they had light skin and a little money. Thank God things had changed, or at least they were supposed to have changed, because I had a huge problem with colorism or classist bullshit. Black folks had enough stress from the outside world. We didn't need to be tearing each other down.

"You have to excuse Martin. He's not having the best of days. Some chick from Brooklyn put it on his ass last night, and he's not thinking straight." Malcolm laughed.

"Fuck you, Malcolm." Martin gave his brother the finger, then tried to clean up his comment. "And what I meant, David, was that Anthony's wife and Mother kind of got into it at the meeting. Considering Mother's age and her status in the community, Mrs. Johnson should give her respect."

"Especially after Mother and Leslie went over there with a solution that should have made everyone happy," Malcolm added.

"Look, I hear you," I said, "but everyone knows your mother can be, shall we say, intimidating." Neither of them spoke up to deny that. "Sydney Johnson is a strong-willed woman. She's naturally going to bump heads with Carolyn. But the Johnsons wouldn't have come as far as they have if she wasn't. She helped Anthony grow that business from the ground up, and she didn't do it by being some demure housewife."

"Okay, we'll admit Mother can be a handful, but if they're such great businesspeople, how come they're willing to over-pay for the land?" Martin asked. "Sounds kinda stupid to me."

"I don't know. One man's trash is another man's treasure. His wife wants a pool. Besides, I don't see y'all backing down, and I respect both of you as businessmen."

Neither was able to reply or make eye contact with me, which meant my point was correct. Anthony and Sydney weren't the only ones making questionable financial decisions because of this land.

"All I'm saying is that y'all fighting over nickels and dimes when we all should be stacking dollars. Fuck that land. Think of the big picture."

"What's your point, David?" Malcolm asked.

"Anthony Johnson's a straight-up genius. The man has over two hundred patents, and Sydney Tech is about to partner up with Singh Transportation to supply all the batteries for their fleet of electric trucks worldwide."

Malcolm raised his eyebrows. "He's partnering with Singh Transportation. That's huge."

"Yeah, it is," Martin agreed, and that's when I knew I had them.

"Ten years from now, he'll be on Forbes Top 100 and have enough money to buy your bank, gentlemen. The time to get in with this guy is now. Trust me. I'm his CFO. Big things are about to happen."

"You think this guy would be interested in doing some business with us?" Malcolm asked like I knew he would.

"I don't see why not. Then again, maybe you should ask him yourself," I said, laughing as I pointed to Anthony, who had just arrived. I had purposely not told them who my partner would be because I was worried they might refuse to come to play. Anthony, on the other hand, just didn't care.

"He's your partner?" Malcolm snapped.

"Yeah. What's the matter? You scared?" I joked.

"Never that," Martin replied. "Kicking his ass will be a pleasure."

"What's up, fellas? I heard you brothers were the ones to beat around here." Anthony greeted them as he made his way over to us.

"That's what they say," Malcolm replied. I guess his competitive spirit wouldn't let him back down, even now that he knew who my partner was. "You any good?"

Anthony nudged my arm. "I guess we're going to find out. Why don't you guys serve first? You're the home team."

"That we are. Come on, Martin." Malcolm walked to the right side of the court.

"Hey, Anthony," Martin shouted as he followed his brother.

"Yes, sir?" Anthony replied.

"Where the hell you get that yellow-ass sweater? You rob Big Bird?" Martin laughed at his own joke as if it was the funniest thing he'd ever heard.

Anthony looked at me. "What's wrong with my sweater? I like this sweater."

"Don't pay attention to him." I motioned for Anthony to follow me to the other side of the net. "He just likes to talk shit."

"So do I. I just know how to back it up," Anthony said loudly enough for both Brittons to hear.

I lifted my hand for a fist bump, and we got into position for Martin's serve.

"By the way, where'd you get those tight-ass shorts? You shopping at Victoria's Secret again?" Anthony yelled out to Martin.

"Oh, shit!" I laughed, and so did Malcolm.

Anthony's comeback comment was refreshing. I'd worked for Sydney Tech for five years, and from what I'd seen, he was always mild-mannered and laser focused on business. We had played tennis in the city a few times, but I'd never heard him talk shit like that.

Martin smashed the ball across the net, but Anthony was ready for it. We volleyed back and forth for a while, and I could see that the Brittons were surprised by my partner's skills.

When Anthony finally missed, Martin almost looked relieved. Of course, he couldn't resist a jab. "Hey, Anthony, this isn't baseball. You don't have three tries. You're supposed to hit the ball the first time."

"Just serve the damn ball," Anthony barked back at him, annoyed.

Martin served it, and Anthony hit back a winner.

"What you think of that, big head?" Anthony jeered.

"Nice shot!" Malcolm said, approaching the net. "I guess you got a little game."

"Thanks," Anthony replied.

"So, David was mentioning that we should partner up and do some business. You open to that?"

Anthony nodded. "Yes, I am. Doing business with our own is very important to me. However, the most important business partner that I have is my wife, and she wants a swimming pool, so until I get some land to build her one, you're going to have to give me a little time."

"I think that's fair. Tensions are high, but things should calm down soon. Let me talk to Mother once the air thins around here," Malcolm replied, getting back in position.

Martin served again, and Anthony used his backhand to return the ball. Martin then hit the ball with such force that it flew past Anthony.

"Dammit!" Anthony shouted at himself. He, like the rest of us, was very competitive.

"Man, Anthony, by the time I get finished with you on this court, your wife's going to be calling me daddy," Martin joked.

"Yo, Martin, chill. That shit's not necessary," Malcolm warned his brother. "Talking shit is one thing, but there ain't no need to be disrespectful."

"Nah, he ain't gotta chill. Give me the ball so I can make him eat it."

When the next serve came Anthony's way, he smashed it so aggressively that it bounced once and then hit Malcolm right in the balls.

I didn't think he did it on purpose, but nevertheless, Anthony was pleased. "Now who's your daddy, boys? Who's your daddy?" he yelled.

It took Malcolm a moment to recover, but when he finally stood up straight, he was enraged. "What did you say?"

"I said who's your daddy!" Anthony yelled back, stomping around the court in a mini victory lap.

Out of nowhere, Malcolm dropped his racket and charged the net. "What the fuck did you say about my daddy? I will fuck you up out here. Say it again."

Anthony looked very confused. He stepped toward Malcolm. "Hey, man, calm down. I'm just having some fun."

"You don't have fun at my daddy's expense."

Before we knew it, Malcolm had jumped the net and decked Anthony with a punch in the face. "But I bet you won't do that shit again, will you?" he said, continuing to pound on Anthony as he struggled to get up off the ground.

"Come on, Malcolm. Get off him! It's cool. It's cool. He didn't mean it!" Martin yelled.

We finally managed to restrain Malcolm, but the damage had already been done. Anthony's eye was swelling up quick.

"Talk that shit now, Johnson!"

Martin held his brother back and escorted him off the court. I helped Anthony up.

"What the hell was that all about? I thought we were just having fun and talking shit." Anthony asked me, wiping the blood from his nose. He looked pissed, and I didn't blame him.

I shook my head and tried to explain. "Malcolm has always had some serious daddy issues. Moses was Malcolm's hero, and he still hasn't come to terms with him being gone."

"That's no excuse for him putting his hands on me like that."

"You're not wrong about that."

Sydney Johnson

32

I sent the kids away to their friends' houses and prayed Karrin was going to be out another night. My job was to get me and my husband back on the same page, and it was not going to be easy, but I was ready when I heard Anthony's car pull into the garage. Wearing the barely-there thong body suit and clear stilettos, I checked my reflection and added another layer of lip gloss as I waited for him to come into the house.

The door slamming a little harder than usual caught my attention, but I didn't think much of it. I posed in the doorway of our bedroom and called out, "Welcome home, baby. Don't worry. Nobody's home but meeeeee!"

I expected him to appear on the stairs within seconds. When he didn't, I carefully descended the staircase and went looking for him.

"Babe, where are you?"

The sound of running water coming from the first-floor bathroom confirmed his location. I tapped on the door before opening it and striking a sexy pose. I just prayed I wasn't going to find him sitting on the toilet, which thankfully, he wasn't. Anthony barely glanced over at me. His attention was on whatever was in the sink.

"Well, damn. That wasn't the reaction I was hoping for," I told him. "Can you at least be a little more excited?"

"Right now, Syd, the only thing that would excite me is beating that motherfucker's ass. I can't believe he did this to my face!" Anthony smacked the countertop with the palm of his hand and lifted his head to look at me.

Startled, I took a step back, now noticing his ripped shirt, busted lip, and the growing bruise under his eye. "What the—? What happened? Oh my God, did you get into a fight?"

"Yes, I got in a fight," Anthony yelled, pushing past me as he stomped to the kitchen.

"What the fuck? With who?" I asked, right on his heels.

"The Brittons. Mostly Malcolm."

"For what?"

"Because I beat their asses in tennis." Anthony snatched a dishtowel from the kitchen drawer and reached for the ice cubes I was grabbing from the freezer. "Then he got mad because I was talking shit. This dude attacked me, Syd."

"Oh, hell no! His ass ain't getting away with this." I was so angry that I could barely see straight. I couldn't believe anybody had the nerve to put their hands on my husband, and the fact that it was one of those damn Brittons made my blood oil even hotter.

I grabbed Anthony's cell phone off the kitchen counter. "I'm calling the police. We're filing assault charges against his ass."

Anthony put his hand on my arm to stop me. "No, we're not. Don't call the cops. You know how I feel about Black people calling the cops on each other."

"But Anthony—"

"Sydney, I said no. We're not calling the police!" His voice was so loud it rattled the dishes in the cabinet.

I lowered the phone. "Hey, I know you're upset, but I'm not the enemy here." I leaned against the counter, fuming.

"I'm sorry." He walked over to me, and I wrapped my arms around him. "I just can't believe he hit me over a tennis game."

I leaned back to get a good look at his injuries. "Yeah, he really swelled up your eye. What a bunch of entitled assholes."

We held each other tight, both of us quiet for a few minutes. I could feel his racing heartbeat finally slowing down.

"They need to be taken down a notch. All of them," I said.

Anthony finally broke our hug. "Give me that phone."

I handed it to him, and he searched the contacts until he found the name he was looking for.

"Hello, Jeffrey. This is Anthony Johnson," he said when the call connected. "I want to raise our offer on the Simpson property." As he spoke, he gave me that confident, don't-fuck-with-me look that always turned me on. "We're not interested in the property on Waterside. The only property we're interested in is the one next to Carolyn Britton."

I blinked in surprise, hoping I'd heard correctly. The physical altercation with the Brittons had stirred something in my husband, and he was fired up. I'd never seen him so enraged. I was nervous and turned on at the same time.

"Baby?" I said carefully after he put down the phone.

"That bastard might have won the fight, but we are going to win the fucking war." Anthony's eyes were dark and piercing as he spoke. I grabbed his hand and pulled him toward the stairs. I couldn't wait to make love to my husband, black eye and all. As crazy as it sounds, he was even more sexy when he was angry.

Malcolm Britton

33

After the fight with Anthony Johnson, I remained silent during the entire ride home, attempting to process all the emotions I was feeling: shock, sadness, a little regret, but most of all, anger. I'd never truly wanted to kill anyone in my life, but for some reason, his words brought it out in me. I wasn't a violent man. I'd actually never had a fist fight until today, other than a few skirmishes with Martin when we were kids. But you don't ridicule my father, not after everything he went through before he left us. Martin and David could think what they wanted, but as far as I was concerned, Anthony Johnson mocked me and my father on purpose. It wasn't just his words. It was his tone.

My father was everything to me. Not only was he the man I looked up to and aspired to be like, but he was also my best friend. He taught me about business and finances, but more importantly, he taught me about respect and pride. He taught me how to be a man. The hurt I felt from his absence was deep and one I dealt with daily. Once those words came out of Anthony Johnson's bitch-ass mouth, all of my pain crystallized into pure rage, and next thing I knew, I was being pulled off of him and Martin was leading me out into the parking lot. Had they not stopped me, there was no telling what I would've done.

We arrived at the house and Martin had barely put my Maserati in park before I was out of the car and headed into the house.

"Malcolm!" He called after me, but I continued inside, heading straight to the kitchen to put ice on my swelling knuckles. "Malcolm, hold up."

"I don't have nothing to say, Martin," I told him as he hurried behind me.

"Well, I do, so you need to stop and listen to me."

I grabbed cubes of ice from the dispenser, tossed them into a clean dishtowel, then placed it on my hand, wincing from the sudden cold. "I don't have nothing to say, Martin. I'm good."

"You ain't good. You assaulted that guy."

"He deserved that shit and more. You heard what the fuck he said about Daddy!"

"I heard, but he didn't mean it. At least not the way you were think—"

I cut him off. "Like I said, I don't wanna talk about it. That motherfucker was wrong."

"You can pretend all you want, but this ain't about him. This is about you and Daddy and that bullshit about you not being Daddy's son."

"Don't push it, Martin." My brother was coming dangerously close to getting what Anthony Johnson got.

"I'm not pushing it. We both know what the paternity test said. You're Daddy's son. You need to let that shit go, man."

What he failed to add was that the first two paternity tests had been inconclusive. How was I supposed to let that go?

"What the hell is going on?" Mother rushed into the kitchen. She looked from Martin to me, and her eyes widened when she noticed me icing my hand. "Malcolm, what happened to your hand?"

I looked down at my disheveled shirt and swollen hand. "Nothing. I'm fine, Mother."

"We were playing a doubles match at the park and it kinda got out of hand," Martin stupidly volunteered.

"Out of hand how? Did he fall?" Mother asked. Martin tried to look over at me for help, but he'd already opened the door, so it was his to deal with now. "Answer me!"

"Things got a little intense during our tennis game with David Michaels and Anthony Johnson. Anthony was trash talking and said something Malcolm didn't like, and one thing led to another."

"What did he say?"

"He asked me who was my daddy," I interjected, now finding it necessary to explain the details so Mother would understand my perspective.

For a moment, her eyes became small and tight, reflecting the same anger I felt. "And what did you do, Malcolm?"

"I punched him," I stated matter-of-factly, as if knocking Anthony Johnson the fuck out was the most natural response in the world.

"Repeatedly, Mother. It took me and David to pull him off," Martin elaborated. "We may be looking at a lawsuit."

Mother had always been hard to read, but at that moment, she was especially so—until she turned to me with a proud smile on her face. "Well, sometimes a man's got to do what a man's got to do. Your father wasn't above punching someone out over principles, and neither should you be. Let's just hope the fallout isn't too big."

Well, that went better than I would have expected.

Suddenly, Mother turned around and stared toward the kitchen door. "You're hovering again, Leslie. What's wrong?"

Leslie, who I hadn't even noticed until Mother called her name, eased into the kitchen from the hallway, looking scared. "Aunt Carolyn, something has happened."

I don't think any of us liked the timidness in Leslie's voice. It could only mean one thing: bad news.

"The Johnsons just made an $8-million bid for the Simpson property."

"Leslie, you told me less than an hour ago that Jeffrey was preparing paperwork for the Johnsons to purchase the property on Waterside Drive. What the hell happened in an hour?"

All eyes turned to me, and Martin said, "A black eye and a swollen lip. That's what happened."

Leslie Bowen

34

For some people, weekends were made for rest and relax-
ation. Not mine. My schedule was full, starting early Saturday
morning at the home of Frank and Delores Mitchell. They
had decided it was time to sell their family home and move
a little farther down the beach to a smaller cottage. I was
looking forward to handling the listing of their current home
as well as the one they were purchasing. The paperwork for
the double commission had been handled, and all I needed
to do was gather their signatures, then continue with my day.

"Good morning." I greeted Delores when she opened the
door.

She was around the same age as Aunt Carolyn but seemed
younger, mainly because of her relaxed, free-spirited nature. I
always felt warm and comfortable whenever I was around her.

"Morning, Leslie. You're right on time this morning."

The big hug and bright greeting I expected was noticeably
absent, but I attributed it to the early hour.

"Yes, ma'am," I said. "I'm just as excited about this as you
and Frank are."

"Come on in. Frank's in the backyard." Delores welcomed
me in, and I followed her to the back of their home, where
Frank was working in the beautiful flower garden in his
coveralls and straw hat, looking more like a farmer than a
decorated army genera.

"Hey, Mr. Frank, those gardenias are looking good over
there," I told him.

"Thank you, Leslie." He walked over, but like his wife, he
didn't offer a hug or the pleasantries he usually had for me.
Something was definitely off.

"Is everything okay, Mr. Frank? You feeling okay?" I asked, hoping their unusual behavior wasn't related to the cancer he'd been treated for a year ago. From what they'd told me, he'd made a full recovery and was in remission.

"Yes, I'm feeling fine, Leslie." He glanced over at Delores, who looked just as uncomfortable.

"What's going on?" I asked, no longer able to gloss over the obvious tension.

"Uh, Leslie, we aren't going to be able to give you the listing," Delores told me. "I'm sorry. We wanted to tell you face to face, and—"

"You decided not to sell?" I asked, trying to keep the disappointment out of my voice.

"No, we're still selling," Frank replied. "We just decided to go with another realtor, that's all."

I couldn't believe what they were saying. Days ago, they'd told me they specifically wanted me to handle the transaction because of how much they trusted and respected me. I was almost like family. Now, they both stared at me as if I were a stranger.

"I don't understand. We've been talking all week . . ." I started.

"We know, but the truth is, we're retired, and although we're financially comfortable, we still need the mortgage on the new property to have a rate that we can handle. That's why Amistad had been our bank for years," Delores explained. "If they deny—"

"Deny? Why would they do that?"

Delores looked at me with what felt like pity. "Well, we got a call from the bank regarding our application and were advised that if you were the realtor, then they wouldn't approve it."

"That makes no sense." I shook my head.

"I agree, but they said the decision came from the head of the bank." Frank gave me a knowing glance. "We're sorry, Leslie, but we can't afford not to get this loan."

"There must be some kind of mix-up," I said, trying to reassure them. "I'm actually going to see Aunt Carolyn this afternoon, and I'll speak with her directly regarding this."

Frank and Delores looked slightly relieved.

"Okay, that's a good idea. I told Frank this had to be a mistake. Your aunt probably doesn't even know about any of this." Delores's smile was a little warmer as she touched my shoulder.

"I'm sure she doesn't," I told her. "But I do need a favor."

"What's that?" Frank asked.

"Can you hold off on giving the listing to anyone else until we get this sorted out? It won't take long." I pleaded with my eyes.

They looked at one another, then Delores smiled and nodded. "That's fair. We can give you a few days."

"Thank you." I exhaled, not having realized that I was holding my breath. "I'll call you in a couple of days."

The farewell as I left their home was much warmer than when I had arrived, and this time included hugs, laughter, and even a dinner invitation for Jeffrey and me. The Mitchells weren't the ones who were anxious now. I was. I tossed my briefcase into the back seat of my SUV and pulled out of the driveway. It was still early, but I needed a drink before my next appointment.

Two hours later, I strolled down the dock toward the USS Carolyn, where the Britton Foundation Annual White Tea was hosted every year. My nerves were on edge, despite the three mimosas I'd had. Instead of chatting with the other ladies clad in all white heading toward the yacht, I remained silent. Trying to talk to anyone was pointless anyway. The only person I needed to speak to was Aunt Carolyn.

Just as I was about to step onto the deck, Kimberly appeared and said she needed to speak to me in private.

"Okay. What the hell is going on?" I whispered when we were out of earshot of the guests.

"There's been a slight change of plans for you," Kimberly said, looking stylish as ever in her white jumpsuit that showed off her tiny waist.

"What kind of change?" My legs suddenly felt like jelly.

"Look, Leslie, I think you should sit this year's tea out," she said. "It would be best."

"So she doesn't want me here. That's what you're saying?" I asked for clarification. "I'm not stupid, Kimberly. I know a 'message' from my aunt when I see one."

"You know how she is, and right now, she's not pleased with you."

I flinched slightly at her words. "It's a charity event, for God's sake, and I'm supposed to give a speech. I'm on the damn board. What am I supposed to do? How is this going to look? People already see that I'm here."

"I'll tell people you're ill and had to leave, and that you still made your donation. Then you can try and fix this situation. Do whatever you need to do to get back into Carolyn's good graces."

"Fix it how?" I exclaimed, my voice louder than I had intended. I lowered it as I continued. "I don't even know what she's pissed about."

"Real talk, I don't know exactly what's going on, but from what I can gather, it most likely has something to do with that land. Its importance has her pulling out all the stops, and nothing and no one is going to get in her way, including you."

I looked around and saw Aunt Carolyn on the yacht, staring at us. The look she gave me was menacing. Her message was loud and clear, and I had no choice but to leave.

I turned to Kimberly and told her, "Please extend my apologies. I'm suddenly not feeling well."

Jeffrey Bowen

35

Saturday was my favorite day of the week because it was the day Leslie's schedule was full of open houses, walk-throughs with clients, and whatever obligatory social gatherings she had committed herself to. It gave me plenty of free time during the day to sail, work out, or nap if I chose to. But then there were Saturday nights, which were our designated date night. I actually enjoyed planning our evening festivities, which always ended with great sex that I'd look forward to all week.

Recently, Leslie and I had been discussing having a baby, which motivated me to step up my romantic game. I made reservations at Capelletti, our favorite restaurant, and picked up a bouquet of calla lilies and a bottle of Veuve Clicquot champagne to set the mood. Tonight was going to be a good night.

"Honey, I'm home," I announced as I walked through the door precisely at six o'clock. Date night officially started at seven, which gave me an hour to shower, change, and get ready. Leslie's SUV was in the driveway, but she didn't answer, and she wasn't in the great room, her favorite spot in the house.

"Les, where are you?"

"Here." Her voice drifted downstairs.

I went into our bedroom and strolled over to the bed, where she was sitting with her sexy, toned legs crossed, looking gorgeous in a white sundress and heels. I dramatically presented the flowers to her.

"For my beautiful wife."

"Thanks." Her voice was flat, and she barely looked at the bouquet.

"How was the tea?"

As I bent down to kiss her forehead, the bottle of Don Julio on the nightstand caught my attention, along with the half empty glass in her hand. If she was drinking tequila, something was up.

"I don't know. I was disinvited." Leslie glared at me. "Aunt Carolyn wouldn't even let me on the fucking boat."

"What?" I put the bouquet on the bed and sat beside her.

"She's pissed, and everyone knows. After meeting with the Mitchells—who, by the way, pulled their damn listing per Aunt Carolyn's orders—I went down to the beach, and nobody in the circle would even talk to me. They were all acting like I was a pariah. And I even brought a very expensive bottle of wine."

"Your beach cronies? You for real, babe?" I shook my head in disbelief. The wrath of Carolyn Britton wasn't anything new to me, but subjecting my wife to her madness was beyond cruel. "You've known those women all your life. What the fuck? That's ridiculous."

"It's Aunt Carolyn. She wants that property at any cost." Leslie gulped her drink. "Why the fuck did you have to put that property up for bid, Jeffrey? This is your fault."

"Mine? Your aunt's irrational behavior has nothing to do with me. What did she say?"

"Nothing! She won't talk to me, and neither will anyone else, other than Kimberly, who seems to think—"

The ringing of my cell phone interrupted her. I glanced at the caller ID on my watch and saw that it was Sydney Johnson. Knowing exactly why she was calling, I decided to ignore it and continue the more pressing discussion with my wife.

"It's Sydney Johnson. I can call her back later."

"No, answer it," Leslie instructed.

I wasn't sure that was a good idea, but the way Leslie said it sounded like a command, so I picked up my phone and answered.

"Hello, Sydney."

"Jeffrey, how are you? I know it's Saturday, but I'm calling to see if the Simpsons accepted our offer," she said.

"I haven't spoken to them yet, Sydney. I told you as soon as I know something, I'll update you, but your bid is still the highest," I explained to her as I'd already done several times. Unlike her husband, who was at least trying to keep this relatively professional, she was becoming quite annoying.

I couldn't really blame her, though, since I was slow-walking the whole process on purpose. I'd decided to wait until after the Fourth to talk to Everett about the offer they'd made. Hopefully by then, the Johnsons would have come to their senses and agreed to buy the Waterside property.

She sighed. "Okay, I guess I'll wait for your call then. Goodbye."

"Enjoy your weekend, and we'll talk next week," I said, hoping she would understand that was a hint to not call back before then.

"They're not going to back down, are they?" Leslie asked when I put my phone away.

"I don't think so. The altercation Anthony had with Malcolm at the tennis court didn't help. They're pretty determined," I said.

"Kimberly was right. This has to do with that land." She reached for the bottle, but I grabbed her hand to stop her.

"Sweetie, look, I know Carolyn is tripping, but it's Saturday night." I leaned close to nuzzle against her neck. "We can't let her ruin the nice evening we've got planned."

"I'm not going anywhere." Leslie folded her arms tightly across her chest.

"We don't have to. We can order in, enjoy champagne in the hot tub, then I can give you a massage. You look like you could use one." I started rubbing her shoulders.

Leslie pushed me away. "I don't want a massage."

"Fine. You can give me one instead," I said playfully. "You can rub my back, then my front."

The look on Leslie's face let me know that she was unamused. "You don't seem to get it, Jeffrey."

"Get what?"

"Until my family gets what they want, I'm not giving you shit. I suggest you get used to rubbing yourself because that's the only person that will be touching you."

"Leslie, you're being as fucked up as Carolyn. You know that, right?" I yelled, shocked by her behavior. "I think you have forgotten that I am your husband, which makes me family too."

"I'm well aware of that, Jeffrey. And if you want me to fulfill my wifely duties, you'd better do whatever you need to do to get my aunt that property." She grabbed a pillow and shoved it at me, along with the throw that we kept on the edge of the bed. "You won't be sleeping in here until then. Good night."

"Are you fucking kidding me?"

"Not one bit."

I stormed out of the bedroom and had barely made it into the hallway before I heard the door slam. This was definitely not the Saturday night I had planned. Not only had Carolyn Britton's wrath disrupted my sex life, but I'd been banished to the guest bedroom.

I had to do something to fix this fast. I'd never done an unethical thing in my entire legal career, but now I was contemplating my options. My cell phone rang again. This time, I did ignore the call. Other than Sydney Johnson, the last person that I wanted to talk to was Everett Simpson.

Anthony Johnson

36

I'd never been a daredevil, and living on the edge wasn't my thing, hence the reason I was holding on for dear life as David's "go-fast" sped through the water. The long, thin cigarette boat had the capability to reach speeds of over 90 miles per hour. David swore he never pushed it past 65, but it felt like we were going 120. Though my grip was tight, I enjoyed the mixture of the strong wind and light spray of water against my face. Finally, he slowed down, and I was able to relax a bit as we drifted against the current.

"Yo, why'd you stop?" I asked him.

"Oh, thought we'd pause and enjoy the scenery." David grinned and tipped his head in the direction he wanted me to look. I turned to see a group of gorgeous ladies watching us from the deck of a nearby yacht.

"Nice."

"Hey, ladies." David waved to them. They giggled as they waved back, then without warning, lifted their bikini tops, offering us a full display. A few of the more rowdy ones even bounced up and down a bit before readjusting their tops.

"Damn, I love the fucking summertime," David said.

"I hear ya." I was married and my wife definitely handled her business, but I was still a man and wouldn't turn away from the impromptu female mob displaying their beautiful assets. "I see why you love being out here on this damn boat."

"Oh, it's an attention getter, for sure. Man, I thought you were getting your own this summer. I know a guy trying to get rid of his if you're interested." David reached into the mini fridge and grabbed two beers, then handed one to me.

"Nah, I'm good." I opened the can and took a sip. "I got more important shit to deal with right now. Mainly, finalizing this Singh contract. Sydney's on my ass about this damn land, and my crazy-ass sister-in-law is still at my crib."

"Relax, dude. The Singh contract is a done deal, and once it's done, you'll have enough money to buy ten boats if you want." David sat back and propped up his feet. "And, if you like, I can take that fine-ass sister-in-law off your hands to help you out. That's what friends are for."

"Man, you definitely don't need those types of problems in your life. Hell, neither do I, which is why I want her gone, ASAP." I shook my head. "That chick is trouble with a capital T. Besides, your wife would kill you and me both."

"What's the deal with you and her anyway?" David gave me a curious look.

Not willing to air my family's dirty laundry, even to my trusted friend, I evaded the question. "It's not worth talking about, man. Just a fucked-up person, and God don't like ugly."

"Well, at least two of your three problems will be resolved soon. The deal and the land," David reiterated. "By the way, your eye looks much better. I guess that cocoa butter works."

I touched my face. The black-and-blue was gone, but it was still tender. "Yeah, I still can't believe dude punched me like that. One of these days, me and Malcolm Britton are gonna have a rematch."

"Man, let that shit go. You're already kicking their asses by over-bidding for the land. Against my advice, I might add." David had made it clear multiple times that he was not in favor of us buying the Simpson property.

"She wants a pool, Dave. You know how me and Sydney are. I'm not the kind of guy who disappoints his wife," I said.

"You're full of shit. This isn't about a pool, or else you would have bought that property on Waterside and saved yourself millions. This is about beating the Brittons." He stared at me, and I had to relent.

"Okay, yeah, it's a little bit personal, but in the long run, it's about making Sydney happy. If they really wanted the property, they could have bid higher."

"But they didn't, which is what concerns me." David gave me a stern look. "Besides, a relationship with a bank like Amistad could be very useful, my friend. There's a lot of moving parts to this Singh deal, and a line of credit with Amistad would have been nice."

"There are other banks, David, and you know how I feel about loans."

"All right, if that's what you want, you're the boss," he said, giving me a pound. "You know me. I'm team Johnson. Whatever you need."

"Good to know, 'cause I need your advice about this property, as a long-time resident and my financial guy."

"What's up?"

"Why haven't the Simpsons accepted our offer? It's been damn near a week."

David looked off into the horizon, then sighed. "Could be the Brittons raised their bid. Carolyn doesn't like to lose, and neither do the boys."

"No, I thought about that, but Jeffrey told Sydney last night that we were still the highest bidders, and he was waiting to hear from Everett Simpson, who's out of town."

David frowned and opened his mouth to say something, then stopped.

"What?" I asked.

"Everett's not out of town. I saw him yelling at the gardener yesterday. He never misses the fireworks show. Guy's like a big kid."

"Then why's he holding out?"

"Look, I've known Everett a long time, and he's not holding out, Anthony. Dude lives a high-profile life and is way too bougie to turn down money, especially millions of dollars of it," David explained.

"So, what's going on then?"

"If I had to guess, I'd say Jeffrey's playing you. From what I'm hearing from my wife, Carolyn's got him and his wife under crazy pressure. They're probably hoping y'all will just go away or come to your senses on the Waterside property," he said.

I shook my head. "Don't Jeffrey and his wife have commissions riding on this thing too? They're making money. It's gotta be something else."

David shrugged. "Says the man who's overpaying for the property. Don't you get it? It's personal for them too. Carolyn is Leslie's family. But if you think I'm wrong, then why don't you ask Everett yourself? Let him tell you."

"I would, but I don't know that guy from the man on the moon. What am I supposed to do? Just call him up and ask him what the hell he's doing?"

David laughed. "No, that is not the way to approach Everett Simpson. He's a pompous ass. You've got to approach him a certain way. Dangle something that's appealing to him."

"I can't approach him any kind of way. Like I said, I don't know him," I explained again.

"Yeah, but I do." David clapped his hand on my shoulder. "Anthony, I got you. We just have to come up with a course of action to get him in front of you."

"You say that like it's simple." I reached for another beer.

"It's damn sure not as hard as you think. As a matter of fact, I know exactly what to do." David turned to me with his game face on. "Everett is keen on three things in particular: good food, exquisite wine, and premium Cubans. From what I can tell, you got all three of those covered."

"I mean, I got a decent wine cellar and a nice cigar collection, but I ain't no chef," I told him. "I guess I can hire one."

"You ain't gotta do all that. I said good food. You might not be a chef, but can't nobody touch them damn ribs you be making."

David's compliment was accurate, if I do say so myself. I was a grill master, for sure.

"I need for you to start prepping because Fourth of July, you're having a nice little barbecue. Everett will be there. Cool?"

I shrugged. "Cool. I still don't know how you're gonna get him to come to the house."

"Leave that up to me." David started the ignition. As the engine roared to life, he turned around and yelled, "Oh, and you need to have beef *and* pork ribs. And make sure your wife makes some of that corn, too."

I braced myself as we took off over the water. David seemed more than confident that he could get Everett to the house so I could talk to him. Sydney wasn't going to be too thrilled about hosting a get together in less than twenty-four hours, but once she found out who the guest of honor would be, I was sure she'd be more than willing to roll out the welcome mat.

Malcolm Britton

37

It was damn near two in the morning when I left Vanessa's house after making my monthly "alimony payment." She'd wanted me to spend the night, but I needed to get some real rest because Morgan would be arriving this afternoon on the Hampton Jitney for the Fourth of July festivities, and I needed my strength.

As I drove home, I thought I was seeing things when a woman suddenly appeared in the middle of the road. I slammed my brakes, stopping just in time. She turned to face me, looking very much like a deer in headlights. We stared at one another for a moment, until finally she continued to the opposite side of the street.

I took a few seconds for my racing heart to settle before letting my window down and yelling to her, "Hey, you okay?"

She glanced back briefly and gave me an evil eye, then resumed strutting down the street as if it weren't the middle of the night. I turned the car around and slowly pulled beside her.

"Miss, I wanna make sure you're okay," I told her.

She stopped and looked at me. "I'm fine. You can go."

The voice and Brooklyn accent was more familiar than the face that I now recognized. It was Martin's friend, the girl he'd brought to breakfast and the one he'd been moping over for the past few weeks. Why she was walking through the streets at night, I had no idea. Her dress was short and tight, and she carried a pair of heels in her hand, along with a small purse and a sketch pad, of all things. It looked as if she'd just left a party or a club, and I wondered if she was drunk.

"You're Martin's friend," I said.

"Was," she corrected me.

The chuckle escaped before I could stop it, which turned out to be a good thing, because the anger in her face faded.

I introduced myself. "I'm his brother, Malcolm."

"I recognize you," she said, still walking along the side of the road. I crept slowly along beside her.

"You're Karrin, right? Martin can't stop talking about you."

It was true. Instead of being focused on figuring out how to get that damn property from Everett, Martin spent more time bitching about Karrin blocking his calls and texts. The man known for his rotation of women during the summer now seemingly had none, and the only one he wanted was nowhere to be found—until now. I took it as a sign from the universe, and being the supportive older brother that I was, I decided to act on it.

"Well, Karrin, I can give you a ride if you'd like," I told her. "It's not safe for you to be out here alone. You could get hit by a car."

Karrin smirked. "Thanks, but I'm not that far from my destination. I'm good."

She was not going to make this easy, but I had to at least make a case for my brother. I needed him focused again, and this woman seemed to be the key to that.

"Listen, Karrin, my brother has been sulking like he lost his favorite pair of sneakers. Real talk, I think you should consider giving him another chance. What happened at breakfast really wasn't his fault. You know that's not on him, right?" I asked. "Our mother can be difficult."

She finally stopped walking and took a step closer to the car. "I know, and he apologized for it, but I don't do drama. I am here to relax this summer, not go back and forth with anyone, including your mother, who Martin lives with."

"If that's what you're worried about, it's an easy fix. You don't have to come to the house or see her."

"Oh, really? Did he move out?" She folded her arms.

She was definitely Martin's type: cute, curvy, and sexy as hell, but this girl was funny and had a little spunk to her. I could see why she stood out from the others. There was a spicy sassiness to her that the typical women Martin dated in the Black Hamptons didn't have. His obsession was starting to make sense.

"No, he didn't move," I said, "but we have other accommodations. Have you been to the yacht?"

"We were supposed to go but never got the chance."

"Well, how about you have a chance now? Martin and I host a phenomenal get together on the yacht for the Fourth of July. You can be a guest and enjoy all the festivities with us."

"Did your brother put you up to this?" she asked.

"How could he? Hell, I didn't know I would almost run you over in the road in the middle of the night. Did you?"

Karrin laughed. "No. I guess that's a good point."

"So, is that a yes for the Fourth?"

She exhaled. "I guess."

"Great. We start at ten in the morning, and the attire is all white." I gave her all the details. "And be sure to wear a swimsuit and pack a bag."

"Okay." Her face brightened up a little.

"And I won't mention it to Martin. It'll be our surprise." I winked. "You sure you don't need a ride?"

"I'm positive," she said. "But I'll be there for the Fourth for sure. Thanks, Malcolm."

"See you then," I said, waving as I drove off.

I'd done my brother a solid, and in five hours, Morgan would be in my arms. It looked like the Britton boys were in for one hell of a Fourth of July.

David Michaels

38

Admittedly, me craving some of Anthony's ribs was one reason why I'd suggested he host a cookout on the Fourth of July. I was also hoping he would open a few of those expensive bottles of wine. However, just as I suspected, the mention of the ribs and wine had been quite useful in luring Everett Simpson to Anthony's house.

"What do you want, David?" Everett asked when I showed up at his house. He had answered the door wearing a smoking jacket, which was pretentious but not surprising. This guy was so uptight and bougie he would make Carlton Banks look like a hood rat.

"Hey, Everett. I'm looking for Pikachu. Have you seen him by chance?"

He turned his nose up and frowned. "Who the hell is Pikachu? I don't even know what that is."

"A white Maltese, tiny little thing. Symone left the door open, and he got out. Thought he might've run over here." I described my wife's dog that was, at that moment, secure in my house.

"I didn't even know you all had a dog. Sorry, I haven't seen it." Everett was about to close the door, but my foot was just over the threshold. He looked down at my foot then up at my face with an expression that said, "Why are you still here?"

"Man, I gotta find this dog, otherwise my wife's gonna lose it. And I don't wanna miss watching the fireworks at Anthony Johnson's house tonight. He thinks he's slick. Called and said he put some ribs on the grill, but I know he's just try'na show off the two bottles of Dominus Estate 2018 he copped last week, lucky bastard." In truth, Anthony had been holding the wine in his cellar for a year.

"You know someone who has *two* bottles of Dom Estate 2018?" Everett took the bait like a fish who'd been starving.

"Yeah, but that's nothing. Anthony's wine cellar is probably the most impressive one in the community aside from the Brittons." I continued luring him on the hook I'd dangled.

Everett scoffed. "Now, I doubt that, David. You've seen my cellar and my collection. The Brittons only have me beat because I lost some stock after Hurricane Sandy."

"I have, but I've also seen his. Look, I gotta go find this dog so I can get to the BBQ. I'll see you later, Everett." I turned to leave.

"David." He stopped me before I had taken two steps.

"Yeah?"

"Tell your friend Anthony I'd love to check out his wine cellar sometime."

I walked back toward him. "Why don't you come over tonight with me and hang out? You were planning on watching the fireworks show, weren't you? I hear it's going to be off the chain."

"Of course. I haven't missed them since I was a kid."

"Then come on through. I'll let Anthony know I invited you."

Everett perked up. "Well, if you don't think he'd mind. I mean, I was planning on making Grandma's cobbler. I can bring that. And I do enjoy some good ribs."

"Then I'll see you there about eight. He lives to the left of Carolyn, right on the beach. The old Peterson place," I told him.

Jesse Britton

39

There was always an early morning start time for the celebration of Fourth of July. At seven a.m., Kenny and I began setting up the preparations for the small gathering of about twenty people that we'd planned. I had convinced my mom to allow us to use her yacht since she wasn't going to be using it, and she hired a Jamaican captain named Manny to take us around. We watched as deliveries of beer, cases of liquor, grocery bags full of snacks, and trays stocked high with sandwiches were carried on board. As for the other essentials—ice for the drinks and plenty of condoms—Kenny and I had made sure to bring those.

"Man, this was the best idea you had yet," Kenny said as we surveyed the inventory. "Partying on the water all day with our own captain, and we'll have the best view of the fireworks tonight, too."

"Exactly. And more importantly, no fucking cops to tell us to turn down the music and interrupt our fun."

"Facts." Kenny nodded. "This time, I definitely kept my guest list to a minimum. I love my frat brothers, but I gotta make sure the ratio of hotties to bruhs is two to one this time."

I laughed. "We're on the same page with that, man." Unlike the pool party, I'd been way more selective about my invitees. Not only was the space more limited, but I didn't want to risk having any underage drinkers like last time. Everyone at this event had been carefully vetted, especially the females.

By noon, we'd showered, dressed, and were greeting guests who started arriving before the noted sail time of twelve thirty. As I looked around at the group, I felt confident about the good time we were going to have. My anticipation became even more heightened as another group of ladies arrived, all AKAs. I was pleasantly surprised by one in particular.

"Wow, I didn't think you were coming." I grinned as I helped Tania step on board along with her sorority sisters. I hadn't seen her since the morning that cop caught us in bed. I'd texted a few times to make sure she was okay, but that was about it. I figured we'd bump into each other sooner or later with her and dude broken up.

"I didn't either," she admitted. While the other members of her group went over to get the party started, she stayed back to talk to me. "It was a last-minute decision."

"It was a good one." I was unable to ignore how amazing she looked in the bikini top and extremely short denim cutoffs that showed off the body I'd enjoyed days ago. "How've you been?"

"I'm fine. Everything's cool." She gave a nonchalant shrug.

"I'm glad. I didn't know how you'd be handling your breakup."

She gave me a strange look. "What breakup?"

"With ol' boy, the boxer dude."

"Peter," she said. "And we haven't broken up. I mean, shit's a little tense right now, but nah, we're good. At least for now."

I was shocked. "Wait. So, y'all are still together after you . . . I mean, we—"

"Got caught?" She finished what I was trying to ask. "Yep. He didn't mention it to me, and I damn sure wasn't gonna tell on myself."

I leaned back against the rail and folded my arms. "What about his dad? He didn't say anything?"

"Evidently not. I mean, I've purposely been avoiding Sargent Lane, and I think he's been doing the same. Like I said, Peter hasn't said anything at all about it."

"That's weird," I said, scratching my head. "Isn't it? Or am I tripping? 'Cause my pops would have told me in a New York minute."

"Look, I don't want to think or talk about Peter or his father." She looked me in the eye. "I just wanna hang out with my friends, get my drink on, and have a good time. That's it."

I smiled and pulled her into my arms. "I like the sound of that."

"Yo, Jesse!" Kenny yelled. "It's twelve thirty, my guy!"

I gave Tania a quick kiss before yelling over my shoulder, "Then let's go! Tell Manny all aboard! And turn the fucking music up!"

Manny took us out past Gardiner's Island to Montauk to see the lighthouse, and we were having a blast. I didn't know what Tania, Peter, or his daddy had going on, but based on the way she and I were on each other during the party, I could tell she meant what she'd said. She was not thinking about them. She remained wherever I was, whether it was sitting in my lap while we talked to our friends, feeding me chips off her plate, or backing that ass up on me while we danced. It was obvious that not only was she into me, but, I had to admit, I was feeling the same way.

However, the fact that she made sure we weren't caught together in any photos or videos didn't go unnoticed. The girl was as smart as she was sneaky, but somehow that made her even sexier.

Manny got us back to the bay and anchored at the perfect time so everyone could *ooh* and *aah* while we watched Uncle Martin and his friends do a crazy light show with Jet Skis and hoverboards as fireworks went off above their heads. I'd never seen anything like it, and I promised myself that next year I would be a part of it.

"Look, y'all, that's my uncle," I yelled as Uncle Martin did a crazy trick on the hoverboard while he held Roman candles. I was puffed up with pride and feeling pretty damn blessed, a mood that was even more pronounced with Tania by my side. We kissed under the fireworks like something out of a romance novel.

"Let's go to the bedroom," I whispered into her ear.

"What?" Tania pulled back a little. "I don't think so."

"Why not?" My fingers ran along the waistband of her shorts before I slipped my hand into the back and cupped her ass.

"Because you know what happened the last time we were in there. I'm not taking any chances."

I looked out over the large body of water where we were anchored. "Uh, you do realize we're surrounded by water, right? I promise no one is going to pop up unannounced."

"What about the rest of the fireworks show?"

"We can still see them from the window in the room."

She gave me a doubtful look.

"Okay, we can hear them," I admitted. "But don't you wanna make some fireworks of our own?"

Tania removed my hand from her ass put a little breathing room between us. She rested her forearms on my shoulders. "Jesse, I don't know—"

The kiss that stopped her was full of so much passion that it left her breathless, and she had nothing else to say as I led her away from our partying friends and down to the bedroom. I locked the door and quickly removed her swimsuit top, putting my mouth on the nipples that had been poking at me all day.

Tania moaned as she grabbed at the string that held my swimming trunks firmly around my waist. I was rock hard before they hit the floor.

"Jesse," she whispered as I unbuttoned her shorts and slipped them off, then removed her bathing suit bottom.

"Yeah?" I answered, hoping her answer would be related to the blowjob that I was more than ready for.

"You know I gotta go home, right? I can't stay all night. He's going to be waiting."

I touched the side of her face. "Come on, Tania. It's the Fourth. No one has a curfew."

"I know, but . . ."

"I promise to get you home early in the morning. How about that?" I placed her hand on my hardness so she could feel that I needed as much time with her as possible.

"Early, Jesse," she said as she wrapped her fingers around me. "Six o'clock. I'm serious."

"That works." I sat on the edge of the bed, and she leaned in to kiss me. I closed my eyes and enjoyed the sound of the fireworks show, courtesy of Amistad Bank, while Tania took my tongue into her mouth. It was the best Fourth of July ever.

Anthony Johnson

40

I was working the grill when David and his daughter Symone stepped out onto the back patio. Our entire home had been revamped with Sydney Tech security features, and I'd just let them in via the app on my phone. Watching them walk across the patio was a visual reminder of why we needed to purchase more property. Our yard was nice, but smaller than most of the others in the neighborhood. The patio and grilling area took up most of the space. Although I could never complain about the perfect water view, the additional land would allow us a pool and more, to make it an ultimate space for entertaining guests.

"Hi, Mrs. Johnson." Symone waved at Sydney, who was setting the table.

"Hey, y'all." Sydney greeted them with a hug.

"Lisa couldn't make it, but she sends her apologies and her deviled eggs," David said, handing her a covered tray he'd brought with him.

"Your wife is so thoughtful. And no need to apologize. This shindig is last minute anyway."

Sydney was too polite to say it, but we had already assumed Lisa wasn't coming. She never came to functions. Hell, sometimes I wasn't even sure she existed, and I'd worked with David for the past five years.

"Gabbie and Tyler are in the game room, Symone. Why don't you go upstairs and get them? We're just waiting on a few more guests, and then we can eat. I'll put these on the table."

Symone didn't hesitate to go back into the house. David made his way over to me.

"That is one big-ass, professional-looking grill, Anthony. And it smells like you know what you're doing on it." David gave me a pound.

"I bet you smelled them as soon as you hit the front door, didn't you?" I said proudly. I had been perfecting my recipe for twenty years, and I knew my ribs were untouchable. I was looking forward to eating more than my fair share.

"I sure did."

"Take a look." I opened the hood of the grill and displayed a smorgasbord of ribs, chicken, sausage, and shrimp kabobs. Then I opened a little side compartment and waved my hand so he could get a whiff of the brisket. "Bro, I been smoking this brisket since last night."

"Damn, that's what I'm talking about." He laughed. "You went all out, bro."

"A little. You sure this dude Everett is coming?" I asked uneasily. "I hope I didn't do all this cooking for nothing."

"Relax. He'll be here. Oh, and heads up, once he's here, you're gonna have to open one of those bottles of 2018 if you want to impress him."

"I was saving those for me and Syd's anniversary next year, but fuck it." I exhaled. "Whatever I gotta do to close this deal, I'll do."

"Like I said, Everett's a money guy. I have full confidence that after tonight, that lot is yours. And just in case, I brought these." He handed me a box of cigars.

"My man fifty grand!" Once again, David was proving that he really was team Johnson.

"Dad, Mr. Simpson is here," my daughter Gabbie announced as she entered the backyard.

Everett was standing beside her, wearing an expensive silk shirt and pressed white slacks that were definitely not what I'd consider casual enough for a backyard barbecue.

"Let's do this," David said quietly to me as we walked over to greet Everett.

"Everett Simpson, this is Anthony Johnson." David introduced me, and the two of us shook hands.

"Anthony, nice to meet you," Everett said in a voice that was about as casual as his attire. This dude was definitely all about being "high society."

"I hear you have a very impressive wine cellar," he said.

I laughed. "I'm new at this, but I'd like to think so. I was just going down to pick out a bottle for dinner. Why don't you join me?"

Everett smiled. "Lead the way."

The three of us ventured down into my wine cellar. Everett didn't say much, but based on the way he studied the labels, I could see that he was impressed by what he saw.

I pulled out one of the bottles of Dom Estate 2018. "This is one of my prized possessions right here."

Everett nodded appreciatively. "As it should be. I've been trying to get my hands on one of these for quite some time myself. May I?"

"Sure." I handed him the bottle, and the way he stared at it, you would have thought he was in love.

"Magnificent," he murmured, cradling the bottle like a newborn child.

"That would be the perfect bottle to use for a toast in celebration of buying that property from Everett," David hinted.

"Yeah, that's what I was hoping." I caught the pass that David had tossed me and slammed it home. "What's going on with that, Everett? I felt the offer we made was more than fair."

Everett handed the bottle back to me. "What offer is that? I haven't heard from Jeffrey in over a week. The last bid I heard was six million from Carolyn Britton."

"My wife and I put in a bid for eight million cash last Friday. Jeffrey told my wife he was waiting to hear back from you." My demeanor was no longer backyard-barbecue cool. I felt a burst of adrenalin that I always got when I was ready to do business.

"Shit. Eight million dollars?" Everett looked stunned. "Are you serious?"

"Yes, sir. Very serious. We can close in a week. How's that sound?"

"That sounds delightful." A wide grin spread across Everett's face. "And here I was thinking Carolyn Britton was stalling on my counteroffer, yet here you are, ready and willing to do business."

"Business is what I do," I said.

Everett extended his hand to me. "Well then, Mr. Johnson, I accept your offer. Why don't you bring that fine bottle of wine upstairs so we can celebrate?"

"Yes, why don't we?"

I glanced at David and mouthed a silent "Thank you." He winked at me as we made our way upstairs and outside. Damn, this felt good.

An hour later, we'd demolished Sydney's corn, Lisa's deviled eggs, and almost all the meat that I'd prepared. From the way Everett licked his fingers, it was clear that he'd enjoyed every bite. Plus, he drank damn near the whole bottle of Dom Estate by himself.

"Well, Everett, while Sydney gets dessert ready, how about we enjoy a smoke?" I took out one of the cigars David had given me.

"Are those Opus Forbiddens?" Everett actually gasped. "They only make those every five years."

"Best damn smoke you'll ever have," David bragged. "Perfect for the occasion."

"You boys enjoy yourself while I heat up the cobbler." Sydney stood up from the table. "You kids come on and help me. Let these gentlemen talk."

We carried our drinks over to the fire pit near the edge of the property, where we cut the cigars and settled into the chairs around the fire, smoking in silence for a while.

After a while, David said, "Gentlemen, it doesn't get better than this, does it? World-class cigars while we sit on our Black-owned beach, looking at this world-class view."

"I'll drink to that," Everett said, raising his glass.

We toasted to our good fortune, then settled back into a comfortable, satisfied silence again.

When his drink was finished, Everett put down his glass and said, "Please excuse me. I have to go make a quick call. Maybe we could visit that wine cellar again when I come back."

"We sure can," I told him.

"Good looking out," I said to David as soon as we were alone. "I owe you, man."

"It's all good. I told you I had you." Then he frowned. "Man, I knew Jeffrey's ass was up to something."

"And you were right."

"I hope you know what you're doing, though, because that's a lot of money for some land, and Carolyn Britton is gonna be pissed."

It was gratifying to imagine how the news would hit her. The woman rarely, if ever, lost. I was happy that Sydney and I would be the ones to conquer the mogul.

"Fuck her and her sons. I'm not concerned about any of them," I said, even though I was a little worried about the neighborhood repercussions. She might have been a cold bitch, but Carolyn Britton obviously still held power over plenty of the residents in our neighborhood. Syd and I might have to do some work to counteract any bad feelings she stirred up against us.

"My wife is gonna get her pool, and that's all I really care about: making my wife happy."

"I bet," David said, then leaning in, he changed the subject. "Um, I gotta tell you, I'd been hoping your fine-ass sister-in-law would be here tonight. I know you said I couldn't touch, but I damn sure wanted to look at her."

I shook my head. "I don't know where she is, but, bro, I didn't make that rule for her benefit. I made it for yours. That girl's a piece of work, and trust me, she's not a road you want to go down."

"Damn. It's like that?"

"Worse."

Everett returned. "Well, gentlemen, I'm gonna take my leave."

"You sure you won't have dessert? What about the wine cellar?"

"No, no, regretfully I won't be able to see your collection again tonight, but I must say thank you for sharing the Dom Estate 2018. It was magnificent—along with the cigar. I'm glad we had a chance to meet face to face."

"Me too," I told him. He was arrogant, for sure, and maybe not someone I'd want to hang out with on a regular basis, but if Carolyn did decide to create social problems for us, then I wanted to start racking up points in my favor now. "You sure you won't stay for the fireworks?"

"No, I have an event I frequent every year on the Fourth. I wouldn't want to miss it. However, I will be talking to Jeffrey."

"Glad to hear that. I'll be looking out for Jeffrey's call," I said.

Suddenly, Everett started laughing. It was the most relaxed I'd heard him sound all night.

"What's so funny?" David asked.

Everett discreetly gestured to the side of our yard that shared a property line with the Brittons. "Do you see that old battleax Carolyn Britton over there on her balcony, pretending not to see us? She must be shitting pickles knowing that I'm over here with you."

Karrin Wilks

41

"Hey, beautiful, where are you going?" Martin mumbled, gently tightening his arm around my waist. My attempt to quietly slip out of bed without waking him had failed, but that didn't change the fact that I had to pee.

"To the bathroom and to find some coffee. I'll be back," I replied.

"Okay. There's a Keurig on the top deck. Bring me a cup too, please." He kissed me then turned over and buried his head in the pillow.

Waking up on a yacht with Martin felt like a dream. After watching him perform in one of the most spectacular fireworks shows I'd ever seen in my life from the deck of his family's yacht, Martin had taken me back to his stateroom and we'd made love all night. I'd been with my share of guys, but he was the most attentive lover I'd ever had. Usually, you could find a guy who could sling it and another who could eat it, and if you were lucky, a guy who might be just okay in bed but made you feel special outside the bedroom. Being with Martin was the first time I'd experienced all three in one person. I wanted this to last forever. I just needed to play my cards right.

I hit the bathroom, then grabbed one of Martin's T-shirts from a drawer. I slipped it on and eased out of the room, venturing up the stairs to find me some coffee. The view from the deck was breathtaking—the bright blue sky, the harbor sparkling in the morning sun, and to my surprise, the glorious smell of weed.

Forgetting about the coffee, I followed the scent to the front of the boat, where I found a tall, athletic-looking guy with deep-set brown eyes and gorgeous, wavy hair. He had that Michael B. Jordan kind of sex appeal. Had I not already found Martin, I definitely would've given him a full court press.

"Oh, shit! You shouldn't sneak up on people like that. I didn't know anyone else would be up this early." He smiled at me with perfect teeth, making no attempt to hide the joint in his hand.

"Good morning. I'm sorry," I replied. "I didn't mean to interrupt. It's so pretty out here."

"It is beautiful and it's peaceful. The perfect setting to wake and bake." He offered me the joint. "Do you partake?"

"Thank you. You just made my day. I ran out yesterday." I took the joint.

"I can hook you up later if you need some," he said as he watched me take a hit. "Yeah, that was one hell of a show and party last night, wasn't it?"

"I've never seen anything like it," I said between pulls. "Rich people know how to party."

"Don't they?" he said as if he weren't one of them. The guy's Louis Vuitton slides had to have cost at least $800, and his shades probably set him back at least a grand. Plus, he wore a white Givenchy T-shirt and shorts that let me know that his style was top tier, and so was his bank account—unless he was like me and just knew how to make up good stories to get "loans" from rich family or friends.

"Where you from?" he asked.

"Brooklyn. Bed Stuy." I reached out to hand back the weed, but he gestured for me to take another pull. "How about you?" I was guessing somewhere Upper East Side or perhaps Westchester.

"Iowa, originally, but I live in Harlem now."

I almost choked on the smoke in my lungs. "Iowa? How the fuck does a Black man come from Iowa?" *Especially a fine-ass Black man.*

He shrugged, laughing along with me. "I know, right? That's why I ran away to New York first chance I got. Fuck Iowa."

I liked him. He was funny, and more importantly, he was down to earth.

"Iowa was bad?" I asked.

"The worst. And I had three strikes against me to start." He raised his hand and started counting on his fingers. "Number one, I'm Black. Number two, I can fight and would never back down, and number three, I'm gay."

Oops. I guess I'd really misjudged. I definitely wouldn't have guessed that this guy was gay.

"Anyway," he said, "I don't wanna talk about Iowa. I wanna talk about those moves you was putting on Martin last night. From what I could see, you had as much fun as I did. I saw you."

"You did? I guess I was kind of in my own little world last night." My whole focus had been on Martin.

"Hell yeah. Everybody did. You were dancing your ass off. And, girl, that swimsuit you had on sure made it hard for anyone to take their eyes off your ass. You looked good as fuck in that damn outfit, and the Versace shades were the perfect touch."

He finally reached out and took the joint back from me. "Martin was smart not to let you out of his sight."

I tried not to blush, both flattered and charmed by his words.

"I did have a good time." I sighed. "I hate that the weekend is coming to an end and I gotta leave this yacht."

"I wouldn't be too worried about that. From what I saw yesterday, you'll be back here a lot."

"You think so?" I asked. From what I could tell, Martin really was feeling me, but having it confirmed by someone else did boost my confidence.

"Listen, I've been around the Britton boys a long time, and—"

"There you are. I thought you were coming back to bed."

I turned around at the sound of Martin's voice.

"I was," I answered. "I came out to look at the water and find the coffee, then we started talking."

Martin put his arm around me possessively. "Oh, okay. I see you met my brother's friend Morgan."

"Yes, I'm sorry. I didn't mean to keep her from you. We were just having a nice little chat, that's all," Morgan said. He put out the joint and got up to leave. "I guess I'll go and check on Malcom."

"Nice chatting with you," I said.

"Same here. I'm sure I'll see you around."

The way Martin rolled his eyes made it clear he didn't really like this guy. I wondered if he thought Morgan was trying to hit on me, so I decided to put him at ease.

"He's really nice. And he's gay."

"I know. That's why I can't stand that motherfucker."

"Martin!" I shouted with disdain. "Are you homophobic? 'Cause I'm not with that gay-bashing shit."

"No! Hell no. I don't give a shit if someone is gay. I hate Morgan because he's the one that makes my brother act a damn fool, and I don't like that," Martin muttered.

"Act a fool how?" I was starting to see a picture, but I wanted him to make it clear.

"Morgan is my brother's lover," he said as if he hated to even utter the words. "He's been playing Malcolm for years."

It took a moment for me to process. "Wait, Malcom is gay?"

"No, I think the term he uses is *fluid*."

Jeffrey Bowen

42

I was going through emails in my home office when the doorbell rang. It was only nine in the morning, and I wasn't expecting anyone. Assuming it was the grocery delivery order that Leslie had placed, I decided that she could drag herself out of bed and get the door. Had she not still been hell bent on freezing me out of the bedroom, I may have been inclined to be a little more gracious, but she was still locking the bedroom door, so I remained at my desk. A few moments later, the bell rang again.

"Damn it, woman. Come answer the door," I mumbled to myself.

When the bell rang a third time, I felt like I had no choice but to answer the damn thing myself. I was surprised to see Everett Simpson on my doorstep, looking far from friendly.

"Uh, Everett, good morning. I wasn't expecting you. Did we have an appointment?"

"No, we didn't," he sneered. "And as much as I dislike doing pop-up visits, I don't have a choice. And neither do you."

Judging from his attitude, I had to assume that word had traveled back to him about the latest bid I'd withheld.

"Well, come in so we can talk." I stepped back and held the door open wide. As he followed me back to my office, my mind raced, looking for the best way to explain why I hadn't updated him with the latest offers. It was proving to be quite a balancing act, keeping this client happy while also trying to make sure my marriage didn't implode.

He sat down in a chair across from my desk.

"Can I get you a coffee?" I asked.

In response, he picked up the decanter that he knew was filled with expensive brandy and poured himself a drink. "Do I need a new attorney?" he asked.

As much as Everett was a pain in the ass, he wasn't a dumb man. I wasn't going to insult him by pretending I didn't know why he was upset. It would be pointless.

"Listen, Everett. I've been meaning—"

"Eight million fucking dollars!" He threw his hands in the air. "Eight million dollars."

"I know—"

"Bitch, I know *you* know. The problem is I didn't know because you didn't tell me."

"I was going—"

"*Was*? What the fuck do you mean, *was*? Anthony Johnson made that bid over a week ago. You had the ethical duty to let me know within forty-eight hours." Everett began pacing in front of my desk. "I knew something was up when I didn't hear from you after Carolyn's last bid. That shark would've had your ass drawing up the paperwork within the fucking hour and then made you tell the Johnsons to kiss her ass."

"Look, Everett, this situation has gotten complicated. There's no way Anthony Johnson and his wife should even be bidding that much for that land just to put a pool in. I'm giving him time to think this through. We've put him in one hell of a situation, not to mention what this whole thing has done to my marriage," I admitted, hoping my woes might help him understand why I'd done it.

Everett scoffed. "They can afford it. And as for your wife, she's not stupid. Leslie is not going to let you run free in the open market. Hell, I might try and turn you out myself."

"You're not exactly my cup of tea."

"You never know until you try." He smirked. "Now, either you're going to get Carolyn to bid higher, or you're going to draw up paperwork for Anthony Johnson to sign."

As if the two of them could sense that they were being discussed, Leslie appeared in the doorway of my office with Carolyn by her side. I was as surprised as Everett to see them and gave Leslie an accusatory glance. My wife had blindsided me and most likely alerted her aunt to Everett's arrival at our house.

"We're in a meeting," I seethed, cutting my eyes at both women.

"Yes, Jeffrey, I can see that," Leslie said in the fake polite voice that she used whenever she was trying not to curse out a customer service rep on the phone. "Aunt Carolyn happened to stop by, and she wanted to say hello to Everett."

Carolyn strode into the room and took the seat next to Everett.

"Well, isn't that neighborly of you, Carolyn." Everett's smile was as fake as Leslie's voice. "Are you planning on wintering in Palm Beach?"

"Cut the crap, Everett." Carolyn glared at him. "Why are you even doing all of this? You know you were supposed to sell that property back to me."

Everett placed his hand on his chest as if to clutch an invisible set of pearls. "Is that so?"

I looked at Carolyn. "Back? What do you mean?"

"When Moses and I were first married, his father was having some trouble with the bank. To help his father, Moses sold the land to Everett's grandfather with the stipulation that if it was ever to be sold, ownership would be offered to the Britton family at fair market value," she explained.

It was my first time hearing this, and it made Carolyn's determination more understandable. I turned to Everett. "Is this true?"

"That *may* have been mentioned a time or two over the years, but it was never put in writing. My great grandfather and Old Man Britton were friends, and they helped each other out from time to time," Everett said, sounding unconcerned.

"You know damn well your father promised to sell that deed back to us right before he got sick. There was no reason to announce the sale at that damn HOA meeting in the first place," Carolyn snapped at him. "I would have given you fair market value."

Everett remained calm. His demeanor was a complete contrast from Carolyn's fury, and he looked like he enjoyed inciting her.

"That was only five million dollars. Now I'm getting eight. Unless you'd like to bid higher, of course. I haven't signed the deed yet."

Carolyn slammed her hand on my desk. "You're going to pay for this, you manipulative son of a bitch!"

"Pot, meet kettle. How's it feel to be on the losing end for once, Carolyn?" Everett turned to me. "Jeffrey, I'll expect that purchase agreement between the Johnsons and me later today, or I will get a new lawyer to handle it and sue you for malpractice in the process." He stood and headed for the door.

"You're going to pay for this, Everett Simpson," Carolyn warned as she got up from her seat.

He paused and turned around with an amused look. "Au contraire, mon cher. I do believe Anthony Johnson is the one paying. Good day."

"We'll see about that." Carolyn turned her ire toward me and Leslie. "And the fallout is on both of you." She slammed my office door as she left.

Leslie and I were left standing in the office, both of us too shocked to speak. Everett Simpson had trumped Carolyn Britton, and Anthony Johnson was going to win. I looked over at Leslie, who wouldn't even glance in my direction. I prayed that Everett was right when he'd said that she wouldn't be stupid enough to set me free. Either way, I had a feeling that it was going to be a hell of a long time before we had sex again.

Sergeant Tom Lane

43

I'd been told it could get crazy, but I never thought you could pack so many people into such a small town. Main Street was ridiculously busy, full of weekend warriors, day trippers, and residents, all fighting for a limited amount of parking spaces. The holiday weekend had everyone excited, and judging by the number of shopping bags people were carrying, it was inspiring them to spend plenty of money. I was watching people stream by on the sidewalk as I finished my doughnut and coffee at a table outside Beach Brew.

"Morning, Tom." Chief Harrington greeted me as he came out of Beach Brew with a large coffee in his hand. "Getting your morning jolt, I see."

"To be honest, Chief, I'm addicted to the stuff. I drink about ten or eleven cups a day."

"Wow, that's ridiculous. I like a good cup of Joe myself, but I'm not quite that bad." Chief laughed as he took a seat at the small table. "You know, I've been meaning to tell you that son of yours is doing a great job working with the auxiliary unit. I'm impressed. Looks like he's got great potential to join the department in the future. Say the word, and I can have him at the Suffolk academy this fall."

"Nah, Chief. I appreciate the compliment, and I'm glad to hear he's doing a good job, but Peter's a boxer. Golden Gloves champion. He's headed to the Olympic trials in a few months."

"Wow, that's great!" Chief Harrington grinned and hit my arm. "You must be proud. That's some big-time stuff right there."

I was beaming with pride. "Yes, sir. It's a pretty good feeling. He's got talent and skills out of this world. As a matter of fact, Bobby Boyd tried to recruit him last month."

"So, Peter's the reason why that rich son of a bitch is hanging out." Chief Harrington snapped his fingers. "I thought it was to throw loud parties and cause disruption."

I laughed. "I'm sure he's doing that too. Had Peter and I at odds for a while."

"Really? How so? They try to lowball him?"

"No, they offered him quite a bit of an advance and the chance to train at their facility in Vegas. Everything would be taken care of. But the Olympics has been the goal since Peter started boxing. It's the one thing that's kept him out of trouble, and even when we moved out here, he's stuck with it. I don't want him to get distracted by the flashiness and fame. He's gotta stay focused on the prize, that gold medal."

"I can understand that, Lane. And I respect it."

It felt good to talk man to man with someone about Peter. It had been a rough couple of days, and having the vote of confidence from Chief Harrington reassured me that I'd made the right decision about a lot of things, including telling Peter he had to decline the offer from BBT.

"Ha ha ha! Jesse, stop it!" The sound of a familiar voice caught my attention.

I looked across the street to where a group of young adults was gathered outside the bakery. Tania was in the center of them, squirming to get away from Jesse Britton, who playfully grabbed at her. Memories of their naked bodies on that yacht came flooding back, and the anger I'd been suppressing since that day began rising. That shocking moment was one I had been unable to forget, no matter how much I wanted to.

"You all right, Sarge?" Chief Harrington asked. "'Cause that coffee cup can't fight back, and you've pretty much destroyed it."

I looked down at the paper cup, which I had gripped so tightly that it was crushed now. "I swear those two are going to push me to the point of no return."

Chief Harrington turned to look just as Jesse finally got a hold of Tania and started tickling her. "Jesse Britton? I know you and him had a little run in, and he can be a handful, but he's a decent kid. And the girl works at IGA. She's one of the sweetest young ladies I've ever met. I've known her parents since before the divorce."

The look I gave him was doubtful. "Oh, yeah? If she's so sweet, why has she been sneaking around behind my son's back with that Britton kid all summer? I caught them butt-ass naked on his mama's boat."

"Peter's dating Tania?" Chief looked surprised.

"Yes, sir, since the week we moved here."

"Damn. I see how this could be a problem. How'd Peter take the news when you told him? I'm sure he was heartbroken."

I stared at him without answering.

"You did tell him, didn't you?"

"No." I shook my head. "I didn't."

"Why not?"

I struggled to explain what I really didn't understand myself. "Mostly because I was afraid of how he'd react. Part of the reason I got him into boxing in the first place was for a healthy way to release aggression. But he really loves that girl, Chief. I'm afraid that if Peter found out about that Britton kid and Tania, he'd kill them both—or at least do some serious damage." I stopped myself for a second, realizing that it wouldn't be in my son's best interest for the chief of police to think he has a serious anger issue. I tried to tone it down a bit. "I mean, would you blame him? What guy wouldn't be pissed?"

Chief Harrington nodded. "Yeah, I remember being young and in love. Lots of feelings you don't know what to do with yet."

"And it makes it even worse that the other guy is a rich prick. Those damn Brittons." I sat back and stared at the chief. "It's like they can get away with anything they want around here."

"It seems like it at times," Chief Harrington said, apparently not recognizing the irony that his friendship with Carolyn Britton was a major reason it was true.

"I can't have those two ruin my son's future. He's worked too hard. I just gotta find a way to keep the truth about the two of them away from my son."

"Look, Lane, I can't tell you how to raise your son, but I will tell you this. Sag Harbor is a small town. He's bound to find out somehow, whether or not you want him to."

"So, what am I supposed to do then? Send him away?" I asked, frustrated.

Chief Harrington looked me dead in the eye. "If you're truly concerned about Peter and his reaction, then that's exactly what I'd do, because when it comes to the Brittons, neither me nor the department can help you."

Malcolm Britton

44

It had been a long but fun-packed three days, and by noon on the seventh, I'd bid farewell and escorted the last of my guests to shore, with the exception of one. To my relief, things had gone better than I expected. Not only was a good time had by all, but my son hadn't caused any trouble, and now that Karrin was in Martin's arms, he was acting like himself again.

Making my way across the deck, I smiled at one of the biggest reasons for my own good mood. Morgan was looking sexy as ever. His sleeveless T-shirt showed off those muscular arms I so admired, a result of his dedication to his two daily workouts. The shorts he wore gave me a great view of his equally toned thighs. I couldn't help but grin. Very sexy, indeed.

"That was one hell of a party. You should be proud," Morgan said. "I don't think I slept but like twelve hours the whole weekend."

"I have to admit, it's been one of the best Fourths ever. I appreciate you being here to enjoy all of it." I reached for his hand.

"I had a fantastic time. Thank you for inviting me."

I led him to the deck chairs, and we sat next to each other. "So, will I see you this weekend?"

Morgan hesitated. "About that . . . I've been waiting for the right time for us to talk. I guess now is as good a time as any."

"Talk about what?" I asked, dreading his answer. Last time he wanted to "talk," we broke up for four months.

"I can't see you next weekend, Malcolm." He stopped and looked into my eyes, taking a deep breath before he delivered the blow to my heart. "Truth of the matter is that I can't see you anymore."

"What the fuck? What do you mean, *anymore*?"

"I mean this. Us. Whatever you want to call it. I can't do it anymore. We're done."

For a moment, I thought he was joking—or at least I hoped he was—in spite of his somber voice and unsmiling face. It took a moment for me to respond as I came to grips with the fact that he was serious.

"Morgan, where is this coming from? Two seconds ago you were telling me what a great time you had," I said breathlessly. "Now you're saying that we're done?"

"I always have a great time with you. There's just no future in it." Morgan's hand slipped from mine, and he stood, pacing as he spoke. "I can't continue having these sporadic moments with you, and yet no commitment. Then I don't hear from you until the next time you decide it's *safe* to be with me. I deserve better, and I deserve more."

I walked over to him and put my hands on his shoulder to stop his pacing. "What do you want, Morgan? I provide you with everything: a spacious condo, an allowance. I make time for you when my schedule allows. I give you gifts—"

He laughed bitterly. "Gifts? You think that's what this is about? Don't kid yourself, 'cause I've got them lining up to give me gifts."

That little jab hit its intended target. He knew how jealous I could be, and the idea of other men after him was not a thought I wanted to entertain.

"You don't think I know that? My point is I love you, Morgan. I show it to you all the time. What more do you want?"

"I want consistency and commitment. I'm tired of being your little secret, Malcolm." Morgan folded his arms. "I want to sleep in the same bed with you every night and wake up beside you every morning."

"Isn't that what we've done all weekend?" I reached for him.

He snatched back before I could touch him. "One weekend is not enough. But it doesn't matter anymore because Everett has asked me to move in with him."

I stumbled slightly from the shock of this revelation. "Everett Simpson?"

"Yes, Everett Simpson."

My eyes closed in response to the anger rising inside me. There was no way this shit was happening. I didn't want to imagine Morgan with anyone else, and the fact that it was Everett made it worse. "What the fuck? You can't be serious."

"Oh, I am very serious," Morgan answered

"Everett Simpson is a self-centered, narcissistic son of a bitch who doesn't love anyone but himself. You do realize that, right? He doesn't love you."

"That's not what he says."

"He's lying. He's doing this to get at me. He's using you," I explained, desperate to change Morgan's mind.

Morgan peered at me. "Wow, and you say Everett is full of himself. Let me give you the facts, Malcolm. Everett has loved me since the day you stole me from him. He's never disrespected you, and only said he wanted me to be happy. Well, I'm not happy."

I felt as if I'd been punched in the stomach. "He can't take care of you like I can."

"That's not for you to say. And besides, he will be able to once he sells that property for eight million," Morgan said with a smirk.

Ugh, that fucking land again. It felt like my whole summer was going to be consumed with drama related to that property. Not only was Everett playing games with the price that had Mother on the warpath, but now he was using the land to steal Morgan from me.

"You can't move in with him, Morgan. You love me."

"You're right, I do. But I can't be with someone who can't fully be with me. As much as I love you, I'll never have that with you." He looked as if he wanted to cry.

I reached for his hand, and he let me hold it this time. "You will. I promise. If a commitment is what you want, then you'll have it."

Morgan shook his head. "We both know that can't happen. It's been ten years, and you've never even introduced me to your mother."

"That's what I'll do if that's what you want," I promised. "I can't lose you. I'll tell her everything and introduce you, and we can go from there. I promise. We can even get married if that's what you want."

"Malcolm . . ." Morgan's look was doubtful. "Don't make promises you can't keep."

I placed his hand over my heart, staring into his eyes as I spoke. "I won't. I swear."

A slow grin spread across Morgan's face, and he leaned in and kissed me.

Carolyn Britton

45

Out of all the rooms in our home, the library was my favorite. It was spacious, with warm wood accents, a Moroccan area rug that covered most of the floor, an extremely comfortable sofa, and a custom-designed mahogany desk in the center. The floor-to-ceiling bookshelves were more stocked than the local bookstore, filled with an array of African American literature and history, classic novels, books on business and gardening, and even a graphic novel collection owned by Martin. I considered it my sanctuary, the place where I did my best thinking.

While everyone else was resting and recuperating from the weekend festivities, I was hard at work, until I was interrupted by the ringing of my cell phone.

"Hello, Malcolm darling," I answered after seeing his name displayed on the screen.

"Hello, Mother. I'll be home in the morning and wanted to speak to you about something important," he said. "Do you think you can carve out some time after breakfast for me?"

"Yes, of course, son," I said. "This doesn't have anything to do with the Johnsons, does it? We need a solution to that problem, and since you had that little incident on the tennis court, I thought you might want to spearhead the effort."

"No, Mother, it has nothing to do with the Johnsons."

"Oh, Lord. What did Jesse do this time?" I sighed, preparing myself to hear about whatever mischief my grandson had gotten into.

"No, it's not Jesse. But it is important."

"Well, we can talk tomorrow. Enjoy your evening." I put my phone down, wondering out loud, "Now, what could that be about?"

"I think I may have an idea what it is."

I hadn't realized Kimberly was standing in the doorway until she spoke. I motioned for her to enter.

"What's that? Did something happen on the yacht between him and his brother?"

"No, not between him and Martin, but him and someone else." The look on Kimberly's face was odd. I'd never seen her look so uncomfortable. "Mrs. Britton, the reason Malcolm wants to talk to you is because he's getting married. He proposed today," she finally blurted out.

"Proposed? To who? Was he drunk?"

"No, he was very sober." She took a long, deep breath before she revealed the part that she knew would set me off. "He proposed to Morgan."

"Morgan!" I blinked, leaning back in my chair. "*Morgan* Morgan?"

Kimberly nodded.

"The man? *That* Morgan?" I couldn't believe those words were coming out of my mouth.

"Yes, ma'am." She nodded.

I'd been aware of Malcolm's admiration for men for quite some time. No, he hadn't told me, but a mother knows these kinds of things about her children. I'd actually expected him to come out of the closet in high school, but then I was pleasantly surprised when he met Vanessa and they started dating. I was even more delighted when he asked her to marry him and Jesse came along.

When their marriage started to break down, Vanessa told me about a man named Morgan, but I assumed she was just a scorned wife making up lies. Maybe that was wishful thinking on my part because deep down, I knew it was possible. But now, here was Kimberly, affirming the suspicions about my son that I thought had been put to rest long ago.

"Are you absolutely sure, Kimberly?"

"Yes. I heard it with my own ears."

"You were with them?" I asked.

"No, not really. I was on the upper deck, so they didn't know I was there. But I heard the whole thing. I just felt that you should know so that you wouldn't be blindsided by anything, ma'am," Kimberly said.

I stared past her, not focusing on anything in particular as I attempted to process what I'd just learned. The room was so quiet that I could hear the palpitations of my heart. According to what Vanessa had told me years ago, Morgan was some kind of hick from Iowa or Idaho or somewhere like that. He could have been born in the middle of a cornfield for all I knew. He was certainly not of the caliber of people that I expected my sons to pair with. He had no education past high school, no real career to speak of, and no family connections that could be of benefit to us. Their backgrounds couldn't have been more different, and I couldn't understand what Malcolm saw in him. As for Morgan, he probably felt like he'd hit the jackpot—a rich, successful man to take care of him.

The fact that he was a man was still a little uncomfortable for me. I was trying not to be homophobic because I knew times were changing, but I still wished my son preferred women. Aside from neighbors silently judging us, I worried that his choices could turn some potential clients away from our bank. Things were not as bad as they used to be, but there was no denying that plenty of people still had a problem with homosexuals.

I also worried about what a marriage to Morgan could do to my grandson. He was so heartbroken when his parents divorced. When his mom remarried not once, but twice, Jesse struggled to accept it. As far as he knew, his dad had never dated another person. I suspected that Jesse still hoped for his parents to get back together. There was no telling how he would feel if his father not only married someone else, but that someone was another man.

Suddenly, all of the confusion and frustration that was swirling around inside bubbled up and burst out of me. "Son of a bitch! What the fuck is wrong with my sons? I swear, the more I try to keep this family intact, the more they go out of their way to ruin it!" I picked up a book from my desk and threw it across the room. "Can't we just pay this Morgan person off?"

Kimberly shook her head. "No, your husband tried that years ago. He wouldn't take the money."

"Years ago? Moses knew about this?" I shouted.

"Yes. He asked me to keep an eye on things in case they got out of hand."

So, this dilemma would require a more creative solution. I needed to think this through, and raging about it would not be productive. I regained my composure. "Well, I appreciate you telling me this information. Thank you," I told her.

"You're welcome." Kimberly looked relieved to be getting out of there as she turned and rushed toward the door.

"Oh, Kimberly?" I called out. "I don't have to tell you to keep this between us, do I?"

"No, ma'am. That's already understood."

Jeffrey Bowen

46

An evening sail was just what I needed to calm my nerves. This situation with Carolyn was getting out of hand, and because of it, tension in the house was at an all-time high between Leslie and me. She'd been ignoring me so completely that I wondered if she would even notice my absence while I was out on the water. I'd checked my phone several times, but she hadn't called or sent a text.

As promised, I drew up the contract Everett had demanded from me, but I still hadn't gotten the Johnsons' signatures, using the holiday weekend as an excuse. I was beyond stressed and so on edge that I'd considered sabotaging the pending sale to Anthony Johnson. In the end, my conscience wouldn't let me. Not to mention the fact that I could lose my law license.

"Fuck!" I yelled in the darkness, frustrated that I couldn't even find comfort in my favorite pastime.

I forced myself to stay out for an hour, then headed back to the dock. Leslie still hadn't called. There was no point in going home, so I contemplated just spending the night where I was. After the holiday weekend, most of the crowds were gone, so I wouldn't be disturbed by people partying on nearby boats. First, I needed to get food and a few supplies, so I tied up to the dock and stepped off the boat to go to the convenience store on Main Street.

As I approached the end of the dock, I saw a quick movement out of the corner of my eye. Before I could turn to look, someone grabbed me from behind and threw a cloth over my head, cloaking me in total darkness.

"Stay quiet!" The voice was gruff.

I felt something cold and hard pressed against my lower back that filled me with fear and silenced my voice. I flinched as my abductor snatched my arms around me and bound my wrists together.

"Let's go!" a second voice commanded, and I stumbled as my captors dragged me away.

I'm gonna die. They're gonna kill me. My thoughts were racing as fast as my heartbeat, and the cloth over my head made it hard to breathe. Beads of sweat that I had no way of wiping poured from my forehead, down my face and neck.

Calm down. If they were going to kill you, they would've done so already. I tried to reason with myself as I listened to the sound of a car door opening. Then, I was pushed so hard that I nearly fell. A set of hands lifted me, and I was tossed inside, landing on my back. The space was wide open, so I assumed they had thrown me in the back of a van. I curled up on my side and remained that way as the van lurched forward and they drove off.

It seemed like they drove for hours, though I was so disoriented that it could have been much less. I tried to listen for any sounds that could give me clues about where they were taking me, but the engine was so loud that it was the only thing I heard. Finally, we stopped, and I was dragged out and forced to walk for another ten minutes. The stench of fish filled my nostrils, and I could hear water nearby.

A boat. I'm on a fucking boat, I realized as I tripped on something.

"Sit his ass there!" the gruff voice commanded, and I was pushed down onto a chair.

It got quiet for a while. I wondered if I was alone. The smell of chum faded, now replaced by another familiar smell: a Bolivar cigar.

Fuck. It couldn't be him. He wouldn't have come all this way just to speak to me. I closed my eyes as if I weren't already in total darkness, fearing what was about to take place.

Someone yanked the cloth off my head, and I opened my eyes only to find that I was blinded by a bright light shining directly into my face.

"Do you really wanna fuck with us?"

The thick Spanish accent sent a shiver down my spine. I recognized it immediately. Now I was certain that the man smoking Bolivar cigars was also there.

"No, I wouldn't do that," I said, squinting to see past the blinding light, even though it was pointless.

"Okay, then give us an update."

"I've got everything in place."

"Then why hasn't it been done? This is taking way too long, Jeffrey. Our patience is wearing thin," he growled, scaring the shit out of me.

"I understand, but it's not me. This isn't my fault. Carolyn won't give up the money," I explained in a panicked voice. "I don't think she believes me. I may need some help."

"This was your task, not ours."

I shifted in my seat because I could smell the cigar smoke getting closer. "I know. I know, but I can't do it without the money. I tried talking to her, but she's concerned that the government is watching her every move." I dared not say that I thought she was stalling.

It was quiet again, and I thought he might have left, until I felt his presence looming over me. This time when he spoke, his voice was low. He was so close to my ear that I could feel his breath with every word he spoke.

"She'd better change her mind, or it won't be good for either of you."

Before I could respond, the cloth was back over my head, and I was being snatched up again. They dragged me out the same way I'd been forced in. I was relieved to be alive, but I knew that if I didn't handle the task I'd been given, then the next time they came for me, I wouldn't be so fortunate.

Anthony Johnson

47

Waking up before six, especially on the weekend, was not my idea of fun, but somehow, David had convinced me that I should go on a fishing charter with him and Reverend Chauncey. With everything going on with Carolyn, I'd been hoping to get to know some of the community leaders this summer, so this trip would give me a chance to get to know the local pastor better.

"Good Morning, Mr. Johnson." Reverend Chauncey waved from the parking lot, where he was already waiting.

"Please, call me Anthony, Reverend." I extended my hand to him.

He shook my hand with a firm grip. I didn't know exactly how old he was, but from his weathered skin and silver hair, I guessed he had to be well into his seventies. There was still some spryness in him, though, and his personality was warm and welcoming.

"Where's David?" I looked around.

"I'm right here." David walked up, pulling a collapsible wagon that held a cooler, fishing rods, and a few other bags and containers. "You fellas ready?"

"Oh, yeah," Reverend Chauncey said eagerly. "You know how much I look forward to this every year."

"Same here, Rev. It's one of my favorite traditions," David said.

"Traditions?" I asked as we all began heading toward the dock to meet the charter boat we'd reserved.

"Yep, David's father and I would enjoy a sunrise fishing expedition every July. Started when we were younger, then

David came along when he got old enough, and then both of my sons until they moved away," Reverend Chauncey told me.

"After Dad passed a few years back, Reverend Chauncey decided to continue the tradition. We still have a good time in his honor." David smiled, and I could see the nostalgia in his eyes.

Being invited to join them this morning made me feel special. "I'm looking forward to having a good time with you gentlemen."

We'd just arrived at the entrance of the pier when Mr. Chauncey asked, "Hey, isn't that Jeffrey?"

I saw Jeffrey making his way down the dock. "Yeah, that's him, but he doesn't look too good," I said. He seemed distressed the way he was kind of hunched over and kept looking over his shoulder.

"I see what you mean," David said. "You think he's drunk?"

"He's not stumbling, but he is acting a little strange." Reverend Chauncey walked over to Jeffrey. We followed behind him.

"Morning, Jeffrey," Reverend Chauncey said.

Jeffrey jumped slightly, startled. "What do you want?" He sounded agitated.

"Just checking on you. Everything all right, man?" I asked.

Jeffrey nodded, but his eyes told a different story. They were darting left and right like he was looking for someone he didn't really want to see.

"You sure you're o—?"

Jeffrey cut me off. "Yeah, everything's fine. If it's the papers you're looking for, you can stop by my office on Monday." He finally looked directly at me. "You wanna take on Carolyn Britton, you go right ahead. But don't say I didn't warn you."

"Jeffrey, you need to—" David went to put his hand on Jeffrey's shoulder, but Jeffrey jerked it away.

"Anthony is supposed to be your boy, right, Dave?" Jeffrey gave David a pointed look. "Well, then you and Reverend Chauncey should let Mr. Johnson in on the Peterson tragedy, so he'll know exactly what he's up against. Because right now, he doesn't have a clue."

Before we could say anything else, Jeffrey scurried away.

"What the hell is up with him?" I asked, bewildered. "And what is this about the Peterson tragedy? Did somebody die in my house or something? 'Cause Leslie sure didn't disclose that when we bought it."

"Jeffrey is troubled," Reverend Chauncey said, still staring in the direction that he had run off in.

"Come on. Our charter is waiting, and we don't wanna be late," David said, pulling the wagon behind him as he headed toward the boat. The look he exchanged with Revered Chauncey didn't go unnoticed, but neither one said anything.

I waited until we were settled and enjoying the sunrise from the deck of the charter boat to bring up the subject again. "Okay, so I'm curious. What was Jeffrey talking about with the Petersons?"

Reverend Chauncey and David shared another glance, then David nodded, as if to say it was okay to talk about it.

"Dale Peterson ran a pretty big auto parts business back in the day. You ever heard of PAPS?" Reverend Chauncey asked as he rigged up his fishing pole.

"Yeah, I remember PAPS. They used to do those crazy superhero commercials," I said.

"If your car is in trouble, it's PAPSman to the rescue." David sang the jingle from those ads, making me laugh.

"Yeah, well, PAPS stood for Peterson Auto Parts Stores," Reverend Chauncey continued. "They had shops all over the city, Long Island, Westchester, and Jersey. Did pretty darn well, too."

"I remember those stores," I said. "What happened to them?"

Reverend Chauncey lowered his head. "Dale Peterson killed himself. Right over there by Cedar Point."

"Really? Why?" I'd never met the man, but I hated to hear about anyone dying that way.

"Rumor has it he just couldn't take it anymore. I think he was just tired of fighting the Brittons." Reverend Chauncey sighed, his eyes remaining on the pole he was holding.

"Fighting about what?"

"You see, Sarah Peterson and Carolyn Britton didn't care too much for each other. Two queens in the kingdom. But when Dale purchased the yacht that Moses Britton had been bragging about buying, it was on."

"They fought over a boat?"

Reverend Chauncey shook his head sadly. "To me, it was more about ego. But after Dale bought the boat, the Brittons purchased both the Petersons' mortgages and threatened to foreclose. And when that didn't work, Amistad bankrolled the competition, humiliating Dale and putting them out of business."

"That's insane." I frowned. "I would never let anyone bring me to the point that I wanted to kill myself over business."

"You never know what you'll do when your back is against the wall, Anthony," Reverend Chauncey said as he pointed to the Britton yacht floating in the distance. "Dale Peterson is proof of that."

Carolyn Britton

48

There were very few things in life that were so unexpected that they caught me off guard. But, when they did happen, it never took long for me to gather my thoughts and come up with a strategy, both in business and personal matters. Sometimes, the solutions would be simple. Others took a little more effort, planning, and acceptance that it must be done for the greater good. I'd learned to be swift when it came to difficult decisions, and this was one of those times. Everything was in place, and I was anxiously awaiting Vanessa's arrival.

Kimberly brought her straight to my office without anyone seeing, as instructed.

"Please, sit." I stood and offered her a seat before turning to Kimberly to ask, "Is everyone here?"

"Malcom just arrived. The rest are gathered in the dining room."

"We'll be there shortly," I told her. Then I said to Vanessa, "Thank you for coming."

Vanessa rolled her eyes. "Carolyn Britton thanking me. This should be good."

"Actually, it is." I walked closer to her seat. "I'm about to . . . how does Jesse say it? Oh, do you a solid."

"How so?" She raised an eyebrow.

"You'll see. But I assure you it's a big one, and one you'll like," I said. "And you of all people know I don't do favors for anyone."

"Which is why I'm wondering what you're up to, Carolyn."

"I'm not up to anything," I told her. "Let's just say I'm in a giving mood these days, and you just happen to be on the receiving end. Needless to say, you will owe me one, and I will expect a thank you."

Vanessa's eyes followed me as I walked toward the door. "Maybe if I knew what I would be thanking you for . . ."

"I guess you've waited long enough." I smiled. "Come. Walk with me."

Vanessa stared at me for a minute before she finally stood up and followed me down the hallway and into the dining room, where Malcolm, Martin, and Jesse were sipping on mimosas. The looks on their faces were all matching as they stared at Vanessa and me, unaccustomed to seeing us together when neither one of us was scowling.

"Hello, gentlemen."

The silence was complete but brief, finally broken when Jesse greeted his mother.

"Mom?"

"Hi, son." Vanessa kissed his forehead. "Malcolm, Martin."

"Hey, Vanessa," Martin said, then looked at his brother.

"What's going on?" Malcolm asked Vanessa. She simply shrugged, so he directed his attention to me. "Mother?"

"Come, everyone. Let's sit and talk. I have an announcement to share. Martin, can you pour Vanessa a glass of champagne?"

"Thank you, Carolyn." Vanessa's smile was nervous as we took our seats at the table.

"Grandma, are you sick?" Jesse's face was full of concern as he sat between his parents.

I laughed. "No, I'm not sick, Jesse. I'm fine."

"Can't blame him for asking," Martin said, handing Vanessa her glass. "I was wondering the same thing. What is this about?"

"Well, this is about our family," I told him. "Specifically Vanessa, Malcolm, and Jesse."

"What about us?" Malcolm asked warily.

I looked at the three of them sitting to my right. "I owe the three of you an apology. One that I should've given many years ago."

"Mother, what are you talking about?" Malcolm asked.

I paused for a moment to consider my words. I needed to deliver them with the right amount of contrition so my plan would succeed. "I may have overstepped my boundaries and caused more chaos than happiness. What I thought was best for our family actually may have destroyed it. And I want to make amends."

Malcolm continued to look at me as if he thought I was crazy. "Again, Mother, what are you talking about?"

"I'm talking about the fact that it was me that caused your divorce. I knew you two loved each other, but I didn't care, and I purposely destroyed it."

While Malcolm and Vanessa looked confused, Martin scratched his neck uncomfortably, and Jesse seemed to be hanging on my every word.

"Mother, I don't know where all of this is coming from, but—"

"It's coming from my desire to make you happy and do the right thing, Malcolm. I realize that one of the reasons for your unhappiness is because of your inability to be with the person you've always loved." I nodded toward Vanessa. "And I'm sorry, both of you. I was wrong and selfish, and I want to make things right."

"Bro, I've never seen Mother this humble, and if she's apologizing, you better accept it," Martin muttered to his brother.

"Well, Carolyn, I for one accept your apology. Thank you for acknowledging the error of your ways," Vanessa said.

Jesse looked at Malcolm. "Dad?"

Malcolm sighed. "Okay, Mother, I accept your apology, but there's something I'd like to say, and maybe it's good you're all here."

"Thank you for accepting, Malcolm, but before I turn the floor over to you, I'd like to finish." I looked at Jesse. "You, young man, are the most important thing in my life. You are the future of this family. And although I had good intentions, I'm the reason you didn't have a chance to grow up with your mother in this household. I'm sorry, and I love you. I hope one day you can forgive me."

Jesse jumped up, rushing over to hug me as I wiped the tear I'd somehow managed to squeeze from my eye.

"I forgive you, Grandma, and I love you, too."

"Now, the best way to resolve this is to make things right. So, I've decided to host a ceremony for the two of you to get remarried this weekend. It will be held right here poolside," I announced.

"What?"

"What?"

"What?"

Malcolm, Vanessa, and Martin all spoke at the same time.

"Are you serious, Grandma? Mom and Dad are getting married again?" Jesse exclaimed.

I nodded toward him. "Yes, we are having a wedding, and although it's a bit last minute, it's going to be the talk of the town. I've already invited the press, and most of our major clients have been informed. Reverend Chauncey has already agreed to do the honors."

Vanessa grabbed Malcolm's hand. She was giddy with excitement. "Carolyn, I don't know what to say."

"Well, you can start by accepting this as a token of my support of your nuptials." I removed the small black box from my pocket and slid it toward her.

She picked it up from the table and opened it, gasping when she saw what was inside. "Carolyn, it's your mother-in-laws's wedding set."

"Seriously?" Martin reacted. "Damn."

Jesse turned to his father, who still hadn't said a word. "Dad, can I be your best man? No offense, Uncle Martin, but you got to do it the first time."

Martin laughed. "By all means."

"Dad, Dad, can I?" Jesse persisted.

Malcolm finally spoke. "Jesse, Vanessa, Martin, can you excuse Mother and me for a second?"

Jesse and Martin immediately stood, while Vanessa was still staring at the rings in her hand.

"Vanessa, please. This will only take a minute." He nudged her arm.

She rose slowly, her eyes locked with mine, and I gave her a reassuring nod before she followed Martin and Jesse out of the dining room.

"Have you been smoking more than cigarettes?" Malcolm hissed once we were alone.

"Of course not. What would make you ask me something like that?"

"This entire conversation. What's really going on, Mother? Everyone in the Black Hamptons knows you hate Vanessa. Heck, you've said on more than one occasion that you'd rather die than see us together." His eyes widened. "Wait, are you sick? Was Jesse right?"

"Hell no, I'm not sick. However, that debacle of a situation with your brother and the hooker he brought to breakfast the other morning woke me up to a cold reality. My interference in your relationships has cost you your happiness, and that was never my intention. I realize that Vanessa makes you happy," I told him.

"I appreciate your revelation, I really do, but my marriage to Vanessa is water under the bridge. I don't see her that way anymore."

"Is that so? Then why are you still sleeping with her?" I stared him in the eye.

He quickly looked away, caught off guard by my question. "Who told you that?"

"It doesn't matter. Fact is, it's true. Even Jesse knows."

"Jesse's twenty-one years old, Mother. He's a grown-ass man who came to terms with his parents' divorce a long time ago."

"Children never get over those type of things, even grown ones. The boy wants to be your best man, Malcolm. If that's not an endorsement for this marriage, then what is?"

"It's not happening. I'm not remarrying Vanessa." He shook his head.

"Okay," I said mildly. "That's fine, but then understand I won't be naming you CEO of Amistad Bank. That was your wedding gift, by the way."

I knew my son, and I watched my words register in his face. Malcolm's entire demeanor changed. He sat straighter in his chair, his eyes now bright, reminiscent of his father's.

"Seriously? CEO? You're just messing with me, Mother."

"No, I'm not."

"Wait. Are you willing to put that in writing?"

"I'll do even better than that." I had to chuckle. He was such a businessman. "As an additional sign of good faith, I'll include it as part of your wedding announcement for Page Six."

Jeffrey Bowen

49

Had it not been my job to protect the Britton trust, I wouldn't have been standing at the front door of the Britton home, especially so early in the damn morning. However, duty called. This impromptu wedding of Malcolm and Vanessa, which I'd only learned about a day before, was happening, and as the Britton attorney, I had to do my due diligence to make sure my client's best interests and financial freedom were protected. In other words, there had to be a prenup. A tight one.

It came as no surprise that it wasn't Malcolm who'd reached out regarding the safeguard contract, but Carolyn. It was one of the rare times that we agreed on something. I personally didn't have a problem with Vanessa, but her track record for massive divorce settlements was a well-known fact. The woman had a knack for making money from marital dissolution, or, as she once told me, "Profiting from heartache and pain."

"Good morning, Jeffrey." Kimberly beamed when she opened the door. "Beautiful day for a wedding, isn't it?"

"I guess," I said with a nonchalant sigh as I followed her to the library.

"Jeffrey." Carolyn glanced up from her desk when we entered.

"Carolyn." I walked over and placed a folder in front of her.

"Thank you." She nodded, opening the folder and scanning its contents. "I trust that you included all of the specifics I requested."

"And a few others you failed to mention. I made sure the trust is well protected should things not work out. Again."

"We'll see what happens," she said. "I've got a feeling the two of them will remain married for a very long time."

"Then why the need for the prenup?" I asked, curious why she suddenly seemed pleased about Malcom remarrying the woman she'd hated for so long.

"Like you said, my son and family still need adequate protection," Carolyn answered. "We wear seatbelts every time we get into our vehicles. We hope an accident doesn't happen, but sometimes they do. It's just a safety precaution. Malcolm has way more to lose than the first time they married. Business still needs to handled."

"Speaking of business needing to be handled." I lowered my voice. "This situation regarding Venezuela needs to be resolved quickly."

Carolyn's voice was sharp. "It will be resolved when I'm able to resolve it. We've discussed it already."

"No, there was no discussion other than your refusal to address it. This shit was supposed to be taken care of almost two years ago, Carolyn."

"Don't you think I know how long it's been?" she hissed. "It's not like I'm purposely avoiding it. There was the situation with the courts, and now that that's handled, I'll get to it when the funds are—"

"You keep saying that, yet you're willing to pay seven million dollars for a piece of land that you don't even need," I pointed out. "All because you want to spite your neighbors."

"You don't know what my reasons are, and I resent your assumptions."

I leaned close to her. "I'll tell you what is not an assumption, Carolyn. This has become a matter of life or death, and I'll be damned if I'm leaving this earth anytime soon. If someone has to die behind this, it won't be me."

"What are you saying, Jeffrey?" Carolyn's eyes met mine.

"I'm saying that you're handling business the way you want to, and now I'm doing the same." The tension between us was thick, and I was certain I'd made myself very clear. I waited for her response.

"Carolyn, you wanted to see me?" Vanessa strolled into the room, providing a much-needed interruption.

"I did."

I turned and smiled, pleasantly surprised at the sight of Vanessa's head full of curlers and her face free of makeup.

"The bride to be."

"Hello, Jeffrey," Vanessa said. "You're a bit early, aren't you?"

"Jeffrey was gracious enough to bring these over so you could sign them." Carolyn held the folder toward Vanessa.

"Sign what?" Vanessa looked tense as she took the folder and opened it.

"Just a standard prenuptial agreement," I told her.

"Excuse me? Malcolm and I didn't discuss a prenup." Vanessa put the folder back on Carolyn's desk. "Does he even know about this?"

"Certainly you didn't think there would be no agreement in place, Vanessa," I told her. "You know better than that. This is not your first or second marriage."

"And you know better than to think I'd sign anything without my attorney reviewing it first," Vanessa snapped back. "Let's be clear. My interests deserve to be protected as much as his."

"Then I suggest you call your lawyer, because there will be no wedding if they aren't signed." Carolyn stood. "Time is ticking, and six o'clock will be here soon, dear."

Vanessa snatched the folder back and stormed out of the office.

"Well done, Jeffrey," Carolyn said. "My husband always said he knew what he was doing when he put you in charge of our legal matters. Sometimes I see why."

I turned to leave without a response.

"I expect to see you and Leslie at the wedding," Carolyn called after me.

I stopped in my tracks and did a one-eighty. "I'm sorry. I wasn't aware that we'd even been invited."

"Why wouldn't you be?" she asked, looking genuinely perplexed. "Why would you even think that?"

"From the way you've been treating my wife, why would I think otherwise? You've made it very clear that she's not welcome around you. And at this point, I don't even know if I'd want her to be."

"Oh, please." Carolyn fanned her hand dismissively. "That was a business strategy, and your wife understands. This wedding is about family. Your presence is not only requested but required. She understands that too, I'm sure."

"Required?" I challenged, almost amused by the unmitigated audacity of the woman.

"I'll see you both promptly at five thirty. Remember, formal all-white attire is the dress code." She returned her attention to the paperwork on her desk. "Please close the door on your way out."

Anthony Johnson

50

When Victor Singh casually mentioned during one of our conference calls that he'd be in the Hamptons for the weekend, I didn't hesitate to invite him to dinner, and he'd graciously accepted. I had already started setting things for production in motion as I waited for the contract details to be finalized, so I was eager to get this deal closed. I needed to recoup some of the capital I'd already spent. Although I knew that breaking bread at an Italian restaurant wouldn't necessarily speed up the process, I hoped it would strengthen the business relationship we were building. It would also provide me the opportunity to introduce him to Sydney and David.

"This place is amazing, Anthony. I've heard about it, but this is my first time here," Mr. Singh said as we left Capelletti. He was a short and portly man in his late fifties with dark olive skin and thick, gray whiskers. The traditional turban on his head matched the dark blue suit he wore.

"Actually, it was Sydney's suggestion. I can't take credit for it." I put my arm around my wife, who'd insisted we dine at the popular casual restaurant, a local favorite, instead of one of the fancier five-star establishments in East Hampton. Her suggestion was spot on, because by the time we finished, our table was full of empty plates, and Mr. Singh wore a satisfied smile.

"Well, Sydney, thank you," Mr. Singh said. "It was an excellent choice."

Sydney smiled. "This is our first time here as well. Anthony has been putting in so many long hours in preparation for the contract that we haven't had much time to dine out."

Mr. Singh gave me a surprised look. "Is that so?"

I shrugged. "Like she said, prep work. I've ordered the lithium materials, secured the warehouse space, HR has started fielding resumes for potential employees and creating schedules for new hires. Shipping and distribution are working on a packaging design along with logistics. We just wanna make sure we're ready once the trigger is pulled on this thing."

The impressed look on Mr. Singh's face was exactly what I was hoping for, and I waited with anticipation for his response.

"Well, you're making me look bad. I feel a slacker." Mr. Singh laughed. "Looks like I need to put some pep in my step."

"Hey, we're ready when you are, sir," I replied, then offered, "Since you're here, we can actually finalize the paperwork while you're in town."

"I'm sorry, Anthony, but my wife insists that I not do business while on vacation. But we'll get things finalized by the end of next week." He gave me a reassuring nod. "I promise. No worries. We're almost across that finish line. I'm glad we were able to have dinner and I was able to meet your lovely wife and Mr. Michaels."

"Pleasure meeting you as well," David said and shook Mr. Singh's hand.

"Anthony, we'll speak soon," Mr. Singh told me, then stepped into the Rolls Royce that was waiting for him.

"That went really well, babe." Sydney squealed and hugged me tight.

"It did," I agreed. "That paperwork is as good as signed first thing next week."

"Let's hope so," David added.

I looked over at him, surprised by his lack of enthusiasm. "Hope? Man, didn't you hear what he just said? Hell, at this point, he feels bad it's taking so long."

David frowned. "You don't think you should've waited to get started on pre-production? Maybe talked to me first? You haven't even seen my budget yet."

"It's gonna be fine, David. I'm just putting a few things in place. Relax, I got this." I clapped my hand over his shoulder.

"Exactly." Sydney's head tilted to the side as her Brooklyn attitude emerged. "Chill. My baby knows what he's doing. He's the reason Sydney Tech is the success it is today."

Sydney's vote of confidence made feel even better, and it was enough to make David retreat.

"All right then, I'll holla at you later," David said then headed to his car.

"We need to get home too," Sydney said suggestively. "I got an itch that needs to be scratched."

"I can definitely take care of that." I kissed her. "I need to thank you properly anyway. For picking a great restaurant, being a great wife, and always having my back." I whispered, "And my front."

Sydney grabbed my hand and began pulling me toward the parking lot. My great night was about to get even better, and I would definitely be going to sleep with a smile on my face.

Malcolm Britton

51

From the number of people who turned to stare at us as the host led us to our table at Baldwin's Seaside, it was clear that word had spread about our upcoming wedding the next day. There was no rehearsal planned, so no rehearsal dinner, but I felt it was fitting that my fiancée and I at least went to dinner together.

"Everyone's looking at us." In true Vanessa fashion, she loved the attention that we were getting.

"I see." I looked around. "I wish they'd stop. It's like they've never seen us before or something."

"Well, many of them haven't." Vanessa waved at a couple who were smiling and whispering nearby. "At least not together."

"Which, I'm sure, made the advertisement in the *Hampton Express* even more confusing," I said, referring to the photo of Vanessa and me that had been published, along with the details of our lightning-fast engagement and wedding.

Vanessa giggled. "Oh, Malcolm, it was a wedding announcement, not an advertisement for Amistad's new lower mortgage rates. You're being ridiculous."

"Mother is the ridiculous one, which is probably why it was a full page." I picked up the menu that I knew by heart.

"Relax. The more anxious you look, the more they stare," Vanessa said. "You should know that by now."

I began scanning the wine selection, thinking that it was going to take at least two bottles, along with several shots of liquor, to calm my nerves. I still couldn't believe what was happening. And because it was all taking place so fast, I didn't have the chance to really think about it, let alone accept it. I was being pressured from all angles: my mother, my son, my ex-and-soon-to-be-again wife, and even my brother. While I was unsettled, everyone seemed to be on board with it, even excited. Hell, two bottles of wine might not be enough.

"So, I believe there are some things we need to discuss before tomorrow," Vanessa said.

"Such as?" I asked warily. The last time we married, she'd demanded a monthly shopping allowance, and I was certain this time would be no different. "Before you start, your alimony payment will now be replaced by your shopping allowance. You're not getting both."

She laughed. "Wow, I hadn't even thought of that. Damn it."

"Too late." I smirked. "The decision has been made."

"Malcolm, as crazy as all of this is, I'll do whatever you want. I'm just happy to be marrying you. I love you. I really do, but . . ." She stared at me very seriously.

"Sir, Madame." The waiter appeared and placed a bottle of chilled champagne and two glasses on the table.

"We didn't order this." Vanessa spoke before I did.

"It's compliments of the couple at the table in the rear, to your left," the waiter said. "In honor of your upcoming wedding. They send their congratulations as well."

We looked toward the back, and my mouth dropped. "Take it away."

"Sir?" the waiter asked.

"I said take it away. Now," I repeated a little louder as I stared at the two people waving at us. Everett seemed damn near giddy as he raised a glass in my direction. Sitting across from him was Morgan, looking just as amused.

I hadn't seen or spoken to Morgan since my surprising engagement, mainly because I couldn't think of a way to break the news to him. Now it was clear that he already knew. My jaw tightened, and I fought the urge to go over to their table.

"Malcolm, don't give them the reaction they want," Vanessa warned me, then she turned her head toward the waiter, who looked as if he didn't know what to do. "Thank you. Please let the couple know that we appreciate the kind gesture."

I looked at her. "What? I'm not drinking that."

"You don't have to." She smiled. "I will. It is a very expensive bottle of champagne."

The waiter poured her a glass, then scurried off. Vanessa lifted her glass and raised it toward Everett and Morgan before taking a sip.

"I can't believe you," I muttered.

"Why? What did I do? Other than refuse to entertain their pettiness."

I turned back around in my chair, now needing a drink even more than before. "Where's the damn waiter? He didn't even take our drink orders. As a matter of fact, let's just leave."

"No, I'm not going anywhere. We came to have dinner, and that's what we're going to do." Vanessa poured champagne into the other empty glass and passed it to me. "Drink this. It's Dom, your favorite. Gotta give it to them. They have great taste, and they're not cheap."

"I'm glad you're so fucking amused by all of this, Vanessa, because I'm not." I snatched the glass and gulped the cond tents inside.

The Dom did help me relax a little, and so did the double shot of bourbon I ordered soon after. By the time our food arrived, I was mellowed out and almost as unbothered as Vanessa—until a wave of noise erupted in the dining area and folks began buzzing with anticipation. Once again, our attention was drawn to the back of the restaurant.

"Oh, fuck no," Vanessa said.

Everett was down on one knee, looking at Morgan, who was about to cry. I closed my eyes, telling myself that when I opened them, that vision would be gone. It was just a nightmare.

"Yes! Yes! Yes!"

I heard Morgan yelling, then the room erupted in applause. This wasn't a bad dream; it was a horrendous reality.

"Malcolm." Vanessa reached across the table and placed her hand on mine. "Breathe."

"I'm fine. I'm fine, Vanessa." I opened my eyes and exhaled, lying to her and myself.

"Are you sure? You don't look fine."

"I am." I nodded. "I most certainly am."

"You want to step outside and get some air?"

"No. I'm fine, really."

"I'll be right back. I need to use the restroom. That display has me feeling a little queasy." She stood and excused herself.

Moments later, Everett floated past our table, speaking into his cell phone. It wouldn't have been so bad, but I knew he'd done it on purpose. "It went perfect, and of course he said yes."

I waited until he was out of the dining area before I went over to the table where Morgan was still sitting. "Congratulations."

"Thank you." Morgan glared at me. "Same to you."

I looked down at his empty left hand. "Don't tell me he proh posed without a ring. Typical Everett."

"Actually, he didn't give me a ring." Morgan pulled back the cuff of his dress shirt and held up his wrist. "He gave me this."

I sneered, unimpressed by the diamond-encrusted timepiece with the leather band he was so proudly displaying. "A watch? That's different."

"Isn't it? It's the Roger Dubuis Excalibur Pink Gold I've always dreamed of owning. I told you about it, remember? I never imagined I'd meet a man who loved me enough to get on one knee and ask me to marry him, let alone with a watch that cost over a hundred and fifty thousand dollars," Morgan boasted. "Look at both of us, Malcolm. Finally getting everything we wanted."

"Morgan, don't do this." I grabbed his arm.

He jumped to his feet and snatched away from me. "Get your fucking hands off me. I'm not Anthony Johnson. I hit back, and you know it. Go back to your Jezebel."

"Malcolm, honey, let's go." Vanessa's voice was in my ear. She put her hand on my shoulder to turn me around. "We have a long day tomorrow, and it's getting late. Perhaps we should leave."

"Yes, I think that's a good idea." Everett appeared by Morgan's side and put his arm around him.

"Come on." Vanessa led me away from the table. We exited the same way we had entered, with people staring at us.

"Malcolm, I want to finish what I started to say," she told me.

"What's that?" I asked, my voice still a little testy.

"This shit with Morgan is over. There wasn't much I could do about it when we were divorced, but now I'm about to be your wife. I expect you to be faithful, no exceptions. I want the two of you to have zero contact."

"Vanessa—"

"It has got to stop, or else I'll be forced to stop it myself. And I guarantee nobody's going to like how I do it."

Vanessa Britton

52

It was my wedding day, and although it was my fourth, this one was special to me. First, I was remarrying my best friend. I still didn't understand what had caused his mother's change of heart after all this time, and I was sure it had nothing to do with wanting to see me and Malcolm reunited, but I didn't care. The second reason it was special was because I'd never seen my son so excited. From the moment he'd found out his father and I were remarrying, he'd been full of joy. Not only was he Malcolm's best man, but he was also walking me down the aisle.

The Britton home was busy with vendors and staff handling wedding preparations. Despite it being considered a small, intimate ceremony, a far cry from the two hundred fifty guests we had at our first wedding, Carolyn had secured a florist, caterer, photographer, videographer, string quartet, and a decorator. Reverend Chauncey had agreed to serve as the officiant, as he had the first time we were married. Everything was in place.

While the groomsmen had gathered in the west wing of Carolyn's home to get dressed, my entire house had been transformed into the bridal suite, complete with hair and makeup artists and my personal stylist, who fussed over me as I got ready.

"Can someone get me another mimosa?" I asked Nadia, who'd graciously accepted my request to serve as my Maid of Honor.

"Sure." She stood up from the salon chair, where she'd been getting her makeup done.

I fanned myself, suddenly feeling hot. The last thing I expected to feel was nervous, but my anxiety had been high since the moment I woke up. That dinner date with Malcolm had been a bit much.

Everett's proposal to Morgan was surprising, of course, and my initial thought while watching him pop the question right in front of us was, *Thank God.* I was relieved because it meant that Morgan would finally be occupied by someone else. I couldn't think of a better suitor for Malcolm's "distraction" than Everett, who I knew would require plenty of Morgan's time and attention. I thought that maybe the stars were aligning in my favor this time.

However, as soon as I saw the look on Malcolm's face as he watched the two of them, I knew I was wrong. He truly looked distraught, and for a moment, I wondered if I should comfort him. Seeing the pain he was enduring was too much for me to bear, so I excused myself to give him some space. I wasn't expecting him to confront Morgan while I was gone. As much as I loved the fact that I was finally becoming Malcolm's wife again and had no doubt of his love for me, I couldn't ignore the truth that he was *in love* with someone else.

"I heard someone needed a drink."

"Alyssa!" I hopped up from my seat so fast that I nearly knocked the curling iron from the stylist's hand as I rushed toward the woman who'd walked in behind Nadia. I was so glad to see her that I ignored my freshly made-up face and allowed a tear to fall. We hugged for a few minutes until finally, she pushed me away.

"Get it together, bitch!" She laughed and dabbed at her own tears. "You act like this isn't the fourth time you've done this. Why are you crying?"

I grabbed a Kleenex from the box the makeup artist held toward us and patted my face. "The same reason you're crying, heifer. Because I'm glad to see my sister, that's why."

"I guess that's okay." She lifted the bottle of Casamigos she'd been holding. "This calls for something a little stronger than weak-ass mimosas, don't you think?"

"You're probably right." I looked at the other ladies in the room. "Hey, can you all give my sister and me a minute, please? It won't take long."

Everyone else exited the room, leaving me and Alyssa alone. She was older by two years, but we could pass for twins. I loved the fact that we looked very much alike because to me, she was the most beautiful woman in the world, and the one person I could always count on for anything. Malcolm was my soulmate, Jesse was my heart, but Alyssa was my sister, and we'd been bonded since I was born.

"I'm glad you made it," I said as I watched her pour the liquor.

"Did you think I wouldn't?" She passed me a shot. "Although this is so damn last minute. If I ain't know any better, I'd think this was a shotgun wedding and you were pregnant again. Are you sure that's not what's going on?"

"Hell no! You know I ain't having no more babies, especially at this age. I wouldn't dare risk all this fineness I've held onto all these years. I'd mess around and not snap back like I did the first time."

"I hear ya." Alyssa shook her head at me. "I still don't understand why you're even doing this for real. You're getting three alimony checks, you live a fabulous life, you travel the world and are free to come and go as you please."

"I'm doing this because I love Malcolm, and he loves me," I told her for the umpteenth time.

"Okay, and? That's nothing new. Y'all have been fucking since the damn divorce and through two other marriages. It was working. Why the sudden need to get remarried?" Alyssa sat in the chair left vacant by Nadia.

I swiveled my chair around and stared at my reflection in the mirror. "I've always wanted to remarry him. You know that. The time is right. I'm marrying the man of my dreams."

"And the man of your dreams, is he still fucking men?"

Alyssa's words were sharp. I whipped my chair in her direction and snapped, "It's not men. It's *man*. It was only one."

"Or was it just one that you know about?"

"You're out of line," I warned her. "It's none of your business."

"I'm your sister and I love you. That makes it my business. I want you to know exactly what you're about to be dealing with. You ready to be looking over his shoulder and checking his whereabouts 24/7?"

"For Christ's sake, Lys, I won't have to do that. Malcolm and I have discussed it, and I told him my expectations as far as his former relationship. He understands. In addition to that, as of last night, Morgan is engaged and about to marry some-one else," I stated matter-of-factly. "Another man."

"And? Married men still do a lot of dirt. Doesn't matter whether they're gay, straight, or bi. They can be the whole rainbow in the bag of Skittles."

"Some matron of honor you are." I sighed. "You're supposed to be here to support me, not cause doubt."

Alyssa walked over and put her arm around my neck. "I do support you, V. I always have. I just want you to be sure that you want to do this."

"I do."

Alyssa took a deep breath. "All right, then. Let's get you married . . . again."

"I love you."

"I love you, too." Alyssa walked over to the door and opened it. "Okay, ladies. All systems are go. We've got a wedding to get ready for."

Nadia and the other ladies returned to the room. Some-one turned on the music, and Alyssa poured more shots and passed them out. Having her there made me feel a little more settled, but her words were also sobering. Marrying Malcolm was a dream come true, but it came with a lot, including the contract I'd been forced to sign.

I looked at my sister, dancing and laughing. "Alyssa, I'm glad that you're here."

"Somebody had to be here to stand beside you," she said. "And to watch your back. You may believe Carolyn Britton has had a change of heart, but I don't."

Martin Britton

53

Although I didn't admit it to him, I had mixed feelings about Malcolm's wedding. On one hand, I was happy that he was getting married, something he'd wanted to do for a really long time. But on the other, I did feel slightly bad for him because of the fact that he wasn't marrying the person he was in love with. He didn't say it, but I knew this probably meant the end of him and Morgan. Despite my outright disdain for my brother's former lover and my slight joy that their relationship was finally over, I felt bad that it came at the expense of Malcolm's heart. I could only hope that he found true happiness with Vanessa. That wasn't impossible, because they truly did care about one another.

As we stood at the far end of the west garden of our home, I focused on my brother in his white tuxedo, nervously holding Vanessa's hand as they exchanged vows.

"Malcolm, do you take Vanessa to be your lawfully wedded wife, to have and to hold, for better or for worse, for richer, for poorer, in sickness and in health, till death do you part?" Reverend Chauncey asked.

There was a brief moment of hesitation, but after a warning glance from Mother, Malcolm replied in a low voice, "I do."

Reverend Chauncey turned to Vanessa and asked her the same question, after which she boldly smiled and loudly announced, "I do."

"If there is anyone here who feels that this man and this woman should not be joined, let them speak now or forever hold their peace." Reverend Chauncey directed the question to the small crowd assembled to witness the bride and groom exchange their vows.

I locked eyes with my mother, the only person other than Morgan who I thought might have objected, even though this event had been her idea. She remained silent, even nodding her head in approval.

My eyes looked beyond her, and I smiled at Karrin as she entered the backyard. She looked beautiful in a gorgeous, sparkling black gown, a stark contrast to the all-white that every other guest wore. She noticed me staring and smiled back.

"Then, by the power vested in me by the State of New York, I now pronounce you husband and wife. Malcolm, you may kiss your bride."

Malcolm took a deep breath before sharing a polite kiss with Vanessa. Then they turned toward the applauding guests.

Jesse looked at me, shaking his head in disbelief as he clapped for his parents. "Yo, did this really just happen, Uncle Martin? My parents are remarried?"

"It did."

While everyone gathered around to congratulate the happy couple and the reception began, I made my way to greet my date for the evening.

"Hello, gorgeous." I took her hands in mine and kissed Karrin softly.

"Damn, you are wearing the hell out of that tux." She grinned, looking me up and down.

"And you came in here trying to outshine the bride, I see." I spun her around.

"The ceremony was beautiful. Well, the little bit I was able to catch. I'm sorry I was late."

"Trust me, it wasn't a long service, and you were here for most of it." I threaded my arm through hers, all the while watching my mother, who was all up in Kimberly's ear. "Come. I'll introduce you to the lovely couple."

"Yes, please. I don't know why I was expecting him to marry someone else," she said.

"It's complicated, and I'll explain later."

"I look forward to it. It should be some interesting pillow talk."

"Very interesting. Shall we?" I pointed toward my brother and Vanessa, but before we could proceed, Kimberly strolled over to us. I prayed she wasn't coming over with some of my mother's bullshit.

"Here comes this bitch," Karrin mumbled.

"It's fine," I leaned and whispered into her ear.

As Kimberly approached, I said, "Kimberly, you remember Karrin."

"I do. How are you?" Kimberly politely said, and Karrin tilted her head in greeting. "Martin, we have a slight problem."

"Mother?" I asked.

"Yes. Unfortunately, your friend is going to have to leave."

Karrin opened her mouth to respond, but I interrupted. "She's my plus one."

"That may be true, Martin, but I've been instructed to escort her off the premises." Kimberly's eyes remained on me. "Discreetly, of course. We're not trying to cause a scene. Keep in mind, there are members of the press in attendance."

"We're leaving." I took Karrin's hand and led her out of the yard, thankful that I had slipped my keys into the pocket of my tuxedo pants. We headed straight to the driveway and got into my car.

She began laughing uncontrollably. "You're ditching your brother's wedding? Oh my God, you are crazy."

"Crazy for you." I leaned over and kissed her. "Come on. Let's get outta here. I'm in the mood for sushi."

I revved the McLaren's engine as I pulled out of the driveway, glancing in the rearview mirror at Kimberly. She was standing in the driveway like a sentry, watching us until we were down the street.

Carolyn Britton

54

Images of the day's events replayed in my mind as I took a late-night stroll along the beach. Malcom's wedding would be a huge hit on Page Six in the morning. The threat of a marriage to Morgan was a thing of the past, thanks not only to Kimberly, but to Vanessa as well. I had no doubt that Malcom would still indulge in his indiscretions with men, but Vanessa would keep him in line. She'd keep up appearances and protect the family name at all costs as the dutiful wife and perfect beard. Now, if I could figure out how to get Martin and Kimberly together so they could bless me with a few more grandchildren before it was my time to leave this earth, I might just die happy.

You'd think that being well into my sixties, I would be able to do as I pleased without worrying who was watching, but I still had to keep up appearances, and what I was about to do certainly did not fit the image that I worked so hard to cultivate. So, I waited until I was farther down the beach, where there were no more houses, before I reached into my pocket and pulled out the items I'd tucked away. Using a gold-plated lighter, I ignited the joint dangling from my lips, took a drag, and then continued on my walk with smoke trailing behind me. Unfortunately, I soon discovered that I was not alone.

Someone grabbed me from behind and pulled me into the dunes. The joint fell from my mouth as I opened it to scream.

"Shhhhhhhhhhh! I'm not going to hurt you," he hissed.

My eyes widened, and I froze, recognizing the voice of the man I could not see. I could smell the strong scent of the cigar he'd recently smoked.

"What the hell are you doing here? Have you lost your mind?"

"That's the exact same question I have for you, Carolyn. You seem to have lost yours," he replied, his grip still tight around my neck. "A sane woman wouldn't be preventing things from moving forward as planned."

"I'm not preventing anything." I felt like my pounding heart might come right out of my chest. I was scared; there was no doubt about that. However, I still had some cards to play.

"Things are going to move forward. I just need time, and you have to have patience and stick to the plan," I said.

"That's not what I was told. What's the problem with the fucking money? Why won't you pay it?"

"Because I can't right now. There's another situation that's come up."

"I don't give a fuck about any other situation. This is not a game. You need to pay the fucking money," he growled in my ear.

I took a deep breath, then spoke as firmly as I could without ending up with a knife in my back. "I don't have the money to pay right now. The Simpson property has become available, and there are people who want to dig it up and put in a pool. Do you know what that means?"

"What? That's not possible." He sounded surprised.

"Oh, but it is. Everett Simpson has placed the property up for sale," I told him. "And currently the asking price is eight million dollars."

He was quiet for a few seconds, but it didn't mean I had talked him out of anything. "Then you need to do both," he said angrily. "It's not as if you don't have the money. You're in charge of a bank."

"I just got the bank back," I said, pointing out the obvious. "The regulators have their eyes on us and probably will for quite some time. I can't afford to do anything that will cause suspicion. It can't be both right now. I can only do one at a time."

"Then choose wisely."

"You know what's on that land. Do you really want it in someone else's hands?"

I could hear his breathing become more intense. "Just know I can't wait much longer, and I'm starting to take this personally." He tightened his grip. "You don't want me to take this personally, do you?"

"No, I don't, but I also don't want that property winding up in someone else's hands."

"Not my problem. This entire Venezuelan situation was your idea, not mine. Fix it or I will."

Suddenly, I felt his hot, wet lips on my neck, and his free hand slid up my dress to feel my ass. I jumped, holding my breath in anticipation of what he might do next, but as quickly as he had arrived, he disappeared into the darkness.

Sergeant Tom Lane

55

I was pleasantly surprised when I stepped out of the shower and smelled bacon. Thinking Peter must've woken up hungry and decided to cook a hot breakfast instead of making a smoothie, I got dressed from the waist down and strolled into the kitchen to assist my son. Cooking together would give us a chance to talk, something we hadn't done in a few weeks because of our busy schedules. There was also the tension of the BBT contract offer that lingered between us. Peter was constantly on edge, hence the reason I delayed telling him about Tania and that asshole Jesse Britton. I didn't want to poke the bear. Thankfully, she'd made herself scarce, and Peter's time was limited. When he wasn't working, he'd been training with Bobby Boyd, which he thought I didn't know about. I didn't want to force the issue because I probably would have made things worse.

"Morning, Mr. Lane."

I stopped in the kitchen doorway, shocked to see Tania at the stove instead of Peter. "Why the hell are you here?"

Tania looked uneasy. "Peter wanted pancakes."

"Where is he?" I ignored the perfectly browned pancake in the pan she was holding toward me.

"He went for a run. He should be back soon." She went back to what she was doing as if she were welcomed in my home.

"Okay, good. Can I ask you a question?"

"Yes," she said timidly.

"What the fuck are you doing here?" I demanded. "I mean really?"

She stared at me for a while, then let out a sigh. "For Peter."

"You weren't here for him when you were laying up with that Britton boy."

"I know, and I have no excuse or explanation."

We stared at one another for a while. I ignored the fact that I was shirtless and walked closer to where she stood. "What's wrong with you? You can't play with people's emotions like this."

She had the audacity to look offended by my questions. "Nothing's wrong and nobody's joking, Mr. Lane. Peter and I went out last night when he got off work. We had a nice time and talked. He asked me to stay over, and I told him no."

"And yet?" I peered at her.

"He insisted, and like I said, this morning, he asked for pancakes." She slid the pancake on the plate with the others she'd already made, turned the stove off, then faced me. "Look, Mr. Lane, I know the last time we saw each other—"

"You were butt-ass naked in bed with Jesse Britton," I reminded her. "Which is why, again, I'm asking why the hell you're here. Not in my kitchen, but with my son."

"I . . . I . . ." Tania shook her head.

"Does this have something to do with this Bobby Boyd contract? Is that why you're hanging around? Because he's not signing that shit, so—"

"No, that's not it at all. I don't care about that. And I actually told him I agree with what you said. He should focus on the Olympics."

I didn't know whether to be grateful or suspect. On one hand, I was glad that the one person who probably had just as much influence over my son as I had agreed with me. Then again, after the salacious deed that I'd witnessed, I had a hard time believing Tania wasn't full of shit.

"Let me ask you a question, Tania. Do you love my son? Be honest."

"I do care about him. That's the honest to God truth. I care about him a lot. Peter—"

"Morning, Dad." Peter's untimely appearance interrupted our conversation. He dabbed at the beads of sweat pouring down his head and neck. His entire body was soaked. His T-shirt and shorts clung to his body.

"Hey," I said, annoyed as I watched him walk over and kiss Tania's forehead.

"You have a good run?" Tania asked him with a smile.

"Great run," he answered, then looked over at me. "I beat my best time, Dad. And I had the weight vest on."

"My man," I murmured.

"Bobby and Mr. Cornelius gave me some pointers, and they paid off," Peter said. "And now I get to enjoy pancakes with the crispy edges just like I like them, compliments of my boo."

"After you take a shower." Tania laughed and pushed him away.

"Yeah, today's gonna be a good day. I'm off, and the party tonight is gonna be off the chain," Peter said.

"What party?" I was surprised to hear anti-social Peter excited about a party.

"Bobby is having a little get-together at his summer rental. He invited me and Tania to hang out," Peter said. "Lots of celebrities, and he wants to introduce me to a couple of potential trainers."

"You haven't signed that contract, have you?" I frowned.

"No, Dad. I haven't. It's actually on top of your dresser. Bobby's just cool like that." Peter sighed, then kissed Tania. "He wants me to win the Olympics."

"Good." I turned to walk out of the kitchen.

"Dad, you're not eating?" Peter called after me. "It's plenty of bacon here, dude."

"I'm not hungry," I replied, no longer able to tolerate being in the presence of either one of them. For months, I'd been hoping that Peter would come out of his shell and become more social. Now that he was happy, I resented the two main reasons: Tania and Bobby Boyd.

Carolyn Britton

56

I'd given strict instructions for Leslie, Kimberly, and my sons to assemble in my office for an emergency meeting two days after I was accosted on the beach. The incident had me spooked, for sure. It was going to have to be dealt with eventually, but not in the manner you might think. For now, there were more important things that needed to be taken care of. I'd put out one fire with Malcolm's wedding, and now it was time to get back to the other one that had been brewing: The Simpson property. Time was ticking, and I needed all hands on deck.

"Have we made any progress with the Anthony Johnson situation?" I asked as I sat at my desk.

They all looked around at each other while avoiding eye contact with me.

"Is everyone on mute? Because I can't hear anyone."

"I think I speak for everyone when I say we've been working on it, Mother," Malcolm volunteered.

"Is that so?" I asked, and they nodded in unison.

"And what exactly have you done so far?"

"To be honest with you, the man is insulated. He's a self-made man who uses little if any credit. He pays for everything with his business up front or within thirty days," Malcolm said.

"What about his wife? What do you have on her? She's his weakness."

"She's a spender, no doubt about it, but again, she only uses debit cards tied to a sizable checking account. They barely have any credit other than two Citibank Visa cards they got in college."

"Nobody is this good," I said. "There has to be another way. Leslie, what's that husband of yours have to say?"

"I . . . uh . . . well, Aunt Carolyn, I have stressed to Jeffrey the importance of doing everything in his power to make sure things go in your favor," she said weakly.

"And?" I folded my arms. "Before you answer, I'd like to remind you that I just allowed you back into the fold."

"Yes, and I appreciate it." She nodded. "I've talked, yelled, fussed, and not to put my business out there, but I've held out for the past month. He ain't seen no parts of the punanny."

"Please spare us the details," Malcolm whispered.

"There ain't no details to tell," Leslie whispered back. "Don't worry."

"Well, if holding out isn't working, then maybe you should offer it up on a platter," I suggested.

"I tried that too when we got home after the wedding." Leslie sat back and folded her arms. "He didn't want it."

"Well, that's odd. How hard did you try?" I asked before I could stop myself.

"Mother, please." Malcolm frowned at me.

"To be honest, Aunt Carolyn, I don't know what's going on with Jeffrey," Leslie said. "He's dealing with something other than this property situation, and whatever it is has him acting strange. I've asked him, but the only thing he says is that it's an overseas business matter, whatever that means."

I decided not to interrogate Leslie anymore, especially since I had a pretty good idea what had her husband so bothered. The last thing I needed was for her to press him to the point that he finally gave in and told her the details.

"Mother, if you really want that property this bad, then maybe . . ." Malcom took a breath, looking like what he was about to say went against everything he believed in. "Maybe we should just go ahead and raise our bid."

I shook my head. "I appreciate your thoughts, Malcom, but raising our bid won't help because this is personal. The Johnsons are making this very personal, so we have to hit them where it hurts."

"I understand," he replied. "Martin and I will come up with something. We're just going to need a little more time."

"We don't have any more time! This shit needs to happen now!" I glared at their faces one by one, and that's when I realized my youngest wasn't in the room. "Speaking of Martin, where the fuck is your brother?"

"He hasn't been home in two days," Kimberly answered. "Not since the wedding."

I sighed. "My God, don't tell me he's still throwing his little temper tantrum over that tramp that showed up."

"Pretty much," Malcolm said. "I've tried calling and texting him, but he won't answer."

"Well, where the fuck is he exactly?"

"He's staying on the yacht," Kimberly stated, then added, "And he's not alone."

I rolled my eyes to the back of my head. "You've got to be kidding me. You mean to tell me he's still laid up with that trashy tramp instead of attending an emergency meeting that I specifically said that he needed to attend?"

"It appears that way, Mother," Malcolm said. "Like I said, I've tried to reach him, but I'm being ignored."

"Fine. I'll deal with your brother and his decision to run away from home later. In the meantime, this Johnson situation is priority. We've got to do something."

"I wasn't going to mention it, but Jeffrey's been dragging his feet getting the final paperwork over to Everett. I do know that," Leslie said.

"Well, I guess that's something," I told her.

"But he promised it would be ready by the end of next week."

"That doesn't give us much time."

Kimberly spoke up. "Mrs. Britton, I think I may have a plan that could work in our favor and make the bank and some of our partners a lot of money at the same time."

"Thank God," I said. "At least someone has been putting their brain to good use around here. What do you have in mind, Kimberly?"

"Have you ever heard of a company called Entech?"

"No, but I have a feeling I'd like to."

"Yes, I think you will. However, we're going to have to act fast," she said, "and we're going to need Martin. It's going to take a certain kind of finesse to pull this off, and we know that's what he does best."

"You and Malcom put together the details and let me worry about Martin," I assured her. "If this plan of yours involves him, I'll make sure he's available. He won't have a choice. Now, please explain."

Everyone leaned in to listen as she shared the details of her plan, which was our best hope of finally ending the Johnsons' ridiculous quest for the land that was rightfully mine.

Martin Britton

57

As fate would have it, Karrin and I found ourselves at the same restaurant where we'd had our first date. After spending the past few days on the yacht, I suggested we come up for air and have a nice meal.

I hadn't talked to anyone since we left Malcolm and Vanessa's reception. I ignored several calls from my mother, brother, and nephew before deciding to turn my phone off and immerse myself in the moment with Karrin.

"Are you sure you're okay?" she asked as she dug into the ribeye steak she had ordered. Because neither one of us had gone home, she wore the same dress she'd worn to the wedding, and she looked gorgeous.

"I'm fine," I told her. "Why do you keep asking me that?"

"Because you literally dipped out on your brother's wedding reception, maybe?" She raised an eyebrow. "And you haven't checked in with anybody. I'm sure they're worried."

"A wedding reception where you weren't welcome," I reminded her. "That shit wasn't cool. And believe me, they're fine. They know where I am."

I hadn't seen her since the reception, but I knew Kimberly had been on the yacht once or twice while we were there. The fresh fruit, swimsuits, and other small household items that showed up hadn't just magically appeared.

"Your mama's probably having a fucking conniption right now," Karrin said dramatically. "I appreciate your display of loyalty, Martin, but she already hated me, and you leaving probably added fuel to the fire."

"She's gonna have to get over it. I mean it." I picked up my wine glass and swallowed the contents in one gulp, then poured another glass. I knew Karrin was trying to be supportive and appreciative, but I didn't even want to think about my family. The night was young, and the only thing on my mind was what I would be doing to Karrin once we got back to the yacht.

"Why are you looking at me like that?"

"Do you really wanna know?" I asked seductively. "Don't act like you don't know what I'm thinking about."

She laughed. "You're a mess."

"So, you really gonna sit over there and act like you ain't thinking the same thing?" I challenged, having already noticed her subtle glances at my crotch throughout the evening.

"I guess we should have them box this up and leave then, huh?"

Her words were like music to my ears. "Damn right."

I motioned for the waiter, who quickly boxed up our meals then accepted the credit card I gave him for payment. Karrin and I finished the bottle of wine while we waited for him to return.

"You know what I want?" I leaned across the table and took Karrin's hand.

"To make love to me all night long until my toes curl?"

"That too, but more than that, I want to take a long walk along the beach under the stars, holding your hand."

Karrin blushed. "That sounds so romantic. How did I get so lucky?"

"I was thinking the same thing," I replied just as the waiter returned to our table.

He leaned in close to me, his voice barely above a whisper. "Sir, I'm sorry, but your card was declined."

"What? That's impossible. That's a Platinum Amex without a limit."

"I'm sure it's some kind of mix-up with your financial institution and not your fault, but we are going to need another card."

I took the card from him and slid it back into my wallet, then handed a different card to him.

"Now, where were we?" I placed my hand back over Karrin's.

"I believe you were telling me how beautiful I am. And that you wanted to take a romantic walk with me."

"I was also thinking that maybe on that walk, we should discuss taking a trip. How does Paris sound, or maybe Morocco?" I became excited as I talked. It had been ages since I'd been on a true vacation, and I couldn't remember the last one I'd taken with a woman. I knew I wanted to travel with Karrin by my side, though.

"I would love either one." She was beaming, but then her eyes went to the waiter as he came up behind me, and her face fell.

"What?" I turned around to see the waiter shaking his head.

"My apologies, sir, but this card was declined as well."

"What the hell? You've gotta be kidding me," I snapped. "I know she's not doing this. No way."

Karrin looked concerned. "Is everything okay, Martin? Do you need me to pay?"

"No, of course not." I took out my wallet again. "You do take cash, right?"

The waiter nodded. "Yes, sir, cash is acceptable."

"Keep the change." I thrust three crisp hundred-dollar bills toward him, then said to Karrin, "You ready to get out of here?"

"Uh, yeah sure." She hopped up. "Are you okay?"

I picked up our boxed food in one hand, then grabbed her hand with the other. "We're going to have to take our walk later. We're going to the yacht, but then I've gotta leave you for a little while to take care of something. I need to talk to my mother."

After taking Karrin to the yacht to make sure she was settled, I went straight home. As I drove, I thought about everything I wanted to say once I got there. Disliking Karrin was one thing, but now my mother had taken things too far. I was a grown man, and she was going to have to accept the woman I chose to date.

The house was quiet, and I ventured into the library, where I knew I would find Mother.

"You canceled my credit cards?" I entered without knocking.

She didn't even bother to look at me. "I did. I blocked your trust accounts as well, just so you know."

"Why would you do that?"

After a brief moment, her eyes finally moved from the computer screen and landed on me. "Because of your reckless behavior, that's why. You think I'm going to allow you access to those funds so you can finance some fly-by-night romance with that floozy? No, Martin, I won't let you do that."

"Let? It's my money, Mother."

"Correction, it's my money, which I allow you to access via a trust, of which I am the administrator. You haven't earned that money. It was given to you, and as such, now it has been taken away."

I tossed my hands in the air. "So, you're punishing me for being in love?"

"No, I'm teaching you a lesson. You act irresponsibly, then you lose certain privileges, for your protection, and mine."

"Irresponsible how?"

"For Christ's sake, Martin, are you so caught up in your feelings for that tramp that you don't even see how erratically you've been behaving?" She looked astonished.

"I'm not the one behaving erratically, Mother. You are. You act like I've never dated a woman you disliked before. But Karrin is special. I have feelings for her. You haven't even given her a chance."

"It's not just the fact that you barely know this tramp. I'm used to that. But you continued cuddling up with her after she cussed me out and disrespected me in our home in front of your entire family. Then, you have the nerve to invite her back to our home to attend a private family event, and after I respectfully asked that she leave, you abandoned your brother on his wedding day to leave with her." Her voice was sharp and piercing, but then suddenly, she became calm.

"Do you think I'm going to allow you to continue wining and dining her on my dime? Now that I think about it, not only are you irresponsible and erratic, but you're delusional as well. All over a random piece of ass. My, my, my, how pussy whipped can you be?"

I was so angry that it took everything in me not to flip over the desk she was sitting behind. Sure, Karrin had been disrespectful, but not without good reason; and maybe me leaving the wedding was a rash decision, but Mother had pushed me to that point. She twisted my feelings for Karrin in such a negative way that it was sickening.

"You're really going too far with this," I said.

"Call it what you want. My money, my decision. What's the problem? Does your new bedmate not have any money of her own?" She smirked. "What does she bring to the table? Where does she work? What about her family? Who are they?"

"You're being unfair and judgmental."

"How? I just asked you a basic question about the woman you claim to have feelings for, and you don't know the answer to any of them. I'm sure she knows the answers about you, though. So, I ask you again, Martin. What do you know about her, other than she has a pretty face, nice tits, a great ass, and probably does things to you in bed that no other woman has?"

"She's a talented artist, Mother," I answered. "And you know how much I love art."

She snickered, making me feel even worse for telling her. "An artist. How cute. Martin, you are my son, and I love you, but you're going to have to make a choice. Either you can go be with your broke Brooklyn boo and live your best broke life, or you can remain in your current position as vice president and help me continue to build the Britton legacy. Now, what are you going to do? Sit in that chair, or walk out that door?"

Fuck! Fuck! Fuck! Fuck! Fuck! She had me backed into one big-ass corner.

I slumped into a chair, staring at the floor, feeling disgusted and disturbed. I hated that everything she said made complete sense, but I also couldn't ignore the fact that despite knowing nothing about her, I did have strong feelings for Karrin. But was she worth throwing away my stake in the family fortune? I didn't know if I could answer that yet, and Mother was certainly not going to allow me time to get to know Karrin better before she forced me to decide.

She walked over and put her hand under my chin, lifting my head as she spoke. "I want you listen to me and listen good. The day that I will stop putting the best interests of this family first, before anything and anyone, will be the day that I close my eyes for good. Do you understand?"

I looked up, and our eyes met. Mine were full of tears. "Yes, Mother. I understand everything."

She kissed the top of my head. "Good, because it's time to get back to business. We need your help with the most pressing topic at hand: destroying the damn Johnsons."

Sergeant Tom Lane

58

Though the weekend had ended days ago, Sag Harbor was still full of people, and the complaint calls were higher than usual. Unfortunately for me, one of them was regarding the Brittons. When I found out where I had to go, I definitely took my time getting to the dock. Even though this was a direct order from the chief, it was not a true emergency, which made me even less motivated to arrive. Trying to fight the urge to just turn back around, I reminded myself that this would give me the chance to gaze upon Vanessa Britton's fine ass. I knew there wasn't a snowball's chance in hell of me ever hitting that, especially since she'd just married Malcom Britton again, but a brother could fantasize.

When I arrived at the dock, it wasn't Vanessa waiting for me. It was another woman, cute, but not as sexy.

"Sergeant Lane?" She greeted me with a pleasant smile.

"Yes, ma'am." I nodded, noticing she was much nicer than I expected.

"I'm Kimberly. Nice to meet you." She gestured for me to follow without offering more detail. "This way, sir."

We continued down the pier, and I dismissed the flashbacks entering my head as we got closer to the yacht where I had discovered Tania's betrayal. The young woman walked past it.

"Wait. I thought we were going on the Britton yacht."

Kimberly gave me a strange look. "We are. This is the Britton yacht."

I looked at the yacht we'd just passed. "Isn't that Vanessa Britton's yacht?"

"Yes, it is." Kimberly pointed at a much bigger yacht. "This one is owned by Carolyn Britton. She's the one who made the complaint. I trust you brought the paperwork with you?"

"I did." I patted the folded paper in my breast pocket. The chief had given it to me before I left the station.

"Good, then I guess we should go ahead and get this over with." She guided me onto the yacht that had to be at least a hundred feet long. It made Vanessa Britton's yacht look like a regular old boat.

I tried not to act mesmerized as we went inside, but it was hard not to react to the luxury and glamour surrounding me. Everything was shiny, lavish, and expensive, impressive even by Hamptons standards. It was one thing to see this kind of opulence on television, but to walk through and experience it firsthand left me awestruck.

It dawned on me that Kimberly seemed unbothered as she led me through the yacht. "Miss, I was told this was a trespassing matter," I said.

"It is." She stopped in front of a closed door. "She's in here."

"She?"

Kimberly turned the knob and opened the door without knocking, then stepped back. The room was dimly lit, but I could see the silhouette of a body under the white comforter.

When I didn't move, Kimberly said, "She's asleep. Should you wake her, or should I, Sergeant?"

My eyes widened. What the hell kind of a situation had I been sent to take care of? "I'll do it," I said, but then Kimberly proceeded to take charge anyway.

"I'll help." She turned on the light then stepped in and said loudly, "Karrin!"

The woman sat up quickly, looking confused and a little frightened. "What the fuck?"

I tried not to stare at the beautiful breasts and tattoos exposed in front of me, but they were hard to ignore.

"You need to leave." Kimberly stood near the foot of the bed with her arms folded.

"I don't have to do shit. I have permission to be here." Karrin looked at me, then grabbed the sheet to cover herself.

"Not from the owner, you don't." Kimberly shook her head. "Martin Britton does not own this yacht. Carolyn Britton does. Now, you need to remove yourself, or I'll have you removed."

"You ain't gonna do shit!" Karrin barked back at her.

"No, I don't have to do anything. He will." Kimberly looked at me.

"I'm sorry, ma'am. She's right. You're going to have to leave," I told her.

"I'm calling Martin." She reached for the cell phone on the nightstand and dialed a number. After a few seconds, she pulled the phone away from her ear to look at the screen with a frown on her face, and then dialed again.

"It's pointless," Kimberly said. "You're blocked."

"He wouldn't do that." Karrin began texting into the phone.

"That text will go unread, and I told you, you need to leave," Kimberly insisted.

"And I told you I ain't going nowhere until I talk to Martin." Karrin jumped up, still holding on to the sheet.

I decided to intervene and prevent the cat fight that was brewing. "Ma'am, you're trespassing, and if you don't leave, I'll have to take you into custody."

"You can't be serious." Karrin's voice softened as she looked at me.

"He is. And he also has a restraining order." Kimberly added insult to the distraught woman's injury. "You're not to come within five hundred feet of any member of the Britton family or onto any of their properties, or you'll be arrested."

Karrin's eyes remained on me, and I nodded, handing her the paperwork from my pocket. She opened it and read it.

"I'll give you a few minutes to get dressed," I told her. "I'll wait for you outside."

She continued staring at the paper. "This is some bullshit. I can't believe this."

"He said a few minutes, so you need to make it quick," Kimberly said. "And don't think about leaving anything behind. You won't be able to retrieve it if you do. It'll be discarded."

"Fuck you," Karrin spat.

Kimberly stepped outside the room, and I followed.

"I'll make sure she leaves," I assured her. "But I gotta ask, was all of this necessary?"

"Carolyn Britton doesn't tolerate anyone intruding on her privacy. If you need me, I'll be on deck."

I sighed. "I think we'll be fine. I know the way out."

It didn't take long for Karrin to get dressed. A few moments later, the door opened, and she stepped out wearing a formal gown. The only other thing she had was a small clutch and her cell phone.

"You have everything?" I asked.

"Yeah. I ain't have shit to leave here anyway other than a phone charger," she huffed. "That bitch is gonna pay for this."

"Let's head on out," I said, unsure of which bitch she was referring to: Carolyn or Kimberly. From what I gathered, either one of them could have earned that title.

She didn't say anything else as we made our way off the yacht. I noticed Kimberly watching as we stepped on to the pier, but she remained quiet too.

I led Karrin to my parked cruiser and opened the door. "I can give you a ride home."

"Thanks," she said, getting in.

I closed the door, and as I walked to the driver's side, I turned and looked at the smaller Britton yacht. I blinked a few times to make sure my eyes weren't playing tricks on me. Standing on the deck, kissing under the moonlight as if they were in the closing act of a rom-com, were Tania and Jesse Britton.

"Fuck," I whispered as I got into the car.

"What's wrong?"

I was so caught up in my thoughts that I'd forgotten Karrin was already inside. I shook my head and pulled the seatbelt across my body. "Oh, nothing. You okay?"

"Yeah, I'm cool. These fucking Brittons are something else, though," she said, staring at her cell phone as if she wanted to cry.

"They damn sure are."

Martin Britton

59

Shark fishing wasn't really Malcom's thing. It was mine, especially since my father was gone. It was the sport he loved the most, and I couldn't get enough of it. For my dad, it was peaceful and built patience. For me, it was about hooking up and bringing in the monsters of the sea. But the early morning charter that I'd booked wasn't about anything in the water. This was about a bigger catch: one that would satisfy my mother, benefit our company, and provide a much-needed distraction from thinking about Karrin, who I couldn't get off my mind no matter how hard I tried.

"I'm glad you were able to come out today," I said to Victor Singh, who was standing beside me on the deck as we floated in the middle of the open water. The captain had taken us far out, and we were sitting somewhere off Rhode Island.

"Yes, thank you. I was pleased to get the invitation. Fishing is a hobby of mine that I've enjoyed for quite some time, but my schedule rarely permits it."

"Some things we have to make time for," I said. "And fishing is one of them."

The background check Kimberly had done on Victor Singh and his company had revealed his love of deep sea fishing. So, when I casually "bumped" into him at his favorite coffee shop in Southampton, I'd acted like he was one of my business heroes and name-dropped a few mutual friends. Just like I knew it would, my act flattered Victor, and he began to treat me like we were old friends. Then, I began talking about my big shark fishing trip and how one of our mutual friends had dropped out.

"You know," I had said as if the thought just came to me. "How about you come in his place?"

"I'd love to," he agreed.

Fully expecting that this would be his answer, Kimberly had already found a charter boat and offered the captain double for the day to secure the reservation during the busy weekend.

"You are a busy man," I said as we cast our lines into the water. "I read a couple of months ago that you were in the process of making a bid for Entech Freight out in Houston. That's a huge move and a great fit for your company."

He looked surprised. "You certainly do know a lot about my company."

"I can't help it if I'm a fan."

"Yes, well, it would have been ideal, had we been able to make it happen." Mr. Singh sighed, and I could hear his disappointment.

"Wow, that's unfortunate." I put my fishing pole in the rod holder and turned toward him. "Deals like that are hard to come by in today's market. If you don't mind my asking, why'd you walk away?"

"Our creditors thought it was too risky to finance. With our balance sheet, we just didn't have the free capital needed to swing it. After much thought, we decided it wouldn't be feasible at this time," he explained.

"It's too bad you weren't banking with us. I would've backed that deal in a minute. It was a no brainer."

He looked intrigued. "Perhaps we should talk about moving some of our accounts to your bank so we can do business in the future."

"I have a better idea," I told him. "We should discuss moving all your accounts to Amistad so we can assist you in the purchase of Entech Freight."

Mr. Singh turned his body toward me. "Are you saying that's a possibility?"

"As possible as whatever that is you've got on your line." I pointed to his pole being pulled by something in the water. "You might want to strap in for this one."

Mr. Singh did just that and excitedly began maneuvering to struggle with the rod. After an hour's fight, he pulled out a twelve-foot shark. His reaction was so ecstatic that I couldn't help laughing and shouting in enjoyment with him.

"Well, that's a catch for sure."

"Darn right it is!" He grinned, standing next the twelve-foot shark for a photo. "It's my biggest catch yet."

I reached into the cooler and passed Mr. Singh a cold beer, then we sat back and shared a toast.

"Well, you've caught the biggest fish of your life, Victor. Now, what about closing one of the biggest deals while you're at it?" I asked.

"If you really think it's possible, it would be my honor, Mr. Britton."

"I do. Between us and our strategic partners, we could have this deal wrapped up by the end of the weekend."

"That fast?" He seemed more than pleased.

"The most profitable deals are the ones that close fast. It's just a matter of flying your lawyers out and putting in the hard work."

"Well, I don't normally do business on the weekends—my wife's rule—but for this, I will have to make an exception."

"I'm sure she'll understand," I said. "However, there is one small detail that we need to discuss first. No cause for concern, of course, but important nevertheless."

"What's that?"

"You currently have a pending deal with Sydney Technologies, right?"

"That deal hasn't been disclosed. How did you know that?" he asked.

"It's my job to know," I replied. It didn't hurt that David had opened his big mouth about the deal while we were playing tennis.

"Yes, Anthony Johnson is quite an impressive young man. His electric battery could be a game changer for Singh Transportation. I'm looking forward to working with him and his company," Mr. Singh said with such confidence that I almost felt bad about what I was about to tell him.

"Sydney Tech definitely has a bright future. However, we have another battery developer that we've been working with that's just as dynamic," I pointed out. "We like to keep things in the family, so to speak."

Mr. Singh had a troubled look on his face. "This puts me in a very uncomfortable position, Martin. The deal with Sydney Tech is pretty much done."

"A pretty-much-done deal isn't a completed deal, Mr. Singh. Until that dotted line is signed, everything is fair game, right?

And I'm sure the pending deal with Anthony Johnson isn't worth losing Entech Freight," I stated.

Mr. Singh didn't answer. He stared into the water, and I could see him deep in thought, reflecting on our discussion. Instead of applying more pressure, I allowed him to come to a conclusion on his own. It was the perfect time for me to rely on the lessons my father had taught me about fishing and put peace and patience to good use.

"Gentlemen, how was your excursion?" Malcolm greeted us when we returned to the dock three hours later.

Mr. Singh shook his hand jovially. "Oh, it was quite successful for several reasons."

"Oh? I take it you made a great catch?" Malcolm asked, glancing over at me.

"The biggest one ever." I smirked. "And, Mr. Singh and his team will be joining us on the yacht until the Entech deal can be finalized."

"Ah, good. I was just on the phone with the CEO of Entech," Malcolm said. "He's flying out tonight. If you're serious, we can have things wrapped up by Monday night."

"I am," Mr. Singh said. "And I look forward to doing business with you."

Malcolm beamed with pride. "As do I."

We all shook hands, and Mr. Singh proceeded to the Rolls Royce that was waiting for him.

"Good job, baby bro." Malcolm nudged me when he was gone.

"Thanks. Just tell Mother. I'm sure she's been calling every fifteen minutes, asking you for an update." I didn't want to talk to her myself, still holding on to a grudge over her treatment of Karrin. I'd done what needed to be done for the sake of the family, but the resentment still lingered.

"Aw, cheer up, Martin. You did a good job today," Malcolm said.

I appreciated my brother's efforts, but it was useless. There was only one person who could lift my spirits, and I had no idea where she was now.

Malcolm

60

My phone rang, and I excused myself from the breakfast table. Martin, Mr. Singh, and a few others from his team were seated on the top deck of our yacht, finishing up a gourmet meal. The attorneys for both Singh Transportation and Entech Freight had worked through the night, gathering the necessary documents and signatures to complete the deal. We'd just gotten word that wire transfers were received, and the deal between the entities was officially done. Singh Transportation now owned Entech Freight, and I'd completed my largest deal.

"Hello, Mother, how's your morning?" I said cheerfully.

"It was fine until I walked out onto my balcony and saw the Johnsons strutting around the Simpson property with a pool contractor like they already owned it," she snapped. "Please tell me you have good news for me."

"I do, Mother. The deal is done," I said with excitement.

"That's exactly what I wanted to hear. You've handled this remarkably, Malcolm. It makes me even more confident in my decision to name you CEO. Your father would be proud."

Her words of praise were unexpected, and to hear her mention that my father would be proud made me smile in a way that I hadn't in a while. "Thank you, and I appreciate your confidence."

"You're welcome," she replied. "So, has Mr. Singh delivered the news to the Johnsons, by chance?"

"No, not yet. The deal was just finalized moments ago, but I can encourage a call right away," I replied.

"That would make your mother extremely happy, Malcolm. And please, give Mr. Singh my regards and let him know we'll meet soon."

"Consider it done. We'll talk again soon."

I made my way back to the table. "Victor, can I speak to you in private for a moment?"

"Certainly." Mr. Singh followed me to a lower deck. "Is everything okay?"

"Yes, everything's fine," I reassured him. "It's just that the press has gotten wind of our deal, and we're going to have to make a statement. Have you spoken to Anthony Johnson to let him know that you're pulling out of your agreement with Sydney Tech?"

"No, not yet." A look of concern came over his face so deep that the wrinkles in his forehead seemed to multiply. "I felt that it would be best not to say anything until after the deal was finalized."

"Well, it's finalized," I stated.

"Honestly, I feel kind of bad. I really like Anthony, and he's going to be very disappointed."

"I understand, but I'd hate for him to be blindsided. Which is why you should call him sooner rather than later. I'm sure he'd rather hear it from you than the press, or on social media."

"You're right. I'll give him a call right now. This shouldn't take long," Mr. Singh agreed, pulling out his phone.

"I'll give you some privacy. I'll see you back up top," I said with an empathetic pat on the shoulder.

I returned to the upper deck and sat next to my brother.

"Everything all right?" Martin asked.

"Anthony Johnson's about to have a ten-ton truck fall on his head," I told him. "I just wish I could be there to see it."

Sydney Johnson

61

One of the first lessons I'd learned once Sydney Tech took off was that money can make anything happen. After the dinner meeting with Mr. Singh, Anthony had given me the go ahead to start planning the renovation of the Simpson property and pool installation. I'd already done my research and decided on Violet Cooper, the celebrity landscape designer from HGTV. So, I made the call.

"I'm sorry, but her schedule is quite full," her assistant had told me. "We might be able to squeeze you in sometime this fall."

"And what if I am willing to offer you triple her normal fee?" I asked. "Does that free up any space in her schedule?"

"Oh, look at that. It turns out she does have time next week for a consultation," the assistant said without hesitation.

Now, Violet was walking the property with me and Anthony as I described my vision.

"I want a huge waterfall here that you can see from the Jacuzzi. I did tell you I want a twelve-person Jacuzzi, right?" I asked.

"Yes, ma'am, you did." Violet made a note on the iPad she carried.

I had a sudden strange feeling that we were being watched, so I turned to the house next door, and sure enough, Carolyn Britton was standing on her balcony, looking down on us. She was already sneering, but I couldn't resist the urge to give her even more reason to be mad. I flipped my middle finger at her. The horror on her face before she rushed away brought me joy.

"It was here, right?" Anthony asked, bringing my focus back to him and Violet. "Where you wanted to put the chairs and ottoman."

"Oh, and the lounge space." I pointed toward the edge of the property that would be ours in a few days. "We can put it there?"

"Yes, that's plenty of space," Violet said. "You said you own all of that area to the edge as well?"

"We will," Anthony volunteered. "So, you can give us everything she wants?"

"Yes, sir. It just comes down to money and how much you're willing to spend."

"Don't worry about money. Money is the least of our concerns," he said.

"Well, in that case, now that your wife has said what she wants, what about you?" Violet asked Anthony.

"Me? I just want my wife to get the backyard of her dreams."

I hugged him from the side. "My husband loves to grill."

"I can design the optimal cooking area for him, complete with granite countertops, hooded grill and oven, all stainless steel, and if you like, we can mount a tv over it as well," Violet suggested.

Anthony lit up like a Christmas tree at Macy's. It was great to see him so excited because he rarely asked for anything. "Wow, that sounds like music to my ears."

Violet laughed. "Then we definitely need to make sure you have surround sound out here as well."

Anthony's cell phone rang. He looked at it. "It's Mr. Singh. It must be important. Maybe he wants to get those papers signed today after all."

"Answer it," I said, feeling excited.

"Good morning, Mr. Singh," Anthony said and then walked a few feet away.

My eyes remained on him as he talked. I couldn't hear what was being said on the other end, but his happy disposition faded quickly.

"I need to grab some pics of the area," Violet said, holding up her iPad and aiming it.

"Go ahead," I said, now more concerned about Anthony's agitated demeanor than the backyard design. I moved closer to where he stood.

"You can't do this! I'll sue your ass for breach of contract!" Anthony's voice was as intense as the look on his face. Something was wrong. Normally, he wasn't easily angered, especially when it came to business. "You son of a bitch. What happened to being a man of your word?"

I waited a few seconds, watching Anthony stare in disbelief at the phone he held in front of him now.

"Babe?" He didn't answer, and I moved closer, thinking he might not have heard me. My heart began racing. "Babe, babe, talk to me."

Anthony dropped the phone to the ground, balling both fists and slamming them against his head. He screamed at the top of his lungs, "Fuuuuuuuuuuuuuuuccccckkkk!"

I heard a sound and looked up to see Carolyn Britton back on her balcony, cackling as she watched my husband react to what I would soon learn was devastating news.

Sergeant Tom Lane

62

"Wow, this is it," I said out loud as I stared at the papers in my hand. Reading Peter's mail wasn't something I did often, but when I saw the sender of the already-opened FedEx envelope laying on the kitchen table, I couldn't help but look inside. After the long day I'd had at work, it felt good to come home and find good news.

"Hey, Dad," Peter said, rushing past me.

"Hey, yourself," I called after him. "Hold up. Come back here."

Peter reluctantly sauntered into the kitchen. "Yeah?"

"What's up? You weren't gonna say anything about this?" I held up the papers.

Peter shrugged. "I figured you'd see them when you got home, and I was right. You did," he said nonchalantly. "Look, I gotta go."

"Wait. We need to discuss this." His lackadaisical attitude was disappointing to say the least. "Son, this is huge!"

"Yeah, I guess. It's not like it's a surprise or anything, right?"

"Well, no." I walked over to him. "But it's still a big moment for you, and I'm proud of you. Shit, the Olympic trials! It's official. You're on your way to being an Olympian."

"Yeah, it is." Peter turned to leave. "I'm out."

"Peter . . ."

"Dad, I gotta go," Peter bellowed. "I gotta find Tania—"

"I don't give a damn about that girl, and neither should you!" The words had escaped before I could stop them, but now that they were said, I felt slightly relieved.

Peter looked both stunned and annoyed. "Well, I do. I was late getting off, didn't get a chance to tell her. Now she's not answering her phone. She's probably mad, so I need to go find her and—"

"No, what you need to do is focus on this damn opportunity right in front of you. There's a deadline for these forms, Peter. You've gotta get a physical, bloodwork, drug test . . ."

"I'm not thinking about that at this moment, Dad." He glared at me. "It's funny how you're so pressed about that paperwork, but you haven't even read the BBT contract."

"That's not true. I did read it, but I wanna get an attorney to read it too, that's all," I told him.

"Have you made an effort to hire one?"

I didn't answer because I didn't want to admit that I hadn't. We would need a sports entertainment lawyer, and that would require a two-plus-hour trip into Manhattan. During the busy tourist season, it was close to impossible for me to take a day off to do that. Now that we'd received the letter stating he'd officially been selected for the Olympic trials, I thought it trumped the Bobby Boyd Camp. Or at least I hoped that it did.

"That' s what I thought." Peter grimaced. "I'm going to find Tania."

"Fine." I closed my eyes and exhaled. "I'll get a lawyer to go over the paperwork from both opportunities."

Peter softened. "You will?"

"Yeah, I will. And then we'll sit down and discuss it. We'll make the decision together."

"Thanks, Dad." Peter hugged me. "I'm glad you're proud of me."

"I'd be even more proud if you get in that garage and hit that bag. Whether it's the Olympics or the pros, you gotta be in top shape. Your old man won't be there to run your workouts. Better enjoy me while you can," I joked. "That girl can wait."

Peter smiled. "A'ight, I can do that. That'll buy me some time, and hopefully Tania will have cooled off by the time we're done."

"And if she hasn't, you'll still be in top form. Come on. Let's get changed." I put my arm around his neck. "I love you, son. More than anything in this world."

"Love you too, Dad."

The fact that I was able to use working out to distract Peter from Tania had been a stroke of genius, but it wasn't going to take his mind off her for long. I was going to have to make a decision soon: either get Peter away from this place before he found out what Tania was up to, or tell him the truth myself.

Anthony Johnson

63

I was standing on the back porch, pacing back and forth and stressing the fuck out over the Singh deal falling apart. I'd tried to call him about ten times, but he never answered, and all I could do was leave a message. I'm sure he was purposely sending me to voicemail, but I continued to call because I really needed to talk to the man and find out what happened. Just three days ago, he had been gung-ho for the deal, and now—now I was fucked.

I pulled out my phone and dialed another number. David answered, cheery as fuck, on the second ring. "Hey, boss. You down for some tennis in the morning?"

"I need you in the office tomorrow at seven a.m."

"You gave me the day off tomorrow, man. Remember it's my daughter's birthday? She's having a party on the beach."

"Yeah, well, buy her a pony or something. I need you in the office at seven a.m. sharp."

"A pony? You do realize that Symone is twenty-one, don't you?" He was being sarcastic, and that just made me even more annoyed.

"I don't give a shit how old she is, Dave! Just be in the office!"

"Okay, okay. What the hell is going on?"

"We're fucked, that's what's going on. Take a look at the Singh file I sent you and see if you can make heads or tails of it. I'll explain the rest in the morning. I gotta go talk to Sydney." I hung up the phone without waiting for a reply. It was going to take David half the night go through the Singh file, but if anyone could figure it out, he could.

"Talk to me about what?" I turned around, and my worst fucking nightmare had just stepped onto the patio through the sliding door, accompanied by my wife.

"Hey, how you doing?" I asked Jeffrey, trying to hold myself together. "How can I help you?"

"I'm good." Jeffrey reached into the messenger bag on his shoulder and took out a folder. "I got the final paperwork from Everett and the title company a little while ago. A couple of signatures and a wire transfer, and the property will be yours."

Sydney squealed and clapped her hands. She was so happy she looked like she was going to explode. "Yes! About time."

"Uh, yeah, about that, Jeffrey. There's been a slight change of plans." I swallowed and shifted back and forth. Then I turned to Sydney. "Babe, we need to talk."

She looked instantly deflated. "What's going on?"

"Jeffrey, can you excuse us for a moment?" I asked.

Jeffrey gave me a confused look. To be honest with you, I was totally intimidated, not by him, but by my wife.

"Sure, no problem." Jeffrey stepped inside through the sliding door.

"Talk to me, Anthony. What's going on?" Sydney asked as soon as we were alone.

I exhaled, unable to look my wife in the eyes. "I fucked up. We can't buy the property."

Sydney raised both eyebrows, looking perplexed as she stepped closer. "That's not funny."

"I wasn't trying to be funny. As disappointing as this is for both of us, there's no way we can buy that land right now. We don't have the capital."

"Baby, listen, I know you're stressed about the Singh contract, but we can still do this. We'll just have to tighten our belts a little."

"It's not going to work." I shook my head, finally looking directly into her eyes so she could understand the severity of the situation.

Just like she usually did, Sydney tried once again to change my mind. "You're acting like we're broke. For God's sake, we own one of the most successful privately owned tech companies in the country."

"Being successful doesn't always mean liquidity, Syd," I explained. "Our patents are worth a mint, but our cash flow is nonexistent, especially after today. I had to use the money we set aside for the land to cover the Singh shortfall, and it wasn't nearly enough. When it's all said and done, we may have to sell this house in order to save the company."

She took a step back. "Sell this house?"

"And possibly the house in Westchester, too. It's either that or sell Sydney Tech and all its patents. We're going to have to weigh all our options."

"No. Selling this house or the other one ain't one of those damn options." She looked me up and down as if we were in grade school and I'd just stolen her ice cream money. "We didn't work so hard all these years to lose everything because of one deal gone bad. What happened?"

"We've been taking chances and moving money around since day one. You've just been turning a blind eye to it."

"That's because I trusted you!" Her eyes widened, and instead of retreating, she became infuriated. "But I won't do that again."

"Syd, I'm sorry—"

She cut me off with a dismissive look. "What is David saying about all this? He's our goddamn CFO."

"He's looking over the file. We're supposed to talk in the morning."

"I don't care what you have to do, Anthony. Put that brilliant mind of yours to work and come up with a way to fix this shit, because ain't no way I'm losing my homes, cars, or anything else. I don't do broke."

"Sydney . . ."

"Figure it out, Anthony. I mean it." Her bottom lip quivered, and I could see that she was about to cry before she rushed back into the house.

I felt lower than I had in years. I was about to lose it all: my business and my family. Sydney didn't say it directly, but I feared that if I didn't live up to her expectations, she would be gone. I had promised to make her happy forever, and now I'd failed.

"Everything okay? Your wife looked pretty upset when she came inside." Jeffrey returned to the patio.

"She's not used to me disappointing her, and I'm not used to doing it. But like I was saying earlier, there's been a slight change of plans, and we're not gonna be able to buy the property after all," I told him.

Jeffrey gave an empathetic nod. "You do understand that the one point six million–dollar deposit you put down is non-refundable?"

"I do, but unless Mr. Simpson would return it out of the kindness of his heart . . ." I suggested, looking for some sign of hope.

"I seriously doubt that." Jeffrey shook his head. "I'm sure he won't even entertain the thought of it."

My shoulders sagged in defeat.

"Good luck to you, Anthony," Jeffrey said. "Sorry about your recent bad luck. But keep your head up. You never know what could happen here in the Black Hamptons."

"I appreciate that, Jeffrey."

We shook hands, and he left.

I looked back at the house, and my heart sank. Buying Sydney her dream house in the Hamptons had been one of my biggest accomplishments, and the possibility of taking it away was too much for me to bear. There was only one solution, and it was going to be the hardest decision I'd ever have to make.

Jeffrey Bowen

64

I'd gone home to make some adjustments to the paperwork on the Simpson property and tell my wife what I knew she'd consider good news. To say she was elated to hear that the Johnsons were no longer in the running for the property was an understatement. In fact, she was so happy that we ended up making love right there on the living room floor.

Now that my love life was back to normal, it was time to get the rest of my life in order. To do that, I had to speak to Carolyn. To my surprise, she was already expecting my arrival when I got to the Britton mansion. Leslie had probably called her the moment I left our house.

"Well, that didn't take long, Jeffrey," she said smugly from the chaise lounge on the balcony, where she was perched as if she were the Queen of Sheba.

"What are you talking about?" I asked, not in the mood to play whatever mind games she was attempting to play. It was bad enough that the news I was delivering came at the expense of Anthony Johnson's downfall. The guy who was usually so jovial and upbeat had seemed broken when I left his home.

"Whatever that was going on over there." She gestured across the way toward the Johnsons' backyard. "Is everything okay?"

I realized that she'd been watching the entire situation play out earlier. "Save the faux concern, Carolyn. We all know you don't give a damn about anything other than the property. So, let's cut the bull."

"Okay, let's." She shrugged. "Do tell. Why exactly are you here?"

"I'm here because the Simpson property is again available for purchase. I assume you're still interested."

"You know I am. Otherwise you wouldn't be standing here," Carolyn replied. "It is unfortunate about Anthony Johnson's company tanking, though."

I shook my head in disbelief. "When the Johnsons backed out, I figured it was your handiwork."

"Nothing handy about it. It's just business, that's all. But I do love it when a plan comes together."

Carolyn's pride was sickening.

"You ruined a man's life over a piece of land."

"Don't be condescending, Jeffrey. None of this would've happened had you just called and let me know the property was for sale. You're just as culpable as anyone."

I balked at her accusation. "So this is my fault because I followed my client's instructions?"

"Truthfully, there is plenty of blame to go around. But what's done is done." Carolyn sat up to accept the folder I was passing to her.

"The paperwork is all in order. I've already amended the name to reflect yours instead of the Johnsons," I said as she studied the pages inside.

"And the price?"

"Same as the Johnsons. Eight million dollars."

She looked like she found that funny. "I don't think so. I'll pay the five million, which I believe was the original asking price."

"Carolyn, be reasonable. Two weeks ago you were willing to pay seven million."

"Two weeks ago I was in the middle of a bidding war with the Johnsons. Now I'm not. You tell Everett that's what I'll pay. And if he drags his feet, my offer will be four million. The stock market's taking a beating, Jeffrey. People don't have disposable funds to pay over asking right now. They're all trying to recover from their losses," she said with a dramatic smile.

"You make a good argument." I took the folder and closed it. "I'll pass your offer onto Everett and let you know."

"Good. I'll expect the paperwork by the end of day tomorrow."

"Now that the matter of the land is finally finished, we can proceed with getting the Venezuela situation settled," I said, hopeful that the dark cloud that had been hanging over my head could soon vanish.

"Fuck Venezuela," Carolyn stated abruptly.

"What?" I asked incredulously. "What do you mean? You can't do this, Carolyn."

"Don't tell me what I can or can't do."

"You know as well as I do that this shit isn't going to just disappear. You don't have a choice. They don't give a damn that you're Carolyn Britton. Unlike everyone else here in the Black Hamptons, they aren't afraid of you."

"Well, maybe they should be," Carolyn said. "Maybe it's time for them to realize I'm the one they should be scared of and not the other way around."

"Do you know how dangerous it is to play with fire?" I tried to make her understand the peril she was putting not only herself in, but me as well. "They're desperate, and you're antagonizing them. This isn't a game."

She shook her head. "Those threats you're speaking of mean nothing to me. I'm untouchable."

"This is pointless," I said, frustrated and disgusted at the same time. "Goodbye, Carolyn. Let me leave you with this— and it's not a threat, it's a promise. Your lack of concern for anyone other than yourself is going to cost you. I've watched you for a long time. If nothing else, I've learned a thing or two. I'd hate for you to get a taste of your own medicine, because I'm sure that it won't taste good."

I didn't bother waiting for her to respond. Whatever last word she had for me, I wasn't there to hear. That mean, vindictive woman had done enough damage, and I was no longer willing to be a participant.

David Michaels

65

I'd gotten up at five o'clock in the morning and drove to the city for my meeting with Anthony. I'd barely had any sleep after reading the clusterfuck of a file he'd sent me. The numbers were right, and we stood to make a hell of a profit from the batteries we were going to supply to Singh Transportation. However, from the panic in his voice, I knew something was wrong. I'd pleaded with Anthony more than once to go easy on preproduction until the contracts with Singh were signed, but my words had fallen on deaf ears, which was evident from the file he'd sent me. He'd already started purchasing raw materials, supplies, and warehousing that added up to more than twenty million dollars. Anthony was a brilliant man, but he had a tendency to be too trusting and make emotional decisions. It was why he had hired me as his CFO to save him from his own worst instincts. Only you can't save someone if they are not willing to tell you there's a problem.

"What the fuck's going on?" I stepped into Anthony's office, ready to explode on him about the file. What I saw, however, stopped me in my tracks. "What the hell is all this?"

"Food?" Anthony looked up from the nachos he was eating as if nothing was wrong and his desk wasn't covered with containers of French fries, tacos, and quesadillas. The meeting table near the window had remnants of burgers, fried chicken, and sandwiches, along with opened boxes of Chinese food. It looked like he was hosting an international food festival for himself.

I picked up a grocery bag filled with cookies and snack cakes sitting in a nearby chair. In the five years I'd known him, Anthony had always been a health-conscious brother, lecturing me on unhealthy food choices, and now here he was eating enough bad shit to give a man fifty heart attacks.

"What's up with all of this shit?"

"Nothing's up with it. I was hungry and couldn't decide what I wanted to eat, that's all." Finally, he looked at me. "I got a lot on my mind. Food helps me think."

"Anthony, man, talk to me. What's going on?" Something was off with him. It wasn't just the massive amount of food. It was also the way he stared off into the distance as he spoke. His normal upbeat demeanor seemed defeated.

I pushed the food away from him and leaned forward on the desk. "Does that thinking have anything to do with this file you sent me last night?" I asked, shaking the printed pages at him.

"Yup, the Singh deal collapsed." He reached over and grabbed a taco and shoved the whole thing in his mouth.

"Man, are you fucking kidding me? Is that why you moved twenty million from the incidentals account?" I tried to understand not just his behavior, but the crazy financial shit that was happening. Anthony was always solid and methodical when it came to business. Now he seemed erratic, and I had no idea why.

"It is," he said with a mouth full of taco.

"You said that money couldn't be touched. It's the company's rainy day fund. Isn't that what you called it?" I resisted the urge to slap the food from his hand.

"That's exactly what it is, and right now, it's raining like a motherfucker and don't look like it's gonna stop no time soon."

Stunned, I dropped into the only chair that wasn't covered with containers of food. "What happened? Why'd they pull out?"

"They just purchased Entech Freight."

I closed my eyes and took a deep breath, now understanding the cause of my boss's sudden binge eating. Hell, there was no way anyone could've seen this coming. From the way Mr. Singh was acting after dinner, the only thing remaining was the formality of signatures. It was a done deal. The man didn't show any signs of uncertainty about anything.

As I exhaled slowly, trying to get my head together, I heard Anthony's phone chime.

"Motherfucker!"

My eyes flew open just in time to see Anthony slam his fist against the large computer screen in front of him. Instinctively, I shifted in my chair, sliding a few feet backward, and waited for him to calm down.

"What the hell is that all about?" I wanted to be supportive, but shit was starting to get a little scary.

"They just announced the purchase of Entech Freight by Singh."

"Okay, and? It's not like you didn't already know it." He was going to have to get past his pride and help me with an accounts payable solution.

"Yeah, well, we didn't know this. Here."

I took the phone from his hand and read the notification from CNBC.com.

Singh Transportation Makes Turnaround Move and Snags Electric Truck Maker Entech Freight.

"You just told me about this. What's the big deal?"

"Keep fucking reading!" he huffed.

I did as I was told, reading the rest of the article aloud until I got to the last sentence. "Financing for the acquisition was through Amistad Bank and its strategic partner, Nations Bank."

I flopped back in my chair. "You think the Brittons did this on purpose?"

"Think about it. It makes all the sense in the world. And from what you and Reverend Chauncey told me about what happened to the Petersons, it makes sense that they have their fingerprints all over this. I just don't know how they knew about the Singh deal to put this all together."

I turned my head, hoping he wouldn't notice the regretful look on my face and figure out that it was me who had told Martin and Malcolm about the Singh deal on the tennis court. *Fuck!* I wanted to scream.

"They're trying to put us out of business," I said.

"Yeah, well, they're doing a pretty good job." His computer screen was already destroyed, so he shoved it off the desk. It flew to the ground, taking the remaining tacos and the container of nachos with it.

"Well, boss, from what I can see from this balance sheet you sent, you're right. We're fucked."

Sydney Johnson

66

When Karrin entered, I was sitting at the kitchen table, doing the same thing I'd been doing all day—crying. I didn't even bother trying to hide my swollen eyes or tear-stained face. I was hurting and no longer cared who saw, including my sister. Our company was in trouble, our marriage was in crisis, and our lives were in shambles. I hadn't seen or heard from Anthony in more than twenty-four hours.

"Hey, Syd, did you—" Karrin stopped in her tracks. "Oh, shit. What's wrong?"

"Everything." I sniffled.

She sat beside me. "What do you mean, everything? Where's Anthony?"

"I don't know. Somewhere mad at me, probably. We had a fight. A big one."

"You acting like y'all getting divorced." She sat back and shook her head.

"We might," I told her, recalling the argument we'd had before he ended up leaving. For some reason, he kept trying to get me to accept the possibility of selling our homes, and I couldn't. I wouldn't. This was one of those times that I needed my husband to boss up, not give in, but he didn't seem to understand.

"Shit is that bad, Karrin."

"What the fuck happened?"

"Anthony got involved in a bad business deal and lost a lot of money. We might have to sell this house and the one in Westchester, too."

"Damn, that's fucked up."

"Tell me about it." I sighed. "So, now he's talking about downsizing and liquidating our assets, meaning the houses and God knows what else. I'm not trying to hear that shit, though."

"Why not?" Karrin asked.

"Because I'm not ready to just give up everything we've built and achieved over the years. Somebody's gotta fight for it." I looked at her. "Anthony is smart. He can figure out a way to keep our shit even if we gotta sell the company."

"I don't get it, but okay. It's your life."

"What don't you get?" I asked. "What kind of wife would I be if I didn't hold him to the standards he's capable of? You think Sydney Tech would be what it is without me supporting Anthony? That's what I've always done. I push him."

"You're willing to fight in order to hold on to the houses. Damn, I might be a materialistic bitch, but you selfish as shit, Syd."

"Me selfish?" I was totally taken aback by her words. "What the fuck is that supposed to mean?"

"Nothing. Forget about it."

"No, say it!"

"Don't get mad, but to me, it would make more sense to downsize now if that's what you gotta do to keep the company, then fight like hell together to get it all back. Shit, you sitting here crying when it sounds like your man got a plan, Syd. You believed in him enough to get y'all this far. Now you're acting like he's a failure."

"I guess I didn't think about that," I admitted. "But you don't understand."

"Sis, you got it good and don't even realize it. That man ain't have nothing when you met him, and look where you landed." She looked around. "Now that you got taste, imagine where y'all can go when you restart. Anthony's a good dude. Instead of bullying him into doing what you want him to do, maybe you should support him in doing what he feels should be done. Like you said, Anthony's smart, and his smart got you here."

Karrin's words were like a slap in the face. She was right. Anthony was a good man, and I'd been out of line. Instead of consoling him and helping him figure it out when he needed me the most, I'd been confrontational, and he didn't deserve that. We'd always been a team, and I'd behaved like a dictator and a spoiled brat. I owed him an apology, and more importantly, my support and help. Who would have ever thought my sister would be the voice of reason?

"Thanks, Karrin." I hugged her, then took out my phone.

"You calling Anthony?" she asked.

"Nope. Someone else." I scrolled my contacts until I got to the name I was looking for, then hit the call button.

"Hello."

"Hi, Leslie, it's Sydney Johnson."

"Oh, hello, Sydney. What can I do for you today?"

"I was wondering if you could come over and do an appraisal of our home. We're thinking about listing it."

There was a long pause before she answered. "Well, certainly. I can go ahead and schedule a time that works."

"Thank you. The sooner the better," I told her.

When the call ended, I looked at Karrin. "I guess we're putting the house on the market."

"Hey, look on the bright side. Selling this house means getting the hell away from the people next door." She tilted her head in the direction of the Britton mansion, and we laughed. "Which works for me."

"Yeah, me too," I replied. "Me too."

Jeffrey Bowen

67

I waited until the next morning before breaking the news to Everett about Carolyn's offer. I sent him a text that read: We need to talk in person.

He replied, Come by my house immediately because I'm headed out of town.

His eagerness was undoubtedly due to the fact that he assumed the paperwork had been signed by the Johnsons, which, of course, wasn't the case. I decided not to mention that over the phone.

The drive from the Britton mansion to Everett's home was short, but I took the long way, hoping to calm down. By the time I pulled into the circular driveway of Everett's house, I had managed to get my ragged breathing under control, but I still dreaded the conversation that was about to happen.

"Jeffrey, come on in." Everett, dressed in a paisley silk robe and slippers, held the door open and welcomed me inside.

"Thank you. I won't take up too much of your time." I stepped into his foyer and waited for him to close the door.

"We can talk in here. Excuse the mess. We're packing up to leave for the Vineyard," he told me as he led me into the house.

"We?" I asked.

"Yes, my fiancé and I," Everett bragged.

"Uh, I didn't know you were engaged," I commented, wondering who the hell had the patience to put up with Everett's aggravating ass enough to actually marry him. Whoever it was must've been tolerant beyond measure.

"I am. We haven't made the official announcement yet because we're waiting on our engagement photos to be ready. And, of course, my check," he said as we entered a large, open family room. There were several large suitcases open on the floor and sofas, surrounded by piles of folded clothes and multiple pairs of shoes.

"Jeffrey, this is Morgan."

I tried not to stare at the guy beside Everett wearing a matching robe and slippers. "Nice to meet you."

"Same here." Morgan extended his hand toward me. "I've heard quite a lot about you."

As we shook hands, I took notice of the impressive watch on his left wrist that I recognized as a Roger Dubuis.

"Congrats," I said to both of them.

"So, I'm hoping you're here with a check in hand," Everett said. "We've got a wedding to plan, and this one here is high maintenance."

Morgan twisted his lip at Everett. "You're the one who keeps spoiling me. I'm not the one who came up with a week-long wedding celebration in Dubai, Mr. Simpson."

"Relax, hon. I was just kidding. Love you." Everett began making kissy-faces.

"Love you too," Morgan replied less enthusiastically.

"So about my check, Jeffrey?"

"Actually, there is no check or wire. Things have changed with regards to the sale." There was no way to break the news gently. "The Johnsons withdrew their bid."

"W-what did you just say?" Everett stammered. "Don't you tell me Anthony Johnson is trying to play games and reduce the price, 'cause Carolyn is still an option."

"Right now, she's your only option."

"Did you tell Anthony that deposit he made is non-refundable? Because he ain't getting it back." Everett folded his arms. "Maybe that will make him think twice."

"I did, but I think he's dealing with a situation where he's just not able to buy it right now."

Everett sighed. "Well, Carolyn will be elated to hear that. I was hoping that bitch had met her match, but I guess the Brittons prevail once again."

"They always do, at everyone else's expense," Morgan commented, rolling his eyes. It wouldn't have surprised me if he had some kind of issue with them too.

"Well, at the end of the day, money is money, and a sale is a sale, even when you can't stand the buyer. When will Carolyn be issuing my eight-million-dollar payment?" Everett moved one of the large suitcases off the sofa so he and Morgan could sit.

"She won't be," I told him. "Once she found out the Johnsons pulled out, she immediately rescinded her bid to reflect the asking price."

"That's bullshit," Everett snapped. "She's gonna have to come better than that, or I'll just sell it to someone else."

"She's not going to bid any higher, and if you don't accept the offer and sign off on it today, she'll lower it." Explaining the corner that Carolyn had backed him into was not easy. Everett may have been a pompous jerk, but he didn't deserve to be strong-armed. "And to be honest, Carolyn and the Johnsons were the only parties interested in the property. We have no other potential offers."

"Are you fucking kidding me? So, it's either accept her low-ball offer or get nothing?"

"For now."

"That doesn't seem fair," Morgan said.

"It isn't, but that's the reality of the situation right now," I told him.

"There's no other option?" Morgan pressed. "Like, maybe not a buyer for the property, per se, but shit, somebody who just wants to beat Carolyn at her own game?"

Morgan's words caused a light bulb to go off in my head. "Oh, shit!" I exclaimed.

"What?" Everett asked.

"Oh, shit, shit, shit." I repeated over and over again as I paced back and forth, formulating the plan that could accomplish two goals.

"Jeffrey, what the fuck is going on?" Everett asked. "You look like you've lost your mind."

I ignored him and continued pacing until it all came together and made sense. Finally, I stopped and announced,

"Everett, what if I told you that I have a way to guarantee you your eight million and possibly beat Carolyn Britton at her own game? What would you say?"

Everett smirked. "Now, Jeffrey, you know me well enough to know the answer to that question."

"Good, because I might just have a way to get both of our asses out of the fire and Anthony Johnson's too."

"Well then, stop pacing around and have a seat."

I did as he asked and settled in a chair.

"You know me, by all means, please do tell."

David Michaels

68

The chaos ensuing at Sydney Tech had me stressed, not to mention watching my boss fall apart was a little depressing. Sensing he needed some time to process things and get on the same page as his wife, I told him, "Boss, I think you should go back out to Sag Harbor to work things out with Sydney." Anthony was a brilliant man, but I'd never seen anybody who lived for their wife the way he did.

"I don't want to go home without a solution," he told me.

I put a hand on his shoulder. "I'll hold things down while you're away. I promise that I'll continue to go through the books and financial records until I come up with some type of resolution."

As soon as he left, I got to work, poring over the company's finances, resources, and ledgers, hoping to come up with a quick fix, even a temporary one, so he wouldn't have to liquidate everything he'd worked so hard to build. I worked through the night and into the next morning, hitting one brick wall after another. I finally decided to take a much-needed break myself and head back out east to the Black Hamptons.

There was still plenty of daylight left when I got out to the beach, so I loaded up my cooler and headed to the marina. Usually, an hour or two gliding across the water at eighty miles per hour was all it took to clear my head, and I hoped that would be the case. Plus, I needed some fresh air. There comes a time in every man's life when he is faced with the decision of whether to stick with something or abandon ship, and that time was quickly approaching for me with Sydney Tech. I didn't want to leave Anthony and Sydney in the lurch, but I didn't know how long Anthony would be able to keep it together. Not to mention the fact that when companies go bankrupt, people tend to blame the CFO, and this was not my fault.

Just as I was preparing to take off, I heard someone calling my name.

"David! Hey, Dave!"

I turned around and saw Jeffrey, of all people, waving at me. I threw my hand in the air to greet him, then started the engine.

"No, wait!" he yelled loud enough for me to hear over the roaring motor. I turned and saw that he was running damn near full speed, waving both arms over his head. "David, hold up!"

I cut the engine, stepped onto the dock, and waited for him, wondering what the hell was happening.

He took a moment to catch his breath before he could speak. "Dude, where's Anthony? I've been calling, but he's not answering. His wife said he's with you."

"Nah, I haven't seen him since yesterday in the city. He's kinda fucked up right now with everything that's going on. He's probably off somewhere thinking. Or eating."

"Damn. I need to talk to him."

"Why would he want to talk to you? Aren't you one of the Brittons' lawyers that screwed him over by helping Singh buy Entech?"

"I don't have anything to do with that. I represent the Britton trust and the conservatorship over the bank. I do not deal with the bank's day to day operations. They have other lawyers for corporate matters. But I might be able to help."

I folded my arms and gave Jeffrey a doubtful glare. I was in no mood for some bullshit-ass ploy he'd probably concocted with Carolyn. "Man, listen. I think I speak for Anthony and Sydney Tech when I say thanks, but no thanks. We're good."

I turned to step back on my boat, but Jeffrey grabbed my arm to stop me.

"David, I'm serious, man," he said, sounding sincere enough to make me turn back around. "No bullshit."

"You're Carolyn Britton's lawyer, Jeffrey. You're just as much a part of why we're getting screwed as she is."

"That's not true. I'm the trust's lawyer," he said as if that technicality freed him from responsibility for the damage being done.

"Aren't they one in the same?" I asked.

"Not exactly, especially when Carolyn's decisions recently haven't been in the best interests of the bank." He took a step closer and looked me in the eye. "How hard would it be for Sydney Tech to come up with four million dollars?"

"Depends. Why?" I asked, now curious about what he had up his sleeve. There was something about the surreptitious and, oddly enough, confident grin he wore.

"Take me for a ride on your boat and I'll explain."

At this point, what did I have to lose?

He stepped on board, and we were off.

Sydney Johnson

69

When Anthony returned home, I threw my arms around him. "Baby, I am so sorry. I never should have pushed you the way I did. I want you to know that I'm by your side, no matter what. I have already called Leslie, and she'll be coming over to do an appraisal, and we will sell this house to make the business whole again. I don't care where we live, baby, as long as we're together. We built this thing once, and we will do it again." The words came out in an emotional rush, but Anthony's response was cold, almost robotic.

"Okay, thanks, Syd," he said, then left me standing there in the foyer while he went into his office and locked the door.

We'd been together more than two decades, and I'd never seen him this way. I feared that I'd pushed him to his limit, and I wasn't sure the old Anthony would ever return.

For the next two days, he didn't come out of that office other than to meet the Door Dash person with his delivery. When I knocked on the door, he respectfully asked me to leave.

"I'm working," was all he would say.

At first, I thought this wasn't too unusual, because it was his process whenever he was working on a new project or invention. The difference this time was that when I finally got inside the office, I found him lying on the sofa, surrounded by food and looking miserable.

"Not now, Syd," he had said, and I backed out of the trash-filled room.

On the third day, he finally emerged from his office. He may not have looked confident, but he did look determined, like he had worked something out in his mind.

"We're going to get through this, Anthony. I believe in you," I told him when he entered the kitchen and poured himself some juice.

"I know, and I promise you will never have to worry about money ever again." He kissed my forehead.

"Honey, I don't give a shit about money. All I care about is you."

"I appreciate you saying that, but we both know the money's important." He smiled at me with admiration, and I wanted to fall in a hole. "I'm going out for a while."

"Now? Where?" I asked. "I've got Leslie coming over here to list the house. She should be here any minute."

He kind of laughed to himself. "You tell Leslie we're not selling the house."

"But babe, you said it yourself. We need the money."

"No, we don't. All our money problems will soon be over. I can promise you that." He kissed me again, then walked off. "Don't wait up."

"Anthony, baby . . ."

"I love you," he said, then headed toward the front door.

"I love you, too," I mumbled. I wanted to go after him, but Leslie arrived at the same time. I watched him get into his car and drive off, telling myself that he'd feel better once we got the process started. No more selfish acts for me. I was going to do my part and lighten Anthony's load. Reality was hitting us both hard.

I welcomed Leslie inside and remained committed to doing the right thing. Despite what he'd said on his way out, I was still going to list the house.

"The upgrades you've made to this place are fantastic," Leslie said as we walked through the house. "Wow, look at this. The flooring you chose is gorgeous."

"Thanks. The original flooring was horrible, and as much as I loved the house, I knew it had to be the first thing to go." I stared at the porcelain marble tile that ran throughout the entire downstairs. I'd loved it so much when we chose it, and soon, it would be for some other woman to admire.

"It was definitely worth it. It makes the house look so much bigger than it is," Leslie said.

I told myself it was a compliment and not a dig. "I think so."

We continued into the kitchen. I made sure to point out the lighting we'd installed under the cabinets, the smart refrigerator, interactive cooktop stove, and motorized cabinets, all designed by Anthony. I could tell that she was not only impressed by those, but also the LED lighting throughout the house and the motion-activated faucets in all the bathrooms. As much as I hated to let it go, there was no doubt in my mind that we would get top dollar for our home.

"So, how much do you think we'll get?" I asked once we finished the tour.

"With all the upgrades you've made, I'm thinking about seven point five million, maybe a little higher," Leslie said, looking at the iPad she'd been making notes on.

"Seven million?" I was insulted. "You're kidding, right?"

"No, that's a fair price for the square footage, especially considering you paid under six million two years ago," she explained. "Plus, there's the fact that you all don't have a pool."

"We were just about to pay eight million for a piece of land. This is an entire house," I said.

"To be honest, that was an unusual circumstance, and you and Anthony knew you were overpaying."

"You do realize the high-level, state-of-the-art tech design of this house, right?" My body stiffened with tension. "The security system in here is better than the one in the White House. Anthony designed and installed it himself. The wireless touchscreens and surround sound in every room, the energy efficient appliances . . ."

"Again, Sydney, I took all of that into consideration. Those things would definitely appeal to some buyers, including myself, but you also have to keep in mind that there are older buyers who aren't tech savvy and won't see the value of that. So, in their mind, they would be thinking about the cost of taking out some of what you consider must-haves," Leslie explained. "That's the kind of thing I have to think about when appraising. It's no different than you getting rid of the original flooring. People like different things."

I looked around and nearly began crying all over again. I hated to think of someone moving in and pretty much destroying what we'd done to perfect the house. It wasn't fair.

Leslie touched my shoulder. "Look, I know this is hard for you right now. I'll put everything into the system and get a more accurate number, then get it over to you. It may be a little higher, but not by much. Either way, I'll do my best to make sure you get a fair offer."

"Thanks." My voice was flat. "Do you think we can get this done by the end of the summer? I really want to get it over with so when we leave, we don't have to come back."

At this point, I was ready to get the sale over and done with, especially since I was going to possibly have to go through the same ordeal with our other house. The quicker we got past this devastation, the quicker we could get back on our feet.

"I can definitely try. Do you have the listing paperwork I emailed for you and Anthony to sign? I need to go over a couple of details."

"Oh, yeah. It's in the office. I'll go get it."

I entered Anthony's office, searching on top of the desk for the contract I'd printed out a few days earlier, but I didn't find it. Then, I shifted a couple of items on the desk, thinking the paperwork had been moved. That's when I saw that he had taken the folder containing our life insurance policies out of the safe. I looked at it for a moment, seeing the thirty-million-dollar policy amount highlighted.

He wouldn't do something that stupid, would he? I wondered as alarm bells started going off in my subconscious.

I opened the top desk drawer, pushing my hand all the way to the back.

Shit! It's not there.

I ran out of the office.

"Sydney, is everything okay?" Leslie asked, seeing the panic on my face.

"Yeah, uh, why don't you see yourself out? I'll bring that paperwork to you tomorrow," I said, rushing up the stairs into my bedroom. I grabbed the lockbox from the top of the shelf in the back of Anthony's closet, fumbling to open it. My heart dropped when I saw that it was empty.

"Karrin!" I yelled, running toward the bedroom suite that was temporarily hers.

"What?" She sat up in bed when I burst through the door.

"Did you take the gun?" I shrieked, holding the empty lockbox toward her.

"What gun?"

"The gun he keeps in his office drawer."

"I couldn't get in his office if I tried. He's got a combination lock on it, doesn't he?"

"Yes, he does." I closed my eyes and tried to breathe. My husband's gun was missing, and so was he.

Jesse Britton

70

It seemed like every day, Tania and I took advantage of my mother's yacht being empty. It was the perfect spot for us to chill whenever she was able to sneak away from Peter's clingy ass. And now that his father knew it was my family's boat, he seemed to leave us alone too. Peter may have been a fighter, but he obviously wasn't laying down correct, because Tania was hooking up with me every chance she got. Not that I was complaining, because I was starting to catch real feelings for her.

"So, I was wondering," I said hesitantly. We'd just made love and she was snuggled up against me while I ran my hand across her smooth skin.

"Wondering what?" She smiled.

Before I could answer, her phone vibrated on the night-stand. Shaking her head, she sat up.

I playfully pulled her back down. "Where are you going? You can't get away from me."

"I'm sorry, but I gotta go, Jesse."

"No." I wrapped my arms around her waist. "Stay with me, just for a little while longer. I gotta go to some party my grandma's giving in about an hour anyway."

"Seriously, Jesse, he's blowing up my phone." She turned the screen toward me. "Look. He's calling again."

She wasn't lying. Dude was seriously trying to keep Verizon, AT&T, or whatever service he used in business. That had to be like the twentieth call in the last hour.

"He'll be all right. It's about time you kicked that clown to the curb anyway."

"You know I can't do that. And I can't stay." She playfully shoved me away, and I stared at her affectionately. My finger ran along her collar bone and across her chest, pointing to her nipples, now erect from my touch.

I smirked. "It's not cold in here, so it's pretty obvious you wanna stay."

Tania grinned and folded her arms across her chest. "You're devious. You know that, right? Erect nipples could mean a lot of things."

I lifted the sheet so she could see that I was aroused. "But I think we both know what this means, and you said you would never leave me unsatisfied."

"You don't play fair." She giggled, staring longingly under the sheets.

"Neither do you. Now, are you going to put that phone down and handle your business or what?"

She thought about it for a second. "Both."

"Both?"

"Both. I'm leaving." Tania hopped out of the bed before I could stop her. "But I'll meet you back here in an hour or two, after your grandmother's party."

"You promise? Because I'm starting to feel something I never felt before."

"And what's that?" she asked.

"Love," I mumbled, barely able to get it out. I'm sure it sounded corny, but it was true. I was definitely falling in love with her.

"Are you serious?" Her face softened, and she looked like she wanted to say something but changed her mind. She picked up the rest of her clothes off the floor and got dressed. "We agreed this was a sneaky link, Jesse. We're not supposed to catch feelings."

"I know that," I replied. I'd fucked up. I shouldn't have opened my mouth. "I can't help how I feel. I think about you all the time. I'm lonely five minutes after you leave, and I can't stop smiling when you're here. I didn't mean for it to happen, but I'm in love with you. I just need you to know."

"You know what the most messed up thing is?" She lowered her head.

"What?"

"I'm in love with you too, but summer is over in two weeks, and you're leaving to go back to school. I'll still be here while you're doing God knows what with God knows who."

She wrapped her arms around my neck, and we shared a long kiss that left us both breathless. When it ended, she touched my face.

"I want you to prove me wrong. I really do."

"Good." I smiled and kissed her again. "'Cause I will."

A noise came from behind the stateroom door in the small hallway.

"Is that your parents?"

"I don't know. I guess it could be, but I told my mom we were coming here."

Tania had an uncomfortable look on her face. "You told her?"

There was a knock on the door that made her jump. At least this time I had been smart enough to lock the door.

"Who is it?" I asked. There was no answer, but whoever it was knocked again. "Mom, that you?"

Tania's eyes shifted uneasily to mine when I didn't get a response. I was about to get up and see who it was when someone kicked the door with such force that I could feel the boat move. Thankfully, the door and lock held, but a few more kicks like that and it would come flying off the hinges.

"Shit! Who the fuck is that?" I shouted.

"Oh God, it has to be Peter!" Tania said harshly, and I immediately knew she was right.

He must have heard her voice because the kicks resumed, one after the other, shaking the door in its frame.

"He's going to break that door down!"

"I can see that. What I wanna know is what the fuck is he doing on my boat?" I looked around the room for a weapon, but everything in the cabin was nailed down. "Shit!"

Peter kept kicking and kicking the door until it came tumbling down. Tania's eyes widened with fear, and she screamed.

"Noooooooo! Jesse, look out!"

I turned around. Peter was closing in on me fast, and I had nowhere to go in the 12 x 15 cabin. I tried to scramble away, but that only bought me a few seconds. The son of a bitch was strong as hell. He was throwing me around the room like a rag doll. Finally, his fist connected with my jaw with such power that he knocked me backward onto the floor. I hit my head against the desk, and the excruciating pain worsened when Peter jumped on me, straddling my flailing body as he delivered one punch after another to my face and torso.

"Peter! Stop! Stop!"

I reached out for Tania, who tried jumping on Peter's back to stop him. He paused only long enough to push her away, tossing her tiny body onto the bed before resuming his brutal beatdown.

"Help! Help! Someone call the police!" I heard Tania screaming as she ran out of the room.

The sweat from Peter's menacing face dripped onto mine, and each blow he landed was accompanied by a loud, animalistic grunt. This dude was aiming to kill me.

Gasping for breath, I struggled to stay awake, but it was impossible. Hoping to find some kind of relief, I gave in and succumbed to the darkness.

Anthony Johnson

71

I'd officially hit rock bottom. I knew this because no amount of food made me feel better, not even milkshakes. In the past, whenever I was stressed, upset, or depressed, food was my comfort, but nothing soothed the disappointment I had for myself for failing Sydney and the kids. Even though she apologized for snapping on me and was trying her best to be supportive, she wasn't wrong. I had acted irresponsibly. The mistake I'd made by prematurely pulling the trigger on production had cost us damn near everything. I was going to make it up to her if it was the last thing I did.

BE AN ORGAN DONOR. GIVE YOUR HEART TO GOD.

Those were the words displayed on the marquee in front of the church. I slowed down and read them again before giving in to the feeling compelling me to pull my car into the parking lot. I wasn't a religious man, but I did believe in God, and I prayed quite a bit because I was thankful for the life I was blessed with. I guess that's why I stopped at the church—to tell God there were no hard feelings. I'd had a damn good run.

I stared at the gun lying on the passenger seat, then read the sign once more before I stepped out of the car, tossing the empty bag of Doritos that fell out of my lap. The door of the church was unlocked, so I stepped inside. There was a single light on, but the place looked empty. I continued into the sanctuary and sat in one of the middle pews. The sun had gone down about an hour ago, and the dim, tranquil light allowed me to collect my thoughts, clear my conscience, and speak to God. Closing my eyes, I began to pray in silence, asking for forgiveness.

"Anthony?" The baritone voice startled me. "Son, are you all right?" The voice got closer, and I turned to see Reverend Chauncey walking down the aisle.

"Uh, hey, Reverend Chauncey. I didn't know anyone was here. I hope you don't mind."

"Nonsense. This is the Lord's house. You're always welcome here." He smiled as he sat beside me.

"Thanks, Rev, but I think I'm done here." I stood up.

"Please, sit. You look like you need to talk." He nodded at me. "And I'm here to listen."

I sat back down and shook my head, staring at the pulpit in front of us. "I don't know what to say, Rev. I saw the sign about being an organ donor, and I think it just got me thinking about . . . things we leave behind after we're gone."

"You thinking about going somewhere, Anthony?"

"Maybe. I'm having a Dale Peterson moment, Rev. The more I think about what he did, the more I understand." I confessed the secret I'd been harboring for the past two days. "At this point, I'm worth more dead than alive."

"That's not true. Not true at all." Reverend Chauncey sighed. "You're looking at this all wrong. It's not the material things that hold value, son. It's the life you live and the ones you love while living it. Material things can be replaced. You can't be."

"I don't have much of a life right now. I've lost it all."

"No, Anthony, you haven't lost all of it." He turned and looked at me. "You've lost your faith, and not even all of it. What little faith you do have led you in here. You didn't just stroll in here by chance."

"You think so?" I asked.

"I know so. You got knocked down, but you ain't knocked out. You just gotta get back on your feet, pick up your faith, and keep pushing. Some stumbling blocks are steppingstones. Dale Peterson was an old man even before that situation with the Brittons happened, and all he had were those auto parts stores. You're a young man, and from what I've been told, innovative. You might be a little broker financially right now, but you're not broken."

"Easy for you to say. Like I said, I'm worth more dead than alive." I stood and went to shake his hand. "Thanks, though."

Instead, he pulled me into a tight hug and whispered, "Dale Peterson killed himself thinking his family would be better off without him. Unfortunately, he didn't know that insurance policies don't pay on suicide claims. He left his wife without a husband and his sons without a father. Two of his boys are drug addicts, and his wife died of a broken heart."

I didn't reply, but I held his gaze for a moment.

"You're a smart man, Anthony. Smart men learn from others' mistakes."

Although I appreciated the talk with Reverend Chauncey, I was still troubled as I returned to my car. I unlocked the door and got in, still pondering what I was going to do as my eyes fell on the 9 mm resting on the seat beside me.

Carolyn Britton

72

As soon as the paperwork for the Simpson property was finalized and the deed was signed over to me, I immediately began setting my next plan in motion. A press release was sent to the entire community, along with an announcement via social media and email, inviting everyone to the Britton estate for a special presentation. The family was on high alert and advised that their attendance was mandatory. Kimberly made sure all of the details were taken care of, while I focused on the purpose of the moment, which only a select few were privy to.

"Mother, what is this all about?" Malcolm strolled into the dining room, accompanied by Vanessa.

"You'll find out along with everyone else." I looked up from the tea that I was stirring. "I promise you'll be pleased, though. It's your legacy."

"That may very well be, but as CEO, don't you think I should be kept abreast of things prior to them happening, rather than after?" he asked, taking the chair out for Vanessa to sit.

"Malcom, you're CEO of Amistad Bank, dear. That has no bearing when it comes to personal matters," I answered. "There's a difference. Rest assured, today's occasion will be enjoyed by everyone in attendance."

"I'm glad to hear that." Martin entered. "I hope it will be a brief one as well. I have an art event to attend."

"It shouldn't take that long," I said. "As long as everyone is on time, we will be fine."

Once breakfast was finished, I called Leslie to make sure she'd completed the assignment I'd given her. She'd been on her best behavior since the Johnson family fiasco, which was the only reason I'd tasked her with taking care of a key component needed for today.

"Good morning, Leslie. I expect that you've secured what we need for the presentation?" I asked.

"Good morning, Aunt Carolyn. I made contact and stressed the importance of it being ready no later than noon. The event starts at two, so we should be fine."

"*Should be fine* does not equate to *will be fine*," I pointed out so that my niece would understand that there could be no room for error, or else there would be hell to pay. "It needs to be *in place* no later than noon. Do you understand?"

"Yes, Aunt Carolyn."

"Good. See you then." I ended the call.

It was all coming together. August was here, and although I'd been faced with several challenges, I'd been the victor in each one: regaining control of the bank, taming the rogue sergeant at Jesse's unauthorized party, Martin's fling with that annoying THOT, Malcolm's near catastrophic proposal to that ingrate country bumpkin Morgan, and the biggest victory of all, the humiliation of that ghetto momma, Sydney Johnson, and her husband, cumulating in the purchase of the Simpson property. I hadn't faltered once, despite being pushed to my limit. The day of reckoning that I'd been waiting for had finally arrived.

At one thirty, guests began to arrive and were escorted to the south garden of the house, where Malcolm and Vanessa's reception had been held less than two weeks before. Instead of circular tables draped in fine linens holding antique china, there were rows of chairs perfectly aligned, facing a podium. By two o'clock, nearly all of the seats were full, and those who opted to stand had assembled close enough to hear what was being said. I took notice of Reverend Chauncey, the mayor, and a few other community leaders, in addition to the editor of the *Hampton Express* newspaper. My sons, along with Vanessa and her sister, Alyssa, were seated on the front row beside me. Conspicuous in his absence was my grandson, who I'd deal with later.

Leslie stepped up to the podium. "Thank you all for coming this afternoon. I'm sure you are anxious to find out why you've been assembled here. As president of the Black Hamptons HOA, I always appreciate when a member of the community extends an act of kindness that benefits us all. It is even more gratifying when that act comes from a member of your own family. Today is one of those extremely gratifying moments for me. To explain why, I'd like to turn the floor over to Carolyn Britton, my aunt." She smiled and gestured in my direction.

I stood and accepted the applause as I approached the podium. "Thank you, Leslie, and kudos for the outstanding job you've done as HOA president."

Leslie nodded and gave a polite smile in response.

"As Leslie stated, we appreciate your attendance here this afternoon. As most of you know, it was recently announced that the Simpson property, which is located to my right, was for sale. I have the pleasure of announcing that I have acquired it," I declared. "This was a very personal and purposeful endeavor for my family, but not for the reasons most of you suspect."

I took a deep breath and looked at Martin and Malcolm before I continued the story that I'd held onto for years. It was one that I'd never told them.

"It's true that this land belonged to the Britton family at one point in history, but they were not the original owners. The land belonged to the Cottman family. Upon my marriage, my husband absorbed it into his portfolio, but it is my family legacy, and I wish to preserve it."

The looks of confusion I had expected came across the faces in front of me.

"Cottman is my family surname, and this land is the only thing that was left of them, passed down through the family from my grandparents to my parents, and then to me." I swallowed the lump that had formed in my throat. "Now that it belongs to me again, I have chosen to use it to honor my family so that they will have a forever place in the community. This acre will become the Cottman Community Garden and Park."

I nodded to Leslie and Kimberly, who stood on each side of a large easel. They removed the sheet, uncovering the large, framed rendering of what would be the park. Leslie had commissioned her architect friend to create the plans, which he had done in record time. The *oohs* and *ahhhs* echoed through the crowd. Some people pulled out their cell phones and took photos of the beautiful poster.

"My hope is that Cottman Community Garden and Park will be a place for families in the Black Hamptons, including mine, to enjoy and grow together for generations to come. Thank you." I smiled and walked over to join my family.

"Mother, why didn't you tell us any of this?" Martin hugged me tight.

"I didn't want to say it until the time was right."

"This was beautiful, Carolyn," Vanessa said.

"Thank you," I said, then looked at Malcolm, who seemed a bit bothered. I knew hearing what Moses had done wouldn't sit well with him, but he needed to know. "Malcolm, I hope you're pleased with the plans for the land."

"I am, Mother." He hugged me. "Congratulations."

"Mrs. Britton, we need the family by the poster for pictures," Kimberly said.

Taking photos and answering questions from the media was a priority. Acquiring the Simpson property was one thing, but once people discovered that the Johnsons suffered behind it, there was certain to be some negative talk, similar to what had happened when Dale Peterson killed himself. Having the land become a community landmark was a brilliant idea, and it positioned me as the hero, not the villain.

"Hello." Chief Harrington approached me, looking unusually grim.

"Chief, I see you're arriving later than expected. I hope there wasn't some type of emergency in town?"

"Actually, Mrs. Britton, there was. There's been an incident." His facial expression told me this wasn't just any incident. This was big.

"What kind of incident, Chief?"

"There is no easy way to say this, but your grandson's . . ." I'd never seen the chief tongue tied like this before. "He's been attacked."

"Attacked by whom? Is he all right?" Anxiety filled my chest as I stared at the chief of police. Despite his rambunctious personality, Jesse was my pride and joy. My hands were trembling.

"He's on his way to Southampton Hospital. He's in bad shape. It doesn't look good."

"Oh God! No!" I shrieked. "Not my Jesse!"

"Aunt Carolyn, what's wrong?" Leslie and Malcolm came running to my side.

"Mother, are you okay?" Malcolm asked.

I didn't answer as my eyes returned to the chief. "What happened to him?"

"He and a young lady were attacked on his mother's boat."

Sergeant Tom Lane

73

I'd been driving like a bat out of hell for the past twenty-two minutes, weaving through traffic like I had a hundred kilos of heroin in the trunk and the DEA was hot on my tail. I'd been up the island in Riverhead, doing a little moonlighting at a stock car racing event, when Nugent gave me a heads-up call about my son being in an incident. He was vague about the details, but he told me enough to convince me I needed to get there in a hurry.

"Sarge, there was a lot of blood at the scene. The medevac helicopter is landing now. You need to come directly to the station house."

"Is my son okay?" I asked.

"Just get to the station."

As I raced back to Sag Harbor, I called the chief and the sergeant on duty to get more details, but neither of them would answer. I pulled up to the station, my tires screeching as I slammed the car into park. I jumped out of the truck and ran into the station. Inside, the usually calm and quiet place seemed chaotic. I felt like I was in the Brooklyn precinct again.

"Lane!" Chief Harrington rushed over to me.

"Chief, they called and said there was a situation and I needed to get over here because Peter . . ." Looking around for my son, my eyes fell on Tania, who was weeping into the arms of another young lady. She was covered in blood. "Tania! Where's Peter?"

She wouldn't even look at me. The chief steered me away from her down a corridor.

"Lane." Chief Harrington's voice was calm, which seemed odd considering the chaos around us. "Do you have a family lawyer?"

"A lawyer? For what?"

"Peter's been arrested."

"Arrested? Why?"

"He had an altercation with Jesse Britton, Sergeant. The boy might not make it," Chief explained.

"He . . . what . . ." I couldn't even think clearly to get my words together. "Is Peter all right?"

My son. My only child. This Britton kid drove him to his breaking point. Fuck these rich motherfuckers!

Distress turned to anger. "Where is my son? I want to see him."

"He has to be processed. Then I'll let you have all the time you need. I just need you to take some time to calm down. Come up with a plan."

"Plan for what?" I asked.

"Listen to me. This is serious. I can only protect you so much. These people are going to go after him and you . . ." The chief put his hands on my shoulders and looked around as if the walls had ears. He continued speaking, but he sounded like the teacher in a Charlie Brown cartoon to me. The only words I caught were at the tail end of whatever he had said.

"Peter's going to need legal representation."

"I'm not thinking about any of that right now, Chief. I just wanna see my boy and make sure he's all right." I shook my head in disbelief. The last thing I was concerned about was a fucking lawyer. I needed to see Peter, and I was certain he needed to see me. Without saying another word, I walked away.

"Sergeant Lane!" The voice belonged to Tania, and it stopped me in my tracks.

I turned and stared at her as she approached me in her blood-stained shirt.

"Can I please go with you to see Peter and make sure he's okay?"

Was she for real?

"You! This is all your fault!"

Her bottom lip quivered, and tears fell from her eyes, but I wasn't moved by any of it.

"Why couldn't you just leave him alone?"

"I'm sorry."

"Sorry? My son is behind bars because of you." I was about to snap just like my son. I took two steps toward her, but before I could leap, the chief and a few other officers grabbed me.

"I'm telling you this one time, and one time only," I said, breathing hard as they pulled me away. "Stay the fuck away from my son!"

Anthony Johnson

74

I left the church and drove to the beach parking lot, which was surprisingly empty. I sat on the hood of my car, listening to the waves and staring off into the dark ocean for the better part of an hour. My circumstances hadn't changed, but as I reflected on Reverend Chauncey's advice, I came to the conclusion that suicide was not the answer. I would have to start attending church more regularly, I decided, because that man's words had just saved my life.

My soul felt a little lighter, but I still had to dig myself out of a big hole before I would truly feel good again. The painful first step on Monday morning would be to sell off the majority of my patents. I had promised myself I wouldn't do that because they belonged to my children and, hopefully, my grandchildren. I was the guy who used to complain about how Black people were stupid for selling off our inventions and land to make other people wealthy. Well, I guess that old saying was right. You should never judge another man's decisions until you've walked a mile in his shoes.

A car pulled into the parking lot, blinding me with its high beams. I raised my hand to shield my eyes. I thought it was probably some kids planning to get it in on the beach, but the car didn't pull into a parking spot. It kept coming toward me until it was a few feet away, the lights still shining in my face. Finally, they went off. While my eyes readjusted, I heard the door open.

"Anthony!" Sydney shouted. I watched my beautiful wife run toward me. "Baby, you had me so worried." She threw her arms around me and held me tight.

"I had myself worried."

She leaned back, looking into my eyes as she asked nervously, "Did you take the gun?"

"Yeah, I took it. It's in the glove compartment."

"Anthony, you weren't gonna . . ." She couldn't even get the words out.

"I thought about it," I replied honestly. "But I'm good now. I don't know what I was thinking."

She squeezed me again. "A moment of weakness. We all have them. I have them all the time, trust me. I'm so sorry I was worried about what everyone else is thinking instead of being good with myself and you. I won't let that happen again," she promised.

"Syd, we're gonna go through a little rough patch for a while, but I promise you we'll be back where we belong."

"Babe, where we belong is together, no matter what. You're not just my husband. You're my best friend. I guess I forget that sometimes. It's me and you against the world." She kissed me. "I'm sorry if I let money and materialism get in our way. But just know, I'm ride or die." She kissed me again, and my hands began to roam. I was no longer hungry; however, I did have an overwhelming desire to make love to my wife. The thought of Sydney and the love I had for her was all I needed to survive.

"Hey, you two. Get a fucking room."

We broke our kiss, and I turned to see David grinning at us.

"What are you doing here?" I asked.

"I came with Syd. Don't ever cheat on her, bro. She'll use that GPS location on your phone to catch you every time." He walked up and handed me a folder. "I have some really good news." His voice sounded promising.

"What's this?"

"Take a look and see. It's the answer to our prayers."

I opened it and flipped through the pages. "Is this what I think it is?"

He grinned. "That's right. It's the Singh contract, just waiting for your signature."

"That's not funny, man."

"I'm not laughing."

I studied his face and realized he was not joking with me. "But . . . how the fuck?" I glanced back down at the folder, flabbergasted. "How'd you get him to sign?"

"Mr. Singh never wanted to kill the deal with us, Anthony. Carolyn and Malcolm made him do it as a stipulation for Amistad to finance the Entech deal."

"I knew it," I said bitterly.

"The only person who could supersede her was in Venezuela. I hope you don't mind. It cost you four million dollars to help bring him back to the States. But then again, it might have saved you fifty."

I glanced at my wife, who was still pressed up against me. "We're back, baby. All you gotta do is sign and we've got a fully executed contract."

"Somebody give me a pen!" I was elated. "I just don't understand how this all came about."

"Let's just say, while Carolyn Britton was playing checkers, worried about the land, Jeffrey was playing chess, orchestrating her worst nightmare." David laughed. "She has no idea how her life is about to change."

Sergeant Tom Lane

75

I wasn't able to see Peter until he'd been processed. They took his fingerprints and a mug shot and entered his information into the criminal database. I cringed at the thought of him becoming another young, Black man in the system. My worst nightmare had come true.

"It shouldn't be much longer, Sarge." Nugent walked over and handed me a cup of coffee.

"Thanks," I said. "Have you seen him?"

"Yeah, briefly. He's gonna be all right." Nugent sat beside me. "He's a tough kid. We've all been in fights before."

Sensing his empathy for me and concern for Peter, I leaned over and whispered, "Look, I need you to tell him don't say shit until we get a lawyer, man."

Nugent whispered back to me. "I already told him that. He knows."

"Thanks, man," I said gratefully. I had had "the talk" with my son about what to do if he was ever stopped by the police. Every Black father has to do that to keep his son safe, even those of us who are cops. But I didn't know if Peter would remember those lessons now. If he was nervous, maybe he'd want to tell his side of the story. I was anxious to get in and see him before anyone started asking questions. This may have been the precinct where I worked, but I'd been around enough cops in my life to know that some of them were not above coercing a confession out of a scared suspect, guilty or not. There was no way in hell I would allow that to happen to Peter.

"Chief, what's up? Can I see him now?" I jumped up, damn near knocking Nugent over to get to my boss, who'd just come from the back where Peter was being held.

"Not yet. They're almost finished with him. It won't be long," he told me as I followed him into his office.

I lowered my voice. "Listen, Chief, I know this has gotta be by the book, but if there's any way we can charge him with misdemeanor B&E and simple assault . . . Peter's a good—"

"I wish I could, but your son did a lot of damage to that kid, Lane. He broke down a locked door to get to him. This is some serious shit." He shook his head. "Not to mention the stink that her highness Carolyn Britton is going to stir up."

"Chief Harrington!"

As if my night couldn't get any worse, Carolyn Britton came storming into the station, escorted by her son Martin. As soon as I saw her, I knew that the shit show that was already brewing was about to boil over, and the target on Peter's back got larger. I stepped aside, hoping to go unnoticed, while Nugent walked over to the Brittons to intercede.

"He's in his office, Mrs. Britton," Nugent told her. "Can I help you with anything?"

"You can help me by telling him to get his ass out here."

"I'm right here, Carolyn," the chief announced as he stepped out of his office. I had no choice but to follow him. "How can I help you?"

"You can help me by making sure justice is served."

"I understand, Carolyn." Chief Harrington nodded. "This situation is very unfortunate."

"And what about his assailant?" Martin asked. "Is he in custody, and have charges been filed?"

"They have," Chief Harrington told him. "An arrest has been made, and charges have been filed accordingly."

"I want to know who the hell did this," Carolyn demanded.

Chief Harrington, Nugent, and the other nearby officers remained silent. A few glanced over at me.

It was going to come out eventually, so I spoke up. "It was my son."

"Your son!" Her head jerked as if she'd been struck.

The chief began, "Mrs. Britton, it appears this may have been a simple fist fight between the two young men, and—"

"Fist fight? No the fuck it wasn't!" Martin shouted. "That monster straight up attacked my nephew and beat him unconscious. Not to mention the fact he broke into my sister-in-law's boat and kicked in the cabin door."

"My grandson is in critical care, and his injuries are serious," Carolyn stated. "I don't give a damn who fathered the monster who did it. I expect him to be charged with aggravated assault, disorderly conduct, felony breaking and entering, felonious assault, and I also understand he assaulted his girlfriend in the process, so add those charges too, along with domestic violence and intimidation."

"Mrs. Britton, do you really think—"

Chief Harrington shook his head to shut me up. Talking to her was pointless.

"Considering the circumstances, it may be best for the County Attorney's office to take over the investigation. Be expecting a call from them within the hour." Carolyn turned on her heels and stormed out with her son, leaving us all speechless.

Chief Harrington was right. I was going to have to come up with a plan and find a good-ass criminal defense attorney for Peter. If I didn't, his life would be over. The Brittons were out for blood, and he was damn sure going to need someone better than the court-appointed lawyer that I could afford.

Epilogue

After unleashing on the police department, Carolyn Britton stormed out of the precinct. She'd held nothing back, and it allowed her to release the pent-up rage that had been building since she'd heard the news about her grandson. It didn't matter who Peter was. She wanted him not only arrested, but thrown under the jail his father worked at.

Now that she'd taken care of making sure Chief Harrington and his subordinate, Sergeant Lane, understood how vigilant she'd be about the prosecution of Jesse's assailant, it was time to get back to the hospital.

"Martin, first thing Monday morning, I want you to go see the mayor. I want Chief Harrington put on notice, and I want a new search to begin for Sag Harbor's next Black police officer. I can't believe such a good day turned so bad."

"Consider it done, Mother," Martin replied.

Little did Carolyn know, her bad day was about to get even worse the moment she stepped onto the sidewalk and saw Jeffrey across the street with Anthony Johnson. Anthony was smiling, looking nothing like a man who'd lost everything. Carolyn studied them, and her instincts told her something wasn't right. She didn't bother to look either way for oncoming cars as she rushed across the street.

They looked at one another, then back to her.

"Hello, Aunt Carolyn. How's Jesse?"

"Jesse's not well. They beat him up pretty bad. You and Leslie should go see him tomorrow," Carolyn replied, her eyes shifting from Jeffrey to Anthony. "What are you doing here, Mr. Johnson?"

"Hello to you too, Carolyn. Nice to see you," Anthony replied.

"Jeffrey?" Carolyn's eyes remained on Anthony as she spoke. "What's going on here?"

"You'll be pleased to know that Anthony, with the help of Everett Simpson, took care of that situation down in Venezuela, so you don't have to." He winked.

"What? What the hell are you talking about?" Carolyn asked, sounding irritated.

"The situation in Venezuela," he repeated. "It's taken care of."

Whatever sick joke Jeffrey was trying to pull wasn't funny, and Carolyn damn sure wasn't amused. She had made the decision that Venezuela wouldn't be handled until she was good and ready for it to be, which wouldn't be anytime soon. She still had to get her ducks in a row.

She grabbed Jeffrey by his tie. "That's impossible. He doesn't have any involvement or knowledge of that. It's a personal matter."

"Not necessarily true. You left me no choice. I had to find other resources." Jeffrey smirked, patting Anthony on the back.

"You son of a bitch! Do you know what you've done?"

"I know exactly what I've done. You should be thanking me," Jeffrey replied smugly.

"No need to thank me, Carolyn. I've been well compensated." Anthony grinned.

"Well, I'd like to thank you," a voice said from behind Carolyn. A tall man stepped from the shadows, smoking a cigar. He shook Anthony's hand and then greeted her.

"Hello, Carolyn."

Carolyn's heart raced as she locked eyes with her handsome husband. Freshly shaved, in a designer suit and Italian shoes, he looked like he'd just walked out of a board meeting. It was a blessing and a curse at the same time. The man she loved was back, but life as she had come to know it over the past seven years would be no more. It was over.

It was Carolyn's actions while serving as the head of the investment banking division of Amistad that had caused the feds to come knocking. She'd taken it upon herself to make some rather risky trades based on insider information without telling anyone, including Moses. When the investigation of their financial institution began, Moses made the decision to take the heat, leaving her and her sons in charge of Amistad, while he fled to Venezuela, a country with no extradition treaty. In a sense, he'd still be free, while Jeffrey worked diligently to find a solution to bring him home.

Sure enough, Jeffrey's tenacity paid off, and he connected with the right political allies. A deal was made, and once the election was over and a change of administration happened, a major donation from Amistad and the Britton Foundation got the ball rolling. Once a second donation was made, all charges against Moses Britton would be dropped by the justice department, and he would be free to return to his family. However, the payment didn't happen. Carolyn made no effort to pay it.

It wasn't because she didn't love or miss Moses, because she did. There were times that she longed for his presence. But once she'd gotten a taste of power, she never wanted to let it go. Moses returning home would strip her of all the sovereignty she'd earned in his absence. She wanted to hold on to it a little while longer, or at least carve out a piece of it for herself. Now, there he was, smiling at her. She began to feel lightheaded.

"Dad!" Martin's voice sounded distant, but he was standing right beside her.

Carolyn tried to breathe as she watched her oldest son run to his father, throwing his arms around him like a cub to a grizzly bear. The moment was bittersweet.

"Mother, are you okay?" Martin asked.

Carolyn said nothing as her eyes closed and she collapsed into her son's arms.